FAREWELL
To DREAMS

Fatal Insomnia, Book One

CJ Lyons

FICTION

FAREWELL
To DREAMS
A Novel of Fatal Insomnia

CJ Lyons

EDGY READS

Copyright 2014, CJ Lyons, LLC

Edgy Reads

Cover art: © Kon / Dollar Photo Club

Library of Congress Case Number 1-1238993351

To Toni for sharing your talent as well as sharing my vision.

"The earth is heavy and opaque without dreams."
~Anaïs Nin

CHAPTER ONE

I'M ANGELA ROSSI. I'm thirty-four years old, and this is the story of how I die.

I'm an ER doctor and victim's advocate—make that former ER doc—and this is the story of how I live.

Most of all, it's a story of redemption.

I hope.

Guess it all depends on your point of view…

⁕

EVEN IF IT'S a rainy Thanksgiving night with the ER's waiting room overflowing and all of our exam rooms filled, cops and firemen will always get first dibs on our attention. They may have to wait if others are closer to death, but they're going to get seen and seen fast.

Here at Cambria City's Good Samaritan, the only trauma center still standing in this corner of Pennsylvania's Allegheny Mountains, we know how to treat our friends, and when you work on the front lines in the ER, first responders are more than friends, they're family.

So when I grabbed the next chart stacked in front of the overflowing rack and saw a cop's name there, I was surprised.

Like most of my colleagues, my job encompasses more than simply working shifts in the emergency department. I'm also medical director of the Cambria Advocacy Center, in charge of forensic evaluations of victims of violence. More than collecting evidence and assisting the police with their investigations, we also provide support and counseling to victims.

Matthew Ryder's name had come across my desk as the replacement for the detective who had been working with us. Poor guy had driven off an icy bridge and died. But I hadn't expected to first meet our new detective as a patient.

I glanced at the registration time on the chart: 17:02. Ryder had been waiting almost three hours already.

"Why didn't you guys tell me there was a police officer waiting?" I asked the clerk at the nurses' station. "I could have eyeballed him between the MI we sent up to the cath lab and the guy stabbed with the drumstick." Drumstick Guy had made our night. ERs are like that; our fun begins when yours ends.

"He didn't want to bother you. Said he was in no rush."

Great. Despite what he said, no cop would take kindly to waiting three hours. Especially not with the ER as crazy as it was tonight. Trust a family holiday to bring out the worst in everyone.

"I did put him in front of the minor cares, especially when I saw all the blood." His words were underscored by the wailing of yet another ambulance arriving. My shift ended an hour ago, which meant the ambulance was someone else's problem, but the least I could do was take care of Ryder—and check out the detective I'd be working closely with starting next week.

Scanning Ryder's chart, I wove my way around two patients parked in wheelchairs outside of X-ray and a family member pacing as he talked on a cell phone.

Amazing what a triage note can tell you about a person. Scalp laceration. Good vitals. Thirty-seven years old, no meds, no allergies, 182 pounds, single. I pulled back the curtain to Ryder's bed space.

Instead of lying on the patient bed, Ryder straddled the rolling office chair meant for physicians, watching the next bed space through an opening in the curtain, his back to me.

"They're scared," he said without turning around.

His voice was pitched low, but had no trouble carrying to me, its intended target. It was that kind of voice. More like a bullet, direct and forceful, than an invitation. His posture was relaxed yet commanding, perfect for a cop or soldier. As if he owned the space, the room, the entire emergency department.

The area beside him was occupied by a family gathered around an elderly woman, wringing their hands, arguing with each other in English peppered with Hungarian. Back when the Pennsylvania Railroad was in its heyday and the coal mines still producing, Cambria City's diversity once rivaled Ellis Island. We're still multicultural and multigenerational, but in the current economic plight, the majority of our citizens now speak the same language: welfare.

Ryder turned and glanced at me. The chart hadn't mentioned his blue eyes, so blue they couldn't be ignored. Blood seeped through the towel he pressed casually against the side of his head. Scalp lacs are like that, bleed like stink.

"You should talk with them. Tell them she'll be all right." He didn't give me a chance to argue, seemed to assume we were in agreement and that he was in charge. "I'll wait."

I washed my hands and gloved up, choosing to ignore his presumptive attitude. I'd spent most of my twelve-hour shift helping the Kowaczs: arguing with their HMO, negotiating with my fellow doctors for space, kissing the charge nurse's butt when the entire clan descended upon us. "She won't be all right. She's dying."

"Damned undignified way to do it. Can't you give them some privacy?"

It was impossible to ignore his stare or the force behind it. If I hadn't been so exhausted after the long day I might have given in and let loose my anger at his impertinence. Instead, I broke free from his gaze and yanked the curtain closed.

"Best I can do for now." A sudden tremor in my left hand distracted me. Damn it, not again.

I'd had problems for the past few weeks, on and off, but chalked it up to overwork, stress, and exhaustion. It'd been since before summer that I'd had a full night's sleep or done more than toss and turn, my limbs restless with the urge to move, move, move. Fatigue I could handle, one of the many skills any ER doc masters. But even a slight tremor could be a problem. A twitch or shake at the wrong moment, say, with your hand holding a scalpel, could be devastating.

My best friend, Louise Mehta, is a neurologist, so I'd promised myself that if the tremor continued or if things got worse, I'd let her check me out. Clenching my left hand at my side, I willed the spasm away. If I could make it stop, then things weren't worse and I could continue to ignore my symptoms.

The tremor wasn't cooperating. Much like the patient before me. "Why don't you lie down on the bed so I can examine you?"

"No, thank you. I'm fine here." He pushed the chair out of reach, preferring a confrontation to an examination. "Why?"

Now both my hands were fisted at my hips, and it had nothing to do with any tremor. "Why what? Why use the patient exam bed for an examination?"

"Why is that the best you can do?" His tone wasn't judgmental. Quite the opposite. As if he genuinely cared about the Kowaczs or my problems. But it had been a hard day, and Ryder was unlucky enough to become my last straw.

"Because I'm a sadistic, heartless bitch who could give a shit. Why do you think? Maybe because there are no open beds in the hospital, and even if there were, we have no nurses to staff them, and even if we did, the Kowaczs' insurance doesn't cover hospice or end-of-life care."

He held my gaze during my tirade, steady as an anvil absorbing hammer blows, finally blinking when I stopped to take a breath. "Feel better now?"

My sigh turned into a chuckle as my mood lightened. My tremor disappeared as well. See? Nothing to worry about. "Yes, I do. I'll feel even better if you tell me what happened and let me examine you."

"It's stupid, really." He removed the towel to reveal a two-centimeter gash above his temple. His flannel shirt and the T-shirt beneath it were splattered with blood. "You know when you're microwaving those frozen dinners and they say remove to stir halfway? I left the door to the microwave open and hit my head on the corner when I went to put the dinner back in."

"Did you burn yourself or black out?" I explored the laceration. Superficial, a few staples would close it nicely.

"No."

"It's Thanksgiving, and you were home alone having a frozen dinner?" I poured Betadine over his wound, releasing the sour scent of iodine into the small space.

"Now who's wasting time with questions that have nothing to do with medicine?"

"Just checking your mental status, seeing if you have any psych problems." Despite my exhaustion, I enjoyed the banter. He was easy to talk to—a plus for a Sex Crimes detective. Interesting that he hadn't played the "policeman" card. I was relieved to see my fingers completely steady as they guided the hair-thin 27-gauge needle along the edges of his wound, infiltrating it with lidocaine.

Before he could answer, the curtain flipped open, its cheerful rattling a sharp counterpoint to the chorus of coughing coming from the hallway beyond it.

"Angie, we need to talk."

If Ryder's voice was one of quiet command, my ex's was gentle persuasion, smooth and warm enough to make you turn as if searching for sunlight to bask in. It was Jacob's strength both in and out of court, and the one thing about him I could seldom resist.

"I'm a little busy." I glanced up at Jacob, then immediately forced my gaze away, knowing what he wanted. Despite being divorced for three—no, four—years, we're still close and usually fall together again around the holidays. Two lonely people who share a past and know how to comfort each other.

He stepped into the room, the curtain whishing shut behind him, blocking out the chaos of the ER. Tall, lean, with a mop of curly dark hair and a gaunt, narrow face, Jacob radiates intensity. He makes you

7

want to listen to him, look at him, agree with him. A snake charmer, his cohorts at the DA's office call him. I concentrated on filling my irrigation syringe, as if the simple four-second task required all my attention.

"Your mother sent me to bring you."

That got my interest. It isn't often that Jacob lies—although, for a rabbi's son, he can do it surprisingly well. Learned how in law school. When he does lie, it's never self-serving. This time it was easy to see whom he was protecting. And it wasn't me. My ex-husband is closer to my family than I'll ever be. To tell the truth, he's closer than I ever was—at least not since I was twelve and my father died.

Killed. In a car crash. My fault.

My dad, Angelo…I'm like him in every way. Same dark, Italian looks; same incessant fidgeting, unable to sit without tapping a song out with my fingers or toes; unable to walk anywhere when I could be running. Restless, unable to just…be.

Those qualities had made my dad the life of the party, loved by everyone. And me? I killed the man who was my mother's entire life, the man who could make her laugh and cry and laugh again all in the space of a single heartbeat. Every time my mom looked at me, that's who she saw.

It's been twenty-two years since my dad died. I glanced up at Jacob, wishing he was telling the truth, that my mom did send him to ask me to join the family. That she wanted me. There, alongside my sister and cousins and the laughter and joy. Silly, wistful thinking. You'd think an ER doc would know better. "No, she didn't."

He didn't waste any breath with a sigh. "All right, she didn't. But everyone else did."

My shoulders hunched in regret, I turned my back on Jacob to aim a stream of sterile water at Ryder's laceration.

"Hey, that's cold," he protested, but he didn't flinch or move away as I doused him and his shirt. That's what he got for insisting on sitting up in the chair rather than lying down.

"Your shift was over at seven, and it's now twelve after eight."

Jacob tried again. He's almost as stubborn as I am. "C'mon. It'll be fun. The whole band is there. Besides, you look tired. Play a few sets with us. It'll work the kinks out."

By that, I knew he meant *we'd* work some kinks out, after my uncle's bar closed down for the night and everyone went home. Usually I enjoy playing fiddle in the ceili band my father had founded. Just as I usually look forward to the physical intimacy Jacob offers. But not tonight. Jacob knew me far too well. My secret wasn't safe from him. If he noticed my night sweats or tremors or the sudden stumbles as my feet forgot which way was down, he'd be pounding on Louise's door, holiday or no holiday, and insist I get a head-to-toe checkup.

I didn't need a checkup. All I needed was a good night's sleep. It'd been so long that the idea of sleep was more appealing than sex. How sad is that?

As I turned to grab the stapler, Ryder mopped the water from his face with his shirt-sleeve.

"Matthew Ryder," Jacob said, showing no embarrassment over exposing our family's—my family's—dirty laundry to a co-worker. "I didn't recognize you under all that blood."

"Hey there, Voorsanger. Minor cooking accident. The kitchen is in worse shape than I am."

"Heard you're taking Harrison's place on Sex Crimes. You up for it?" His voice held a challenge.

I glanced from one man to the other, wondering if there was a reason why Ryder might not be ready to take over Mitch Harrison's case load. Particularly the string of sadistic sexual assaults that had plagued the city the past few months. All tied to one assailant using a street drug nicknamed Death Head to subdue his victims. Harrison had been frustrated as hell by the case, chased down every lead, but at the time he'd spun out on that bridge two weeks ago, he'd gotten nowhere.

Ryder didn't answer Jacob right away. Instead, he held his gaze steady, meeting Jacob's dead-on. "Yeah. I'm up for it. Soon as the doc puts my scalp back together, that is."

Taking my cue, I wielded the surgical stapler, breaking up their touching reunion. "Jacob, I'm sure they're waiting for you back at the bar." My Uncle Jimmy's bar hosted all our family holidays. "And you," I pivoted Ryder back into place and planted a firm hand on his head, "hold still."

The sharp clack of the stapler firing snapped through the room, making them both jerk.

"I'll figure out something to tell your mother," Jacob spoke as if granting me a royal boon. "Call me when you're done here." He left, the curtain rattling shut. I was surprised the blood hadn't scared him off earlier. Like I said. Stubborn.

Then he poked his face through the curtain again. Beckoning me to come closer. I leaned toward him.

"You sure you're okay?" His low baritone was for my ears only, as was the concern on his face.

"Go. Have fun with my crazy family. I'm fine."

He gazed into my eyes, effortlessly read the lie there, and brushed my hip with his palm, an open invitation. "Right. Just checking. Call me."

Then he was gone again. I turned back to the job at hand, ignoring Ryder's amused look.

"So you and Voorsanger…" Ryder said as I finished stapling his laceration.

"Were married. Once. A long time ago." It wasn't a secret. "You do know I'm medical director of the Advocacy Center?"

"Actually, you never introduced yourself."

I covered my chagrin by hastily clearing away the suture tray. Had I really not introduced myself? I snapped my gloves off and turned back to him. My chest and neck flushed with embarrassment. I'm not used to tripping up over little things like simple manners. It's usually bigger things that get to me. Like my fight with the HMO that had deteriorated into a shouting match and still left Mrs. Kowacz stranded in my ER instead of in hospice care where she belonged. "I apologize, Detective."

He pushed out of the chair and turned to me with a full-wattage smile. "No problem. Let's start over. I'm Matthew Ryder."

I took his outstretched hand and shook it. His hand was large enough to swallow mine whole, but he didn't squeeze too hard. Instead, it was a brief, firm contact. "Angela Rossi."

"Nice to meet you, Angela Rossi. If what Voorsanger said was true," he jerked his head at the curtain Jacob had disappeared through, "and your shift is over, then how about joining me for dinner?"

I hesitated. Something I hardly ever do. Usually I'm the first to leap into a situation, trusting my instincts and my ability to tap-dance my way out of problems. But even I know better than to date patients or co-workers. Ryder fell under both categories. Still, something in me wanted to take him up on his offer. And I hesitated.

Hesitation is never a good thing in the ER. Moments of doubt are when patients die. Things happen at lightning speed during those moments, things you can never take back again.

Before I could answer Ryder, the curtain was thrown aside, and two security guards rushed in, carrying a woman's body between them. "She was dumped out of a car, bleeding everywhere," one said breathlessly as they heaved her onto the gurney. "Christ, doc, do something!"

Ryder jumped back, startled. I slammed the code alarm and reached for the woman's head, checking her airway while controlling her c-spine. She was pale, her complexion almost matching the gray hair matted to her scalp. "Hand me that oxygen mask."

He placed the non-rebreather mask onto the woman's face as I wrenched her shirt open, exposing two gunshot wounds to her chest. A nurse jogged in to see what was going on, took one look, and shouted for someone to call a trauma code. She grabbed the monitor leads while I jammed a 14-gauge angiocath into the woman's arm and hooked it up to a bag of saline, no pump or anything, just let it pour in.

"Sats are dropping," Shari, the nurse, said once the pulse ox was hooked up.

"Bag her. Heart sounds are muffled. I have to needle her."

Before I could try to drain the blood collecting around her heart, the monitors alarmed. "No pulse!"

"Chest compressions." Damn it. This woman needed to be in an OR. Now. Instead, she was on a bed in a suture room with no surgeon in sight.

"Ryder, hand me that bundle, the one labeled vascular." He spun around and rummaged through the shelf behind him, finally reaching the sterile vascular set.

"What are you going to do?" He handed me the instrument tray.

I wrenched the sterile sheets open, exposing an array of clamps, sutures, needle drivers, scissors, and a scalpel. "I'm cracking her chest."

Shari's hands stuttered in their rhythm and I saw the question in her eyes, but she knew we had no choice. She scooped up a bottle of Betadine and flooded the left side of the woman's chest with the brown surgical soap as I snapped on a pair of sterile gloves. Ryder took over chest compressions without being told.

"Damn it, where is everyone?" I asked, holding the knife, poised for a skin incision. I really, really didn't want to do this: It was a last-ditch effort, doomed to failure, but the woman was already dead. It wasn't like I could make her any deader.

"That MVA coded up in the ICU. They were rushing him back to the OR," Shari answered.

"Hold compressions." Ryder eased back, his face dripping sweat onto my semi-sterile field. Least of my worries—or my patient's. I sliced through my patient's flesh. I had to put some muscle into it, pushing my way through the tough connective tissue that held the rib cage together.

"Pull that apart and hold it." I used Shari as a rib spreader. Sliding my hand between the ribs, I pushed the spongy lung tissue aside.

I held my patient's heart in my hand. It felt boggy, like a half-filled

water balloon. Pericardial tamponade. Fluid built up
heart, strangling it so it couldn't beat. From the amou
there was probably a major vessel torn as well. One th
First, I clamped the aorta.

Next, I needed to release the tamponade. Cutting a simple flap in
the membrane covering the heart would do the trick.

Except for one thing. I knew what I had to do. In fact, I could see
the steps of the operation to create the pericardial flap and then
repair any holes in her heart or blood vessels. I could see it all like a
dizzying complex series of textbook pages flipping through my vision
in 3-D Technicolor.

But I could not move. My body was locked into place, rigid,
unresponsive to my brain's frantic commands.

"I know her," Ryder was saying. His voice sounded normal, as if
there were nothing wrong. "It's Sister Patrice. She works over at St.
Timothy's."

"She's a nun?" Shari said.

In my head I was cursing. Screaming. This woman was dying
under my hands, but Ryder and Shari were too distracted to notice I
was frozen, unable to move or function. Panic surged through me.
Had I gone crazy? Was this really happening? How could they not see
me standing here like a zombie, my patient dying right in front of
me?

Then I realized it wasn't only my voice I heard. There was music.
Gorgeous, angelic chords so crystal clear they made my heart ache.
Women singing. *Ave Maria.* The notes swirled around me, lifting me
up beyond my body. Soaring and dizzy, I was looking down on the
scene below me. Yet at the same time, I was tethered to the earth,
totally paralyzed.

Panic and disorientation flooded me even as the music seeped into
every cell of my body, bringing a sense of harmony and peace. The
paradoxes tugged at my senses, leaving me reeling.

Then everything stopped, the world as frozen as I was.

I forgive you.

Who said that? It was a woman's voice, each word sparking golden notes shining bright and perfumed with honey, but I couldn't move or respond.

Help the girl. Save the girl.

The voice dropped to an urgent whisper, becoming bruised indigo blows against my flesh, strained with pain, copper-heavy with blood. A dying gasp—inside my head.

This was no time for a detour into *The Twilight Zone.* I was this woman's last chance. Her only chance.

Anger sliced through my panic. Rage, fury, whatever it was, it burned hot. A fire raging inside me, out of control. My vision blurred, I couldn't blink, couldn't focus, couldn't speak. Hell, the things I couldn't do were infinite. Starting with saving my patient.

A shudder roiled through my body, and suddenly, I could move again. My hand spasmed, squeezing the woman's heart, but no one knew except me. In fact, Ryder and Shari didn't seem to have noticed that anything was wrong.

But I knew. Something was terribly wrong.

Shoving my fears and questions aside, I grabbed the scissors and sliced a window in the pericardium. I milked a blood clot out, did internal compressions, waiting for the heart to fill and start to beat on its own. It never did.

CHAPTER TWO

DEVON PRICE HAD spent the drive from Philly barricading his memories. From the Town Car's backseat he watched as the mountains turned to concrete and brick, ribbons of fog and rain obscuring derelicts and despair.

The Town Car slid to a stop. Devon stepped outside and glanced up at the weathered seven-story concrete slab with its 1970s utilitarian design. His childhood home, Cambria's notorious gang-ridden housing development, the Kingston Tower.

All the hopes and fears and pain and guilt that had driven him away hit like a sucker punch. Except he wasn't a sucker. Not anymore.

Reining in his emotions, he took a breath. Despite the rain, the air stank of urine and unwashed bodies. "Some homecoming."

He didn't wait for his driver, Harold, to bring the umbrella, forcing the larger man to jog through the rain after him. Devon ignored the puddles of icy water and kept his focus on the walkway and stoop that guarded the Tower's entrance.

"Become the change," he muttered, taking in the Tower's graffiti-covered concrete walls, the scattered trash, the broken windows patched with cardboard, plastic, plywood.

Still, it was a definite improvement over when he was a kid and junkies shot up on the Tower's stoop, creating an obstacle course to negotiate on the way to and from school. Devon had grown up here with the other invisibles, the wished-they-had-work less-than-poor.

Kingston Tower. His playground, his school, his prison.

When he'd left Cambria eleven years ago, he'd vowed to never return. He'd broken that promise. Had to.

She'd called.

A pair of shiftless gangbangers huddled in the entranceway, eyeing Devon and the Town Car with suspicion. Tyree's crew. He'd noted them when the car pulled up to the curb—there had been three of them to start with.

"Word's gone ahead. There'll be a welcoming committee," he told Harold as the taller man opened the umbrella and held it over Devon's head. "Fair warning. Tyree will not be inviting us to Thanksgiving dinner." He'd be lucky if the gang leader didn't greet him with a MAC-10 on full auto.

Devon glanced at the car, wondering if it was a mistake leaving it here. Back in Philly, the black Town Car had become his trademark, differentiating Devon from the dealers with their white Escalades and the runners with their jacked-up rice burners. Thanks to his partnership with the Russians, Devon had moved beyond the street gangs. He now controlled his own operation, his own people, his own destiny.

At least he had until she'd called. Bringing him west through the Pennsylvania industrial wasteland, switchbacking over mountains and through his past, until he'd finally arrived back where he'd begun. Cambria City. The Tower.

The prodigal returned home. No, that guy was greeted with feasting and parties. No one would be throwing a party for Devon, although some wouldn't mind throwing him a funeral.

More like Hamlet. Except that hadn't turned out so hot. Devon stared at the Tower, squaring his shoulders, stretching the Italian silk of his suit. Hamlet was a whiny-ass pussy. Not a street fighter like Devon.

"Everything's ready," Harold assured him. Devon's second-in-command had a mind like a CPA, always calculating, collecting details, and the body of a WWE wrestler.

"Remember, no guns."

"The men have their instructions." Harold nodded to the SUV pulling up behind them. A Yukon hybrid. Dima and Alexi had scoffed when Devon wrangled his way to the top of the waiting list at the dealership. Russians. They'd pinch a penny until it cried then waste a thousand on imported vodka. As thoughtless and greedy as the gangbangers but twice as ruthless.

Harold stepped forward as three more from Tyree's crew appeared from the shadows in front of the building's entrance, flanking the two already at the door, lining up on either side of the crumbling concrete stoop. Devon waved Harold back and faced the men. Time to run the gauntlet once again.

"Tyree says go up to his penthouse," one of the original two said, holding the glass door to the Tower open.

Devon waited, his gaze targeting each member of his welcoming committee. They were a ragged bunch, even by Cambria standards. Unlike Philly gangs, these bangers crossed racial boundaries. Cambria was like that—progressive, leading the country in poverty for all. Tyree had gotten one thing right: silly to squabble about ethnic divisions when you could band together and rule. At least that was the line of bull he'd used when Devon was a kid. An equal opportunity exploiter.

The men—boys, really—lined up, some with fists ready, others assuming cocky postures modeled after hip-hop vids. The requisite gold caps and bling revealed their relative rank and worth to the Royales, Tyree's gang. A variety of handguns, stuck into the waistbands of low-rider too-baggy pants. Eyes cold, hard, bleak, and empty.

Despite their posturing, these punks wouldn't have lasted a minute on any Philly street corner. Less than that going up against the Russians. Devon made certain his smile made it to his eyes as he strode past them, Harold on his heels. The doorman blocked their way, arms crossed in front of his chest.

"Just the Runt," he said, nodding to Devon, using the label that had followed Devon throughout his childhood, back when he had worshipped Tyree and been a wannabe. Devon hated the name. So innocuous. As if Devon was powerless.

We'll see about that. Devon paused to take the umbrella from Harold and folded it closed as he crossed the threshold. Didn't want anyone getting seriously hurt. Not until he saw what Tyree's intentions were.

Harold didn't slow as he grabbed the punk by his jacket lapels and lifted him to the side. "Where he goes, I go. And it's Mr. Price to you, bitch."

They kept walking, ignoring the sound of a slide being pulled on a semiautomatic. Didn't bother to look back, although Devon appreciated Harold's bulk between him and the punk. Behind him, he heard someone muttering to let it go, what was a skinny-ass runt and one fat white guy against Tyree's army?

Army? Devon rolled his eyes. He'd seen better organized Cub Scout troops. As he crossed the lobby, he did notice a difference. Despite the outside appearance of the Tower, inside, things were decidedly better. There was still graffiti, but no garbage, no junkies passed out in the corners, the floor could pass for clean.

Was this the work of Tyree's so-called army? Or had the women of the Tower finally been able to make a difference in their environment? He hoped it was the latter. After all, that's what his mother had devoted her life to. Before Daniel Kingston, owner of the Tower and most of the souls who resided within its concrete walls, had destroyed her.

Devon grabbed hold of the old anger and used it to bolster his resolve. Last thing he needed was for anyone, especially Tyree, to see exactly how difficult it was coming back here. Too many betrayals— too many people he'd betrayed.

Maybe this was a mistake. Eleven years was a long time. She would have changed, built a life without him. Stupid to return here, trying to reclaim a fantasy.

But she'd called. How could he not come for her?

Two more "soldiers" waited at the elevator. One to guard the door and the other to join them inside and punch the button to the seventh floor. The elevator had also changed. Used to be it worked only sporadically and was a great place to get jumped. Urine, feces, and used condoms had once littered the floor, and blood had seeped into the cracks in the fake wood-paneled walls.

Now it had walls of mirrors, shag carpet on the floor, and smelled of Pure 50 cologne.

"Surprised Tyree didn't add some Muzak," Devon said.

The punk manning the buttons nodded. "Had it rigged up. Man, it rocked, shook the whole damn building. But the speakers blew." He shrugged. "Whatcha gonna do?"

"All the elevators like this now?"

"Hell no. This the only one running. Tyree's private ride. You're lucky he didn't make you walk up the stairs like everyone else."

"He has the entire seventh floor as his, ah, penthouse?"

"Oh yeah. For him and some of his top dogs, we have rooms up there. The ho's as well. Gotta put them somewhere we can keep an eye on them."

Devon restrained himself. He couldn't abide drugs or prostitution. The Russians had mistaken that for a weakness—at first. Until he showed them how to turn a higher profit for less risk. His financial savvy was the only thing worthwhile that he'd inherited from his father. "How about Tyree's sister? She get to stay up in the penthouse?"

"Nah, man. Sister'd have none of it." The punk turned to look at Devon for the first time. "You really gonna buy this place from old man Kingston?"

"That's the plan." It was a hastily constructed lie, a convenient excuse to cover the real reason for his visit home. If Tyree knew the truth, that Jess had called Devon, he'd kill them both.

While he'd cruised the block, taking stock of the situation, Devon couldn't help but notice that every storefront had either a *GOING OUT OF BUSINESS* or a *FOR SALE* sign on its door. Real estate prices what they were, Daniel Kingston had to be taking a huge loss. Devon had cash to burn—well, launder, technically. What better way to solve everyone's problems than to buy not only the Tower but also the rest of the block?

The more he thought about it, the more he liked the idea's sheer audacious poetry. He'd have to make the offer anonymously. Mr. Daniel Came Over On The Mayflower Kingston would never sully the family name by selling to a former resident, most especially Devon. And even though Tyree and his Royales ran the Tower as their turf, Devon was certain Daniel Kingston's lily-white ass still controlled Tyree. No way in hell would things have changed so much that Daniel would have ever relinquished his hold on the Tower.

Devon had carved a niche for himself in the Russians' sphere of influence. Surely it was time to declare his independence. Return home and finally make good on the dreams his mother and the women who'd raised him had had for him?

They had wanted him to become their champion. Had told him he had the power to make a difference in the Tower—their world.

Before Tyree had run him out of town with a death price on his head.

Back then, when Devon was seventeen, he'd been a reader, a lover, not a fighter. A runt.

Eleven years had changed all that.

The elevator doors opened on seven. Two more of Tyree's men got onto the elevator, and one pushed the button for the roof.

The roof? Now Devon was intrigued. Growing up, the roof, with its all-too-optimistic playground, basketball court, community garden, and Victorian-style greenhouse—the Tower's pride and joy back in the day—had been off-limits unless you were looking to score drugs or get a beat-down.

They arrived, and the doors slid open. Tyree's men lined up, one on each side of Devon, the third hanging back with Harold. Devon paused before exiting, taking it all in.

What had once been an open-air basketball court was now

enclosed—not very well, from the draft snaking around Devon's ankles—to form a reception hall with a wall of windows at the far end. Red velvet drapes hid the walls, but Devon caught a glimpse of unpainted drywall. The roof was sheets of translucent corrugated fiberglass perched on two-by-fours, the rain creating a thrumming undercurrent as if a wild animal paced above them, while the floor was cracked concrete with a stretch of red carpet extending from the elevators to a large executive desk—exquisite, hand-crafted mahogany—perched on a plywood dais in front of the windows. A single leather chair stood behind the desk. Tyree's throne.

An impressive way to greet visitors—and to control who came and went. As Devon approached Tyree, he immediately scanned the area, noting exits, strategic positions, the number of bodyguards—four—and the number of guns—at least six, since Tyree always carried two, had ever since a cheap semi had jammed on him in the middle of a firefight.

A firefight that had involved two teens hopped-up on crank, an unpaid tab, and an unarmed sixteen-year-old prostitute. The prostitute had been the only casualty. No great loss, Tyree boasted whenever he told the story. He'd gotten his money from the teens, and the ho had been costing him more in rock than she'd been bringing in.

Of course, Tyree never mentioned that the "ho" was his own cousin.

He hadn't changed with the years. Still the same unpolished, braggart bully. Devon could see that in the way Tyree leaned back in his chair, steepling his fingers, smiling as if he were royalty granting an audience to some lowly peon. Cunning, wily, street smart, but with little wisdom.

"So the Runt finally grew into his big-boy pants," Tyree said, crashing his chair down onto all four legs. He was eight years older than Devon's twenty-eight and had several inches on Devon's six feet, plus about forty pounds, all of it the bulging muscles that came from steroids and heavy lifting. In other words, all show. Useless in a real fight.

Since fleeing Cambria and working his way up through the Russians' organization, Devon had been in more fights than he could count—physical and mental. The physical ones had been by far the easier. Before the Russians had totally accepted him, after he'd shunned Philly's black street gangs, he'd killed two men with his bare hands.

It'd been awhile, but he could do it again. Might even enjoy it in Tyree's case.

"Happy Thanksgiving," Devon said, wondering if Jess's message had been right. She'd left him a voice mail this morning at 7:28, either dodging talking to him directly—she knew damn well he never got up before noon—or because it was too urgent to wait. Probably both. Her voice had been panicked, a whisper begging him to come, that she needed him, and not to say a word to her brother, Tyree.

He sucked in his breath, drawing oxygen down into every fiber, the memory of her final words, that she needed him—him, the outcast, the runt—singing through his mind, repeating until he could block out the panic underlying them. He and Jess, they were meant to be together. Make a family together. Now, finally, maybe, they could.

He'd initially thought he'd swoop in, bluff his way past Tyree, rescue Jess, and escape. After seeing this place, what Tyree had done with it, the decay and ugly filth, he was tempted to stay. Claim his birthright, defy both Tyree and Daniel Kingston.

With Jess at his side, he could do it. Hell, if Tyree didn't wipe that shit-eating grin from his face, Devon might just do it.

"Hear you want to buy the Tower," Tyree said, absently snapping his fingers. Instantly, two women emerged from the shadows. Both wore shear negligees, a throwback to the 1970s like the rest of the cheap bordello decor. Tyree had obviously seen *Shaft* one time too many.

One girl bent over to insert a cigar into his mouth. The other lit it for him as he puffed, his lips pursed like a fish, teeth clamped down. "I reckon it's better to work with you than that white mofo,

Kingston, so," he blew out a lopsided smoke circle, "you have my permission."

Devon held back his laughter. He didn't need anyone's permission. And the more he thought about taking over the Tower, massacring Tyree and his crew, sticking it to Kingston, the more he liked the idea. "Er, thank you."

"Yeah, I think it's fine. You kick back ten percent of the rents you collect, and my boys will continue to provide protection and other services."

Services like mugging old folks, terrorizing women and children, selling drugs and sex.

"That's mighty kind of you."

Tyree narrowed his eyes. Not so dumb after all, he'd caught Devon's edge of sarcasm. "You want to see my sister while you're here, I suppose." He chuckled. "Bitch is gonna drop a cow she hear you back."

) ⚶ (

TYPICAL OF TYREE, after their royal audience, he wouldn't let Devon and Harold use the elevator, instead sent them down the stairs to the third-floor apartment Tyree had once shared with his grandmother and sister. The apartment had been Devon's second home while growing up. He'd pretty much been raised by the entire collective of the older generation of women in the Tower. Cece, Jess's gram, had been one of the best of the bunch. Would tan his hide if he cracked wise, but also was quick to encourage his natural abilities, got him reading, learning about money, how the real world beyond the Tower worked.

After Jess's accident and everything that followed, he'd promised Cece that he'd take care of them. And he'd tried, sent back money after Tyree ran him out of town. Enough so Cece and Jess could have left the Tower. But they hadn't. Even after Cece died last year, Jess still wouldn't leave. He was certain the fault lay with Tyree, who'd never relinquish control over his family, allow them to escape.

23

Jess had made Devon promise to never come back. At the time, Tyree had vowed to kill them both if he did. He'd also sworn to protect Jess if Devon stayed away.

Yet, she'd called Devon this morning. Not Tyree. And she'd been terrified, sounded afraid for her life.

Tyree wasn't a man of his word.

Unlike Devon. If he shook on a deal, that deal was done. If he said he'd come through, he came through.

If he said you were a dead man, you'd best pick out an outfit for the casket.

After a business associate had defaulted on a loan and Devon had inherited a Laundromat and its contents, that had become his calling card: sending a nice suit, compliments of Devon Price. Your first and last warning to make things right before the funeral.

Even the Russians got a kick out of that.

As he strode from the staircase down the dimly lit hallway toward Jess's door, he wondered, not for the first time, if Tyree was setting him up. Forcing Jess to call him home, making him break his vow, only to find a funeral suit waiting for him.

No red carpets here. Just bare concrete floors trumpeting his approach to residents huddled behind triple-locked doors. Walls covered with Royale graffiti, the stench of onions, dirty diapers, and surrender.

By the time he reached Jess's door, his chest was heaving—from fear? Or the excitement of seeing her again after eleven years? Both. He was glad Harold was too far away to notice him run his palms against his suit jacket. Sweat gathered in the scars, constant souvenirs of his childhood here in the Tower.

Get with the game. Her phone call hadn't been a booty call— she'd been panicked. No, terrified. Had to be to reach out to him after all this time.

He knocked on the door. Stopped when he saw it wasn't latched shut. He stood away from the threshold, nodding to Harold, who sidled down to a position where he could cover both Devon and the stairs. Drawing his gun and hugging the wall, Devon pushed the door open.

The smell hit him first. Not a good smell. Copper, salty, tangy-sweet. The smell of death.

The hairs on his arms stood at attention as he edged a glance around the doorframe. A single light bulb burned in the room beyond. It was more than enough to show him what he didn't want to see.

Jess lay on the floor, arms sprawled toward him. She could have been welcoming him home.

Except for the blood.

CHAPTER THREE

NO ONE KNOWS how long it takes to die. Not even us doctors. We know that once blood stops flowing to the brain, it takes only a few seconds to lose consciousness—but that could mean a faint, a coma, or death.

If it's a faint, then gravity helps out and once the brain falls below the heart, blood rushes back to it and you wake up. If a coma, all bets are off on when or if you'll regain consciousness. And death? Well, much as the surgical hotshots might argue, there's no cure for death.

Dead is dead. Science's best guess is that it takes around four to six minutes without blood flow and oxygen for a brain to die.

Which means that when the nun spoke to me, she wasn't quite dead yet. Only in a coma. Her heart might have been stopped, but her brain still had some electrical activity. Neurons gasping their final breaths, firing off random impulses hurtling down synaptic connections.

Figuring that out didn't make me feel any better.

The surgeon arrived in a breathless rush, swearing at the primitive conditions inside the suture room. He shoved me aside to explore the "mess you made" and found a gash in Sister Patrice's vena cava. Then he stripped his Tyvek gown and mask away, told me to call sooner next time, and stalked out.

"Jesus," Ryder said, the nun's blood mixing with his own on his clothing. "Who would want to shoot Sister Patrice?"

I had my own cosmic questions. Why had I frozen like that? Where had that voice come from?

Staring down on the ravaged body of my patient, I didn't think I was going to like the answers.

Then it was only Ryder and I left in the room. And the dead nun. The one who shouldn't have been talking—especially with me being the only one who could hear her.

Ryder surprised me by taking her hand for a brief moment. Technically, once there was a corpse and foul play was suspected, the cops weren't supposed to touch the body, only the medical examiner. But he wasn't a cop right then. He looked down, his lips moving as if praying, then he dropped her hand and stepped back.

His shirt and jeans were covered in blood, as were his hands. Ribbons of it streaked his face, but as his gaze scoured the scene and his posture straightened, I could tell that Sister Patrice had now become a body, evidence.

"We need to secure this room until the medical examiner gets here. I don't care how busy you are, I'm not taking any chances with losing evidence." He didn't wait for me to nod. "I need to talk to those guards, check out the security cameras."

He stepped past me to leave, but I stopped him with a hand on his arm. His muscles bunched tight beneath my touch. "You knew her?"

"Yeah. She was a good person. Worked with Father Vance over at St. Timothy's." He shook his head, as if shaking away the memory of the nun as a person. "You'll get someone to stay with her?"

"I'll stay with her."

He met my gaze, nodded solemnly, his lips tight. "Thanks, doc. I'll be back."

He strode out of the room, leaving me alone with the corpse.

I stared down at the dead nun, wishing I could cover her up, embarrassed by her nakedness, but she was evidence now. Less than human.

The only thing that marked her as a nun was the small cross around her neck, stained with blood. Her eyes were open; they were brown. Despite her short-cropped gray hair, she didn't look very old.

Maybe mid-forties. But I remembered that when I was a kid our priest had never appeared to grow old, never had the worry lines and fatigue that made other adults seem used up before their time.

I stared at Sister Patrice, and she stared back, saying nothing. That was good. A step in the right direction.

I was half-tempted to rap on her skull with my knuckles. *Knock-knock*, anyone home?

Instead, I wrenched my gaze away and began cleaning up at the sink. My scrubs were ruined. I'd change into my regular clothes as soon as the coroner's folks or a police officer arrived to stand guard. But right now it was just me and the dead nun. And my maybe-sorta-could-be crazy head.

Stress. That's all it was. Cracking a chest is the biggest adrenaline-rush you could ask for. Holding someone's heart in your hand…that had to be it.

Overworked, overtired. Same excuses I'd created for my other symptoms: the not sleeping for months, the occasional stumbling gait, the unexplained fevers, the new more worrisome tremors. Stress. Nothing a vacation wouldn't cure.

Except with not-quite-dead nuns talking to me, I had to wonder if any vacation plans should include a trip to the psych ward. I was tempted to call Louise, despite the fact that she'd be in the middle of her holiday family dinner.

If it had even really happened. I held my hands out in front of me. Steady. Not a quiver or shake.

I was about ready to believe it hadn't happened. Just my imagination.

Except…who was the kid who needed help? *Help the girl. Save the girl.* That's what Sister Patrice had said. Why would my mind conjure a hallucination it couldn't understand?

As the warm water swirled over my hands, I tried to re-create those few seconds when I'd been catatonic. I didn't even know what to call the episode. Partial complex seizure? Given the auditory hallucinations that had accompanied it, temporal lobe epilepsy was most likely.

Except, when I had stood frozen, holding Sister Patrice's heart, it hadn't been only her voice that had filtered into my brain. It had started with the bone-aching, beautiful music along with flashing lights that morphed into images blitzing by at superspeed, too many for me to process. I tried now to focus, to relive the episode in slow motion, dissecting it.

Sounds crazy, dissecting a hallucination, but what else was I going to do, trapped in a room with a dead nun?

If there is one thing I'm good at, it's weeding out the nonessentials to zero in on what's important. Mental triage. And right now, understanding my...event...seemed very important. To me, to Sister Patrice.

To an unnamed girl.

A single pure note pierced my soul. High B in a warm timbre coaxed from the G-string on a violin. My fingers curled to form the note as if I held my fiddle, but as the tone grew in volume and depth, bright lights whirled around me, and suddenly I was frozen once more, locked inside my body.

Images swarmed my mind, skittering and buzzing, clamoring for attention as I strained to bring them into focus. This time I didn't have the feeling of someone talking to me, rather it was like searching a musical score, notes and chords moving back and forth, rewinding, then slowing to a note-by-note replay.

A girl, too-skinny, with dark skin, gaunt cheekbones, black hair braided into an intricate pattern. She was a sparkling A-string glissando. Maybe eight, ten, twelve—like the nun, it was hard to tell her age. The music dropped, grew low and ominous. The girl looked scared. Blood streaked her clothing as she held Patrice's hand, and they ran.

I shivered, felt physically there, with them in the dark. The music faded, leaving behind only the dull thud of rain against pavement. It was an alley, nighttime, cold wind knifing through my wet clothing. *My?* Patrice's.

The girl yanked as I—Patrice—stumbled. Then I was fumbling with a key, my hands slick with blood. Shot, I'd been shot. The key finally turned, and I opened a heavy metal door, shoving the girl inside. "Climb high," I told her, but it was Patrice's voice I heard. "Watch for Tyree's traps."

No time to say more, they were almost here. Urgency scratched my nerves, a misfingered minor chord. I closed the door and turned back to face the darkness. I took one step, two. Now I could feel the pain my panic had blocked. Every breath agony. I stumbled away from the door, away from the girl, toward the darkness at the end of the alley.

"Where is she?" A voice screamed at me, loud and angry, I wasn't sure if it was a man's or a woman's. Too close, it was too close. Fear clouded my mind. I reached for the one thing that had always provided comfort. Prayer. *Dear God. Save her, please.*

I—Patrice—expected an answer. Nothing came. Only the grim rain drumming on a dumpster's lid.

I tried to keep running but ended up on my hands and knees, crawling, still praying.

Whispered voices came from behind me. "The girl saw us. We have to find her."

A rat scrambled out of my way as I tumbled into a trash can, dumping it on its side. They stood over me, crowding out all light. "Last chance. Where is she?"

I closed my eyes, denying them answers. A shot sounded, crashing through my mind. As darkness descended, a sudden calm overtook me. My fingers searched for my cross, but my body was beyond my command. All I could do was pray.

Help the girl. Please, Lord. Save her.

The pound of a tympani crashed through me along with a rush of heat that left me gasping. Me, not Patrice. But her shadow clung to my psyche. My chest burned where she'd been shot. I fell forward against the sink, the water still running over my hands. That wasn't me praying, that wasn't me getting shot, dying.

Patrice. Somehow her memory had been embedded into my brain, worming its way into my consciousness.

My hands, no, every part of me shook at the realization. I could barely manage to turn the water off before slumping against the wall, staring at the nun's body. I'd somehow become the answer to her prayers.

If this was real, I was being punked on a supremely cosmic level. Especially as I hadn't believed in God or stepped foot in a church since my dad died.

Ironic, since I'd been hoping maybe God would talk to me at Dad's funeral. I'd been praying for forgiveness, but had known it could as easily go the other way with hellfire and damnation. No way anyone would let me off easy, not after killing my dad, even if it was a tragic accident. But I was only twelve and still believed, so it somehow all made sense in a warped, Catholic schoolgirl kind of way.

My family and Father Kersavage and just about everyone had thought it best if I skipped the funeral, so I had. Not because I was used to doing what everyone—or anyone—told me to do, but because I'd known missing saying good-bye to my dad would hurt me more than them, and back then, hurting me had seemed more important than anything else.

Would even God wait twenty-two years to exact payback? I was all grown up now, skeptical of who or what God was, and sincerely doubted He/She/It would take time out of His/Her/Its busy schedule to mess with me.

Which left Option B: a severe deficiency of vitamin H. H for Haldol, a powerful antipsychotic. Or in layman's terms: nuts, crazy, psycho, loony, daft, insane....

I glanced at the nun. She wasn't talking, which was a relief.

Even if she did, how could I be sure it was really her? I sidled over, half-expecting her to sit up, let loose with some pea-soup special effects, and spin her head around on her neck. But she lay there like a good dead nun should.

Feeling like a thief stealing from the poor box, I grabbed her cell phone from where it had fallen onto the floor. Couldn't let possible evidence be lost, I told myself as I flipped through the numbers stored in the contacts list. The one dialed most recently was labeled: Jessalyn. The one marked In Case of Emergency was labeled: Rectory. And the one called most often was labeled: Office.

I called the office number. It rang twice and went to voice mail. A woman's voice said: *This is Sister Patrice, I'm not available right now, please leave a message.*

I jumped back, dropping the phone. It *was* her. The voice in my head *was* the dead nun on the table before me. Shit, shit, shit. What the hell?

If the nun in my head was for real, did that mean the girl was as well?

The image of the little girl filled my mind, bringing with it melancholy tones of grief and fear. Lost, she was so lost—and scared.

I had to help her.

But how?

CHAPTER FOUR

MATTHEW RYDER OPENED the door to the Good Samaritan security office, expecting a few square badges sitting around with their thumbs up their asses. He was pleasantly surprised to see that although they were crammed into a room smaller than his first car, an '89 Toyota Corolla hatchback, and had less-than-state-of-the-art equipment—Videotape? Who the hell still used tape?—they seemed on the ball, already pulling up footage and scouring it.

"Did she make it?" one of the two guards who had brought Sister Patrice in asked. His uniform was streaked with dried blood, and his voice held a tremor.

"No. Tell me about the car." Ryder took the seat between the two at the monitors. The three of them were wedged in so tight their shoulders touched.

"Here it is. Walt's duping a copy for you, and Zimmerman's on the phone with dispatch now." He nodded over his shoulder to where an older man, the supervisor, no doubt, paced as he spoke on a phone. "We gave them the license plate. He's waiting to see if the patrol cars were able to track it."

Ryder was less interested in where the car went than where it came from: his crime scene. The Major Crimes guys would eventually muscle in, but he was the detective on call. For now, this was his case. "Show me."

The guard, Tinker, his name tag read—bet those jokes got old fast—hit some buttons, and one of the screens went blank then started up again with a grainy picture blurred even more by the rain.

The ER ambulance bay. One ambulance was leaving, obstructing the view, then as it pulled away, a low-slung light-colored sedan came into view. American, looked like a beat-up old Caprice, primer patches marring the paint job. White, maybe silver or tan. Couldn't see the driver through the rain drumming against the windshield.

The car barely slowed, swinging sideways alongside the sliding doors leading to the ER. The car's rear door sprang open. A man's hands—Hispanic or light-skinned black, maybe dark-skinned Asian—rolled a woman's body from the car as the driver pounded the horn. As soon as the first security guard appeared at the ER entrance, the car sped off, water spraying Patrice's body.

"There's the plate." Tinker froze the frame. Ryder made a note of it. Dispatch already had the manhunt going, although if the actors were smart, they'd ditch the car. It was a good bet they weren't the ones who'd shot Patrice—not if they were risking getting caught bringing her to Good Sam.

"Show me where it came from," Ryder ordered.

Tinker looked flustered for a moment, rewinding the tape. "Can't see."

The other guard, a thin man in his sixties, shook his head and leaned across the console. "Try looking at a different camera. If they came down Empire, they'd be on the clinic camera."

"Clinic's closed. It's a holiday," Tinker argued.

"Camera doesn't know it's Thanksgiving," the other man retorted.

Tinker punched a few buttons, and another image appeared. "What time did that call come in?"

"Call? What call?" Ryder asked.

"There was a call to the hospital operator at 20:23," the older guard explained. "Male, bad connection, lots of static, saying they were bringing in a gunshot victim. He hung up before she could get any details."

"They record those calls?"

"No, sorry. But these guys showed up less than four minutes later."

"Call-ahead seating, like we're some freaking restaurant," Tinker muttered. "Okay, look here."

Another blurry image. Where did they get their equipment anyway? Ryder's nine-year-old nephew had better gear than this shit. "Came from the east, down Empire."

"Probably from the Tower."

"Or St. Timothy's," Ryder said. His stomach knotted at the thought. Would he find more bodies waiting for him there? He pushed to his feet, already heading toward the door. "One of you guard the body until my guys get here."

He headed out the ambulance bay, the cold hitting his wet clothing so hard and fast that his heart stalled for a second. "Shit." He swung back around and returned inside. Not because of the cold, but because his phone was in his jacket pocket. And his jacket was still inside the exam room.

Tinker was already there, standing guard outside the curtain. "You need something, Detective?"

"Just my jacket. It's hanging on the cabinet." Ryder grabbed it while Tinker made a note. The security guy was obviously relishing his role as potential witness in a homicide. "Where's Dr. Rossi?"

"Went to get cleaned up."

So much for their dinner date—hope it was good for her. After all, how many chicks got to get involved in a murder on the very first date? Most guys probably waited at least until the second or third for that. He shook free of his thoughts and called dispatch. "I need a unit over at St. Timothy's."

"Sam-11 is already there. Responding to a shots-fired call."

"Any casualties?"

"Unknown. Reporting witness was a Father Vance."

Figured. The only person who'd dare to notice shots fired in that neighborhood would be Marcus Vance. "Patch me through to them."

There was a moment of silence on the line, then a male voice came through. "Officer McInerny."

"Detective Ryder. You there with Father Vance?"

"Yes."

"Where were the shots fired?"

"He reported them from the alley outside. Just got here, haven't had—"

"You in a two-car?" Budget cuts had left most of the patrol cars staffed by one cop, but they still tried to do two to a car around the Tower.

"Yeah."

"Stay with Vance. Don't let him leave. Don't let him take any calls. Send your partner out to the alley. Tell him it's a crime scene. Don't know what he'll find with the rain, but he needs to protect anything he does. I'm on my way."

"Will do."

Ryder hung up. Vance wasn't hurt. Good. But Ryder didn't want anyone else to break the news about Patrice, which meant he'd have to do it himself. He started to pull his jacket on.

"Detective, don't think you want to do that," Tinker said.

Ryder had already stopped before he could smear blood all over his favorite leather bomber jacket. Damn. Couldn't face Vance drenched in Sister Patrice's blood.

☽ ⚜ ☾

DEATH WAS A BITCH, *but she hadn't won yet.* The thought knifed through Daniel Kingston's brain each breathing moment, in between the pain and the gut-wrenching nausea and the goddamned babble of the idiots invading his last days on Earth, determined to sabotage every good thing he'd worked his whole life to accomplish.

Right now, the idiot causing him the most heartache was his son. Daniel Leopold Kingston the second. "Junior" to his mother before she'd passed. "Leo" to everyone else—including the leeches who surrounded Leo and called themselves his "friends." Like that loathsome gang leader, Tyree Willard. Bad enough Daniel had to do business with Tyree to protect Kingston Enterprises' interests in the

Tower, but to have his son treat the gangbanger as an equal...

From his position outside their rooftop conservatory, Daniel watched as one of the waitresses inside the Victorian glass structure maneuvered between tables, her tray held protectively in front of her as she tried to outflank Leo. The holiday party Daniel was hosting for one hundred and sixteen of Cambria's elite was to celebrate Kingston Enterprises' takeover of Narcis, an Irish pharmaceuticals company. A takeover engineered to give Leo a position after leaving—translation: being ignominiously dismissed for research improprieties—his position with the National Institutes of Health.

Not that Leo appreciated his father's efforts. No. Instead, he focused his time and energy on terrorizing serving girls.

Daniel caught his son's eye and beckoned him to join him outside the glass-walled greenhouse, away from curious ears and the temptation of long-legged beauties. "You know there will soon come a time when you'll be the one hosting events such as this one. You'll be expected to represent the Kingston name."

Leo didn't bother to mask his eye roll. Ignoring his father, he checked his cell phone.

"Leo," Daniel persisted, trying to stress the urgency. He didn't want to tell Leo how short his time was, refused to be turned into an object of pity during his final days. "Tell me truthfully. Are you in trouble?"

"No, of course not," Leo lied, almost as effortlessly as Daniel himself. "Just arranging to meet up with Tyree and the guys later. Seeing where the parties are going to be."

Parties? Leo was thirty-one years old, much too old for partying. When Daniel was his age, he'd already wrested control of Kingston Enterprises from his own father. Of course, he'd had Mary, his wife—a woman as voracious for prestige as Daniel was for power—to help him.

Daniel sipped at his wine, the mellow merlot turning to vinegar as he swallowed his anger and disappointment. "Leo, these people are here to celebrate your new position as CEO of Narcis

Pharmaceuticals. You can't abandon them to go clubbing with a gangster."

"No, Dad. These people are here because they're your paid lap dogs and you told them to sit and beg. Nothing to do with me." He waved his hand, a magician making an elephant vanish with a gesture. "Sorry, gotta go, big plans."

As he watched his son walk away, fear of what his son's "plans" entailed churned through Daniel's gut.

He turned back to face the conservatory. Inside the glass, mingling with exotic blooms forced to flower at Daniel's convenience rather than nature's, men and women sipped champagne, toasting Cambria's future—a future that depended on the Kingston family's continued prosperity.

At the base of the wrought iron pillar beside the door was the date the conservatory had been completed: 1846. The crowning achievement to a house that had taken two generations of Kingstons to build.

Daniel touched the toe of his shoe to the date. For luck. A habit ingrained in him as a child and then later when he was barely thirty and had taken the family company from his father, a man with frivolous tastes and an even more frivolous mind. At that time, the mid-seventies, Kingston Enterprises had been stripped bare, only this house and a single, weed-infested lot on the least-desirable block of the city left to its name.

Now look at him. He'd gambled everything they had by building Kingston Tower. He remembered how proud he'd been when they'd erected a smaller model of this same conservatory on the roof of the otherwise squalid concrete tenement. The greenhouse with its wrought iron and Old World charm had done the job—soon he'd had all the funding needed to complete the project.

Funding that had been diverted into more land acquisitions, a commercial shipping company, several manufacturing plants, two malls, three high-end office complexes and, most recently, Narcis Pharmaceuticals. All of which combined to keep Cambria and the hundred-odd citizens guzzling Daniel's expensive wine inside the conservatory from going under. When he'd saved his family's fortune, Daniel had also saved the city—a city now controlled by men Daniel had handpicked and placed into power.

He raised his glass in silent toast, across the lights shimmering through the mist, to the Tower in the distance. Without the Tower, none of this could have been possible. Mary had been pregnant with Leo—making Daniel superfluous as far as she was concerned—so he'd thrown himself into the project, often showing up on the job site and grabbing a tool, working alongside his men, goading them on to work harder, faster. And after, once the pitiful ragtag families had poured in, he'd personally managed the building, eking every dime out of the public coffers—and some not-so public ones, including the gangs who coveted the Tower's turf and potential customers.

Tyree Willard, leader of the Royales, would say Daniel made the Tower his bitch. The thought made him smile. He hadn't stepped foot inside the Tower in almost two decades, but he still used the lessons he'd learned there in his business dealings. Lessons of grit, perseverance, never surrendering.

Now those lessons were all he had left as he faced his greatest challenge. Cancer. Testicular cancer—the irony wasn't lost on him. How many women from the Tower would be howling with delight if they ever knew?

But no one could know. Not now, the way the Internet twisted private scandals into virtual public executions. Kingston Enterprises would be sunk. And Leo would be left with nothing. If there was one thing Daniel Kingston understood, it was the importance of legacy. The Kingston name was everything. *Omnes nominis defendere*. The family motto: Above all, defend the family name.

"Not too late for you to adopt me and disown him." A ghost separated itself from the shadows, emerging into the light. Not a ghost, but a slender African American woman dressed totally in black: designer suit, shirt, tie, and skin-tight lambskin driving gloves. "Your board of directors would sure as fuck approve."

"Don't be vulgar, Flynn," he said absently. He'd groomed the girl to blend into any crowd, knew she was trying to goad him with her foul language. "How bad is it?"

"Bad." Using her gloved fingers—Flynn never took her gloves off, at least never that Daniel had seen—she selected a choice sliver of dark meat from the Limoges plate she held and, her fingers brushing his as she slid his glass from his hand, chased it down with the remnants of Daniel's merlot. Somehow she made eating with her fingers seem elegant yet primal, sensual yet revolting. Like everything about Flynn, a paradox explored at your own risk.

He waited, reining in his impatience. Daniel made it a point never to let the help see any weakness. Flynn was the one exception to the rule, the only living person aside from the doctors and nurses who knew about his cancer, but he'd be damned if he'd give her any further advantage over him.

She licked the grease from her lips and set the plate down. They stood together, neither bothered by the chill night mist. Music swirled from the conservatory, providing a buffer zone between the idiots trapped inside the glass and Daniel's idiot son, with whom he was trapped as his only acceptable heir. "Another girl from the Tower has gone missing. Exactly like the others. I'm still not sure where he's keeping them, but—"

"We can't have any more surviving victims. The police are getting too close." He'd been able to silence the last meddlesome detective, but another death so soon…too risky.

Daniel shook his head. How had he raised such a fool? It wasn't what Leo had done—was doing—that bothered him. He'd always believed morals were for losers, the weak, so they could feel good about themselves when they ran away, tails between their legs.

Rules meant nothing to Daniel. A strong man forged his own rules, didn't let others dictate to him. No, he could care less about what Leo was doing. It was the risk he abhorred. The family name must be defended at all costs. Yet his son persisted in taking foolish, senseless, needless risks.

Daniel couldn't abide the thought that Leo was all he had left—and he might lose him.

"Find the girl. Deal with her."

"Sure thing, boss." Flynn blew him a kiss before disappearing into the shadows.

CHAPTER FIVE

STANDING IN THE shower in the ER's women's locker room, hot water pummeling my body, scouring it clean, all I could think about was the scene in *The Sixth Sense* where the little boy tells Bruce Willis he sees dead people. The anguish on his face, the despair. Etched into my mind as deep as a scar.

"I don't see dead people." I said the words aloud to give them weight. "I only *maybe* hear not-so-dead people." Well, okay, not maybe. Possibly. Probably.

Definitely.

No, that was too freaky, insane, couldn't be true.

Resisting the urge to scream—only crazy people scream at themselves, and I wasn't crazy, right?—I rinsed the shampoo and soap away, stepped from the shower, and grabbed a towel. Surprised myself when I realized it wasn't just water heating my face but also tears.

Had I just killed a patient? I sank down onto the bench in front of the lockers, hugging myself. Had my stubborn pride, vanity that I could handle my symptoms—denial that they were even symptoms at all—led me to freeze right when my patient needed me most?

To hell with my delusions of hearing dead nuns…what about the reality that she might be dead because of me?

I grabbed the blow-dryer, trying in vain to drown out the recriminations. Of course I'd lost patients before. What ER doc hasn't? But I'd never felt responsible, to blame for it. Like I said, there's no cure for death.

But what if Patrice had had a chance? If I hadn't frozen, if I had moved faster, could I have saved her?

You know how sometimes it feels like the world around you is tumbling past, too fast to see or grasp hold of, as if you're caught in a giant washer and your mind is the agitator, shouting: This can't be happening, this is *not* happening, and there's nothing you can do except accept that this *is* happening? That's how I felt. Numb, uncertain, scared about everything I was denying. Which left me in a state of surreal calm.

My hair still damp, I changed into my street clothes: a pair of cargo pants and a fleece pullover. My stomach clenched against fear, I did what I'd been too cowardly to do before: I called Louise.

Louise Mehta is my best friend, a neurologist, and one of the smartest people I've ever met. Plus, she's whiplash funny. You have not heard a dirty joke until you've heard it told by a middle-age, meticulously dressed Indian woman with a posh British accent.

But Louise does have her faults. She loves routine, likes everything to follow a precise order. Her life is governed by bullet points.

Not me. As an ER doc, chaos is my constant companion. Lists and practice guidelines, standard operating procedures, paperwork in triplicate—they all give me hives. I like being flexible, juggling a bunch of ideas—often contradictory—playing devil's advocate.

Drove my mom nuts. I was the kid ignoring the silly coloring books and getting busy playing Michelangelo on the living room walls. But this new chaos overtaking my life? Too much even for me. I needed a sober voice, someone who could make sense of it all.

"Hello?" A man answered on the fifth ring. Geoff, her husband. He's a biostatistician—even more regimented than Louise, but somehow still fun to be around, although I almost never understood half of what he was talking about. The price for brilliant friends.

"It's Angie. Is Louise free?" Sounds of kids laughing and grownups talking filled the background. Right. Thanksgiving. A night when normal families got together and did normal family things. Don't ask me what those are. My family congregates at my uncle's bar to play music and get drunk. Turkey and apple pie optional.

"She's kind of tied up, Angie. Tiff ate two-thirds of a mincemeat pie and threw up all over her favorite dress. Louise is up giving her a bath and trying to save the dress before she melts down completely." Their three-year-old fashionista is named Tiffany—both Louise and Geoff swear it was the other's idea. "Is this an emergency?" he asked. "She's not on call, but—"

Was I really going to ruin my best friend's holiday with a crazy story about a dead nun and hearing voices?

Proof. I needed proof. Then I'd have something solid to fight.

"No," I told Geoff. "Just calling to wish you all a happy Thanksgiving."

"You, too, Angie. Take care." He hung up.

I couldn't leave the ER without stopping at Mrs. Kowacz's bedside. I'm no saint. More like a glutton for punishment. I needed to see if I could make it, this thing I had no name for, happen again. Mrs. Kowacz was the only not-quite-dead-yet person I knew.

After all, muscle tremors and insomnia are one thing. Hallucinations? Catatonia? Seizures? Fits that leave patients dead? Those are symptoms that get you kicked out of medicine. Fast.

Whatever these spells were, I was going to do it. Try to…I didn't even have a word for it. Communicate?

"Could I have a moment with her, please?" I asked Mrs. Kowacz's extended family, interrupting their prayers. Three generations gathered around her, the youngest great-grandchild asleep beside her on the hospital bed, her children holding her hands, patting her shoulders, one granddaughter combing her hair smooth. "I'm leaving for the night and wanted to check her one last time."

The eldest son—in his late sixties himself—gathered the others and shooed them beyond the curtain, giving me some privacy. "Thank you, Dr. Rossi," he said as he exited. "I can't tell you how much we appreciate this."

I forced a smile, feeling lousy for taking advantage of them and pushing them away even for a few minutes. "You're welcome."

I made sure the curtain was closed and approached Mrs. Kowacz. She looked like she was sleeping. She was, in a way. Just wasn't going to ever wake up, not from this nap. She looked so peaceful, I hated to disturb her.

Who said I was? Maybe nothing would happen.

My hand trembled as I took hers. Her hand was dry, the skin wrinkled along the back of it, tendons tough like gristle against my fingers. Nothing. No sounds except the whistle of the oxygen through the mask on her face.

If I did hear Mrs. Kowacz's voice, then what? I had some newfound psychic gift? Bullshit. It just meant my delusions were organized—didn't make them any less delusional.

This was a mistake. So typical of me, curiosity outweighing commonsense.

Every fiber of my being screamed at me to drop her hand, walk away before something *did* happen, before I found out something about myself that I really, really did not want to know.

I couldn't move.

I was frozen again, unable to blink, unable to do anything as the world around me shimmered with color and sounds. That damn angelic chorus again, this time humming a melody that was both spritely and haunting. Liszt, maybe?

With the music, images blossomed in my mind, bright lights and hypersaturated, blinding color. Sights and sounds and smells that were foreign, that didn't belong to me. As if I'd been catapulted into some bizarre 3-D movie with smell-o-vision. Hurtling through time and space, leaping from the pain of a skinned knee of a girl in pigtails to a gold wedding band slid on my finger back to a knuckle-rapping piano teacher then to a cotillion, crinolines rustling, silk swirling, feeling all jittery inside yet at the same time calm, certain. All because of him.

Then he was in a casket, decades older, worn and frayed by time, but superimposed over the old man, I saw the nervous young man who'd been pushed forward by his friends to dance with me at the cotillion so long ago. Harpsichords whirled us around in a waltz while the entire universe held its breath in anticipation. First love, true love.

Nine decades' worth of living kaleidoscoping around me, moments falling away like an aria's final notes dying. But it wasn't my life. I felt nauseated, seasick, unable to defend myself from the cacophony of emotions, sights, and sounds bombarding me.

Finally, that same sensation of heat seared through me, announcing my release. The music in my head faded to empty silence, a void cupping its hands, wanting to be filled.

I blinked, staggered back a step. My knees shook, my stomach quivered, threatening to rebel. I sagged against the countertop. Glanced up at the clock. Four minutes I'd been standing there, all awareness of the real world banished.

I shivered, even though my skin was hot and sweaty. Four minutes lost. Anything could have happened.

In four minutes I'd plummeted through ninety-three years of living. Remnants of Mrs. Kowacz's memories crowded my thoughts. One stood out. The gold ring. Her wedding band. I glanced at her left hand, taking care not to come close enough to touch her again. No ring.

"You want it back, don't you?" I whispered, fully aware that what I was suggesting was crazy. Insane. Career-ending. Very probably symptomatic of something much, much worse going on inside my head.

But I couldn't help myself. For the first time in decades, I believed. In what, I had no idea. But I believed.

"Aw, fuck," I muttered, turning away from the almost-dead woman.

Of course Mrs. Kowacz's son took that moment to pull the curtain back. "Dr. Rossi?" he said, frowning in disapproval at my language. "Everything okay?"

No! my brain shouted. How had I done that? Touch, that seemed to have been the trigger the first time with Sister Patrice and again now. But then what had I done to make it happen the second time, when Sister Patrice had been across the room and I'd been able to dissect that first episode?

"Just fine. Take care now." I started to leave, more confused than ever. Right. Because that's what delusions were—illogical.

And yet…I stopped, memories that weren't mine flooding my mind. I swayed, caught in both realities. "Um. This may sound funny, but did she have a wedding ring?"

He nodded. "Since she got sick, it's too big for her, kept falling off."

"This might be a good time to bring it." The words sounded awkward and weird. As they should, coming from a madwoman. "She'll want it. For the end."

His mouth opened and closed again. Then he shrugged. "Sure. Anything you say."

Not me. I didn't say it. *She* did.

I stood there, trying to decide what to do next. Spend the night with my family? Playing the fiddle, making love to Jacob after, trying to ignore the possibility that I was losing my mind.

Somehow the prospect didn't fill me with excitement.

Find the girl. Yeah, right. How the hell was I supposed to find a girl when I had no idea who she was and I couldn't tell the cops how I knew she was lost?

Save the girl.

Sister Patrice wasn't going to stop nagging. As stubborn as I am, it seemed. I tugged on my parka. Looked like I was headed back to church—two decades too late.

CHAPTER SIX

THE CRISP NIGHT air and the softly falling rain cleared my head as I drove the three blocks between Good Sam and St. Timothy's. Those three blocks pretty much tell you everything you need to know about Cambria.

They're the difference between a kind-of-bad neighborhood and a don't-go-out-at-night, never-walk-alone, triple-deadbolt 'hood. Especially the block St. Tim's is on. Bounded by Empire, State, Union, and Broad, that one square block accounts for the majority of the city's blood and tears.

All because of a failed housing project, Kingston Tower. Home to a thousand souls, give or take—Census workers tend to avoid the Tower. As do social services, truant officers, immigration agents, code inspectors, and the police.

For the women and children who live there and have nowhere else to go, it's like living on the wrong side of prison razor wire. Life as a constant negotiation. Neutral clothing, avoiding any gang colors. Stray dollar bills tucked into places a casual street thief wouldn't find easily: a baby's bottle hugger, the hem of a skirt. Schooling children in the art of dodging bullets. Bunker mentality.

For the men who ruled, especially the members of Tyree Willard's Royales, the Tower is opportunity. I can't tell you how many gangbangers I've patched up who, when I ask them why they do what they do, say it's their ticket "out."

"Out" to where, they have no idea. They all just want out.

St. Timothy's itself isn't exactly a bright spot. Built of sandstone charred black by almost two centuries of coal dust and smog, it's as menacing in its own way as the Tower. Walls thick enough to shrug off cannon balls. Gothic spirals stabbing up into the night, gargoyle sentries perched at every corner, smirking and deriding the futile antics of the humans living in the shadows below. Doors bound by iron, so massive that allowing anyone entrance would take an act of God.

A fortress of blackened stone cemented by the souls of the faithful.

I sat inside my Subaru, parked across from St. Tim's, unable to take my eyes off the gaping maw of the front doors, shadowed by an overhang that arched up to a razor-sharp point. On either side of the point were twin stained-glass windows depicting some saintly action. Barely lit from lights within, they looked like demon eyes reddened by flames. The entire building snarled, daring me to draw near.

I hadn't been inside St. Tim's or any church in twenty-two years. Not since my dad died.

Looking at the looming edifice, I couldn't swallow, scared spitless. I'd rather walk alone through all seven floors of the Tower, facing gangbangers and crackheads, than step inside St. Timothy's. That's how powerful childhood suggestion can be. The monster under the bed, it grows and swells with time as you cower in fear, hiding under the covers, too terrified to fall asleep. Until you defy the stomach-wrenching panic that makes your pulse pound in your fingertips and you pull back the covers and, holding your breath, dare to look.

My phone rang, cutting through the noise of my breathing. Startled, I banged my knee against the dash. Jacob. I didn't really want to talk to him, but answered anyway—delaying tactics.

"I'm guessing you're not coming." His voice radiated disappointment and disapproval. In the background I heard the sound of bagpipes and a bodhrán. "You know you have a family—a real family, not just anonymous patients revolving through the ER."

Every now and then, Jacob appoints himself the voice of my

conscience. Which brings out the bitch in me. One of the reasons we split up. "I'm sure my family is enjoying your company more than they would mine."

"You know that's not true."

"I've got to go." Facing the dark and looming church was more appealing than talking to a man I'd once loved—still love.

"What's so important—"

"A little girl. She's missing. And I think I'm the only one who can find her." I hung up.

Pushing the car door open, I left my sanctuary and stood in the night, sleet slipping down my collar and clinging to my still-wet hair. My lips trembled, and it had nothing to do with the cold. Icy water splashed into my shoes as I crossed the street, my gaze never leaving my destination. I knew if I looked away, I'd run.

One soggy, heavy foot after the other, I climbed the steps to the church, feeling as if I should have been crawling on my hands and knees. Finally at the front door, I reached out a hand. The frozen iron burnt my flesh.

I jerked away. My breath came so fast and hard I thought I would vomit. Pressure squeezed my head and heart in a vise-grip of pain, ready to explode.

Panic attack. A stray fragment of rational thought made its way front and center. I clung to the idea—so much better than a new symptom I couldn't explain—as I turned my back on the door and ran.

I made it all the way down the steps, slamming against the Subaru, out of breath. My chest tight, I gasped but couldn't get any air. Breathe. Just breathe. So simple, did it every minute of every day, but right now I had to remind myself how to. Breathe. In. Out. In again.

Oxygen pierced my brain fog as frigid air shattered against my lungs. Tiny sparks of cold that thawed my fear. I spun to face my enemy.

Only a musty, old church. I didn't believe anyway, not anymore. There was nothing to fear, nothing at all. These words and other nonsense repeated in my head as I hauled in one breath after another, my vision hazy.

Besides, Patrice hadn't led me to a church with her thoughts, but to an alley.

Idiot. I straightened, my vision clear once more. Wanted to smack myself in the forehead, but settled for taking off at a jog, circling to the far side of the church, finally back in control.

The Tower sat on the corner of Empire and State while St. Tim's sprawled across the corner of Empire and Broad. Hidden behind both buildings were several smaller buildings, a courtyard, a "play" area—mainly used for drug deals—and several narrow alleys that ran the gauntlet between them.

Patrice had been shot in one of those alleys. I just had to find the right one.

I rounded the corner and had gone a few steps into the dark before I realized a flashlight would have been a good idea, except I hadn't thought to grab one from my car. The church was totally dark on this side. The only light came from the Tower.

Still, the alley felt familiar. I'd never been here before…but I remembered the graffiti's neon colors, visible even in the dim light. And the dumpster splashed with paint and mud. The door had been just past it.

A blinding light seared my vision. "Can I help you?" came a woman's voice.

Instinctively, I raised my hands—in surrender or defense, either way I was ready. The light lowered enough for me to make out the woman's form. She stood several feet away, one hand near her hip. Cap on her head, parka, dark uniform, shiny badge.

"What are you doing here, ma'am?" Her voice was polite but edged with suspicion.

I suck at lying, so I tried the truth. "Looking for a little girl."

That seemed to take her aback. She paused, the light dancing over me, assessing my intentions. "What girl?"

"She's around ten. Dark skin, dark hair done in cornrows. I was

51

told she ran away somewhere around here." I didn't tell her who told me. How could I? "I thought maybe she found a side door into the Tower."

"There's an exit there at the sidewalk." She jerked her chin behind me to Empire Street.

I looked over my shoulder. Shook my head. The fire exit was up a flight of stairs, had a red-lit sign. The door Patrice had shoved the girl through had been down several steps and had no signs. Maybe an entrance to the basement? "Is there another way in?"

"What's your name?"

"Angela Rossi. I'm an ER doc over at Good Sam's."

She squinted through the dark and rain, took a step closer, relaxing her posture. "Dr. Rossi. Sure, I remember you. You stitched up my partner's arm when he sliced it up on a broken bottle. Doug McInerny."

"I remember Officer McInerny." I should. That laceration had taken me the better part of an hour to repair. Four layers of sutures. He'd been lucky there hadn't been any nerve or tendon damage. "Officer Petrosky?"

"That's me." She stood beside me, now sharing the light instead of interrogating me with it. "Doug's inside with Father Vance. We weren't told anything about a missing girl."

"I promised a patient I'd look for her. Can we check the alley?"

She shook her head. "Sorry, no. I can't let you go down there. It's a crime scene."

"Couldn't I just take a look? I won't touch anything." I couldn't hear Patrice's voice, but my insides screamed that this was the place. If I was right, and that door led down into the Tower's basement, the girl could be in grave danger. A lot of my patients came from the Tower—not just in the ER, but also at the Advocacy Center. Victims of assaults so horrendous they made the word rape seem too small to encompass the devastation.

"No, ma'am." Petrosky's voice was firm. "When was the last time this girl was seen? Do you know her name? I'll call in an Amber

Alert."

Of course I didn't have the answers she wanted. As I drummed my fist against my thigh in frustration, behind us came the sound of a car door slamming shut.

"Whatcha got, Petrosky?" Detective Matthew Ryder's voice sliced through the rain drumming against the pavement. Should've known he'd head here after leaving the ER.

Petrosky's attention slid away from me for a moment. That was all I needed. I ran past her, skidding away from her outstretched arm, down the alley.

"Stop!" Petrosky shouted.

Too late. I ducked behind the dumpster, Patrice's last images filling my brain like a weird holographic overlay on reality. Past the dumpster, on the right, a stack of concrete blocks, past the graffiti, there, recessed into the side of the building, a rusted railing. Slippery concrete steps leading down, no light, but I knew there had to be a door down there. The door. Leading to the girl.

I reached the railing, but before I could start down the steps, strong hands grabbed me from behind, a not-quite tackle that spun me around, my back to the Tower's concrete-block wall.

"Rossi, what the hell do you think you're doing?"

CHAPTER SEVEN

RYDER STARED AT Angela Rossi, surprised. Her dark hair curled with the wet, sparks of light dancing from the icy sleet caught in it. She met his gaze, unafraid, despite the fact that her back was to the wall in a dark alley in a part of town where even cops didn't walk alone at night.

She should be afraid, he thought. But he wasn't thinking like a cop. Not with her body pressing against his, not with those lips opening as she caught her breath...

Idiot. He backed away before his mind could finish stripping her naked. Shoved the adolescent X-rated images aside and took another step back, the rush of icy water sloshing into his shoes bringing him to full attention.

"You changed," she said.

I hope so. But she didn't mean it that way. She meant his quick detour home to wash the blood off and throw on clean clothes. Work clothes: a suit and shirt ripped fresh from the cleaner's wrapping.

"So did you." He shook off the banality and straightened to his full height, giving her his best cop stare. The one designed to inspire obedience and truthfulness. "Why are you here?"

"There's a girl missing. I think she went through there." She jerked her chin toward the dark stairwell beside her.

"What girl? When? Was she a witness to Sister Patrice's shooting?" Too coincidental to be otherwise—except how the hell had Angela Rossi gotten tied up in it? "How do you know this?"

Her lips tightened with determination, giving her a look of ferocious innocence. Before he could question her further, she darted to the side, twisting down the steps with a clatter that echoed through the darkness.

"Rossi!" He dashed after her, crashing into her when the stairs came to an abrupt stop four steps down. His weight hurtled her against a metal door. The top of her head brushed beneath his nose, overwhelming him with the scent of springtime sunshine. She squirmed beneath him, shoving him back as she tugged at the door.

"It's locked." She turned to him. All he could make out in the dark were the whites surrounding her eyes and the faint sheen of rain giving her face a pale glow. "Can't you get someone to open it?" She was pleading now. "I know she's down there."

"Who's down there? How do you know?"

She pressed one palm flat against his chest. Not pushing him away, not at all. More like pulling him closer. "I can't tell you. All I know is that she's down there. Somewhere. Lost."

"You expect me to risk losing evidence in a homicide, call in guys from their Thanksgiving dinner, and send them to search the Tower?" Was she nuts?

She nodded, her gaze locked on his. "Trust me."

For a long moment he gazed at her, her hand pressed over his heart, the rain surrounding them in a misty curtain. He remembered how she'd looked, hands dripping with blood from holding Patrice's heart, trying so very hard to save her. He wanted to trust her. But could he?

"You need help down there?" Petrosky shouted, breaking the spell.

"No. Yes," he shouted back, spinning on his heel and taking the steps up to the alley two at a time. "I need a key to that door, an Amber Alert called in, and every man you can get to search the building for a little girl—" He stalled, turned to Rossi, who had followed him up.

"About ten years old, maybe four feet tall, black, hair braided in cornrows, wearing jeans, a gray sweatshirt." Then she faltered. "I think there's blood on the shirt." Her voice trailed off as if she'd surprised herself.

"You heard the lady, she might be injured. Let's move. Call the nearest firehouse, get the hose jockeys off their Barcaloungers and down here to help. And call in a mutual aid request to the staties and the county."

"But, Detective, you can't really expect us to search the Tower—especially not starting down in those tunnels."

"Why? What's down there?" Rossi asked.

Ryder answered her. "A cop's worst nightmare."

☽ ✹ ☾

DEVON HAD SEEN bodies before. He'd had blood on his hands.

But not Jess—Jess couldn't die. She was forever immortalized in his mind as the sassy, beautiful sixteen-year-old he'd loved and left behind.

"No!" His voice didn't sound like itself. It was a strained whisper, too frightened to shout. Shouting might bring others, and bringing others, seeing, hearing, touching, would mean this nightmare was real.

He grabbed on to the doorjamb for support, his legs emptying out from beneath his weight. Even though it felt like time was frozen, nothing he did could push it backward. Could push that blood puddled on the cheap carpet—so much blood—back into Jess's body, could push her back up to standing, could push life back into her eyes. He fell forward, onto his knees, and reached a tentative finger out to touch her face. Avoiding the scars around her eyes, he traced her jaw, touched her lips. Cold, too cold.

"There's no sign of anyone else here," Harold said after making a quick search of the apartment. "We should go."

"Did Tyree do this?" Devon asked, talking to himself more than

56

Harold. No. If Tyree had staged this, he'd be here to witness Devon's devastation.

Then he realized what was missing. Jess's daughter, Esme. His daughter. Where was she?

He whipped around. The hall was empty. Silent.

Too silent. Which meant someone knew what had happened here, had heard, seen something.

Devon climbed to his feet, rage giving him strength, filling the void. "Start knocking on doors," he told Harold, shrugging free of the larger man's grip. "Tell them it's me asking. Tell them I want to know what happened here. Tell them I won't take no for an answer."

CHAPTER EIGHT

I WASN'T SURE if I was more surprised by Ryder's willingness to trust me or frustrated because I couldn't explain exactly how I knew what I knew...*if* I really knew anything, which had yet to be proved.

The rain had turned to a foggy mist, the few overhead lights sparking off the droplets, making the neon graffiti on the walls beside us glow and shimmer. The illusion was so lifelike, as if the letters had separated themselves from the concrete to dance in the night, that my head spun and I had to put a hand out to balance myself.

"What's down there?" I asked Ryder, hoping he hadn't noticed how unsteady I was.

"Middle of the Cold War, the city put a huge underground bomb shelter under these streets, extending north from City Hall and Millionaire's Row. The Tower was built on top of them. Tunnels going every which way for half a mile or more, rooms stacked on rooms, dead ends. Half the shit down there no one's seen in decades."

I stared at the closed door. Someone had painted a skull and crossbones on it, a jagged crown perched jauntily on the skull. "She's down there somewhere. What about getting the people who live in the Tower to help?"

He stared at me like I was asking to fly to the moon. "Tyree Willard and his gang run the Tower. If anyone's got the stones to shoot a nun, it's Tyree. You really want me to put the people who might be wanting this girl dead on her search party?"

I craned my head up, focusing on the few lights scattered across the seven stories of the Tower. Swallowed against another wave of vertigo. "How long?"

"Seven floors, two wings, 280 doors to knock on, and best guess, about 1,100 people, most of whom won't talk to us. And that's just the Tower. Doesn't include the miles of tunnels down below. You do the math."

"What about calling in help? Search dogs or something?"

"You got a scent for the dogs? A name or knowing where she's from would help. We'd at least have somewhere to start."

I felt his disappointment as I shook my head in silence.

Petrosky rejoined us, frowning. "The deputy chief said he's coming down. No mutual aid request until he gets here and 'surveys the situation' himself." She said the last in an officious nasal tone. "The fire guys have building plans and can put together a search grid. Said they weren't going to knock on any doors, though, unless you give them an armed escort. Sounded like they've been here before and didn't like the welcome wagon."

"We're not going to get anywhere without getting Tyree's cooperation." Ryder scowled at the lights blazing from the top floor. "As soon as your backup arrives, tell Tyree's goons I need to meet him. ASAP. C'mon." He took my elbow to guide me away from the stairwell and toward St. Tim's. "Let's get out of the rain."

"I want to help." I needed to see.

He didn't slow his pace, yanking open the side door of the church, and not exactly shoving—more like escorting—me inside, his motions as automatic and controlling as if securing a prisoner in a jail cell.

We were in a small alcove, an ecclesiastic mudroom. A single naked bulb overhead reflected off of white-washed plaster walls adorned with a large wood and brass crucifix. A collection of umbrellas and rain slickers hung on a coat stand near the exit, and a small bowl of water was attached to the wall beside the interior door. It was an intimate space, overcrowded with just me and Ryder.

I felt flushed—not a bad feeling, given that I was drenched with sleet—but none of the heart-racing, overwhelming sense of doom and panic I'd felt earlier when I'd tried to enter the church. Turning my focus away from my symptoms and back to the problem of finding the girl, I spun free of his grasp, pivoting to face him. "You can't stop me—"

"Actually, I can." His voice was calm, that same confident tone of command that had so irritated me in the ER. "If you know about a missing girl, a witness to Sister Patrice's shooting, then I need to know who told you. Someone came into the ER after I left. Was it a patient? Is that why you didn't tell the cops there? Some kind of doctor-patient confidentiality bullshit?"

My anger simmered down to a low boil as he gave me the answer I'd been struggling to find. "I can't say." I pulled my shoulders back in a posture of righteous indignation. "It'd be a breach of ethics."

"Look," he said, obviously exasperated. If he only knew how equally frustrated I was. "I saw what you did for Sister Patrice. I know we kinda almost had a moment back there in the ER. But I can't let you stop me from doing my job. I need to know everything you know. And I need to know it now."

I almost told him. Which would have been even crazier than the crazy voices in my head, talking to not-quite-dead people. But he wanted to help the girl as much as I did. And he'd trusted me this far. He seemed like someone I could also maybe trust.

So I was going to tell him. The truth. All of it.

The door to the sacristy opened. A priest stood there, a uniformed officer beside him.

"Ryder, what the hell's going on?" the priest demanded. "Why are the cops stampeding my church like a bunch of goose-stepping Nazis?"

<hr/>

JESS WAS DEAD.

Harold was at the end of the hall, knocking on doors, but Devon hadn't moved. Couldn't leave Jess. Not again.

So he stood in the doorway, staring at blood and flesh and a broken body.

Jess was dead.

It couldn't be. It was impossible. All the million fantasies about her, about them, about coming home. Those thoughts had given him strength, saved his life. Jess *was* life. No way she was dead.

It was as if his insides had been hollowed out, raked clean by some animal wielding a giant claw. Jess was dead.

And Esme gone.

Thudding footsteps and the noise of a shotgun being racked spurred his body into a reflexive posture: standing tall, hands up and ready, gaze assessing the threat.

Tyree and two of his bangers, scowls fissuring their features, leading with their bulldog chins, stampeding down the hall. Amateurs. It'd been too long since Tyree had been in a serious fight. A fight for his life.

Mood he was in, Jess's blood stinking the air, Devon was happy to accommodate.

Not waiting for Tyree to reach him, he rushed the trio, slamming Tyree against the nearest wall with a sucker punch to the gut followed by another to the throat.

"Was this you?" Devon ignored the guns aimed at him. "What did you do to her?"

Tyree shook his head at his men, Adam's apple bobbing as he worked to breathe, then launched off the wall, taking Devon with him. They slammed into the opposite wall, cracking the plaster. "What you talking about? I got your guys shoving in my front door and the cops coming in the back."

Devon ducked Tyree's fist, shot his own into Tyree's exposed armpit before one of Tyree's goons dragged him off.

"Tyree, you got to see this." The other was pointing through the open door at Jess.

Devon shook free, plowed into the second goon. "Don't you look at her. Don't you dare!"

The words were an incoherent mess that matched his thoughts. Before he could pull himself together, start thinking sense, Harold was there, accompanied by a woman in her sixties. Devon recognized Mrs. Anders as he shoveled in a breath and stomped down his anger.

"Jess!" Her mournful keen competed with Tyree's cursing and the screaming inside Devon's brain.

Mrs. Anders sagged in Harold's arms while Tyree swiveled his bullhead away from the sight of Jess's body, his tiny eyes pierced with fury, and aimed his bulk at Devon like a bullet. They crashed into the opposite door with a force that rocked it on its hinges.

"My sister! This is your fault, goddamn you!" Tyree's fists rained down on Devon.

Devon pushed him off, and they faced each other with the width of the hallway between them. "She called me. Said she was in trouble. That's why I came back. What did you do? You promised to take care of her!"

Tyree's expression was crushed pea gravel. Devon wasn't sure if the other man even registered his words. "What's going on here, Tyree? Who did you piss off? You tell me, now. How the hell did Jess end up—" He couldn't finish, couldn't even glance in the direction of Jess's body.

"Nothing to do with me." Tyree spat the words out, laced with bitter hatred. "She doesn't talk to me. Thanks to you."

"Where's Esme?" Devon didn't like the way his voice climbed to a higher pitch then snagged on the way back down when he said his daughter's name. The daughter he'd never met. Thanks to Tyree.

"Shit," Tyree bellowed, charging through the doorway into Jess's apartment and reappearing moments later. "She's not here. Neither is the dog."

"Ozzie's at my place," Mrs. Anders said. "Jess asked me to watch him."

"Do you have Esme?" Devon asked. A cold gnawing in his gut made him think he already knew the answer.

His need and fury pushed the old lady back a step. She shook her head no.

Devon reached inside the doorway, yanked a framed photo, a copy of the one Jess had emailed him last year before Cece died. Cece with Jess and a chocolate Lab—Ozzie, no doubt—wearing a seeing-guide-dog's harness. Jess's scars hidden behind sunglasses and a smile brighter than a sunbeam. Between her and Cece, swinging against their hands, a playful grin on her face, was a little girl. Esme.

"I told you, you ever came back here, you'd loose them both." Tyree's voice ricocheted from the walls, high-pitched and verging on mania. As if he'd won some kind of cosmic bet. "Just like I told Jess if she ever tried to leave, I'd do to Esme what you did to Jess. I'd cripple her blind."

Devon ignored the urge to shoot Tyree and instead swung the cheap photo frame against the doorjamb, splintering it. Yanking the photo free, he held it up to his face, needing to get closer. This was the family he'd never had. The family Tyree had denied him.

"Cops looking to talk with you, boss," one of Tyree's goons announced, touching a Bluetooth earpiece.

"Let's go." Tyree hauled his breath in with audible effort and straightened, back in control. He turned his back on Jess's body without another glance. "Spread the word. No one mess with the cops. But anyone knows anything about this, they talk to me first if they want to keep on breathing. Nobody touches my family and gets away with it."

Tyree and his men beat a retreat back the way they'd come. Leaving Devon and his ghosts.

"We'd better go." Harold touched Devon's arm as if guiding a blind man. Devon shook him off.

"Leave me be." His words sliced through the air. Harold dropped his arm, took a step back.

Devon raised his face to the heavens, his eyes shut tight, wanting to roar with the pain of it all. He had lost Jess. Might lose her daughter. His daughter. Their daughter.

Eleven years of knowing he had a daughter but not knowing her had grown into a twisted fantasy of an imaginary family—one he cherished in secret, like an addict protecting his stash, telling himself that family would be his someday.

Instead of screaming, instead of kicking his way through the wall, he grabbed on to the image of the girl. His girl. Jess's girl. Esme.

"Come inside, child." Mrs. Anders' voice navigated through his maze of pain. "You come with me now." Gnarled fingers latched on to his arm with surprising strength, leading him down the hall to a room painted sunflower yellow and smelling of raisins and wine. "Sit down now. You've had a shock."

Devon's body obeyed her as automatically as he had as a child, listening to her Bible stories told in her singsong lilting Nigerian accent. Forty years she'd lived here and still sounded like she'd just gotten off the plane from Africa.

An old bedspread, the kind with little puffy balls of yarn hanging out everywhere, now covered her threadbare tweed sofa, but otherwise nothing seemed to have changed. Still the rocking chair by the window, end table overflowing with books beside it, lamp with the rose-colored shade behind it. Still the Blessed Mother on one wall and a crucifix with a palm snagged in the cross on the other—mother and son locked in an eternal staring contest. With Mrs. Anders the implacable referee between them.

He brushed his palms against his designer slacks, even the fine Italian silk rubbing his scars harshly. How he'd feared and hated Mrs. Anders and the others like her. So quick to blame him and his mother anytime Daniel Kingston went on one of his rampages.

When he was a child, Mrs. Anders had terrified him—but also offered him hope with her Jesus. Not just salvation for his soul, salvation for his mother. He remembered looking up at her, her face always haloed in light. But it was only a childhood illusion.

She was just a gnarled old woman lost in her ways. Powerless. No one to fear. Not anymore.

A big brown dog bounded in from the kitchen, nosing at Devon's knees as if expecting someone else to be sitting where he was.

"That's Ozzie."

The dog licked Devon's hand, then rested his chin on Devon's thigh when Devon ignored him.

"What the hell's going on here, Mrs. Anders?"

"Language, boy. Mind your manners." Mrs. Anders had been a teacher in a Catholic school in Lagos way back when, and she still went to Mass every day. Sometimes twice a day. At least she had when Devon was a kid. He figured that, just like her apartment, she hadn't changed.

"No, goddamn it, I won't mind my damn manners." He stood up. The dog didn't growl but did move to stand toe-to-toe with Devon, placing himself between Devon and the old lady. Dog had good sense. "I'm not a kid anymore. I'm a grown man, and I want some answers. Now!"

"Only God has the answers, child. You know that. We should pray." She bowed her head, hands folded together, shoulders rocking, lips moving, but he didn't hear her words.

He felt as if he were falling, plummeting down an elevator shaft with no idea when he'd hit bottom. He squeezed his fists tight, trying to grab hold of something, anything, and finding nothing.

Memories sharp as broken glass pierced his vision. Jess laughing. Her smile. The way her forehead got that little knot in the middle when she was angry. The taste of her lips against his. Those eyes—brown with flecks of light that danced when they made love.

Until the night he'd killed that light forever.

Jess was dead. His little girl gone. Missing. Or taken?

He knuckled his fists against his temples. "I need to find her." He swallowed, dared to say her name, breathing life into the fantasy. A fantasy that had suddenly become his worst nightmare. "Esme."

"Amen." Mrs. Anders stopped her singsong cadence and looked up. "Take Ozzie. He's your best chance. Start at St. Tim's."

"The church?"

"Sister Patrice was here earlier. Maybe she knows something about—" Mrs. Anders shivered violently and avoided looking at the door Harold leaned against.

So many questions thundered through Devon's head. He didn't have time for questions—or answers. He grabbed the leash hanging beside the door and hooked it to the dog's collar.

"Harold, you wait five minutes, then call in a 911 about Jess. I don't want her lying there alone."

"I'm coming with you," Harold protested.

Devon shook his head. He needed to talk with this nun, Patrice, alone. Find Esme, get some answers. "No. You and the others wait here, keep an eye on Tyree. I know he's behind this, somehow. Or he knows who is. I'll call you when I need you."

"But—" Harold swallowed his protest, obviously not liking the change in plans. "No problem."

"I'll watch her," Mrs. Anders said. "Jess. Hold vigil."

Devon whirled on her, her soft voice of contrition igniting his fury. "You? Lot of good your prayers ever did anyone. Worse than useless, you and your God."

His words flew at her like a slap, shaking her. For the first time, he noticed how skinny she was, her skin so thin you could see the veins and blood running through it. Old. When had she gotten so old?

"Living long as I have around here, you learn not to see or hear anything." Her bony shoulders barely creased the thin cotton of her housedress as she shrugged. She didn't meet his gaze as she spoke. "But I don't know who did that—who hurt Jess. I don't think Tyree does either. He's been watching out for the folks here since you left." Finally, she looked up. "He's changed, Devon."

Devon's anger spiked through his body, rooting him to the ground. Tyree? Changed? No way. Tyree was a liar, a user, a master manipulator. He'd never change.

Finally, he was able to draw in a whistle of air through his gritted teeth. He nodded to Mrs. Anders, yanked on the dog's lead, and walked out. The dog whined and tried to stop when they passed the door to Jess's apartment, but Devon refused to yield. He wound the lead around his hand so tight it choked the blood from it. He had no time for distractions, no time for pain. Had to focus on what was important.

Jess was dead. Esme was alive.

And Esme was his. Had been his for eleven years, eleven years stolen. She was all he had left.

He was going to kill Tyree.

No, first he was going to save Esme. Claim what was his.

Then he'd make Tyree pay.

Even if it meant burning the Tower to the ground.

Tyree was as good as dead.

CHAPTER NINE

LIKE MOST CATHOLIC schoolgirls, I had a crush on our priest, Father Kersavage. After my dad died, I never stepped foot inside St. Tim's again, but I still had to go to school. The kids knew the whole story behind my father's death—everyone in the parish did—making me the center of gossip and unwanted attention. Plus, of course, I felt guilty as hell.

I was only twelve, would have blamed myself for war, famine, poverty if you gave me half a reason to. My self-involved need to feel some semblance of control over this messed-up world ranked second only to my need for reassurance that the bad things that happened really weren't my fault or in my control.

Of course, no one gave me that. Because my dad's death *was* my fault.

Father Kersavage was the only person who would talk to me about Dad. Said it wasn't up to me to try to understand the Lord's plan. That would be an act of hubris. Instead, he said all I could do was accept it, ask for forgiveness for my sins, and abandon my willful ways. In other words, I needed faith more than I needed my father.

All that normal Catholic guilt bullshit. We can't control anything, but we're still responsible enough that we should feel guilty even if it's all pre-ordained? What kind of twisted logic is that?

So, yeah, my schoolgirl crush morphed into resentment. At the Church, at Father Kersavage, at the entire universe.

I couldn't change what happened to my dad. I'd have to live with it every day for the rest of my life. But, damn it, I didn't have to be their Judas goat.

So I'd fled Cambria as soon as I could drive. Got a job, got a GED, got emancipated. Worked the system to get through college and medical school, fell in love, married a man from Cambria, and wound up right back where I'd started. How's that for irony?

But you can never go home again. Living my own life seems to have given my family only more reason to resent my role in my father's death.

Father Kersavage is now dead and buried—alcoholic cirrhosis. And he was never anything like the priest who stood before me now.

This priest, Father Vance, looked more like a pro basketball player than a priest. He wore jeans and a U2 T-shirt smeared with white paint. A jagged scar raked across the corner of his jaw and down the side of his neck, disappearing beneath his collar, while his hands had more scars across the knuckles. I imagined Father Kersavage would have given this priest the same condescending lectures he'd saddled me with. Penance, he called our little talks. Instructions on humility.

The priest before me didn't look like he'd put up with that kind of bullshit. Not at all.

He stared at Ryder, seeming to effortlessly read between the lines furrowing Ryder's face before pulling him into a bone-crushing hug. Brief, manly, but telling. They knew each other fairly well. They looked about the same age, although Vance carried a few more pounds on him and had a few inches on Ryder's six feet.

The men stepped into the sacristy, and I followed.

"Hell." Vance made the epithet sound like an apology. "No way you'd send the goons to babysit me and come here looking like that unless it was something bad."

Ryder said nothing, just nodded. Vance sucked in his breath, braced himself.

"Is there someplace we can talk?" Ryder asked Vance.

"If it's bad news, no place better to hear it." Vance took a seat in the front pew and it looked like it would take a bulldozer to budge him. He folded his hands as if in prayer but didn't bow his head. Instead, he looked at Ryder straight-on. "Tell me."

I liked the priest. Liked his no-nonsense style, the way he didn't go all cold and remote but still seemed to have human feelings and wasn't ashamed of them. Not trying to be holier-than-thou.

Ryder's face fissured with pain. The uniformed officer saw it and cleared his throat, looking away.

"McInerny, why don't you go help Petrosky." Ryder's voice was strong, his expression one of command. "She's in the alley coordinating the search for a missing girl."

"Missing girl?" Vance said. "Ryder, what's going on?"

McInerny left, his boots ringing against the marble floor. Ryder leaned his back against the altar rail, arms crossed, frowning. Candles flickered on either side of him, shadowing his face more than illuminating. Vance arched an eyebrow, nodding to the crucifix hanging above him. Rude to turn your back on your savior. Ryder straightened, looking two decades younger for a flitting moment, his hand jerking up in a quick sign of the cross as he pivoted and took a seat beside Vance.

"Sister Patrice is dead. Shot." Ryder's words were blunt, his tone compassionate. I could tell he'd done this before. He knew it was better to say the words in plain English, no sugarcoating or dancing around.

"Patrice? No." The last word came out drawn and quartered. At first in confusion and disbelief, then denial, and finally, despair. "No. Not Patrice. Who—"

"We don't know. We think it happened in the alley behind the church. Did you see anything?"

"No." The priest's voice was choked. "No. I was downstairs painting. Had the window open for ventilation and heard the shots, but I couldn't see anything with the rain. By the time I got upstairs and ran out to look, there was nobody there. I had no idea—" He bowed his head, lips moving without sound, eyes closed.

I watched him pray, amazed at the sudden calm that drifted over his grief-stricken features. No amount of praying had ever done that for me. Maybe I was doing it wrong? Or it worked only for people who believed.

Ryder gave him a moment. Vance crossed himself and looked back up.

"Dr. Rossi," Ryder nodded to where I stood behind a marble pillar, doing my best to stay out of sight of the crucifix, "says there's a young girl, around ten, missing."

"Esme. Patrice was going to see her, her and her mom, Jess. Was she shot as well?"

"We don't know. Who's Esme?"

"Esme Willard. Lives with her mother in the Tower. Apartment…" His face blanked, then morphed to frustration. "Damn it, I can't remember."

"Did Sister Patrice have an office?" I asked.

Both men stared at me, Ryder with approval and Vance with relief. "Yes. Yes, she did. Come with me." He stepped toward me, then stopped, looking down and blinking his eyes clear. "I'm sorry. You are?"

Ryder intervened. "This is Dr. Angela Rossi. She tried to save Sister Patrice." And failed, he didn't add. I was thankful for the omission. For some reason, I wanted Vance to like me. Killing a nun didn't seem like such a good starting place.

Vance took my hand, folding his around it as if praying. "How did you know Esme was missing?"

"Not sure. I just know a ten-year-old black girl was with Patrice when she got shot. Patrice sent her into the Tower to hide."

Vance nodded as if that made perfect sense. He genuflected, then turned and kept walking. Ryder, however, grabbed my arm. "How did you know she was there when Sister Patrice was shot? How did you know Sister Patrice was there at all?"

Whoops. Well, hell, it wasn't like I'd gotten messages from not-quite-dead people before. And I'm a terrible liar. Much better at knowing when others lie. I've had tons of practice in that: Everyone lies in the ER. Just a fact of life.

"Esme's mother was the last person called on Patrice's cell phone." I went with an edited version of the truth.

"You went through Sister Patrice's effects? That's tampering with evidence."

"It was on the floor of the trauma room. All I did was pick it up before someone stepped on it." Thankfully, we arrived at a side hallway lined with two wooden doors before he could ask anything more.

Vance opened a door and gestured for us to go inside. "Patrice and Sister Monique work out of this office."

"And Sister Monique is where?" Ryder asked, his notebook at the ready.

"At the Mother House for the holiday. Patrice drew the short straw, stayed behind to make sure I didn't starve to death and to see to any emergencies." Vance picked up a photo from one of the desks. "Here's Patrice and Esme."

I held the picture, not sure if I should be relieved that I hadn't imagined it all or terrified that somehow Patrice really had spoken to me as she lay dead, my hand on her heart. Decided to focus on finding the girl. I'd figure out the rest later. Ah, the power of denial. "That's her, that's the girl."

Ryder shot me a how-the-hell-could-you-know look. "Can you get me Esme's contact information?" he asked Vance. "And I'll need to take this, to make copies."

Vance nodded, getting busy at Patrice's computer. As he waited for the machine to boot up, he asked, "She made it to the hospital alive? I don't suppose anyone was able to give her last rites?"

Ryder sucked in his breath but otherwise maintained his unemotional facade. I'm sure we both were remembering Patrice's ravaged body after I cracked her chest. His cell rang, leaving it to me to answer Vance's question.

"I'm sorry," I told him, fighting the urge to bounce my weight from one foot to the other like I was a kid back in catechism class.

"It happened too fast."

Whatever Ryder was hearing, it wasn't good news. "What do you mean you can't open it? I don't care if you have to wake Daniel Kingston. I don't care if you have to wake the mayor. We need to get that door open. Have the fire guys cut through it, if you need to."

He pocketed his phone. "I have to go. Are you sure you can't think of any reason someone would want to hurt Sister Patrice or that little girl? Anything going on around here that might be tied in to this?"

I noticed how his questions weren't as direct when they were aimed at Vance. Was that because he was trying to give the priest an out in case something had been divulged during a confession? Or because they were friends? Ryder didn't seem the kind of guy who would cut someone a break for old times' sake—not when murder was involved. And he'd known Patrice, as well. No, he wasn't letting Vance off easy, I decided. If Ryder didn't get the information he needed, he'd be back for more.

Vance seemed to understand that as well. He gave Ryder's questions serious thought, his fingers still at the keyboard, gaze unfocused. Finally, he shook his head in a motion that rumbled through his entire body. "No. Nothing."

Vance returned to the computer. "West tower, apartment 304. That's where Esme lives."

Ryder dialed a number. "Get some men over to apartment 304, west wing of the Tower. See if you can find me some witnesses on this girl's disappearance. Yeah, yeah, I'm on my way."

He hung up once more, shoving the phone into his belt holster like it was a weapon. "Thanks, Vance. I'll be back to talk with you more as soon as I can."

"When can I see Patrice?" Vance asked.

"It will be awhile. I'll see what I can do." He started out the door, then stopped and held it open. "We'll need to check everything in this office and Sister Patrice's room. I'll send some men."

There was an awkward pause. Then Vance stood and walked past

Ryder. I followed. Ryder closed the door. "Can you see that no one goes in there?" he asked Vance.

A smile barely surfaced on the priest's face. "Glad to see I'm not a suspect."

The smile faded when Ryder didn't answer. He glanced at the door, then shrugged as if realizing the futility of locking it. There would be more than one key. I wondered how deep the friendship between the two men ran if Ryder was willing to risk evidence on it. Of course, if Vance had killed Patrice, he had plenty of time to destroy any evidence before he called 911.

"I'll be back." Ryder took two steps down the hall, toward the massive front doors, then stopped at a station of the cross surrounded by candles. He glanced at the painting then back at Vance. "I'm sorry for your loss."

His words didn't sound empty. Or like a last-minute thought. Vance nodded.

"Find Esme," Vance said, echoing Patrice's last words.

I shivered and hurried after Ryder. I needed to get out of this place where my every movement was followed by the spying eyes of a dead god.

Ryder and I walked together to the front of the church. He opened the thick oak door leading to the vestibule for me, and I crossed over. The door closed with a sigh. No hollow thud, like you'd expect from such a tall, heavy, ancient door. Just a tired exhalation, carrying with it the grief of a thousand lost souls.

I placed my hand on the cold iron of the even larger exterior door, ready to push it open, when I realized Ryder was no longer at my side. I looked back. He stood, barely, slumped against the oak-paneled wall, his face crisscrossed by shadows.

His eyes met mine. He said nothing. Didn't have to. I understood his grief, his pain. I'd carried them myself. Maybe not for Patrice or his friend the priest, but for other victims.

I stepped toward him, settled my hand over his, and stood with him. That was it. No words, no sentiments, no tears. A simple, private pause. Breathing room before facing the outside world.

His exhalation echoed in the small space, a plaintive note that spoke volumes. About the world, about the waste, about how weary he was. Fighting for justice when justice always came too late. Losing the fight more often than not. Returning to the battle every waking day.

I heard him. Each unspoken word.

Not like I had heard Patrice's words. No, this was more normal—one exhausted professional recognizing another. Comrades in arms.

His gaze rested on mine, his face edged by the chiseled glare of the overhead light caught in its ornate cage, and I felt closer to him than I had to anyone since my dad died. Even closer than Jacob, when we were married.

As if he knew every inch of me, inside and out.

A scary thought. More scary: It didn't frighten me.

Was it one more symptom? Another diversion from reality? Yet, Patrice's voice had been real.

Was this feeling I had truth—or delusion? I wanted to believe it was real, but I knew nothing about Ryder, nothing at all to explain this sudden feeling of harmony. This certainty of *rightness*.

For one frozen moment in time, we were closer than any two people could be. It felt very much like the moment when I had held Patrice's heart in my hand—poised between life and death, between surrender and denial, between action and consequence.

Then it was gone.

He blinked. Released my hand. "I'd better get back to work," he said, his voice as rough as if we had kissed, even though we'd barely even touched.

I didn't move away from him. Not because I was frozen—because I didn't want to leave. I wanted time to stop again, wanted to re-create that sense of belonging.

A wicked wind blew a stray draft through the crack in the outside doors, leaving goose bumps in its wake. He flushed as I kept staring, then he looked away. Embarrassed? Had I scared him off?

Disappointed, I stepped back, turned to the door. His phone shrieked, bouncing echoes off the stone walls. "Ryder. Yeah, on my way." He hung up. "They found another body. A woman. In the Tower."

"A woman?"

"Not a girl," he reassured me. "Preliminary ID is a Jessalyn Willard."

Esme's mother. Two women and a child. Why would a killer target them?

"Stay here with Vance, will you?" He pulled the heavy outside door open. "I hate for him to be alone."

"I want to help find Esme."

"I'm not letting any civilians into those tunnels. You'd only be standing in the rain doing nothing." Now he turned back, his body half-hidden in the shadows of the overhang. "I'll call as soon as we find anything." My doubt must have been evident, because he met my eyes with a smile, brushing my arm with his hand. "I promise."

He was gone, the thick door clicking shut behind him. I stood alone in silence. The high-ceilinged vestibule was an echo chamber, my own breathing suddenly bombarding me like cannon salvos from heaven.

One door leading outside to the storm, one leading inside to sins I refused to confess. I hesitated between them, not sure which one led to the greater hell.

CHAPTER TEN

DEVON HAD TO force himself to walk, not run, past the cops rapidly surrounding the Tower. Just another black man out for a stroll in the rain with his dog. No, that's not a gun, take no notice, Officer. Nothing to see here, nothing at all....

Good thing the police were more interested in getting Tyree's boys under control. Good thing they were short-staffed because of the holiday. Good thing it was foggy and dark since there was no fuckin' way he could control the waves of fury and panic roiling off him, colliding with the raindrops popping against his skin.

His daughter. His goddamn daughter. Everything he'd done, he'd done for her and Jess. His fingers twisted a corner of the photo he'd shoved into his pocket. Esme. She looked just like Jess. Except her eyes. She had Devon's eyes. All he'd ever hoped or dreamed was for her to have a life different than his.

He couldn't stand the thought of her alone in the dark. Running scared. Had she seen Jess get killed? Terrified. She must be terrified. And if the men who killed Jess found her before he did?

For a moment he couldn't breathe, couldn't even swallow his own spit. First time since that awful night with Jess in the tunnels that fear overwhelmed him, a fear so deep it made the blood in his veins tremble.

They'd been two kids, crazy in love. Crazy enough to break Tyree's rules and trespass on his territory in an effort to find a private place that was theirs alone. Only to have their night of pleasure turn into a horrifying inferno.

Thanks to Tyree and his paranoia. He'd set a fire bomb to protect one of his stashes. And Jess and Devon had triggered it. Devon's pace quickened at the memory of Jess's screams, the searing pain, flames dancing across his skin as he dragged her to safety...

The damn dog decided it was a good time to take a piss. Devon about strangled the beast. Turned out for the best, because as the dog raised his leg against the storefront, a man dashed out of the church doors. Not just a man, a cop. The cop in charge from the way the others ambushed him as soon as he approached the alley choked with patrol cars.

"Good dog," Devon muttered. A fire truck pulled up, double-parking, blocking the street, and he used its bulk as cover to approach St. Timothy's. *Dayut-beri,* the Russians would say. When you are given, take it.

He jogged up the steps, the dog at his side. Never thought he'd be coming back here to St. Tim's. Not in a million years.

Pulling the heavy wooden door open, he let the dog enter first. He followed, bounding across the vestibule to reach the inside door before noticing the woman standing there.

Not Patrice. Instead, a too-skinny white girl with dark hair, too-small tits, and a nice ass. Eyes dark, very dark. Serious, as if she might actually know something worth knowing.

"Where's Patrice?"

She said nothing, like one of the goddamn statues littering this place. He brushed past her, didn't have time for this shit, and ran into the church proper, yelling for Patrice.

"She's not here," the woman said, following him.

Before he could answer, a tall black man appeared, his hands fumbling as he adjusted a clerical collar and the final button of a black shirt. Holy shit. Marcus.

Devon hadn't thought of Marcus Vance in years. But as soon as he saw the man, he remembered him. Remembered those beefy fists pummeling him when he was twelve, being jumped into the Royales. Remembered the fight with rival drug dealers from Baltimore that left

Marcus with the scar on his face.

Marcus used to be Tyree's right-hand man, his enforcer. And now he was a fuckin' priest?

Startled laughter escaped Devon, laughter mixed with frustration and confusion and fear. Alice in freakin' Wonderland, that's where he was. "Where the hell's Patrice?"

Marcus came to a stop in front of him. Hands shoved into his back pockets, rocking on his heels, just like when they were both a decade younger. Marcus was in his late thirties now, but damn, he looked the same as Devon remembered. Except the constant smarmy smirk—that had vanished. The smile that replaced it was sad, sorrowful, as if Marcus wished Devon had stayed away.

"Hello, Devon."

"I asked you a question. Where's Patrice?"

"Why do you want to know?"

"I need to fucking know. She ran off with—" He almost said "my little girl" before stopping himself. "She ran off with Jess's girl, Esme."

"Do you know where Esme is?" The woman from the foyer had moved into the doorway but stopped there, watching the two of them warily. Devon turned so he could keep them both in his sight. The dog had a thing for the woman, was yanking on his leash to go to her, so he dropped it, let the mutt do as he pleased.

"No. That's why I need to find Patrice."

Marcus and the woman exchanged a glance, and Devon knew the news was bad. "What happened?"

Marcus touched Devon's arm. "Maybe you should sit down."

"No. I don't have time to sit down. Jess is dead, do you understand? Dead. Killed. Esme ran away. They said Patrice knows where she is. We need to find her."

"Patrice is dead." This from the woman. Her tone was gentle, but the words still staggered him. He didn't sit, but reached for the back of the nearest pew to brace himself.

"Esme?"

79

"Patrice hid her from the people who killed her. Sent her down into the tunnels."

Marcus looked surprised at that, frowning at the woman. She continued, "The police are organizing a search."

"The police won't find squat," Devon said, shaking his head, trying to rearrange the new facts in his brain. "Not down there. But I can."

The woman finally took a step into the church proper, the dog following on her heels, nosing at her leg. "You know the tunnels?"

"Practically lived down there when I was a kid getting chased by folks like him." Devon nodded at Marcus.

"Runt." Marcus smiled as he used the old name. "If anyone can find Esme, he can," he told the woman. "And Ozzie."

The dog perked his ears at his name and sat beside the woman's leg. She absently scratched his head. "This is Esme's dog?"

"Her mom's."

"Just who the hell are you anyway?" Devon asked, tired of being kept in the dark while seconds ticked past.

"Devon Price," Marcus made the introductions, "this is Dr. Angela Rossi. Works Good Sam's ER. She's the one who took care of Patrice."

Devon gave a grunt of acknowledgment. He didn't have time for this shit. "The police have the alley covered. I'll need to get in through the basement here."

"There's an entrance to the tunnels here?" the doctor asked. She eyed Marcus with suspicion. "Why didn't you tell Ryder?"

"You never said Esme was in the tunnels. All the entrances are supposed to be locked. To keep kids from wandering down there." Marcus's frown deepened, and Devon knew the priest was remembering the night when Jess—when Devon—lost everything. Down in the tunnels.

"Patrice had a key," the doctor, Angela, continued. "She used it to let Esme in."

"I don't need no goddamn key." Devon grabbed the dog's leash and pushed past Marcus when the priest didn't move out of his way fast enough. Man still kept in shape despite the priest collar. Wolf in sheep's clothing.

What the hell had happened around here after Devon left home? He jogged down the middle aisle, not bothering to pause at the altar, took a sharp left and circled around behind the altar to the staircase there. To his annoyance, both Marcus and Angela followed. He didn't need anyone tagging along, slowing him down.

"Who are you?" Angela shouted. "Why are you carrying a gun?"

"It's all right," Marcus assured her. "Devon would never hurt Esme."

Devon shot a glance over his shoulder at Marcus. Did the priest know Esme was his? Had Jess told him? She and Cece were the only people besides Tyree who'd known, but it wouldn't have been hard for someone like Marcus to guess the truth.

They reached the basement. Devon led the way past the boiler room, past several storage rooms, one covered in plastic and reeking of wet paint, then down another half-flight of stairs to a metal door. He jangled the doorknob. Locked.

"You sure she's in there?" he asked the doctor.

"Yes."

He handed her the dog's leash and dug out his wallet. Sliding free two thin strips of metal he kept hidden in the seams, he bent to the door. Hadn't done this in ages. He had others to do this kind of work now, but he hadn't lost his touch. "You'd best call Tyree, let him know the cops will be crawling through his space."

"No. We should call Ryder," Angela argued.

The lock clicked open. Devon straightened and turned to face her. She didn't appear at all intimidated. Instead, she held her ground. The dog, traitor, wedged himself between the two of them, protecting her with his body. This was why he'd never liked dogs. Too noisy at all the wrong times, and they bartered their allegiance to anyone for a biscuit or pat on the head.

"A little girl's life depends on us," Angela said. "We should help the police find her."

"I can find her faster than they can. There's places in there that won't show up on any map. Places that strangers stumbling into them could lead to folks getting hurt."

"You mean booby-trapped?"

"If Tyree's still playing his same old games." He glanced to his side, where Marcus stood listening, considering, all Mr. Man-of-the-Cloth-King-Solomon-like. "You tell me, Marcus. Should we send the cops in?"

"No. He's right. I'll call Ryder, warn him." He patted Angela on the shoulder. "It's the best way."

The doctor didn't look too convinced. In fact, she looked downright suspicious of them both. Smart lady. If Patrice had had a key to the tunnels, it was a good bet she'd negotiated a truce with Tyree and was using them for her own purposes.

"We gonna surprise anyone nasty down there?" he asked Marcus.

Marcus didn't bother looking innocent. "No. Patrice moved the last group out a few days ago." He sighed and turned to Angela. "Wish you'd told me about the tunnels before. Patrice uses a few rooms off this end to hide people on the underground railroad—a few illegals, mainly women running from abusive partners."

"She wouldn't set booby traps for that—"

"No. But Tyree would. He has several stashes down there. No telling what kind of security he has set up near them."

"You any idea where they are?" Devon asked, swinging the door open. There was a bookcase on the other side with a bunch of flashlights lined up on it. He grabbed one, made sure it worked and stuffed it in his coat pocket, then grabbed one more. Last thing he could risk was wandering in the dark. Not down there.

"No. I'm long out of that."

Devon stepped over the threshold, aiming the light down the tunnel. The air was fresh here, smelled of laundry detergent and bleach. Patrice cleaning up after her guests. Farther in it wouldn't be so pleasant. "Call Tyree. Tell him Esme might be down here."

He drew his breath in, surprised at how much effort it took. He'd been calmer staring down men aiming guns at him. But this time there was more than his life at stake. And the tunnels…Christ, he'd never, ever wanted to return to the tunnels, to that awful night eleven years ago. Jess's screams tore through his mind, followed by his own choked sobs as he tried in vain to help her. And the smell, that godawful stench of burnt flesh. His stomach heaved at the memory.

He stepped into the darkness, reached back for the dog's leash. Damn thing better be able to find Esme, fast. His heart stuttered at the thought of her down there, alone, in the dark.

To his surprise, the doctor refused to relinquish the leash. Instead, she also grabbed a flashlight and followed him. "I'm coming with you."

CHAPTER ELEVEN

RYDER STUMBLED DOWN the steps of St. Tim's, back out into the rain, cursing himself for a fool.

Christ on a pogo! He'd lost it, lost it good. He couldn't explain what had come over him inside the church. Suddenly, there they were, shut up in the small, dark space, and Rossi had smelled so very good, and he was so very tired and lonely and…and he didn't even know what. Just that he was sick of this empty feeling that greeted him every morning and haunted him every night, and he had no idea how to fill the void.

Until now. Rossi had filled it quite nicely, thank you. The way heat roiled off her, as if she was feverish. Or he was. That strong jaw, stubborn—as if he hadn't already figured that out for himself.

What the hell was he thinking, letting a woman distract him? During a goddamn murder—make that double murder—investigation.

Dig a hole and bury him now. Maybe the brass was right. He was losing it. Make that, lost it, past tense.

Sleet battered his head and neck, tiny snips of ice, making him wish he'd never left Rossi.

Forget Rossi. Time to go look at another body. At least it wasn't the kid's.

Petrosky waited for him at the bottom of the steps. They wove between the haphazard collection of vehicles. In the distance, he could see sparks from the firefighters cutting through the steel door down the alley.

"What've we got?"

"Female occupant of the apartment, dead from multiple gunshot wounds, obvious forced entry, no signs of robbery."

The fire crew chief spotted him and waved him over to a makeshift command center at the back hatch of their Tahoe.

"Has the deputy chief gotten here yet?" Ryder asked Petrosky as they detoured over to the FD lieutenant.

"No. You're still ranking PD."

Christ. Goddamn brass wouldn't let him call in mutual aid or do this thing right but also couldn't be bothered enough to leave their turkey dinners and come out in the rain. You could bet, soon as the press showed up, they'd be here, squawking to get their five minutes in the limelight.

Ryder couldn't care less about the credit. He just wanted to find the girl—alive—and work his two dead bodies. Hard to do that when he was also coordinating a search of seven flights of apartments, negotiating a truce with the gang that occupied them, and gaining entrance to the tunnels below. His head ached. He circled it with his hands, palms pressing against both sides of his skull, only to unleash a new wave of pain when he snagged one of Rossi's staples.

"Son of a bitch."

The fire department lieutenant looked up and nodded, thought he was describing the situation. "You got that right."

"You got a plan for the tunnel search?" Ryder asked, peering over the firefighter's shoulder to a ragged stack of blueprints spread out in the cargo bay of the SUV.

"These maps are the best we have," the LT said. "Not even sure you'd call them maps, really. More like wishful thinking."

"Why are so many areas blank?" Ryder asked. Bad enough he had two homicides to cover, witnesses to question, but finding the kid took precedence. Couldn't do that without some decent intel.

The LT rolled his eyes. "Security. The tunnels were built as a big fall-out shelter. Emergency evacuation center, they called it. Only part of it is under the Tower. It spreads out over five blocks in every direction. It's a freakin' city down there. You remember Three Mile Island? This," he rapped his knuckles on the map, "is where they evacuated the governor and the whole damn state government to. I know two people been down there in the last few years, and only one of them is still alive."

"Someone got killed down there?"

"Nah. He died of a coronary, fighting a two-alarmer over on Congress."

"Who's the one alive?"

"You're looking at him. We got sent down for a fire inspection after we pissed off the chief. Made it maybe twenty yards in before calling it quits. Place is a shithole, a fucking maze. Phones and radios won't work."

The SWAT commander jogged up to join them. He glanced at the blueprints, shaking his head, rain flicking off his helmet, splattering the map. "Hope you're not planning on any frontal assaults. Talk about your goddamn fatal funnel. No room to maneuver, no sight lines. We need better intel."

No shit, Ryder thought, but he kept his voice clear of emotion. "We've a missing ten-year-old girl, and she was last seen going into those tunnels. They connect to the Tower, so we need to work both locations. My men have the Tower covered, but we'll need backup on the perimeter, especially if the Royales get antsy. Plus, we've a homicide scene in the Tower, so an extra presence there wouldn't hurt."

"I'll spread my guys out, team up with yours until we have a plan of action ready to go." He spoke briefly to his second-in-command.

"Have them start a door-to-door on the third floor where the body is, work their way down, then back up again. But no one goes on the seventh floor until I have a chance to talk with Tyree Willard. Last thing we need is to start a war with the Royales."

"We knocking or kicking?" the SWAT guy asked. Wanting the rules of engagement—and making it Ryder's responsibility if things went wrong.

"Kicking, but go easy on the furniture. We've exigent circumstances to look for the kid—nothing else. Of course, anything you see in plain sight…"

"Got it. Let's go!" he shouted to his men, waving them into action.

Petrosky stirred at Ryder's side. "You want me to go with them?"

"No. Stay with me, monitor the radio while I try to sort out this mess." Ryder turned back to the fire lieutenant. "This kid might be injured. We need to gain access to the tunnels and start searching. There has to be someone who knows them."

The fire LT scratched his jaw. "You remember the alligator guy? Burned down that warehouse down by the wharf?"

"The one with the rabbits?"

"Yeah. Should have seen that place—cages on cages of burnt-up rabbits. He was feeding them to the alligator he was keeping," he explained when Petrosky raised an eyebrow. "One night the alligator tried to sneak a snack, knocked down some cages onto a space heater and *whoompf*, charbroiled rabbit all around. But the gator lived."

"What's he have to do with my girl?" Ryder interrupted.

"Point is, Gator Guy lived down in the tunnels for years before Kingston's men found him and forced him out. He could tell us all about them."

"He's in Rockview." The state penitentiary was two hours away. "We can't wait that long."

The LT shook his head. "Nah. He only got eight months, and with overcrowding, they kept him here. He's in county lockup."

Good excuse to bypass the brass and get some mutual aid from the sheriff's department. Ryder got on his cell, explaining the situation to the ranking deputy on duty. As he hung up, the sparks from the tunnel door died down, and a triumphant cry went up from the firefighters gathered there. "We're in!"

A crowd of uniforms surged toward the end of the alley. Ryder's phone rang. He answered it. "Ryder here."

"It's me again." Vance sounded stressed. "Listen, don't go into the tunnels. Tyree and his gang have them booby-trapped. It's not safe."

"Shit. Okay, thanks." He hung up and turned and yelled, "Hold up, guys!" Then he grabbed Petrosky's arm. "You. Go get Tyree Willard and haul his fat ass down here. Take backup with you. If he gives you any trouble, you give it right back. All I need is for him to be able to talk to me, you get it?"

Petrosky's eyes went wide at Ryder's menacing tone. He didn't care. He was so sick of Tyree and the Royales running this block like they were freakin' kings, beyond the law. Not tonight, goddamn it. Not with two bodies cooling and a little girl's life on the line.

"What are you waiting for?" he snapped when Petrosky didn't move fast enough. "Go. Now!"

۞

FLYNN WAS HALF-TEMPTED to deal with Leo herself. A final solution. He was no good, worth less than mud scraped off his father's shoes.

But she didn't. She couldn't. She owed Daniel everything. After she'd died and been reborn, she'd woken up in the ICU in a bed beside his. She'd gotten good news: She'd live. He'd received a death sentence: terminal cancer.

They'd bonded, the girl with no name and no past she was willing to claim, and the sixty-seven-year-old tycoon who'd needed someone he could trust with his secret. He'd taken her off the streets, given her a home. More than just the job and money and opportunity, it was the trust—no, not trust, faith. Daniel asked her to do things verging on the impossible, and she did them, simply because he believed she could.

Biggest adrenaline rush ever.

Before Leo returned home in disgrace earlier this year, Daniel's missions had entailed corporate espionage and spying, helping him to bring down competitors, ferreting out secrets he could use to solidify his power. It had been exciting, challenging—especially for a girl who hadn't even finished high school before Daniel provided her with an all-access pass to anything she wanted to learn.

Daniel had taught her that knowledge was power. Nights alone in the empty mansion—before Leo spoiled it all—she would sit curled up on the floor, laptop surrounded by notepads and textbooks, and he would supervise her studies: modern psychological warfare, cybersecurity, leadership tactics of Genghis Khan, economic game theory. No topic was off-limits—as long as it kept Daniel amused and served to sharpen Flynn into a more effective weapon for him to wield.

For Daniel, it was a way to keep the pain from his cancer treatments at bay. For Flynn it was her ticket to a new life.

Most people hated the tunnels, feared the anonymous creatures— human and inhuman—that wandered the blackness. Not Flynn. She enjoyed being able to blend in, becoming invisible as she stalked her prey: Leo.

He used expensive night vision goggles to travel from the Kingston brownstone to his lab hidden deep within the maze. None of the tunnels—the largest as wide as a single-lane street, the narrowest with space for only one person at a time to travel through—had working lights.

Flynn avoided the pedestrian paths, instead climbing up past the multicolored pipes at ceiling height to the maintenance catwalk that ran between the pipes and the concrete roof. Below, the maze of rooms was enclosed by walls and thick metal doors, but up here in the cramped space of the catwalks, she could move past walls and doors and access most of the underground compound.

Unfortunately, Leo had turned her search for him into a game, moving his lair frequently while setting traps and false trails for Flynn. Everything was a game to Leo. Including what he did to his victims. But now things were spiraling out of control.

Best way out of this for everyone was if she snatched his current victim and paid the girl off with a one-way ticket out of town, no muss, no fuss. She'd done it before when she'd first discovered his "laboratory," before Leo had moved his base of operations out of the brownstone and into the tunnels. He'd acted so superior after that, thinking she couldn't interrupt him or stop him down here where he operated under Tyree's protection.

Worse than superior. Smug.

He'd promised Flynn that someday, when her guard was down, he'd take her. Show her firsthand what games he and his guests enjoyed. In the meantime, he satisfied himself by leaving blood-stained clothing on her pillow; jewelry bent and twisted, melted by intense heat, the stink of burnt flesh clinging to it; once, a lock of hair tied in a ribbon, a piece of scalp still attached.

She didn't bother Daniel with Leo's lame attempts at psychological warfare. Mainly because she didn't let Leo bother her. Refused to let him get past her guard.

But this was the last time, she swore to herself. She was done playing games.

CHAPTER TWELVE

THIS WASN'T THE smartest thing I've ever done. Following a stranger into a subterranean labyrinth. But if Devon Price could lead me to Esme, what choice did I have? Wait for Ryder and his men to finish searching the Tower, negotiate a truce with Tyree Willard, have him and his gang show them the hidden traps in the tunnels, all while investigating two crime scenes?

I stepped forward, the tunnel's darkness seeping around me like walking into an inky pool, stones in my pockets. The dog followed at my knee. I was glad for someone I could trust in here—two against one, better odds. I patted the dog as we walked. He tilted his nose up and licked my palm. Even that slimy companionship was comforting. I'd had worse things on my hands tonight than doggy spit.

The man in front of me did indeed seem to know where he was going; at least, he didn't hesitate as we passed out of range of the last remnants of light escaping from the church. Then he made a sharp right-hand turn into complete darkness.

I waved my flashlight. It was a bright LED model, yet seemed as ineffective as a child's toy when it came to piercing the blackness. The roof was high above us. At least twenty feet, but I couldn't see to the top through the maze of pipes suspended at ceiling height and the metal catwalk above them. Big pipes, little pipes, all color-coded and letting out the occasional bang, hiss, or whoosh. Unsettling. Especially since I had the feeling the noises weren't all coming from inside the pipes. What could be living down here?

The air didn't smell dank or musty like a cellar. Rather, it had an acid bite to it, a chemical tinge. The walls were cinderblock, painted white and lined with metal shelves that extended from the floor up twelve feet overhead. The floors were gray concrete with color-coded lines—like they used to have in hospitals to direct patients and staff. The place must have been set up in pods or wards, because we'd pass a group of same-colored metal doors, then nothing, bare walls for ten, twenty yards. There should have been dust, cobwebs—but there weren't.

Somehow, that scared me more than anything.

Devon made another abrupt turn. "Nothing down here runs in a straight line," he muttered.

"Do we have to worry about flooding?" I asked, mentally marking my path back to the church sanctuary.

"No. They're not that kind of tunnels. Not like storm drains or sewer pipes. Ever been to Disney? Hear about the tunnels that connect all the attractions? There's a whole city underground there. Heck, they have special cars they drive around in. This place was designed the same way."

"If this place is like underground Disney, why doesn't it have lights?"

He chuckled. "If you're afraid of the dark, it's only gonna get worse."

"Just saying, finding Esme would be easier with the lights on. She's hiding from the men who shot Patrice, so she's not going to come out just because she sees our flashlights or hears our voices."

He was silent for a moment. "How do you know so much? Did you see what happened to Patrice?"

Yes. Images of Patrice's final moments raced through my mind, her voice repeating her last message, insistent, demanding. *Find the girl. Save the girl.* "No. I'm just putting myself in Esme's shoes." It sounded lame even to me. "If you're not a cop, who are you? Why are you carrying a gun? What do you care about Esme? Are you a relative?"

His back ignored my questions.

"Hey. I'm serious. Who the hell are you? One of Tyree's men?" I tugged on his jacket. It was designer silk, much too nice for a gang member.

He shrugged his shoulders, freeing the fabric from my fingers. "No. I don't work for Tyree." His pace didn't slow, but his words did, as if weighing each of them. "Esme is very dear to me. Her mother is…was…a good friend."

"So she'll recognize you, come out of hiding if she sees you?"

His steps stuttered. "She's never seen me. Has no idea who I am."

"Great. First we have to find her in this maze, then we have to convince her to come with us?"

We turned another corner, and the dog pulled me up short, snarling as he bared his teeth. I felt the same way. The darkness before and behind us was oppressive enough, but now there was the unmistakable stench of burnt flesh. It was faint, as if something had happened here years ago—something bad.

Devon halted as well, one hand back, warning me. "Stay still."

"What is it?"

"One of Tyree's places. He used to keep a meth lab here." His voice was hushed, tight as if he didn't want to be overheard. *Was* there someone here to overhear?

"Why are you whispering?"

"I'm not," he snapped. "Hold still while I look around."

One of the first things I teach new interns when they start work in the ER is: Look twice, think twice, act once. This wasn't the first time I wished I'd taken my own advice. But taking action while others are scratching their heads is the only way I know. It's gotten me into trouble, a lot of trouble. It's also saved me or my patients more times than I can count.

Still. Swallowing darkness, trapped in a maze with a stranger and potential lethal IEDs, made me yearn for the relatively quiet chaos of the ER.

Of course, if I was scared, how terrified would Esme be?

"Do you see anything?" I asked Devon, swinging my light to focus on the door he'd stopped at. Originally painted a bright yellow, it was scorched and charred around the edges as if flames had tried to escape. The dog stopped at my side but didn't sit. Instead, he tensed, ready for action, his nose in the air, ears flattened.

"Bad memories." Devon's tone was blacker than the darkness surrounding us, so low I barely caught his words.

He strode forward, and I had no choice but to follow. Staring at the back of his head was driving me nuts. I hated not being able to see ahead of us, felt claustrophobic, with my back exposed.

Reminding me of the second thing I teach newcomers to the ER: Trust no one, assume nothing.

Yet, here I was, trusting this stranger and assuming I was sane enough to make the choices needed to save a girl's life.

I checked my cell. No signal. I'd been hoping to call Ryder, get some good news. Like they'd already found Esme and we could abandon this subterranean expedition. Or at the very least that they knew how to turn the lights on. Or maybe just to reassure myself that the outside world still existed.

It'd been only twelve minutes since we left the church. Felt like twelve hours. I definitely was not cut out for life underground. If the apocalypse happens, I'll ride it out topside instead of burrowing in the dark alongside the rats.

The steam pipes overhead whispered their agreement, sounding eerily like voices. The dog let loose with a guttural noise that was almost below my hearing threshold and lunged against his lead. The hairs on my arms leapt to attention. Primitive fight-or-flight reflexes heightened all my senses.

"Do you hear that?" I asked Devon. He had stopped, was listening. "I don't think we're alone."

The dog went silent, his teeth bared, lunging and about to yank my arm from its socket.

"It's not Esme," Devon whispered. "Turn out your light."

I clicked my flashlight off, and he did the same. Silently, we let the dog lead us through the darkness. Up ahead there was a wide T-shaped junction. A dim glimmer of light slithered from the right-hand side. "That leads to the hospital." Devon's voice was barely a breath in my ear. "The left leads to the Tower."

The noise came again. It sounded like footsteps but not that regular. More like shuffling. It was impossible to tell which direction they came from. The echoes sounded from all directions at once. Even above us.

Then came the sound of heavy breathing. Not strained, more like excited. Bad porno breathing.

The dog's fur wrinkled beneath my palm like canine goose bumps. I tightened my grip on his collar. His head pivoted, first left, then right, then left again.

"Which way?" I whispered as we reached the junction.

About thirty feet down the tunnel on the right, light sliced across it. Sharply angled as if a door had been left open. Shadows fled, twisted inhuman shapes stretching toward that scratch of light.

The tunnel to my left was completely black, just like the tunnel we'd come from.

The sounds of breathing hushed. I imagined they were still there, only stifled. Someone holding their breath, watching, waiting to see which way we would go.

The dog pulled left, into the darkness. Despite the fact that my hospital, safe haven that it had always been, was in the opposite direction, I was inclined to agree. The black was less frightening than the gray.

We'd gone only a few steps when Ozzie jerked to a stop, turning back to nose my palm. Low, throbbing bass notes wormed their way into my marrow. Warning, warning, the ponderous chords sang. I wanted to ask Devon if he heard it as well, but my body was frozen.

Colors flooded my vision. Firecracker bursts that shimmered into blackness. Shit. Not again. I could feel everything—the dog pressed against my legs, offering me support; a whisper of air sighing against the back of my neck as if a door was being closed behind me; the weight of the flashlight in my hand. Even more, I felt the strain of my muscles, locked into place around the flashlight's rubber grip, the spit gathering at the back of my throat, the cramp in one quadriceps as my weight settled unevenly on that leg.

Underneath it all, a slow, crescendo of panic as I lost control of both my body and my mind.

Time slowed in me, around me. Except for my brain. That was on hyperdrive, whirling like a computer processing too much information, every sense at full alert. The path we'd taken from the church, details of the tunnels that I hadn't paid attention to—shelves filled with boxes labeled potassium iodide; plastic jugs of water; cartons of medical supplies with recent dates on the shipping labels; metal cases large enough to carry weapons, sporting heavy padlocks; cartons of MREs with expiration dates in the next decade. This place might have been built during the Cold War, but it was clear someone was preparing for a new war.

And one more thing: the subtle, citrus scent of a man's cologne.

That explained the lack of dust. And the heavy breathing. You wouldn't leave a fortune in supplies unguarded.

"What's wrong?" Devon's voice barely blipped onto my mental radar screen. I was too busy processing the barrage of information pounding through my brain. How was this happening? It was the same feeling I'd had when Patrice had poured her memory into my brain, yet I wasn't touching anyone.

My mind continued to spin, scanning all the data my senses had gathered even though I'd been conscious of only the tiniest percentage. Until now. Sights, sounds, smells thundered through me, accompanied by that weird subliminal music that made my bones ache. It was as if for the first time in my life, I saw the world the way it *really* was, uncensored by my brain's internal editor.

Devon shook me, waved his hand before my eyes, aimed his light at them. It hurt, but I couldn't blink. The dog pushed against me, harder now as my muscles trembled with the effort to stay locked in a position that was totally unnatural.

Then, with a rush of heat, my weight plummeted forward, into Devon's chest, and I was released.

He caught me, spun me against the nearest set of shelves, and sat me down on a crate of bottled water. "What the hell was that?"

Ozzie wasn't so rude with his concern. He settled for pushing his way below my arm, snuggling between my arm and chest, and licking my face.

"How long?" I asked. It had felt like no more than a second to me. Or maybe a decade. Like being in a dream where time collapses and stretches simultaneously.

"I don't know. Three minutes or so. Scared the shit out of me."

Me, too. I blinked hard and fast. My eyes felt dried, scratchy, but I didn't think my corneas were damaged. My muscles ached worse than after playing a marathon session with the band, burning with lactic acid. I was going to be sore in the morning.

"What is it? Epilepsy or something?"

"Or something." My mind whirled with a list of possible diagnoses: temporal lobe epilepsy, multiple sclerosis, aneurysm, tumor, encephalitis…and that was just the top five. Louise was going to have a field day when I finally found the courage to tell her.

"What should I do? You going to have another one? Do you need medicine?" The sudden string of questions seemed out of character for Devon, who until now had acted like the king of macho one-liners. I figured he was as freaked out as I was.

"I don't know," I uttered the three dread words. My admission tasted like acid, burning my throat.

"What do you mean you don't know? Has this happened before?"

"Started tonight. While I was working on Patrice." I told him about freezing, mid-resuscitation, her heart in my hand. It felt good to tell someone, safer to tell a stranger—plausible deniability if he ever repeated it—as if I was rehearsing for when I'd have to explain this all to Louise.

"Shit." He stared at me for a long moment. "Is that what killed her?"

"Wish I knew." Tired of not having any answers, I struggled to my feet, using the shelf for support. Ozzie nudged me with his nose, as if trying to convince me standing wasn't a good idea. The head rush that followed agreed, but I ignored it. "We have to find Esme."

"Didn't your vision or whatever show you where she is?" He sounded irritated. I understood. With a little girl's life at stake, if my episodes weren't helping us find her, that made me a liability.

Devon pulled me alongside him, and we let the dog lead us. Devon had his gun out. He carried it casually but alert, as if he was used to carrying a weapon. I wondered again about him.

Apparently, he was having second thoughts about me as well. "What if you have another...spell, whatever, and something happens?"

"Leave me. Find Esme, get her out of here."

We continued for several minutes. There were no more weird sounds of breathing, no disembodied footsteps. Somehow, that only made the darkness stretching in all directions all the more oppressing.

"So, what's wrong with you?" he asked. It sounded more like a request for information—like a patient filling out a triage form—rather than because he cared about me. Why should he? He didn't know me.

I wasn't about to admit to ignorance. So I exercised my right to remain silent.

"If you're sick, what are you doing working in the ER? Not very smart for a doctor." He was playing dumb to goad me, and it worked.

"I told you, these...spells...didn't start until tonight. No one knows about them."

"Don't you think they should?"

"Then I'd have to stop practicing medicine. I couldn't be a doctor, all I'd be is..."

"A patient. Human, just like the rest of us poor slobs."

"It's not that—"

"Sure, it is. When you're a patient, you're vulnerable. You lose control of your life, of everything." He glanced over his shoulder at me. "You're scared."

Of course I was. Saying it out loud wouldn't make it any easier to swallow. "Is that why you don't tell people you're Esme's father? Because you're scared, too?"

Silence as we both slowed our steps. It wasn't just a guess. Somewhere in that last dizzying spate of information my brain had processed, it had overlaid an image of Devon's face with Esme's. They had to be closely related. I almost hoped I was wrong. There are treatments for things like temporal lobe epilepsy or hallucinations.

But I'd never even heard of anything like what was happening to me. I wished we were back up on the surface where I could call Louise—to hell with the late hour or holiday—and ask her opinion.

He turned to me, the gun pointed casually in my direction, muzzle aimed down at the concrete floor. Then he surprised me and nodded, as if making up his mind about me. "Yeah. She's mine. And, yes. I'm scared shitless. If the wrong people find out..."

I could fill in the blanks. "I won't tell. Does she know?"

He shrugged. "No. It was the price we paid for her safety. Eleven years I've been gone. I thought when Jess, her mom, called me, begged me to come home... Hell, guess for a moment I was that seventeen-year-old kid again, wanting to play knight in shining armor. Stupid."

"You're from here?" I remembered Father Vance saying Devon had known the tunnels as a child.

We turned another corner, and he reached past me to tug Ozzie to a halt. "Hold on a minute. We're under the Tower. Entering Tyree's territory."

Right. Tyree, who liked to play with meth labs and booby traps. "Surely he'd keep any traps farther away from the Tower," I said. "Like the one we found back near the church in the room where the fire was."

"Took him too long to get there after his early-warning system went off." He sounded like he'd thought about it. A lot. "He'll keep things close to home now."

I was sweeping the area with my light. "I think you might be right."

Less than a foot in front of Ozzie, the glint of fishing line filament crossed the tunnel at knee height. Sister Patrice's voice echoed through my mind, warning Esme to climb high. Now I understood what she meant. I hauled Ozzie back, but Devon didn't seem surprised.

"Good. I was worried he'd go all high-tech, get motion detectors or the like." He knelt, tracing the line with his light. It ran through an eye hook and behind a set of metal shelves. Devon peered between the boxes that lined the lower shelf, taking care not to move them. Then he pocketed his gun and pulled out a switchblade. He stretched his arm into the space behind the boxes.

I backed off, holding my breath and the dog. Couldn't help but flinch when the fishing line snapped, whipping through the air.

We were still there. I relaxed and joined Devon as he crawled out from under the shelving. In his hand he held a sawed-off shotgun with a length of fishing line hanging from the trigger. "Good thing Tyree hasn't changed his ways much."

"Good thing."

He handed me the shotgun. "You know how to use one of these?"

"Yes." My little sister, Eve, a girlie girl, hated tramping through the woods or the idea of hunting, so that left me and my dad, alone in the silence of the dawn, hunkered down in our stand. The best times were the long walks back to where the truck was parked, hauling a field-dressed deer or brace of birds more often than not. We'd talk then. About everything—crazy things Mom would have rolled her eyes at. Like how every culture has the same mathematical basis for its music, but it all sounds different. Same with food. Or about religions. Or stories about Dad's time in the Army when he'd traveled all around the world—well, really just to Panama and Germany and someplace I couldn't pronounce in Turkey. But to a girl from Cambria, it had seemed like he'd seen the world.

I never asked him why he came back here. Maybe I should have.

I checked the gun, made sure both barrels were loaded, and snapped it shut. Looping the dog's lead around my hand with the flashlight, I motioned for Devon to go on.

We found two more booby traps, both easily dismantled. One, another shotgun. The second had several M-80s wired together with some kind of detonator. That one pissed Devon off. All I could think of was how much damage an M-80 could do to a girl Esme's size. And how easily a fire could be started down here. With the tunnels acting as chimneys, it would spread blocks in every direction, fast as lightning.

The shuffling sounds and loud breathing returned. I was certain someone was following us, but every time I looked, the space around me was empty. Still, I felt better having the shotgun.

Ozzie was getting as impatient as I was. It was hard to keep him in check, so I finally gave up on the leash and grabbed hold of his harness instead. I knew from his anxiety that we must be close to Esme.

Devon stopped in the middle of another T-intersection and placed his flashlight on one of the ubiquitous metal shelving units so that it shone down one tunnel. He pulled his second light out and waved it down the opposite tunnel.

"Esme?" he called, stepping into the light so that he could be seen. These shelving units were lined with boxes and plastic containers stacked on top of each other. Myriad places for a skinny kid to hide behind or between the crates. "Esme, you can come out now. It's safe."

His words bounced off the walls, sounding more ominous than reassuring.

I gave it a try. "Esme. I'm Doctor Rossi. I'm here with Ozzie. He misses you. Won't you please come out?"

Ozzie yanked against my hand. He led us down the left-hand tunnel where three sets of shelves filled with blankets had been pulled away from the walls and clumped together, creating a bottleneck we couldn't see past. Ozzie danced in front of the shelves, tail wagging, barking.

"Esme, are you there?" I called. "Are you hurt? Do you need help?"

Devon let me do all the talking. I glanced back at him and realized he'd taken a defensive position behind me, gun drawn as he scanned the space behind us.

Ozzie sat, his nose aimed up, tail thumping the floor. I looked up as well, aiming my light at the top of the shelves, just below the pipes. I squinted into the blackness. Barely made out the metal catwalk suspended above the pipes. Then a blur of motion came from the top of the middle set of shelves.

"Esme, is that you?"

My light caught more movement as a shot sounded, followed by a girl's scream.

CHAPTER THIRTEEN

RYDER WANTED TO pull his hair out by the roots. Would have if he hadn't been busy coordinating thirty men, if he'd had two seconds to breathe, and if his scalp hadn't been held together by office supplies. Damn staples. Itched like hell. He settled for pacing in front of the dark maw that was the entrance to the tunnels.

Water sluiced off his overcoat, creating rivulets that ran inside his collar and between his lapels, soaking him inside and out. His trousers, heavy with the wet, sagged against his belt.

Such was the glamorous life of a detective.

CSU and Major Crimes had taken over the homicides, leaving him free. Finding that little girl was now his priority.

Darkness beckoned from the door leading into the tunnels. He'd been lost in the black himself, too many times to count. Paktika had been riddled with tunnels and caves so deep and dark that even with modern night vision gear, some guys lost it down there. It'd been Ryder's job to bring them back up into the light.

Rainwater swirled over his shoe tops. Daggers of his old frostbite stabbed through his toes. Hospitality gift from the Taliban. He remembered the early days in Afghanistan—no support, endless duty, no relief, no frame of reference, just slogging from one bottomless hole to the next, dropping wearily into the black, wondering what piece of yourself you'd leave behind this time. Soul-sucking bitch of a country.

He'd brought all his men home, but he hadn't really brought any of them back whole.

Most of his time there was a blur. Except for the fear he'd had to swallow each and every time he'd entered the black. He'd kept count at first, but after the first dozen times, it hadn't seemed to matter— the fear became part of the routine, like double-checking his gear, taping down anything that jangled, triple-checking the batteries on his lights and NVG, clearing his weapons of the godawful dust that crept into everything.

The fear was always there. It never left. It simply became part of the weight they all carried. One more thing to be stowed and secured.

The kid lost inside these tunnels didn't have Kevlar or NVG. She didn't have a team with her. She was all alone in the black. Maybe hurt. Maybe dead already.

The thought weighed more than the memories.

Petrosky appeared at the far end of the alley, hauling Tyree Willard along with her. Tyree's hands were cuffed behind his back, but otherwise he looked none the worse.

"Let me go! I know my rights!"

Ryder waited for them to come to him and released his scowl, exposing a few of his more raw emotions. The ones with fangs. "Rights? You don't have any rights. Not when a little girl's life is at stake."

"You found Esme?" Tyree lunged forward. Petrosky yanked him back. Impressive work, given Tyree's bulk. "Is she okay? Where is she?"

"What's she to you?"

"She's my niece, you shithead. Where the hell is she?"

"In there." Ryder pointed to the open door.

Tyree sagged, just for a moment, then straightened. "You got to let me in there, man. It's not safe for her, wandering the dark."

"He clean?" Ryder asked. Petrosky nodded. "Uncuff him."

He grabbed Tyree's shirt by the collar, wadding it into a knot so tight it rocked the bigger man onto his heels. "We're going in there together. We're going to find Esme and bring her out again. You will behave yourself and not give me any problems. Do you understand me?"

He didn't need to voice any threat—Tyree knew what the consequences were. Any problems from the gang leader and only one of them would be leaving the black alive.

"Told you, she's my niece. I just want her back."

"Should have thought of that before you booby-trapped the tunnels."

"No one's supposed to go down there except me and mine. Everyone knows that."

"Wait out here," Ryder ordered his men. No way in hell was he risking anyone else's life on Tyree's cooperation. Besides, if it was just him and the gang leader alone in the dark, Ryder had more room to maneuver beyond rules and protocol. Without witnesses.

Ryder grabbed two flashlights from the firefighters, handed them both to Tyree. Best to keep the gangbanger's hands full. He had his own SureFire light as well as his Glock.

They crossed the threshold into the tunnels. He hadn't realized how loud the rain had been until the sound was snuffed out, along with the noise of men working, engines running, people shouting.

Ryder's senses pinged at full alert, his adrenaline peaking to battle-ready. His hormones thought he was back in Paktika, clearing yet another Taliban cave. His weight moved to the balls of his feet, hushing his footsteps and keeping him balanced against any attack.

He used his light sparingly, leaving Tyree front and center, an easy target. Kept his gun aimed, trusting his other senses more than his vision, as Tyree's light sliced the blackness into sharp-edged slivers.

"There's no traps here," Tyree said, as close to an apology as he'd give. "As long as she stayed near the door, she's okay. Esme! Come out, girl!" His voice crescendoed and died.

"She thought the men who killed Sister Patrice were after her. Probably kept running."

"Shit. Patrice is dead, too? Who the hell would want to kill her and Jess? I mean, a nun and a blind girl—that's cold."

Ryder didn't have any answer. Still wasn't sure Tyree and his boys weren't the answer. He wasn't going to think about it until he got Esme out of here.

They came to a side tunnel. "Where's that go?"

"Leads below the Tower to the elevators. But I got them all locked off, 'cept the one I use myself."

"What about the stairs?"

"Locked up as well."

Making their search upstairs a complete waste of manpower. Shit. Ryder continued on, deeper into the dark. If he didn't find anything else to arrest Tyree for, he could always use vandalism and destruction of private property—if Daniel Kingston agreed to prosecute. Which he might not, since that would make the real estate tycoon liable for fire-code violations. Seemed that Tyree and Kingston both knew how to work the system to get the most bang for their buck, with the occupants of the Tower paying the price.

Tyree pulled up to a halt. "Hang on." He knelt, examining a transparent line sagging loosely across the passageway at shin level. "Goddammit. Someone's been coming through here." He yanked the line, revealing a magnet securing it to the metal shelving that lined both sides of the hallway. Then he bent behind the stack of plastic water containers and reached his arm between the wall and the shelf. He emerged holding a double-barreled sawed-off shotgun.

"Drop it," Ryder ordered, leveling his .40-caliber Glock at the gangbanger.

Tyree broke open the shotgun and handed it to Ryder. "They removed the shells. Left the line intact so I wouldn't know to look. Sons of bitches."

"Probably saved Esme's life," Ryder reminded him.

Tyree grunted at that and continued down the passage. Ryder left the shotgun—didn't want his hands full—but mentally marked its location. Double barrel at close range could take the legs off a man. At least cripple him, which was the point.

During the next twenty minutes, they found three more

dismantled booby traps and had cleared two side passages before Ryder spotted light coming from ahead. The reverb of a voice shouting filled the blackness.

He pushed Tyree faster. They arrived at the junction of two wide corridors. Tyree's light caught another black man in its glare. Standing in front of the man was Angela Rossi. Holding a shotgun. A dog stood beside her, pulling hard against his leash.

What the hell? Ryder didn't have time to finish his thought before a gunshot cracked through the dark. Coming from behind him.

A girl screamed. Rossi dropped her shotgun and rushed forward, arms outstretched, as a young girl fell from the darkness above them.

CHAPTER FOURTEEN

EVERYTHING HAPPENED IN a blazing blitzkrieg of action. First, seeing Esme. Alive, climbing out from her hiding place on the top shelf to my right. Then a shot coming from behind us.

Ozzie's howl, the gunshot reverberating as if the sound was ricocheting off the concrete surrounding us, and Devon's shout of anger and dismay collided.

Esme fell forward, her body caught in a crossfire of flashlight beams.

Before she could tumble off the shelf and into space, someone reached down from the darkness above Esme and grabbed her. Esme hung there for a moment, one foot caught on the top of the shelving unit, the rest of her body dangling by an unseen person above her, gloved hand gripping her arm. Another shot splintered her cry of panic.

Then she was gone. Vanished into the shadows above the pipes.

It wasn't until I was halfway up the nearest set of shelves, scrambling from one handhold to the next, that I registered the third gunshot. Or heard the shouting. Adrenaline must have blocked my hearing for a few moments, because then all the sudden below me there were men yelling at each other, their voices a shockwave hitting me, punctuated by Ozzie's barking.

"Lower your weapon," a man shouted. Ryder. I glanced down for a split moment. His gun was aimed at Devon. Had Ryder fired the shots aimed at Esme? No. That made no sense. But the shots had come from that direction. Another man, tall, bulky, carrying two lights, stood to one side. "Now!"

"I didn't do anything," Devon protested, crouching to set his gun on the floor and stepping away from it. "You're the one who shot her."

"Wasn't me." Ryder's tone was tight with adrenaline. He kept his gun aimed at Devon but had shifted position so that he could cover both Devon and the corridor behind us—where the shots had come from. "On your knees. Hands behind your head."

I was almost to the top of the shelving unit. Close enough to see, in the scattered light of the flashlight clutched between my teeth, that Esme wasn't anywhere to be found on the shelves.

"Where is she, Angela?" Devon shouted from where he lay facedown on the floor.

"Shut up." Ryder cuffed his hands behind his back.

I clawed my way onto the top of the shelving unit, tumbling a few boxes to the ground, glad this unit was securely anchored to the wall. I wasn't at all sure that the freestanding shelves Esme had hidden on could have taken my weight climbing them. "She isn't here. But there's a catwalk above the pipes."

"Rossi, get down here," Ryder called. He had Devon and the other man both on their stomachs, in cuffs, and was standing with his back to me, pointing his gun into the darkness.

I couldn't see any blood on the shelves where Esme had been. That was the good news. The bad news was that I also couldn't see which way whoever had taken her had gone. Between the creaks and clanks of the pipes and the noise of the men below, I couldn't hear any footsteps or any sounds of Esme crying. Had she known the person who had taken her? Saved her, really. Risked their life to rescue Esme. That gave me hope.

Still, I was half-tempted to try to follow. Holding on to a pipe for balance, I stood. The catwalk was at my waist. I could have easily climbed onto it. I touched it, felt faint vibrations but couldn't tell which direction they came from. Ryder shouted my name again. I aimed my light down the catwalk in both directions and saw only shadows. With a shooter out there in the dark and no idea which way Esme had gone, it was foolish to try to follow, so I reluctantly climbed back down.

Ryder stood like a soldier, his face closed down, gaze searching for unseen enemies in the shadows. "What the hell were you thinking?"

Ozzie came to my defense, aiming a snarl in Ryder's direction.

"We need to get out of here, now," Ryder said.

"No, we can't leave her," Devon argued.

"Shut up." Ryder's voice lashed out at Devon even as his light whipped through the darkness where the shots had come from. "We have two targets now. Esme and the shooter. We need to get more manpower, coordinate a search, get the lights turned on, do this thing right."

I didn't want to leave Esme behind, but I knew he was right. My one glimmer of hope came from the fact that whoever had taken Esme had been protecting her from the shooter.

"We're too exposed here. We need to move." Ryder motioned to Devon and the other man to get back on their feet. "Tyree, on your feet. You, too—what's your name?"

"Price. Devon Price."

"Let's go." Ryder ushered the two men to march in front of him, his gun still trained on them. I retrieved Ozzie's leash and joined him. Ozzie tugged, didn't want to come at first, but then, with a whimper, he obeyed.

Ryder frowned and gestured for us to move faster. "I've no cell coverage here, and the radio doesn't work either. It's a good twenty minutes back the way we came. We need to hurry, get the perimeter shut down before they can escape."

"We're closer to Good Sam than the Tower," Devon said.

"He's right," the man named Tyree said. "That tunnel," he jerked his chin to indicate the junction we'd passed a few yards back, "goes down to Good Sam's basement, near the heating plant. It's the fastest way out."

I finally put two and two together and realized Tyree was the drug dealer Father Vance had warned us about. Up close he was even bigger. Bulky. My first thought was steroids, which made me wonder what other drugs he was doing. I was glad he was in front of me. I didn't like the idea of having him in the shadows behind me.

Ryder's mouth twisted, and I knew he was worried about the drug dealer leading us into a possible ambush. But he nodded. "Show us." Then he turned to me, seemed to sense that something was wrong. "You okay?" he asked, his voice a low whisper.

"Of course." I appreciated his concern, but I wasn't about to lower my guard enough to admit that, no, I was very much *not* okay. Didn't want to admit that even to myself. My nerves jangled with adrenaline, and I kept stumbling in the dark. Thankfully, no one noticed. "I'm fine. Who's the big guy?"

"Tyree Willard, leader of the Royales, the gang that runs the Tower. Esme's uncle. Who's your new buddy?"

"Your friend the priest introduced us. Devon knows Esme and her family. Ozzie is her mom's guide dog, and Devon thought he could lead us to her."

"You came down here alone with a perfect stranger?"

I ignored the rebuke coloring his words. After all, he had a point. It hadn't actually been a well-thought-out plan. Wouldn't even really call it a plan at all. "I couldn't just sit around praying like Father Vance. Any idea who was shooting at us?"

He grimaced and shook his head, falling silent once more. Intensity radiated off him as we traveled through the dark corridors.

Ozzie galloped ahead of me, straining at the full length of his lead, barking twice at each intersection we crossed as if warning anyone to leave us alone. I couldn't hear any more footsteps or the creepy heavy breathing, but still couldn't shake the feeling that we were being watched.

Ozzie's lead went slack as he suddenly circled back to me, ears at full alert. He twisted his body lengthwise against my legs, blocking my path. I was getting ready to admonish him and tug him aside when a barrage of music, discordant brass and percussion, blinded me.

This time I knew what was coming. The music tugged and pulled at me as if it had a physical presence. Demanding my attention. I could see the men as they walked away, moving so slowly they looked like astronauts on the moon. Ozzie was caught lowering his head to nuzzle my knee, an old-fashioned movie flicking one frame at a time in infinite slow motion. Above the clang of the music, I heard everything: the creak of his leather collar, the jingle of the ring that held his leash, the whoosh of atoms displaced by his movement.

I stood frozen, able to hear and see it all. As if I was everywhere at once, absorbing every molecule surrounding us.

In my mind's eye, I could plot the course through the maze of dark tunnels all the way back through the twists and turns to the church. I heard footsteps and voices in the far distance, could smell the familiar scent of disinfectant coming from not too far away. Smelled something else. Closer.

Candle wax, blood, burnt flesh…and something sickly, sweet, too sweet. I'd smelled it before…with a rush, my vision exploded into a whirl of images as my mind sped back through memories, searching.

That smell…we'd seen an uptick in assault victims coming into the ER and Advocacy Center over the past few months, the most recent just four days ago. All women, drugged, kept several days, raped, and tortured.

In my mind's eye, the me from three months ago raised the first victim's ragged T-shirt, ready to place it in an evidence bag, when the sickly sweet stench of the liquid saturating it overwhelmed me.

We'd tested her and the shirt for drugs and had found traces of paramethoxamine. PXA, a street drug known as Death Head because dying was preferable than overdosing on it. It's in the same chemical family as ketamine but longer lasting with much worse side effects. Instead of pain relief, PXA actually increases pain sensation and, instead of a euphoric high, produces a dysphoric dissociative state. Think the worst LSD trip imaginable, only you're unable to move your body.

That first woman and three more who followed all ended up in the psych ward, catatonic, their minds so clouded they couldn't care for themselves or distinguish reality from the imaginary hell the perpetrator had created.

It was that smell that filled my mind now. I wanted to gag, to hold my breath, but my body was frozen and beyond my control. All I could do was endure, fight past the stench.

The others were still doing their slow-motion walk. Ozzie's head had barely made it all the way around, mouth open but no sound coming yet, his whimper frozen midair. And my mind kept soaring, freewheeling through time and space, all of my senses exploding, on overload.

As I was buffeted by all the sensory information, I fought to find something to anchor me as this psychic tornado ripped through my reality. I clung to the stench of the PXA, focused my entire being on it, ignoring the maelstrom of other sights and sounds hurling themselves at me. Where had it come from?

A dark corridor we'd just passed. It had no shelves, only blackness at the end. Lined with large metal doors, unlike the others. Wide, thick, fitted with airtight gaskets—walk-in refrigerators and freezers? I could hear air circulating through a fan above the last door at the end of the row.

And a whimper. A child's whimper. Forlorn, despairing, it broke my heart.

With a fever rush so dizzying I thought I would vomit, I was back again. Muscles cramped, eyes dry, drool hanging from my mouth.

I staggered forward and wiped my mouth. Ozzie finished his spin around, coming full circle. The men were only a few feet ahead of us, oblivious. The entire time I was trapped in my fugue state—which had seemed like hours, though my burning muscles screamed weeks—only a few seconds had passed in the real world.

Disorientation hit me with a wave of red spots swimming before my eyes. I blinked and cleared them. "This way." My flashlight shook as I pointed away from the tunnel leading toward Good Sam and down one to our left, leading deeper into the maze.

Tyree and Devon halted, looked to Ryder, who stared at me like I was crazy. If he only knew.

"Can't you hear it?" I asked. "Listen."

Ozzie heard it. He dashed down the tunnel, his leash slipping from my trembling grip, and vanished in the darkness.

"I don't hear nothing," Tyree said.

"I don't eith—wait, what was that?" Devon said.

Ryder was silent, moving backward, keeping the two men in range of his gun, heading toward where I heard the child's whimpering. He frowned, glanced at me, then looked at his two prisoners. It was obvious he was torn between securing them, getting me out of there, and the faint sounds coming from the end of the tunnel.

For me it was an easy decision. I started down the tunnel, following Ozzie and my instincts, leaving the men behind.

Ozzie waited for me at the end of the corridor, scratching at a heavy door. It was a walk-in refrigerator—large, like the kind they held sides of beef in. Or bodies.

The door was ajar and surrounded by a thick rubber gasket that was torn and frayed, crumbling between my fingers. This was how I could hear the child's crying despite the thick walls.

There was a heavy padlock hanging from the door latch. Why leave it unlocked? To invite us in or let the child trapped inside out? The men reached me just as I hauled the door open. A wave of odors poured out: a pungent combination of candle wax, burnt flesh, urine, feces, unwashed bodies, that sickly sweet scent of PXA, blood, and terror.

Ryder shone his light inside, alongside mine. The flashlight beams skipped around the room. It hadn't been only one child sobbing.

Young children huddled together in a ball so tight I couldn't tell if they were boys or girls, the oldest maybe eight, the youngest three or four, all races: Hispanic, black, white, Asian. The noise they made wasn't a cry. It was the keening of wild animals caught in a trap.

The light caught them, and they screamed, skittering away from us into the depths of the refrigerator, clinging to the shadows for protection. They all wore dingy white T-shirts that came down past their knees, clinging to their moving bodies like foam on ocean waves.

I took a step inside, following them, but Ryder pinned me with his arm. "Me first."

"They may be hurt." Of course they were hurt. What was I saying?

"Wait." He stood inside the door and systematically aimed the light to all corners, as if slicing an imaginary pie. Crucifixes, dozens of them, covered the walls as well as full-length mirrors painted in bright colors, as if they were stained-glass windows. The light swept across the floor littered with water buckets, rotting food, blankets bunched up into a nest, before finally coming to rest on the glint of chains.

Ryder hesitated, his light spearing a naked teenage girl, wrists and ankles secured by manacles with another length of chain joining them behind her back, leaving her essentially hog-tied, lying facedown. I stepped forward again, but he grabbed my arm, holding me back while he completed his search.

As I chased the younger children with my light, I held my breath and counted. Seven little ones, in addition to the girl chained up and motionless on the floor.

Devon pushed past us. "Esme!"

His voice shook as it careened from one metal wall to the next. No answer.

"She's not here," I told him.

Ryder hauled Devon back by his handcuffs and shoved him against the wall alongside Tyree.

Tyree's expression had grown stony, and he stared at his feet, avoiding any chance glimpse inside the room. I wondered how much he knew about what was going on down here. Maybe those booby traps back in the tunnels hadn't been designed to keep people out so much as to ensure that no one escaped.

Holding my light down at my side so it wouldn't blind the children, I tried to prioritize. The little ones gave out a collective squeal of fright when I stepped inside the doorway. They ducked their heads down, huddled together in a ball of terror.

I approached the unconscious girl slowly. Ozzie was bolder than I was. He dropped to the ground, slunk on all fours to the girl, licked her neck. When he got no response, he looked to me, tail dragging, then to her, and began to echo the children's moaning with his own primal warble. The hair on my arms stood up, ready to fight or flee.

"I'm going to need some help."

"Let me," Devon said from the doorway.

Ryder frowned, considering all the angles. We'd gone way off the map of protocols, rules, or regulations, but he didn't seem as worried about getting in trouble as he was for my safety and the children's.

"It's okay," I told Ryder. "Uncuff him."

Ryder sucked in his cheeks, then nodded, holstering his gun so he could unlock Devon's handcuffs. "You try anything—"

"She's safe with me," Devon said.

Ryder stared him down, but he didn't flinch.

Devon joined me in the dim light and helped me roll the girl onto her side so I could assess her.

"She okay?" Ryder asked. He stood at the doorway, gun drawn on Tyree. Protecting his crime scene, protecting his prisoner, protecting all of us against whoever else stalked the darkness.

"She's breathing."

Devon slid his lock picks free and began working on freeing the girl from her restraints. Ryder saw what he was doing, gave him a look, but then nodded. Guy talk for, "I'll let you slide this time."

"Why don't they run?" Devon asked. "The door's open."

I glanced over my shoulder at the children watching us warily from the farthest corner. How long had they lived here in the dark? "Same reason why they haven't come to us for help. The people who did this to them were people they trusted. Now they don't trust anything—or anyone."

The girl's eyes stared straight ahead, unblinking. Her hair was matted with sweat, blood, and dirt. I brushed it away from her face. Patches of it had been ripped from her scalp, leaving oozing sores behind. Ozzie licked my hand, as if letting me know he hadn't forgotten about me.

Music hit me like a tidal wave. A piano filled with melancholy, grief-stricken, making my heart weep.

My mind felt like it was being spun around by an unseen dance partner, images colliding, sounds flashing, smells and tastes and colors all swirled together. Nothing coherent—nothing except pain and despair.

It was coming from the girl. No words, not like Patrice, but impressions kaleidoscoping together.

She had been injected with something, and from then on everything was a blur. Faces surrounded her, warped like Dali's melting clock. She'd been forced to kneel, her back lashed. Burning. Something branded into her flesh. Electrical shocks searing through the most sensitive areas of her body. More pain and atrocities pummeled my mind. So much that it was hard to tell where the pain was coming from. It seemed to dance along her nerve endings in a never-ending stream of anguish.

Finally, thrown into the darkness, chained up, drugged, and left to die.

CHAPTER FIFTEEN

As DEVON KNELT over the girl, guiding the lock picks with a light touch, he glanced around. This place, he'd never been here before, but something about it felt so familiar...a lost memory danced out of reach, then was banished once more as he focused on Esme.

She wasn't among the ragtag group of children. Was that a good thing or bad? Did it mean she was already dead?

No. Whoever had saved her from falling from the shelves had risked getting shot. They must want her alive—he had to keep hold of that hope.

One lock snapped open, and Devon started in on the final one. God, the smell. It'd been a long time since he'd done any grunt work, been forced to endure a stench like this.

"Hold it," the cop, Ryder, shouted from outside the door. A thud came from the hallway. Fool that Tyree was, sounded like he'd tried to run.

"You knew, didn't you?" Ryder's voice sliced through the darkness.

Devon glanced over just in time to see the cop shove Tyree into the wall, the handcuffed man stumbling. Tyree wheeled around, his eyes dark with fury, the muscles in his forehead drawing together into two knots the size of walnuts.

"Answer me!" Ryder wasn't shouting, not yet. Devon had the feeling the cop was the kind of man who seldom had to shout to get what he wanted.

"Fuck you! You think cuz I live in this shithole, cuz I run with a bunch of punks, I'm an animal? That I'd hurt little kids?"

Tyree. Such a consummate actor. He actually believed his own bullshit. Because Devon knew for a fact that the answer to all of the above was an unequivocal yes.

"Like you give a shit." Ryder obviously wasn't buying Tyree's innocent act. "I saw the look on your face. You knew something was going on. Who did this?"

Tyree shrugged his massive shoulders. "You want anything, talk to my lawyer."

The cop tilted his head, looking at Tyree as if Tyree was nothing more than a paper target. Easy to shoot, easy to forget. Devon had seen that look before. He held his breath, thinking he might not have to worry about Tyree for much longer.

The cop blinked, the tiny movement seemed to take more effort than lifting a two-ton weight, lowered his weapon, shook his shoulders free of tension. He glanced inside the room, met Devon's gaze without flinching, then turned to focus on the darkness down the hallway behind them.

Devon found himself exhaling in disappointment. Tyree was responsible for this and so much more—including Jess's death, Devon was certain—that it might have been nice to have him taken care of, once and for all. Especially at the hands of a cop, with Devon able to watch without taking the rap. Yes, that would have been nice.

Nicer still would be Devon doing the job himself. Face to face, eye to eye. Jess deserved that much.

As soon as he had Esme back, he promised himself.

He popped the final lock and turned to Angela, expecting at least a smile or nod. Instead, she sat frozen, eyes unblinking, one hand caught in the girl's hair.

Shit. Not again. Ozzie made a whining noise, his nose pressed against Angela's arm, as if he knew she was having another of her fits. Devon didn't know what to do. She was breathing. Should he move her? Put his wallet between her teeth so she didn't choke?

Maybe he shouldn't try to wake her. Didn't that kill sleepwalkers?

That's what she most resembled—minus the walking, of course. Her muscles were bunched up, tense like she was awake, but paralyzed.

Last place on earth she should be was stuck down here, especially not with men with guns wandering the tunnels. Last thing he should have done was let her tag along with him.

"Angela? Come on back now," he whispered. She'd helped him—he'd keep her secret. For now, at least. He touched her hand, gently removed it from the girl's hair before she could jerk or fall and hurt the girl.

Angela shuddered as if electricity had jolted her. Blinking rapidly, she looked around, fear tugging at her features, mouth open, ready to scream. She scrambled away from him, but then snapped her mouth closed, her gaze becoming focused once more.

She waved him off, chest heaving as she gasped for air. Bent over double, body racked with spasms, he thought she was puking, but nothing came out.

"Are you okay?" Doctor or not, she wasn't going to be much help to anyone if she kept getting these spells or seizures.

She shook herself and dared to push back up to a sitting position, steering clear of touching the girl again.

"I was with her," she gasped. Tears slid down her cheeks, but he didn't think she even noticed them. "Inside her. I saw, I felt—everything that happened to her."

Devon stared at her. Now it was his mouth hanging open. Give him the dirty double-dealings of the Russians any day. Because he had no idea what the hell to do with this psycho-crazy bullshit.

☽ ⚜ ☾

"YOU GUYS OKAY in there?" Ryder didn't try to mask his impatience. They were sitting ducks down here at the end of this fatal funnel.

The pipes overhead gave out an occasional moan that made the hairs on his neck jump to attention. There was no movement in his field of vision, but who knew what lurked beyond the shadows? Or above them on the catwalks. Not like he could recon, not without abandoning Rossi and the children. Most he could do was check the doors lining the corridor within the limited vision of their light. All padlocked. No sounds coming from within.

What if there were more kids behind them?

No time for what-ifs. Had to work with what he had here and now. Work this problem, move on to the next.

Jesus, he was sick of these tunnels, wanted to get the hell above ground again, get back to finding that little girl. And the punks who took her. And the ones who'd left these kids here.

Animals.

He glanced inside. Rossi sat cross-legged in front of the dog and the younger kids. The little ones pushed behind the dog's bulk, using him as a shield, making themselves as small as possible.

"Hey there," she said in a soft, low voice, pretending to be talking to the dog. "My name's Angela. What's yours? Ozzie? That's a funny name for a dog."

The dog helped out by wagging his tail and licking her cheek, showing the kids she wasn't a threat.

A timid pair of eyes met Rossi's in the dim light. Instantly fled again. Ryder leaned his weight forward, tempted to go in, but knew he'd only spook the kids further. Someone had to keep guard.

Price emerged from the room, carrying the unconscious girl in his arms. Up close, Ryder could see she was only sixteen or so, Asian. She was limp, arms and legs dangling loose, eyes wide open, staring at nothing.

"Any of you guys want to go home?" Rossi asked the other children in a singsong voice. She hummed softly, her body moving to the rhythm, head nodding, until the kids began to mirror her.

Heads nodding, shoulders hunching. A few sobs. Two more hit-and-skip glances.

Rossi tried another tactic. "Who's hungry? Anyone?"

One, the tallest, slowly raised his hand. Emboldened by his example, the rest did—the youngest one last, looking to the others first.

"Okay. You want to come with me and get something to eat? What do you want?"

Silence except for the shuffling of bare feet. The dog now sat at her side, facing the kids, but they didn't run away. Progress.

"McDonald's," came a hoarse whisper, Ryder couldn't tell from which kid. "Pizza," came another.

"Ice cream!" a girl, one of the smallest, sang out.

"Anyone else vote for ice cream?" Rossi asked.

"Me, me, me!" Now they were all looking at Rossi, hands raised again. She stood up without using her hands, one smooth, graceful movement. The children grabbed on to her. She entrusted the dog's leash to the oldest ones and shepherded them out into the hall.

"Let's go." Ryder grabbed Tyree's arm, his hand barely fitting halfway around, and spun him back down the hall that ended up beneath Good Sam. They led the way, followed by Price with the girl and Rossi playing the Pied Piper.

The air grew warmer, and a rushing noise filled his ears as they reached the end of the corridor. To their right was a set of metal double doors. The noise came from beyond them. It was growing louder, a steam locomotive stoking its fires.

Ryder tried the doors. They opened. He blinked against the sudden light. Only a few fluorescent bulbs lined Good Sam's basement corridor, but compared to the darkness they'd been in, it was as blinding as staring into the sun during an eclipse. The kids clamped their hands over their eyes, peering through slits made by their fingers.

He holstered his gun, exchanging it for his cell phone, calling Petrosky. "I want Daniel Kingston on scene by the time I get back," he ordered. "Lock down any exits from the tunnels and get the lights on down there. No one gets in and no one gets out."

"Kingston's here," she said, her voice almost drowned out by the rain. "The brass are kissing his ass, apologizing, and none too happy with you. He's threatening to bring charges."

"For what? We had exigent circumstances—"

"They don't fucking care, Ryder. Kingston's pissed off we barged on to his private property, and they need someone to blame. Guess who's front and center?"

Ryder didn't give a shit about Kingston or his bruised ego. Once the word about the kids got out, all that would be secondary—shit, the press. He couldn't risk them hearing. "Lock down all the exits from the tunnels," he repeated. They reached the hospital's elevator bank, and he pushed Tyree inside the first one that arrived, held the door for the others. "Meet me over at Good Sam's ER. Bring a CSU team. I've got a crime scene that needs babysitting."

"What did you find down there?" She sounded half-excited and half-scared, as if he'd successfully returned from an expedition to the South Pole. "Albino alligators?"

He flashed on the vision of the children alone in the dark. The press was going to feast on this like maggots on a rotting corpse. But Petrosky knew how to keep things clamped down, give him time to do his job without the media interfering. "Just hurry."

CHAPTER SIXTEEN

I WAS USED to being pulled in conflicting directions by the needs of my patients—but not literally. The bright lights and noises and people in the ER scared the little kids, and they tugged at me from behind. One of the youngest had stopped, buried her face against my thigh, gripping my legs in a death hold, so that I couldn't move.

Carmen, the ER nurse I'd grabbed when we came out of the elevator, looked over in dismay. "I don't have beds—" Her gaze said so much more, but like any good nurse, she didn't voice her real emotions in front of patients.

"I don't think we can separate them anyway. Not yet," I said.

Devon gently deposited the unconscious teenage girl onto a gurney parked outside an exam room.

"Carmen, take the girl into a room. She'll need a full assault workup, tox screen—I think she's been given PXA." Thankfully, Shari, one of my Advocacy Center nurses was working the ER tonight. The girl was in good hands. "Devon, help me take these little guys into the Center's observation area."

He'd been looking toward the stairwell, and I knew he wanted to get back into the tunnels, continue his search for Esme.

"The police are closing the tunnels, and whoever took Esme saved her from the shooter," I reminded him. "There's nothing you can do for her right now."

It took him a moment to nod in agreement. "Which way?"

He peeled the little one away from my legs, scooping her up into his arms. She squealed, at first in fright, but then in laughter when he made a squinchy face and blew a raspberry. Then she broke my heart by squelching her laughter with a fist shoved against her mouth and cringing as if waiting to be punished for the joyful noise that had escaped her.

With Ozzie's help, we herded the kids down a side corridor and pushed through the double doors to the Advocacy Center.

The Center has two fully equipped sexual assault examination rooms, plus a large interview room that resembles a dentist's office waiting area with vinyl love seats, a low table perfect for kids to sit and draw at, tubs of age-appropriate toys. Of course, most dentist offices don't also boast a one-way glass wall, video cameras, and anatomically correct dolls.

The kids tumbled into the room but then withdrew into their huddle again, taking Ozzie with them. The sudden silence, broken only by their sniffling, was heart-wrenching.

Some of the older ones tugged at the hems of their T-shirts, obviously embarrassed at being half-dressed. Despite its casual decor, the room was too bright, too formal. They shied away from the furniture, not touching anything.

Again, I wondered what had happened to them. How long had they been imprisoned underground? Not long enough to suffer nutritionally. They looked skinny and hungry, but not dehydrated, and there'd been evidence of food containers in the room where they'd been kept prisoner. I'd spotted a few flashlights as well, but it was obvious that they'd spent a lot of time in the dark. Did they feel safer hiding in the shadows? Or was it a simple matter that the flashlights had died?

There were no obvious physical injuries. In fact, they appeared to be in good health. Their T-shirts weren't torn or terribly soiled, and it was obvious that they'd bathed recently. Someone had cared for them, even as they'd been locked away from the world.

But abuse didn't have to be physical. I was far more worried about the psychological impact of their captivity. Other than the few words

I'd coaxed from them to get them out of their prison, they hadn't made anything more than guttural sounds of confusion and fear.

Devon deposited the little girl he carried onto her feet, and she ran to join the others, the larger ones separating for a brief moment to let her sidle between them, placing her at the center with the other smallest ones. A herd protecting its weak. He reached to open the door, and they began keening as if in pain.

"I don't think they want you to go."

He looked at his hand, still on the doorknob, looked at the mass of children standing in the center of the room, swaying as if they shared a heartbeat. Then he glanced at me. Pain and fear and frustration gathered on his face. "Esme."

"Ryder's doing everything he can. If you go back down there alone, you might end up making things worse. Get shot by the police during their search or by whoever shot at us."

His exhalation circled the room, and his shoulders slumped. "It's been too much time anyway. They'll be long gone."

"Maybe these guys can help. They might know something if we can get them talking."

He didn't look convinced, but he nodded and pulled his hand away from the door. The kids relaxed, and the air in the room felt calmer, as if an electrical current had been shut off.

None of us at the Center work full time here—no way could our funding accommodate that luxury. In addition to Shari, I have three other ER nurses also certified as sexual assault forensic examiners; a local psychologist who volunteers her time; an ever-changing assortment of volunteers from the DA's victim's assistance office; and two social workers, neither of whom were on call for the holiday.

Which meant, until Shari finished with our nameless assault victim and the on-call social worker arrived, it was just me. And Devon. I was glad he'd stayed. Not just for the second pair of hands, but the kids seemed to respond to him. Right now, anything that kept them feeling safe and secure was the best thing for them.

I opened two bins of toys and scattered them onto the floor. Then

I sat down myself and began bouncing one of the rubber balls. Devon took the hint and sat across from me, looking a bit goofy as he awkwardly folded his legs beneath him, tugging at the knees of his designer slacks. We played catch, exaggerating our smiles and encouraging each other. He hesitated when I began to sing *Row, Row, Row Your Boat* in time to the ball's bouncing, but then joined in, adding to the harmony.

A few minutes later, we had a threesome, then five, until finally all the children were playing, passing the ball back and forth, singing the simple yet calming tune. I found another ball, this one the size of a kickball, and began rolling it between our loose group, keeping the rhythm and the kids focused.

"My name is Angela," I sang, punctuating my words by using the ball like a bongo drum. "Angela Rossi."

I passed the ball to Devon. "My name is Devon," he chanted, catching on fast. "Devon Price."

He rolled the ball to the oldest-appearing kid, a skinny black boy who looked to be around eight or nine. The boy caught the ball, hesitated, and for a second I thought he was going to freeze. But he began bouncing the ball between his palms, slid a look at me without ever raising his face, and said, "My name is Andre. Andre Brown."

I smiled at him. "How old are you, Andre?"

Still bouncing the ball, he replied, "I'm Andre, and I'm eight."

He looked at me for approval, and I nodded. "Good job. Who's next?"

Devon leaned forward. "Do you know a girl named Esme? Esme Willard?" Urgency spilled into his voice. "Have you seen her?"

I glared at him while Andre pulled away, dropping the ball and hiding his face in his hands as if waiting to be hit. Before I could say anything, Devon realized his mistake and, to my surprise, lowered his body so he crouched below Andre's eye level. He touched the boy's knee.

"Hey, Andre," he said in a low, man-to-man voice. "Sorry, man. You did good, real good."

Andre peeked between his fingers. Said nothing. Neither did the other kids watching—waiting for his lead.

"C'mon, man," Devon coaxed, still keeping his head low, giving Andre the position of power. He scooped the ball up and rolled it against Andre's legs. "We can't play the game without you. So far you're winning."

Andre blinked, and his hands came down. The tension in the room eased. He didn't smile, not a normal kid smile, more like the shy glint of the sun caught behind a storm cloud. "I'm the winner?" He bounced the ball, regaining his rhythm. "Cool."

Crisis averted. Devon sat up. I arched an eyebrow at him. He shrugged and turned his focus on the kids. Lesson learned. I hoped.

❂

AFTER HANDING TYREE over to patrol officers and giving Petrosky the details about their new crime scene—emphasizing the need for both officer safety and secrecy—Ryder followed Rossi to the Advocacy Center and settled into the observation room, turning it into a command post.

He started with the SWAT commander, figuring he could better persuade Kingston to grant them permission to search the tunnels, but he also alerted his own commander, who in turn reached out to the deputy chief for more manpower, including the bomb squad, and the DA's office for a warrant. Unfortunately, they had too little time. In fact, odds were it was already too late to stop whoever had taken Esme from escaping from the tunnels—too much ground to cover—and it was far too dangerous to send troops down there with Tyree's IEDs littering the area.

Tyree could have helped but had chosen to invoke his right to remain silent. Ryder expected nothing less from the gangbanger. Self-preservation came before saving his own niece.

As he juggled the phone calls, coordinating the Amber Alert and search for Esme, as well as a missing person's database search with the NCIC for the other victims they'd found in the tunnels, he watched Rossi and Price handle the kids. Damn, she was good.

He already knew Rossi was a skilled physician—the way she'd cut open Patrice, even a grunt like him knew that had taken guts and brains—but watching her with the kids, he was stunned. Never should have razzed her about that dying old lady when they first met. It was obvious Rossi wasn't the kind of doctor who thought the best medicine came through pills and objectivity. No, she threw herself into her cases with passion, risking everything.

The observation room had a computer. There was little he could do until they were cleared to enter the tunnels or until he had IDs on the kids, so he gave in to temptation and did a quick Google search on Rossi. To his surprise, the first item that popped up was a page filled with videos.

Music videos. Intrigued, he clicked on one. It was obviously shot in a club or bar. Shadowed in murky lights filtered by cigarette smoke, was Rossi. Playing a violin.

As she stroked the bow across the strings—a movement that sent her head arching back, flinging her hair past her face, exposing her neck—Ryder felt a stirring in his groin. Jesus, who knew a violin could be so sexy? She coaxed a long, complicated phrase from the instrument, her face twisted in anguish, sweat dripping from her chin, eyes squeezed shut.

The shot pulled back to reveal the crowd. They were as mesmerized as Ryder. The entire room, jammed with spectators, paused between breaths. It reminded Ryder of the moment right before Patrice died, that sense of anticipation, of wanting something more but unable to reach it. The note filled the air, circled through and above and around them, setting nerve endings on edge, then shuddered and died.

There was the smallest of pauses, a primordial silence. Finally, Rossi jerked her chin forward and down, her body following, and life began anew. Music erupted from the violin, toe-tapping, hip-swaying, hand-clapping music that was irresistible.

The crowd breathed again, and others in the band began to join in. All men. One playing a round Irish drum, an accordion player, and Jacob Voorsanger puffing on a tin whistle that looked like something a kid would find in their Christmas stocking.

Jealousy flared through Ryder at the sight of Voorsanger up there beside Rossi, sharing something so powerful and intimate. Maybe the lawyer was bigger competition than Ryder had imagined.

He frowned and clicked the computer off, despite the fact that he wanted to watch more. He had a job to do, no need for distractions. Like that moment he and Rossi had shared in the church—what the hell had he been thinking?

Rossi's voice coming from the speaker connected to the room beyond the observation window grabbed his attention. She'd gotten one of the kids to tell her his name. As Ryder listened, he made sure the DVR was recording, grabbed his notebook, and began taking notes. Only the two older ones gave both a first and last name, not much help there.

He called the precinct and waited for the computer tech to search the NCMEC and NCIC databases. Rossi asked the kids about their pets and school, avoiding the topic of what happened in the tunnels, easing into it. Kids were tricky. You couldn't push too hard or fast, had to let them tell things their way.

The tech came back on the line. "Nothing."

"What do you mean nothing?" Ryder drew a question mark on the page of his notebook, his pen impaling the dot at the bottom. "You telling me we have seven kids and no one reported them missing?"

"Yessir. What do you want me to do?"

"Get me their family contact information."

"I can't—not with last names like Brown and Taylor. Not without something more like a date of birth or address. We don't have any database of underage children, and it's not like they're in the DMV."

Shit. He hung up and stood. The oldest kids may know their addresses. Maybe all the kids knew each other. Maybe that's how they all came to be abducted?

Glancing to confirm that the red recording light was on—he wouldn't miss anything—he left. One sure way to get anyone talking was to give them what they wanted. Rossi had promised the kids ice cream, so he'd deliver on the promise.

On the way to the cafeteria, he checked in with the troops. Still no cooperation from Tyree, which meant they were crippled, forced to clear the tunnels inch by inch. It was going to be hours before he'd be able to get anywhere near his crime scene. Jane Doe hadn't regained consciousness, according to the ER nurses. No sightings of Esme out on the street, at least none reported. Par for the course in this neighborhood where seven kids could go missing with no one noticing.

His only hope was to get the kids talking. Which meant letting Rossi work her magic.

A few minutes later, he was juggling two trays laden with bowls of soft serve from the cafeteria's machine and knocking on the door to the room where the children were. Price answered, taking the trays from him.

"I need home addresses," Ryder told the other man in a low tone. "And details of their abduction."

Price frowned. "They're just kids. Haven't they been through enough already?"

"You want the animals who did this roaming free on the streets?"

Price's face twisted with fury. "Any word on Esme?"

And why the hell did Price care so much? According to what little Ryder had been able to find through a quick NCIC search, the man lived in Philly, no wants, no warrants, and wasn't related to Esme. He'd reached out to Philly PD for more but hadn't heard back yet. "No. We're working on it. The kids know anything?"

"Haven't gotten there. Every time Angela pushes closer, they shut down."

"It's always hard with kids. Just give her my message, okay?"

"Yeah. Thanks." Price closed the door again, and Ryder returned to the dark space behind the one-way glass. While the kids squealed with delight and dove into the ice cream, he used the DVR to watch what he'd missed while he was gone. Nothing helpful—Rossi was doing a good job getting the kids to open up, but still, they shied away from anything that got too close to what had happened to them.

Ryder wondered at that. Why hadn't any of them asked for their parents? And the older ones, you'd think they'd be volunteering more info. They were old enough to be excited about helping the police— at least his niece and nephew would have been. But not these kids.

Rossi kept trying. The older two both said they lived in the Tower. When she asked if anyone else lived there, the others all nodded.

Seven kids missing, and no one had reported it. All from the Tower.

What the hell was going on there?

CHAPTER SEVENTEEN

THE ICE CREAM wasn't helping. The kids mentally retreated every time I got close to asking about their captivity. The most I got was one of the youngest saying she didn't want to "go to church no more."

I'd passed the point of exhaustion hours ago—typical for me these past few months. I couldn't sleep more than a few minutes at a time, my body ricocheting between primed and hyperalert, running on adrenaline, and complete shut down. I felt almost there now. Maybe not physically drained, but emotionally.

After the on-call social worker finally arrived, I left to check on my other patient, the unconscious girl we'd found.

Despite the awful things I see at the Advocacy Center, I usually enjoy the work there. It's different from the ER in so many ways. Quiet, intense, focused. Everything at the Center is controlled, the chaos already finished.

One patient at a time. How luxurious it is to give one patient my full and undivided attention for as long as it takes. There is something just as rewarding in that as there is in juggling several dozen cases from a multicar pileup on the Turnpike.

I had just stepped through the double doors leading to the ER when it hit me again. After tonight, I might not be able to do either job. Hard to trust an ER doc with uncontrollable tremors and abrupt-onset catatonia. Harder still to trust her testimony on the witness stand when she was hearing voices of not-quite-dead people in her head.

Aw, hell. I was so screwed.

As if to drive the point home, I tripped over nothing, stumbling into the wall, banging my elbow. Anger and fear tangling like live wires in my gut, I pushed open the door to the critical care treatment room.

The sight of my Jane Doe, still unconscious, eyes staring unblinking at the ceiling tiles—now coated with ointment to protect her corneas—doused me in a wave of guilt that drowned out any self-pity.

If Jane Doe was going to be my last case, she was sure as hell getting everything I had to give.

Shari Bartholomew, one of my sexual assault nurse examiners, stood at the counter beside the sink. "Evidence of repeated sexual assault," she told me as she finished labeling her specimens for the rape kit. "Physical assault as well. Similar pattern of injuries to the two cases we had last month."

"The ones drugged with PXA?"

She nodded.

"Anything new?"

"Yeah, but it's not good news. I think she might be our first PXA overdose. Her kidneys are shutting down. They're planning to start hemodialysis as soon as they have the bed ready in the ICU. Liver function isn't so hot, either."

Our other PXA assault cases had all been conscious, although confused, when they were found. While they hadn't suffered any major organ damage, their brains had been scrambled—so far, it seemed permanent. All four women were still in the psych ward, none with any sign of improvement.

Why had he given Jane Doe more? He obviously was an expert chemist to be synthesizing the PXA and titrating its effects over the days, weeks, he'd kept his victims. What had changed?

"He didn't clean her up as thoroughly as the others," Shari told me. "I found traces of secretions."

A spark of hope sprang to light. Finally, real evidence. Which meant real DNA that might be in the system or at least matched to a suspect—if we ever found a suspect. We hadn't found any obvious DNA evidence on the other victims, they'd all been thoroughly washed before being dumped, but their rape kits were pending, so there was still a chance they might reveal traces of DNA.

"The brand on her chest, it's more clear than the others," Shari continued. "Not as swollen or inflamed. Here, I printed a copy for you." She handed me an image that looked similar to those satellite images from outer space that almost look like letters or designs when they're really river deltas and mountain ranges. Still, it was a step in the right direction.

"Do me a favor and follow up on the other victims' rape kits," I told her. "See if they found any DNA we can use as a comparison." If there was, at least we could determine if it was the same perpetrator—and if he acted alone. I was surprised the lab hadn't already gotten back to us with results. It was one of my few accomplishments in this era of budget cuts that I'd been able to coordinate our evidence evaluation with the crime lab so that active sexual assault cases went to the top of the queue, second only to homicides.

The techs had resisted at first, complaining that they'd get blamed for any delays in processing other evidence, but quickly found that by doing our cases first, they often cleared several cases at once, helping to ease their backlog. Unfortunate but true: Most rapists don't stop at one assault or one victim.

While we waited for the ICU transport team, I did a quick examination of Jane Doe, taking care not to touch her again. Shari was right, she fit the pattern of our other victims. Restraint abrasions, evidence of electrical burns, ligature marks on her neck, parallel lines of being lashed, and the hallmark all the victims had borne: an oddly patterned circular burn just above her left breast, over her heart, a centimeter and a half in diameter.

Shari finished sealing her evidence and signed it over to the waiting police officer. Ryder didn't officially start with the advocacy team until Monday, but he was going to have his hands full already.

"Ready to help me examine our other victims?" I asked Shari after the ICU team had wheeled Jane Doe away.

"The kids? What's the plan?"

"First, we'll collect their clothing, photograph and document any gross injuries. That's probably all we'll be able to do tonight." I explained the tricky situation and primitive group dynamics the kids exhibited. "No way they'll tolerate being separated."

"We should start with the oldest, show the younger ones that there's nothing that hurts."

"Right. Make a game out of it. We'll give them PJs to change into, let them have fun getting their picture taken."

She winced when I said the word "fun" but nodded in understanding. It was a fine line, trying to collect evidence and assess injuries without psychologically damaging the kids more than they already had been.

"What if they want to wash up?"

Tricky. I didn't want to lose any possible skin evidence if any of the kids had been sexually assaulted. Hoped they hadn't, but given the girl's exam, I couldn't rule that out.

"We'll play that by ear." We stopped to grab some kid- and toddler-sized pajamas and put a call into pediatrics asking for a few nurses to help.

Then we returned to the Advocacy Center and got to work.

※

RYDER WATCHED AS Rossi and a nurse talked to each child, persuading them to change their clothes and get their picture taken, while Price entertained the rest and the social worker took notes between phone calls trying to figure out where to place the kids on a holiday. At first the children balked, grabbing at their T-shirts like they would never let go. But a few quiet words and a smile from

Rossi, and they'd pull the T-shirt over their heads, drop it into the paper bag the nurse held, stretch their arms up and twirl around as the nurse took photos with a digital camera, before climbing into the new pajamas Rossi offered them.

Despite Rossi's best efforts to turn the proceedings into a game, none of the kids smiled. Or fully relaxed. Not until they were back with the others, able to throw themselves into the group and distance themselves from the adults.

The last little girl, about five or six, broke Ryder's heart when she kept repeating over and over as she let Rossi examine her and re-dress her, "I'm sorry, I'm sorry, I'm sorry."

Rossi sat back on her haunches, blinking rapidly, watching the girl rejoin the others. The girl didn't say anything more, instead simply sat beside the dog, arms curled around her knees, rocking, as the kids around her devoured second helpings of ice cream.

Price, of all people, saved the day, plopping down on the floor in front of the girl with a bowl of ice cream. He held it between them, offering it without saying anything, and waited. The girl didn't move until her gaze flicked up to search his face. And spotted the spoon hanging from his nose.

Soon, he had her eating ice cream, even let her smear some on his chin, and had coaxed her into giving him a hint of a smile.

Rossi stood at that and left. A minute later, she sat beside Ryder in the small, dark observation room, face buried in her hands.

She wasn't crying. He figured she was years past tears. Just like he was.

"You're doing a good job," he told her after a few minutes of silence except for the occasional shy giggle from the kids as Price showed them how to let the dog lick ice cream from their palms.

She shrugged, her shoulders heaving as if throwing off a burden.

"You are. People respond to you. It's a gift."

"Yeah, some gift. Damaged kids, dying old ladies, victims—no wonder I do so well with men."

"You do just fine with me. And I'm not a victim, not damaged, or wounded."

"Aren't you, Ryder? Aren't we all?" She paused, gestured past him to the kids devouring their ice cream. "I mean, otherwise, why would we be doing this job, poking into the dark corners of the soul that normal people run away from? The stuff of nightmares. That's what we live with, every day. There's got to be something wrong with us, right?"

"You mean like we feel a connection to the violence we see every day?"

"I mean, like, somewhere inside, deep inside, hidden away, don't you ever wonder what it would be like to just let go, break all the rules, run amok like the psychopaths you hunt?"

Hard to say anything when he'd asked himself the same question and had no answer. He remained silent, wondering if she had seen him when he almost lost it with Tyree, if she knew how close he had come to killing the bastard.

"Any news on Esme?" she asked.

Her expression was bleak, and he knew she knew he would have told her immediately if he had. "I've got as many people on it as possible. Even have the crew in dispatch calling all the local businesses near any exits from the tunnels requesting surveillance tape if they have it."

"On Thanksgiving night?"

"It's a little girl. But you're right, for most we won't have anything until morning. Other than an Amber Alert—not much use without a vehicle or description of who took her—there's nothing we can do until we can get into the tunnels. My guys are working on that, but it's going to take time."

"Devon's right. Odds are, whoever took her is long gone. He obviously knew his way around down there, wouldn't have risked getting caught by staying in the tunnels." She sighed, the sound heavy.

"Give me another place to look, and I'm there." His phone rang. Before he answered it, he reached across the space between them and squeezed her arm. Wished he could give her more.

"Ryder here." He stood, turned to Rossi. "It's Philly PD about our mutual friend." He nodded to Price, his designer suit now smeared with ice cream. "I have to take it."

He stepped outside. The hall was silent, as quiet as a hospital got outside the morgue. But somehow the sights and sounds—all those kids, Rossi—clung to him even as he raised the phone and listened to the voice on the other end of the line. He placed one palm flat against the door to the observation area, kept his voice business-like, just the facts, but found himself unable to totally pull away from the emotions in the room beyond.

His job would have been so much easier if he didn't feel anything. Maybe he'd even be a better cop, divorcing his emotions. But he had so little left, he just couldn't bring himself to bury what remained.

Hoped like hell that wasn't a huge mistake.

☽ ❋ ☾

FLYNN WAS CONFUSED. She despised being confused. Over the past three years she'd deliberately pared down her life to the bare essentials. No room for indecision. No room for confusion. Black and white, she knew what to do and she did it.

She was in control.

Until tonight.

She'd lost track of Leo but then had stumbled across the girl hiding on the top row of shelving. She'd assumed Leo had screwed up and let the girl escape. Snuck up close, ready to grab her, and was surprised to see she was young—even for Leo. Had hesitated, was about to sit back and watch, see who the new people on the scene were. One of them was definitely a cop, and Tyree she recognized, but she had no idea who the other guy was.

The woman she knew—would never forget her face. The doctor from Good Samaritan who had saved her life, started her on this path. What the hell was she doing here, so far below ground, in the

139

dark, walking her dog?

Then the really weird shit started.

The girl—Esme, Dr. Rossi had called her—climbed out from her hiding place. And someone hidden in the shadows on the other side of the tunnel started shooting at them. Shooting at the girl—no way he'd seen Flynn.

What was she supposed to do? Let the girl get killed?

Flynn caught the girl's look of terror, and it echoed in her own memories. No way could she trust Tyree or any cops who were with him. She might have been tempted to trust Dr. Rossi if the doctor had been alone, but the man with her had a gun. Who knew whose side he was on? Bullets flying towards them, she'd grabbed the girl and run.

Now that she had time to think about it, she regretted acting so impulsively. She had a girl on her hands—just a little kid, stunned into silence when Flynn showed her her gun—strangers crawling through the tunnels, a cop with them, which meant more cops coming soon, plus Leo on the loose. Was he the shooter? If so, could she risk going back to the brownstone? And then there was Daniel Kingston, waiting for her to save his son's ass, once again.

Fuckinhelluvamess.

She didn't swear, not out loud, not often. Daniel didn't approve, and she'd left that street crassness behind. But sometimes there were just no other words to do justice to the chaos that swarmed her when the world got too much to handle. It was like a beast let out of control, rampaging through her body, ready to kill.

No. That was the old her. Three years ago and blood on her hands. She could control the beast, beat it at its own game, use its strength without letting it use her.

She could. She would.

Her thoughts fell into the rhythm of her silent footsteps, calming her as she moved along the catwalk, the girl slung over her shoulder. Good thing the kid was skinny.

But what the hell to do with her?

CHAPTER EIGHTEEN

THE KIDS WERE still eating—graduating to chicken nuggets and fries—and pediatrics had freed up a nurse to watch them. The social worker had been able to negotiate a truce with Children's Services. Given how traumatized the children were and their need for further observation and psychological evaluations, we'd been given permission to keep them overnight. So far we'd been able to keep news of them out of the press, but I knew that wouldn't last long. Thankfully, the Advocacy Center is self-contained, so we could keep them safe here.

Ryder went to arrange for a police officer to stand guard outside the Advocacy Center's entrance, while I asked an orderly to bring blankets and pillows. There was no way we'd be able to separate them tonight. They probably wouldn't sleep anyway. Other children I'd cared for after being isolated for prolonged periods had the same hyperenergized buzz these kids exhibited. Between their day/night cycles being disrupted and the adrenaline pumping through their systems—not to mention the sugar high—it would be awhile before they crashed and slept.

But the kids were safe. For tonight.

It rankled that that was as good as I could make things. In fact, once we unraveled the tangle of custody issues, found out who was behind all this, and the news broke, tonight might be the best memory they made for a long time.

The kids all said solemn good-byes to Ozzie, giving him hugs he patiently sat through. I don't think they even noticed Devon and I leaving with him.

Reluctantly, I closed the door behind us and turned down the hall leading back to the ER. "Come on, Ryder's waiting for us."

Devon shot me a look. "I have to get back out there, look for Esme. Can't you just pretend I slipped away and you didn't notice?"

"Do I look like the kind of woman who wouldn't notice a man and a dog wandering through her ER?"

He sighed and addressed Ozzie. "That's what I get for letting her come with me."

"Letting me? I should have made you give me directions and gone alone."

"Alone? You'd be lost or worse—" He stopped, his face clouding, and I knew we were both thinking of Tyree's booby traps. Those would have been a nasty surprise.

"Still, I work better alone."

"So do I."

We crossed into the ER. "Is Ryder going to lock you up?"

"The gun's clean, and I don't have any warrants. But the cops won't get anywhere with Tyree."

"You will?" I remembered the animosity between Tyree and Devon when they'd met in the tunnels. "Besides, he's Esme's uncle. If he knew anything, he would have already either told someone or sent one of his men to get her himself."

He bounced back and forth, glanced over his shoulder at the doors to the Advocacy Center. "I was hoping those kids might know something." He blew his breath out. "I don't even know where to start."

"Ryder's doing everything he can." Devon's expression turned skeptical. "He's a good guy. Don't underestimate him."

As if my words had conjured him, Ryder appeared down the hall, coming from the security office. He nodded to Devon, stopped and waited, giving us a few more moments of privacy.

"You'll take care of the dog?" Devon handed me Ozzie's leash.

What the hell was I going to do with a dog?

Ozzie raised his head and nosed my palm until I scratched between his ears. Devon shook his head as if abandoning a lost cause. "Or maybe he'll be taking care of you. He seems pretty clued into these fits of yours."

I'd noticed that as well. Some dogs can sense things like seizures, are used as companions for patients. Patient. There was that ugly word again. Devon read my mind. "You are gonna have a doctor check you out, right?"

My glare had no effect on him.

"You could've gotten us both killed if you'd had one of those spells at the wrong time."

"You going to tell Esme you're her father when we find her?" I countered.

He scrutinized the bulletin board on the wall beside us as he locked his emotions away.

"I saw you with those kids. You'd make a good father."

"Can't tell her. Might get her hurt. If she's still—" He drew in a breath, turned back to me, all business now. "If for any reason I'm not around…I mean, if something, anything—"

"I won't stop looking. I promise."

He nodded, sealing our bargain. "Guess that means you'd better get yourself a clean bill of health. For Esme's sake."

I hated to admit that was highly unlikely. Whatever was behind my symptoms, it was escalating in strange and mysterious ways.

We joined Ryder at the end of the corridor near the ambulance bay entrance beside the security office.

"I checked you out, Price," Ryder said. "Philly PD says I should lock you up first chance I get."

Devon met Ryder's challenge head on, extending his wrists for handcuffs. "Got something to lock me up for, go ahead."

It wasn't animosity that crackled between the two men, but it wasn't friendship either. More a leery mutual respect. "Wish I did. You're free to go."

"My gun?"

Ryder arched an eyebrow as if surprised that Devon would push things. "You can get it back as soon as ballistics is done with it."

Devon considered that, nodded.

"Thanks for your help down there, Price." They didn't shake hands, barely made eye contact, but it seemed to be enough.

Devon started toward the exit, then turned and looked over his shoulder. "Take care, doc."

Sounded like he meant it.

I waited while Ryder escorted Devon to the doors, watching him walk away, as if his glare would be enough to hustle Devon past the city limits and out of his jurisdiction.

By the time he turned back to face me, I'd bullied my exhausted psyche back into my usual facade of professionalism. Or at least a pretense of it. Had to admit, though, it was a bit reassuring to see the expression on Ryder's face before he knew I was looking: haggard with a hint of despair, echoing my own feelings.

"Who did this, Ryder? Why lock up those kids?"

"I wish I knew." He sank against the wall beside me, the dog sitting between us. "According to Petrosky, things over at the Tower have deteriorated into a block-party-slash-riot. Tyree's lawyer got him released. The chief wants my head for calling out the troops without his permission, but that's not keeping him from smiling for the cameras."

"Does the press know about the children?"

"Not yet. So far they think it's all about finding Esme and investigating a double homicide. I'm keeping it that way as long as possible. Top things off, Daniel Kingston wants my badge. That man," he rolled his eyes, "makes Donald Trump look like a choirboy."

"Why would he care?"

"He owns the Tower and the tunnel complex beneath it. Was livid we were trespassing. At least until the camera crews showed up, then he was all sunshine and rainbows, concerned for Esme's well-being."

The anger coloring his voice surprised me. "Daniel Kingston's money and charitable contributions are about the only thing holding this town together."

"Yeah, like that banker, Potter, in *It's a Wonderful Life*. He wants this city for himself, his personal fiefdom."

"Never knew a conspiracy nut who liked *It's a Wonderful Life*."

"I'm not a conspiracy nut. Just someone who's seen too much."

"I know that feeling."

"You must be exhausted. You're not working today, are you?"

"No." I glanced at the clock. One twenty. I wanted to meet Louise as soon as she got into work. I had to know what was going on in my screwed-up brain, for better or worse.

"Want me to call someone to take you to your car?" Ryder asked.

I shook my head. "No, thanks. I'll walk."

Ozzie recognized the magic word and nosed my knee.

Ryder's frown was there and gone in a flash, replaced by a smile that made his face seem young and his eyes seem old. "Should've figured. The worst three blocks in the city, and you want to walk them at one thirty in the morning."

"After those tunnels, they don't seem so bad. And the rain's stopped." We strolled through the sliding doors and back outside into the night. "Okay. Maybe a police escort wouldn't be such a bad idea after all."

He chuckled but didn't take my arm. Instead, he positioned himself on my right side, keeping his gun hand free. I switched the leash to my left hand, and now Ozzie guarded me from the other side. Couldn't ask for better protection.

Or company. Ryder's gait matched mine, even though I walk very fast. When we were married, Jacob, despite his longer legs, was always rushing to catch up with me. Which pretty much sums up our marriage as well. Two people in love, but totally out of sync.

I couldn't help looking over at Ryder. Wondering what went on behind his cop-neutral facade. Hoped maybe I'd have time to find out. After I got a clean bill of health from Louise.

"I know you're probably exhausted, but I'll need you to give us a statement," Ryder said, finally breaking the silence. His arm brushed against mine, but other than that, it was business as usual. He was a cop on his way back to a crime scene, and I was a witness. "I need to know everything you saw down there."

"Devon can tell you more—"

"I need to hear it from someone I can trust." An expression flitted across his face, shadowed by the green glow of a traffic light, giving me the feeling he didn't use that last word very often.

His life and job were very like my own. Trust no one, assume nothing.

I told him everything. From meeting Devon and learning that Father Vance was a former gang member—he nodded like he'd already known that—to Ozzie leading us to Esme. Only things I left out were my little "spells" and Devon's relationship to Esme.

Felt guilty as hell about it. Ryder trusted me, but I wasn't trusting him. Even though I wanted to. But some truths weren't mine to share, and others were simply too risky. I knew how easily lawyers could destroy a case by labeling a witness unreliable. Until I knew more about my condition, the less he knew, the less compromised his case would be.

The closer we got to St. Tim's and the Tower, the more distant he grew. The red and blue flashing lights filled the sky from two blocks away.

"How much trouble are you in?" I was certain that Ryder's entering the tunnels with Tyree was totally against regulations. Not to mention pissing off Daniel Kingston, the most powerful man in Cambria.

"Same as usual. They'll give me a lecture on getting emotionally involved. Again." His tone was wry. "They already busted me from Major Crimes to Sex and Juvie. Only thing lower down the rung is Traffic."

That rankled. I'd fallen into my position at the Advocacy Center after working several nasty cases where the system had broken down.

So I'd decided to take the system on and fix it. I'm proud of the work we do there. Not just for the victims, but for all the crimes we prevent, getting predators off the streets.

I stopped. If I really was…sick, incapacitated, about to lose my job, I wanted only the best people there to take over for me. Ozzie sank to his haunches, watching as Ryder took two more steps before realizing I wasn't following, and turned back.

"What?"

"I know what cops say about working with the Advocacy Center. I've heard the jokes. If you don't want the job, I'll find someone else."

His mouth opened, then he clamped it shut, trying hard not to say something. He stared at me, red and blue lights flashing behind him. Then he nodded. Just one quick jerk of his chin, up and down. Making a decision. About me.

"Want to know why I got sent down to Sex Crimes?" He answered without waiting for me to say anything, "When I worked Major Crimes, they called me a hotshot. On the fast track. Until," he gave a one-shouldered shrug, "there was this case, and suddenly, it just all didn't seem to mean anything anymore. Yeah, it's great nailing a homicide, but most of them are either no-brainers or stone-cold whodunits that you'll never solve because no one dares to come forward. Not like working with your kind of victims."

I studied his face, searching for permission. "Tell me about the case."

He drew in a breath but immediately released it, as if the air tasted bad. "I was interviewing this shithead. We had him on possession, but the DA made a deal in exchange for testimony on a shooter we were looking for, let him walk. Whole time he just kept on smiling at me, like he knew something I didn't.

"Anyway, we arrest the shooter, then a few days later go to take our star witness, aka the shithead, in for a deposition. We get to his squat and find this girl, eleven years old, living there all alone. And she's mad—at us. Fighting and cursing and scratching. Says we drove him away and he left her behind because she was getting too big—but he took her little sister…"

He trailed off. Didn't need to finish. I could fill in the gaps well enough. "You find her?"

"Feds did. Outside of DC. Body dumped at a rest stop off the interstate. Guy had taken them both from his girlfriend, probably the only reason he hooked up with her to start with, been raping them for years. Never found the shithead. Guess I kinda lost it with the ADA who'd pushed the deal."

He caught my look. "No, it wasn't Voorsanger. Your ex is actually a pretty decent ADA. Listens to us peons, even if his boss doesn't. Anyway, insubordination, my boss called it. But I'm glad—maybe working Sex Crimes, I can stop some of this shit before there's a body, before there's another dead little girl."

"You know that's not necessarily true."

"I know. Doesn't mean I can't hope. Some days that's all I got." He looked up, stretched his mouth into a fake smile, saw I wasn't buying it and relaxed. "Anyways, I'm where I want to be. You've got my A-game."

I started walking again, a bit more slowly. "Good to know. Anything I can do to help with your bosses?"

"Don't worry about it. I get them results, they're not going to do more than throw paper into my jacket."

I wondered at that. Most of the detectives we've had at the Advocacy Center, while devoted to the victims whose cases they worked, still had ambitions, saw their time in Sex Crimes as a stepping stone to greater things. Usually, they were on their way up to Major Crimes or another promotion—not on their way down, like Ryder.

"You talk like this is the end of the road for you. Careerwise."

He looked away, his gaze caught by the emergency vehicles crowding the street. "Maybe so. It's not a bad ending. Not if we get the job done."

My sentiments exactly.

We arrived at my car at the edge of the tangle of official vehicles. "I want to help."

He scowled at that. "You've done enough already."

"Take Ozzie. Maybe he can lead you to Esme or at least track her once you've got the tunnels clear and can go back in."

He took the leash I handed him. Ozzie looked from me to Ryder, tail wagging, no complaints. "Thanks. That's a good idea."

He lingered, both of us wanting to say more. Neither having any idea what to say. I fished out my keys. "You'll call me if you hear anything?"

I didn't say "please," but I knew he heard it. "Of course."

"Take care of Ozzie."

"I will."

Wanting to linger but running out of reasons, I risked touching his arm. "You'll find her. I know you will."

He looked away, didn't seem as certain. Just like me in the ER— never making promises I couldn't keep.

CHAPTER NINETEEN

RYDER JOINED THE men at the back of the fire lieutenant's SUV. Figured it was better to hold off on showing his face to any higher-ups, hoping the brass and media would get tired and go away, let him work in peace. When in doubt, regroup, recon, reacquire the target.

He now had victims scattered over four crime scenes; seven of them with families to locate, notify, and interview; one still a Jane Doe; and one of them a critical missing juvenile—which took priority over everything.

Despite all this, or maybe as a respite to it, his skin tingled with the memory of Rossi's touch. It'd been a long time since any woman had had that effect on him. He was a little scared to think about it too much, even more frightened to actually acknowledge any feelings other than simple attraction. Remaining comfortably numb was a far safer strategy.

"What're you smiling about?" the fire LT snapped, sluicing rain water from his Tyvek maps with the side of his hand.

"Just enjoying a good clusterfuck." Ryder gestured to the chaos behind them.

"Got that right." He reached down to pat Ozzie on the head. "Nice dog."

"Where we at?"

"Good news is that Gator Guy came through." He nodded to a man sitting in the backseat wearing a DOC jumpsuit and sipping coffee from between manacled hands. Ryder nodded back to him and

150

the guard beside him.

"Thanks for joining the party."

"No problem," the guard grunted, looking bored.

Gator Guy—the name on his jumpsuit was Jessup—squirmed around in his seat so he faced Ryder and the LT. "You tell him about the power, right? You guys can't turn the juice on, not unless you want to see it all blown sky-high."

"What's he talking about?"

"The electricity." The LT sighed. "The tunnels were originally wired in the fifties—"

"1952," Jessup put in. "Good, solid work. Not like that cheap '70's shit that came later."

"When they built the Tower," Ryder said.

"Right." Jessup talked like he owned the Tower instead of Daniel Kingston. "But that chickenshit wiring over at the Tower needed patched and repaired, cobbled together basically. So finally they hooked into the tunnel's infrastructure."

"But then folks like Jessup came along and jumped onto the grid on their own," the LT chimed in.

"Hey, man, my plants needed their sunshine, ya know?"

"You grew pot down there?" Ryder asked.

"Back in the day. Before I got chased out by the gangbangers and the rich guy's security goons." Jessup shook his head, half-reminiscing, half-regret. "You wouldn't believe the shit I saw down there. Sometimes I wasn't even high."

"That why you got an alligator when you moved your operation?"

"Hell yeah. Lizzie was the best security money could buy. Until she got peckish for a midnight snack and burned down my place. Of course," he brightened, "any evidence of hydroponic activity got burned as well, so all's I got is a Class D, easy time."

"Tell me about exits from the tunnels." Ryder wanted to calculate where he should be searching for Esme, which direction her abductor might have taken.

"That's the bad news," the LT said. "Not only can we not turn on the lights down there—"

"Not without ka-boom." Jessup raised his hands with a whoosh that made his coffee jump.

"Jessup also gave us intel on five unofficial exits not on the map." He gestured with his pen. "Here, here, and here. The other two are the church basement and the sewer line that runs right under this street."

Ryder followed on the map. "Access the sewers, and you can go anywhere in the city."

"Bingo."

Which meant it was too late. Whoever had taken Esme could be free of the tunnels and on the other side of the city by now.

The SWAT team leader ambled over, coffee sandwiched between hands encased in Nomex shooting gloves. Ryder looked at it longingly.

"Ryder, you made it back in one piece. Might not last long. Deputy chief's looking for you."

The brass could wait. "How much ground have you guys covered?"

"Now that Tyree is back and cooperating, the uniforms are progressing with the door-to-door in the Tower."

Ryder grunted. He'd bet the Major Crimes guys were happy about that. Made working their homicides easier, but he was certain Esme wouldn't be found in the Tower. The knot in his stomach writhed, a tangled nest of vipers baring their fangs. He'd lost her. Failure tensed his shoulder blades. "How's it going in the tunnels? Tyree give you what you need?"

The SWAT guy nodded. "Intel on his IEDs. But his group wasn't the only one using the tunnels. Besides that room where you found those kids, we found more evidence of some kind of satanic voodoo cult or something. I'm telling you, there's some freaky shit down there."

Ryder thought of the children's prison, covered in crucifixes and mirrors. "Tell me about it."

"It's slow-going. We were only able to clear your new crime scene and the area immediately surrounding it before we got pulled."

"Pulled? Who pulled you? Why?" Any trace of Esme was growing colder by the minute.

"Are you kidding me? I did. We're not equipped. No lights, shit everywhere. Place is a fucking death trap. And with those damn catwalks, we have to create a perimeter, clear them of any possible snipers, secure the high ground. Only then can we start to clear the rooms below. And once those are secured, we have to leave men behind on the catwalks to guard our flanks. You got an extra hundred men hiding in your back pocket?"

Ryder glanced across the crowd. The deputy chief stood beneath a hastily erected awning, safe from the rain. Beside him was Daniel Kingston. Both men wore tuxedos, were chatting, obviously comfortable with each other. "You gave the order? Not Kingston?"

"Kingston? What's he got to do with anything? I gave the chief my tactical assessment, and he agreed. Orders are to wait until morning when we can team up with the county bomb squad and the staties, get the dogs down there sniffing. Even with their help, we'll be going inch by inch. Might have the place cleared by Christmas if we're lucky."

"What about using thermal imaging? At least make sure there's no one else trapped down there." His stomach twisted at the thought of finding another room with little kids imprisoned in it.

"Way ahead of you," the fire guy answered. "We tried both our units and yours. Nothing works. That place was built to literally withstand a nuclear holocaust. No way our gear is getting through those walls."

Ryder rubbed his temples, trying to ease the headache squeezing his brain. Esme was long gone.

Still, he couldn't help but hope. It was his greatest weakness. Probably would get him killed someday if he wasn't careful, but he just couldn't help it. Extinguish that tiny flicker of hope that kept him warm enough to sleep at night, and he'd be no different from the walking dead he'd seen during the war. Men with dead eyes, dead hearts, just waiting for the rest of their bodies to catch up and die as well.

☽ ☀ ☾

WHEN RYDER WALKED away, I leaned against the Subaru, trying to figure out what the hell had happened to my life. I hadn't had a perfect life, but between the ER and the Advocacy Center, it was a full one. I kept busy, thought I was doing well.

Now it seemed my life had devolved into a cosmic joke. One I didn't know the punch line to.

I stood there, surrounded by too many questions, including: How the hell was I getting home? It was clear I couldn't drive, not until I could prevent my mind from spinning away beyond my control. Good thing it was only half a mile or so to Jimmy's Place, my uncle's bar, above which I rented an apartment.

But still I stood there, doing nothing.

As I sifted through the night's events, trying to arrange them into some kind of sense, I couldn't stop staring at the church across the street. Remembering the scent of candle wax, the crucifixes surrounding the children's prison, I wondered if my newfangled hypersensory fugue-spells could be put to good use. Maybe I could figure out a way to trigger one on command, somehow force my mind to make the subliminal connections it had while I was down in the tunnels when a fugue led me to the children.

After all, if you're losing your mind, might as well make the best of it, right?

Which is exactly why doctors make the worst patients. Not because we know too much, but because we can rationalize and deny just about any symptom. We're the ultimate control freaks, and *we* decide when something is wrong and how to fix it. Or so we'd like to believe.

So, instead of finding a safe bed to crawl into or a nice padded cell, instead of walking to my uncle's bar and snagging Jacob for a marathon night of steamy sex, I left the car and trudged back up the steps of St. Tim's.

Pausing at the top step, palpitations making my body sway, sweat trickling down my spine, I stared at the sea of red and blue and white lights that fanned out on the far side of the church. It was easy to pick Ryder out of the crowd of testosterone. His posture was that of a man going into battle—and he didn't seem too happy about it.

Wishing him luck, I turned to fight my own war and grabbed the ice-cold handle of the church's door. Half-hoping Vance had locked it behind me, I tugged.

Bad luck. It opened.

I entered the vestibule, couldn't help remembering how intense my connection with Ryder had been—here, in the ER, out on the street. It felt dangerous. He felt dangerous. Not like he could hurt me. Rather, if I didn't take care, I might hurt him.

One more crazy, tangled flavor to add to the night's Molotov cocktail.

The church was dark except for the light over the altar, a sunbeam from heaven smiling down on Jesus nailed to the cross. I slid into a pew—not kneeling, I wasn't here to pray—and sat. Just sat. One blessed quiet moment.

Everyone has their breaking point. No matter if you're a tough cop with years on the job, a swelled-ego surgeon, a seasoned nurse, a brave-hearted firefighter, or a tired ER doc who'd lost track of the last time she'd slept.

Sooner or later, we all break. Crash and burn. Shatter.

I was there. Finally. As close to rock bottom as I'd ever been. I slumped in the wooden pew, my emotions churning into an exhausted frenzy. My head felt like a bowling ball that had hit the gutter too many times while my hand was twitching in time to the *Flight of the Bumblebee*.

Add a little drool, and I'd look like a refugee from the psych ward. Which was maybe where I belonged.

I sat there, eyes closed, desperate for sleep. Instead, all I got was a whirlwind of fear dragging me down: How sick was I? What new symptom would appear next? Would it hurt?

Was I going to die?

As soon as they found Esme, I'd call Louise, get myself checked out, tell her about all the crazy shit going on in my head. As soon as they found Esme.

If they found Esme. If they found her alive.

If she was still alive....

That was it. I hit bottom.

No strength to push off and resurface to breathe any hope into those ifs. I sat there, lips trembling like I was a twelve-year-old girl again, alone in the dark and rain, my dad's blood on my hands, drowning in fear and uncertainty—two emotions I despised. In the ER, with a patient's life at stake, I could ignore them, shove my ego aside, ask for help. Now, like it or not, I was the patient.

Fingers trembling, I dialed Louise. To hell with it being the middle of the night, to hell with waiting until tomorrow, to hell with my own stubborn pride. If I was going to help find Esme, I needed to first find out what was wrong with me—and learn how I could use it like I had in the tunnels when it led me to the kids and Jane Doe.

Five rings. Six. I was ready to hang up when Louise's voice came through, chipper and oh-so-confident. "This is Dr. Louise Mehta. I'm looking forward to returning your call. Please leave a message."

Tempted, I was so very tempted to hit the END button. Instead, I pulled the phone closer to my lips and whispered my confession.

"It's me. Sorry, I know it's late. But something's happened. To me. I'm not sure what. I need your help." Shit. How to even begin to explain it all? "Look. I know this sounds crazy. But it happened, I swear. I was in a trauma resuscitation, this nun got shot, had her heart in my hands, when I froze. Not like scared, like catatonic. Maybe a partial-complex seizure, I'm not sure."

I swallowed a hysterical laugh. The number of things I wasn't sure about were quickly building into a tsunami of ignorance. "Anyway, I saw, I heard things, things I couldn't possibly know—but she knew. I heard her voice. In my head, Louise. No one else heard it. Just me. And her memories, I saw, felt—I can't explain it, it was like I was there. With her. When it all happened."

Tears choked my voice. I swallowed, once and again. Glanced at the saints surrounding me, safely ensconced in their stained glass as they looked down at me. The phone felt heavy in my hand. "Anyway. Call me. Thanks."

I hung up, feeling both humbled and humiliated. Not because I'd asked Louise for help—I could trust her, and she'd never judge.

Humbled because I'd finally realized just how much bigger what was happening to me was compared to what I as a physician was equipped to handle. I'd told Louise about only one symptom and hadn't even been able to adequately describe it. And there were so many more: the insomnia, the restless agitation, the night sweats and hot flashes, the muscle tremors, the anxious paranoia—although, that might be more of a result, less of a symptom... Who knew? Anymore, I couldn't even decide what *was* a real symptom.

And the humiliation? That was pride. How could I sit here, in this church of all places, pouring out my heart to Louise, when I'd never been able to confess or ask forgiveness from my own family?

My father was dead because of me, my mother in pain every time she glanced my way, none of them understanding my life. Yet, I was powerless to leave. I needed them to...what? Punish me? Accept me? Forgive me? How could I ask for any of that when I couldn't forgive myself?

Despair wrapped its cold fingers around my heart and squeezed. What if whatever was wrong with me wasn't treatable? What if I was dying?

The music and bright lights found me, of course. No outrunning them, it seemed. Organ music this time. Bach. No time warp or freaky hypersensory acid trip accompanied it. Just a memory.

The tang of Betadine. Ryder, his arms pumping up and down on a naked woman's chest. Sister Patrice's heart in my hand, a soggy bag

157

of blood. Dead—or almost dead—like the rest of her.

Except for her voice in my head.

I forgive you. Find the girl.

Save the girl.

CHAPTER TWENTY

DEVON TOOK THE long way back to the Tower from Good Sam. He needed to think without seeing Daniel Kingston's monstrosity looming over him, taunting him.

It had been a mistake, coming back here.

That hadn't really hit home until he was in that room with those kids, saw the hell they'd gone through. They were all from the Tower, he was certain. Tyree had known—he was certain of that as well. Wouldn't be surprised if somehow Daniel Kingston himself wasn't involved. The man enjoyed exerting his power over the people forced to live in his Tower. Just look at what he'd done to Devon's mother.

It wasn't like Devon was an angel himself. He'd seen things. Hell, he'd *done* things...

But the thought of something happening to his little girl, the thought of someone touching her, hurting her—

Devon gagged, turned into the narrow space between two shuttered storefronts, his weight lurching forward as he emptied his stomach. He stood there, inhaling the sour stench of vomit and, for the first time in years, found himself truly and utterly disgusted.

It was a feeling he'd thought he'd outgrown. Left behind when he fled the Tower.

That was before he made that little girl laugh. A noise so pure, so filled with joy that it split his heart wide open.

He'd never heard his own daughter laugh.

For over a decade he'd nurtured the fantasy of playing hero and rescuing Jess and Esme. Now he realized there was a damn good reason he'd never actually done it. Tyree's threats were just an excuse, as were Jess's refusals to leave the Tower.

He was no kind of man to ever be a father or a partner. First time anyone ever needed anything from him, other than running away when he was told to, and he'd failed. Failed to save Jess, failed to find Esme. With absolutely no idea where to even start looking.

It would be so easy to call Harold to bring the car, escape again, return to his life in Philly.

Reality was, he was never going to be a father to Esme. He understood that now. But he couldn't get the music of that laugh out of his mind. It was addicting. He wanted to hear it again and again.

He should call Harold, go back home. Give up on the fantasy. The bricks he leaned against scraped his scarred palms, and he didn't care. Embraced the pain. If he stayed, there was going to be a whole lot more pain, he was certain.

If he stayed, he might just hear that laugh again, this time coming from his daughter.

☽ ⚜ ☾

AFTER LEO HAD gained access to Flynn's private quarters at the brownstone, she'd established safe houses scattered around the city. Since she had no idea how long his cat-and-mouse game would go on—if Leo had his way, he'd made it perfectly clear that it could go on as long as she could stay out of his hands and alive—she decided the best course of action was to be prepared for anything.

Which was fine by her. That had been pretty much her philosophy ever since Dr. Rossi saved her life three years ago.

So she carried Esme, not to the gates of the Kingston estate but, rather, to the park across the street and around to the rear of the boarded-up carousel, out of sight of anyone. She lowered Esme, a finger to her lips as a warning. The girl huddled on the ground, seemed to realize Flynn was her savior, not a bad guy—good choice seeing as how Flynn had risked her life for the girl when the bullets were flying.

Flynn recognized the girl as the daughter of the blind woman, Tyree's sister, Jessalyn Willard. For some reason, Daniel Kingston was obsessed with Jess, with an almost paternalistic protective attitude. Flynn had decided Jess was one of the reasons why Leo had chosen the Tower as his latest hunting grounds. As if by hurting other women who came from there, he was hurting Daniel.

Or maybe it was Tyree whom Leo was trying to hurt. It was so damn hard to tell, all these secrets woven around her like tangled fishing line able to cut to the bone if you made the wrong move.

She didn't care about Leo or Tyree. It was Daniel she wanted to spare. If she could shoulder this burden for him, protect the Kingston name and find a way to stop Leo without bringing his activities to the attention of the authorities, then Daniel's final days would be peaceful.

After that, all bets were off. But she'd be damned if she'd let Leo hurt any more women. Because this wasn't a game, not to Flynn.

She checked her phone. The motion-activated cameras she'd placed above the carousel door hadn't been triggered. Not one to leave anything to chance, she kept watch on the phone's screen as she moved forward to the door. The cameras both came on, revealing her back and frontal view in a split screen.

Still not satisfied, she went through her careful routine, checking her other security measures before unlocking the city-issued padlock securing the door. No signs that Leo had found her safe haven.

She slid the heavy door open and ushered the girl through, closing it before risking the lights.

"Thank you for being so quiet, Esme," Flynn said in a voice she gathered from her own past, way back when she'd rocked her baby sister to sleep. It was obvious Esme was in shock. Flynn reminded herself to take things slow. But she needed to know who was after the girl. Was it Leo? Esme was much younger than his usual victims. "It was a big help. Are you okay? No one hurt you, did they?"

The girl didn't answer, just looked around as if searching for danger. The lights were slowly coming on. First, the strands surrounding the mirrored inner workings of the carousel, then the ones along the outer perimeter, and finally, as if by magic, one row after another, the old-fashioned incandescent bulbs over the animals.

Esme opened her mouth wide and gasped when she saw her surroundings. Flynn couldn't hide her smile. The place took her the same way, every time. Mirrors and lovingly applied bright enamels, hand-carved animals—horses, lions, tigers, unicorns, even a dragon waiting to be tamed. They combined to create a fantasyland unlike any that a girl raised in the Tower had ever seen.

Esme reached a hand out as if afraid she'd break the spell and stroked the mane of a golden-gilded lion. "Can you make it go 'round?"

Her voice was a whisper, but it echoed through the dark like a gunshot, bringing Flynn back to the urgent reality. A reality where someone wanted this girl dead.

"No. It's been broken a long time." Esme's chin sank in disappointment. "But we can sit here." She guided the girl to a bench supported by two gryphons, their wings forming seats. "And you can tell me what happened tonight. Why you were in the tunnels." And who was shooting at you, she didn't add.

Didn't have to. The girl knew the score. She was only nine or ten, but growing up in the Tower was like dog years. Especially with a man like Tyree as your uncle.

Esme looked up at Flynn, blinking fast as if holding back tears. Still saying nothing. Flynn may have saved her life, but obviously that didn't mean she'd trust her with the truth. Smart kid.

Flynn couldn't resist her urge to shelter the girl with an arm around her shoulders. "Your Uncle Tyree was down in the tunnels, looking for you. Do you want me to call him so he can take you home?"

Esme shook her head no. Looked scared. Made sense. The kid had hidden from Tyree down in the tunnels.

"I can ask the police to—"

At the mention of the police, Esme grew panicked, squirming in Flynn's embrace as if she wanted to run away. Flynn squeezed her tight. "Okay. No police."

Esme calmed.

"Do you want me to call your mommy?" Flynn tried again, although last thing she wanted was to venture back out on the streets with a little girl marked as a target. No. The girl had been running away from the Tower. With someone trying to kill her, Flynn couldn't take her home, so better not promise her that. Then it occurred to Flynn: What if the mother, the blind woman, Jess, was in danger as well? How the hell was she going to get to her and protect them both? "Let her know you're all right?"

That did it. Esme fell apart, grabbing Flynn as if Flynn was a lifeline, curling her small body into Flynn's as she cried, tears and primal moans of grief pouring out. Flynn didn't know what to do, other than to hold her and rock her. She didn't lie, tell the girl it would be all right—it most obviously was not.

A few long minutes, and the girl's moans calmed. Flynn dared to try again. "What happened, Esme?"

"They killed my mommy." The words emerged as a wail. Esme bunched her fists to her mouth, trying to deny the truth. "And, and, Sister Patrice. That's a sin. A bad sin. Killing a nun. They're gonna go to h-e-l-l."

"They sure are, sweetheart. Who killed your mom and Sister Patrice?"

Terror filled the girl's face, and she pulled away, now shaking her head, her palms smothering her lips and any words that might sneak past.

"They're coming." Esme spread her fingers just far enough to let the words escape. "To kill me."

CHAPTER TWENTY-ONE

RYDER TOOK OZZIE with him as he made his way through the crowd to plead his case with the deputy chief. He hoped to persuade him to resume the search in the tunnels, even if on a limited scale.

Only local media had arrived so far. He was surprised to see them still on scene. A body found in the Tower wasn't news, not here in Cambria, but add in a dead nun and a missing girl, and it was enough to get them out on a holiday.

No one was talking about the other kids they'd found in the tunnels. Good. That gave them a bit of breathing room while Rossi's team worked to find their families. But sooner or later the story would break. Some CSU guy or a SWAT team member or maybe one of the fire guys…someone would want to play hero and grab some time in the spotlight. Always happened.

Daniel Kingston and the deputy chief still stood beneath the canopy, and now the son, Leo Kingston, had joined them. The kid—somehow it was hard to think of Leo as an adult when he stood beside his father who possessed a gravitas that made him seem larger than life—had had a few run-ins with the law, mainly possession charges.

Nothing his father couldn't buy his way out of with well-placed campaign contributions. In fact, Ryder was surprised it wasn't Kingston's voice that came out of the mayor's mouth any time he opened it.

Father and son. Ryder had never met either man before, but as soon as he laid eyes on them, he knew they were wrong. Nothing he could prove, nothing he could even explain if pressed. Just a subliminal pinging, like the radar a bat used to fly in the dark, waking primal protective instincts in the far recesses of his brain.

The father spotted him first, the son a millisecond behind. Both turned polished, too-friendly smiles his way, exposing their teeth, eyes meeting Ryder's without hesitation. Eyes that glittered with their own agendas.

Definitely wrong. Sociopath, psychopath, narcissist….whatever the current medical term, here were two perfect specimens.

If Ryder wanted those tunnels reopened, he'd have to play nice. He strode forward, plastered a smile on his face, and reached out a hand to the father. "Mr. Kingston. It's a pleasure. Thank you so much for your assistance."

A flicker in Kingston's gaze. Had Ryder laid it on too thick? But Kingston took his hand, nodding indulgently, as if granting Ryder a royal boon. "Of course. Always happy to help, Detective—"

The deputy chief stepped in. "This is Detective Matthew Ryder. The man I was telling you about."

"The hero who braved the tunnel complex despite warnings posted at every entrance and the fact that he was trespassing on private property," Leo Kingston put in, his smile more a sneer.

"A girl's life was at risk." Ryder didn't shake Leo's hand, instead merely stood there, meeting Leo's gaze, forcing himself to relax. Up close, Leo looked like a petulant teenager, all smoothed edges and crease-free.

"Leo," his father said. A caution.

"I'm sure Detective Ryder had no idea of the repercussions of his actions," the deputy chief put in. "Especially the cost to the city."

Cambria had walked the knife edge of fiscal disaster for years. What the hell did that have to do with saving a girl's life?

The deputy chief answered for him, gesturing to the uniformed men swarming around the alley, St. Tim's, and the Tower. "This overtime will break us. We might need to furlough a good portion of our manpower if we don't shut it down. Fast."

Ah. Now he understood. The brass wanted it to be Ryder's call. Either way, he'd be to blame—for shutting things down too soon, failing to find Esme in time…or for bankrupting the city, forcing pay cuts and furloughs, leaving the city without adequate protection during the holiday season.

His smile now genuine, he turned back to Daniel Kingston. "I don't think we can shut down operations now, sir. Not with thousands of citizens at risk from the dangerous incendiary devices we've discovered on Mr. Kingston's property. I'm sure he'll agree that the price of us cleaning it up for him now is much, much less than the price he'd pay if something went wrong and innocent people were hurt."

Kingston's eyebrows revealed his irritation, although his smile never wavered. "Of course, I'll pay any necessary cleanup costs incurred by the city," he conceded.

The deputy chief nodded and beamed. Ryder half-expected the man to drop a curtsy or genuflect.

"In that case," Ryder said, "I'll tell the men to resume operations down in the tunnels immediately. Even with the safety restrictions, we could start the work until more resources arrive."

Kingston bristled, communicating his displeasure without saying a word. The deputy chief spoke up, "That's not your decision to make, Ryder. We'll continue our work in the Tower for now, but the operations in the tunnels will have to wait until we can better ensure officer safety."

Officer safety, his ass. There was something down there Kingston didn't want anyone to find. Ryder was certain of it. He was about to protest when Leo stepped forward, inserting himself between his father and the chief. "I'm sure neither of you were aware that Detective Ryder forced a civilian, Mr. Tyree Willard, to accompany him down into the tunnels, despite the danger," Leo said, talking like he was Tyree's lawyer. "Or that Detective Ryder then unlawfully restrained the civilian and assaulted him."

Surely this was about more than a little shove?

"Detective Ryder, is this true?" the deputy chief demanded.

Ryder wasn't about to lie, not even to save his job. And he sure as hell wasn't going to explain his actions to these assholes. "Yes, sir."

"Perhaps it would be best for all concerned if Detective Ryder confined his investigation to a less active role, such as interviewing witnesses? After all, we wouldn't want the city to have to deal with any liability issues," Daniel Kingston said after giving his son a look Ryder wished he could interpret. Part disgust, part suspicion, and part...fear? Was it Daniel Kingston who didn't want Ryder back in those tunnels or his son?

Every instinct that had kept him alive during three tours in Afghanistan was now screaming at high alert. Ozzie, standing beside him, made a low sound, his fur rippling, corrugated by an unseen wind. Ryder said nothing, instead focused on the non-verbal interplay going on around him.

The deputy chief, as usual, was clueless to anything except saving his own ass. "Detective Ryder, you'll start your new assignment with the Advocacy Center effective immediately. Which means that you no longer have any business on this crime scene." He gestured to Petrosky, who stood nearby. "Please escort Detective Ryder and his dog," he gave Ozzie a dirty look that the dog returned by baring his teeth, "beyond the barricades."

Ryder gave them a nod, turned smartly on his heel, and left, Ozzie at his side. He trusted the dog to guard his back more than anyone else there.

"The Tower is your primary beat?" Ryder asked Petrosky as they worked their way through the throng to his car.

"Yep. Community policing and all that. Why?"

"Any strange activity lately? Kids gone missing?"

"Missing? No. We had a few runaways right after school started, but none since. Too cold at night. Brings them to their senses, and they head back home."

So not only were the seven kids not reported as missing, there was no unusual talk about them. Ryder glanced up at the Tower. His gait wobbled the slightest bit, as if instead of being safely home in Pennsylvania, he had one foot still back in Paktika.

"What's the deal with Leo Kingston and Tyree Willard? Why would the son of the most powerful man in the city give a shit about a low-rent pimp and drug dealer?"

Petrosky shrugged, but her posture tensed and her pace picked up. Like she didn't want to be answering questions. Or maybe she just didn't want to be associated with a detective whose career was taking a sudden meteoric fall from grace. "Leo has a few possession busts, meth and cocaine, scores from Tyree. And Tyree and the old man have always been tight."

"What do you mean?"

"Other than the gangbangers, most of the residents in the Tower are single moms and their kids. Story goes, back in the day, we're talking twenty, thirty years ago, Daniel Kingston liked to make sure they knew their place so that nobody gave him any trouble."

Ryder stopped, not sure he understood. Waited.

Petrosky didn't turn back, but she did slow down. "Kingston used to come visit—anyone who gave him grief, didn't pay the extra 'rent' he charged for protection, tried to organize folks into protesting the conditions—anyone he thought was a troublemaker, he'd visit their family. Personally. Especially liked to spend time with the women. Would pick one, make a special example of her to keep the rest in line."

"What's that got to do with Tyree?"

"Story goes, Kingston handpicked Tyree to lead the Royales. It's been over twenty years since the old man has been back, but he still keeps a tight grip on things over there. Sentimental reasons, I guess."

"I thought Tyree ran the Tower."

She shrugged. "Tyree might run the place, but it's Kingston who owns it. In every sense of the word."

Maybe it was Tyree who'd gotten the search shut down and persuaded the Kingstons to get Ryder kicked off his own crime scene. Tyree had damn good reason to keep Ryder out of those tunnels—at least until he had time to finish covering his tracks and moving his drug operations. Did that mean he knew where Esme was and was hiding her until he could deal with her mother's killer?

Petrosky left Ryder at his car. He turned back, staring up at the Tower, lights scattered across its gloomy countenance—most of them on the top floor and roof, Tyree Willard's domain. Ryder squinted through the dark as a curtain of fog flowed across the Tower's lights, obscuring them, burying their secrets in its haze.

CHAPTER TWENTY-TWO

A HAND TOUCHED my shoulder, and I opened my eyes, half-expecting to see Ryder or Father Vance. But it was Devon Price. He stood with his back to the altar, the crucifix hanging directly over his left shoulder, aimed at his heart.

"You okay?" he asked. "Having another one of your spells?"

I cringed. He was much more comfortable with my problem than I was. "No." I could tell he saw through my lie but was kind enough to allow me the dignity of denial. "Any word on Esme?"

"No." He sank into the pew beside me. "Figured it was best to start at the beginning. Was on my way back to the Tower when I saw you come in here and had an idea."

"What?" I asked, wondering at his vagueness. The Devon I'd come to know was nothing if not direct. Part of why I liked him. "Will it help find Esme?"

"I hope so." He slid from the pew, and I followed. Funny how we both bobbed and caught ourselves halfway through the sign of the cross as we left the pew—two sinners, fallen from grace.

Devon noticed as well. "How long has it been for you?"

"Twenty-two years. How about you?"

"Almost eleven." He stopped, looking up at the stained-glass windows depicting St. Timothy's martyrdom. Devon barely glanced at the one of St. Tim smiling down on us benevolently, preferring the more ferocious images of the stoning. "This place was like home. When things got too bad. Jess and I..." Sorrow shuttered his face.

"Did you go to school here as well?"

He nodded. "Had a scholarship. Most from the Tower never come here. Think the Church is thumbing its nose at them, all gold and silk when they're fighting for food and running water and heat in the winter. Nice to know Kingston finally cleaned up his act."

"What do you mean?"

"Inside the Tower. Outside, it looks as bad as ever. But inside, it seems like things are a little better. Folks taking pride in where they live instead of using it like a urinal. Tyree made it sound like he forced Kingston to fix things up, but that doesn't sound like Tyree. My money's on the women. After all, it's them that take care of this place." He nodded to the immaculate altar with its embroidered silk drapes and shiny gold candlesticks. "Mrs. Anders, she used to drag me here at least twice a week, on top of the Mass we attended every morning as part of school. Said I had the devil in me, needed an extra dose of Jesus."

I nodded, remembering that daily parade from the school on the other side of St. Tim's into the church. God help you if you straggled or whispered or stepped out of line. "I went to St. Tim's, too. Would have been a few years ahead of you."

His gaze was still lost among the stained glass above us. In the darkness, the saints glowered down on us, ignoring poor St. Tim as he was stoned to death. "Always swore I'd never be him. That I'd fight back."

"That's what I told myself as well."

Devon gave himself a shake and dredged up a tired smile for me. "Guess we both got the devil in us."

He had no idea. But I smiled back at him. Felt a little less tired and uncertain, even though nothing had changed.

We made it to the front vestibule. "You know how you said you could read that girl's mind? Could you do that again?"

"That's your idea?" I stopped, afraid to look at him—afraid of how I looked to him. "I don't read minds. I'm not sure what happened, just somehow we were…together."

"Whatever. Could you do it again?"

Damn, he was stubborn.

"No. I don't know." Embarrassment flushed my cheeks. Last thing I wanted was to explore my newfound craziness. "Maybe. But only certain minds."

"What kind of minds?"

"People in comas." Before I could lose my nerve, I quickly told him about Patrice and Mrs. Kowacz. And about my other spells, the ones that seemed to be triggered by extreme emotions and adrenaline. To my relief, he listened without judgment. Instead, he accepted what I could do—more so than I did myself. I didn't feel anything like acceptance. What I felt was terror. Pure, kick-in-the-gut terror.

"That's how you knew where to find Esme? And those kids? Can you make it happen again? Use it to find her now?"

"That's the problem. According to medical science, this is impossible."

"But you knew where Esme was when we were down in the tunnels. You were right about that. And that old lady's wedding ring." He paced across the marble floor of the vestibule, head swinging as he considered all the angles. He reminded me of Ryder right then, a warrior preparing for battle. "Maybe when you get frozen—"

"Fugues. I decided to call them fugues." It was a small, gentle word. Shades of Bach and chords of organ music rather than nerve-jangling panic.

"Fugues, whatever. Maybe somehow your brainwaves match the coma patient's? Like you're on their wavelength so you can hear what they're thinking?"

"Maybe the moon is made of green cheese and magnets cure cancer. I'm a doctor—this is all impossible." Leaning against the thick wall, I closed my eyes, trying to wish him, the world away. No such luck. "Maybe I'm the one in a coma, and you all are just a hallucination."

"Damn strange hallucination." A smile edged across his lips. "But if so, this hallucination is very grateful you found Esme. Even if we lost her again." He hesitated, and I knew what he was going to ask.

"You want me to try again with Jane Doe." The girl currently in the ICU, fighting for her life.

"Maybe once the drugs are out of her system, she can tell us what happened. Then we might know who took Esme."

He made it sound so logical. Easy. But I remembered the pain, the terror that had overwhelmed me when I'd touched Jane Doe the first time. Wasn't sure I could face that again.

Devon didn't give me a chance to voice my misgivings. He held the door open and together we left the church. A large man was jogging up the steps, his gaze on Devon.

"Harold," Devon said. "What's the news?"

"Esme's not in the Tower. The cops are withdrawing from the tunnels. We'll look there next."

"Wait," I said. "The cops finished searching the tunnels already?"

The man looked from me to Devon, a question in his eyes.

"She's okay," Devon vouched for me. "Harold, this is Dr. Rossi. She's helping."

Harold favored me with an appraising gaze followed by a nod. "Pleasure. The cops didn't finish their search. Kingston sent them away until they can get more manpower and equipment. Best I can tell, we'll have the place to ourselves."

"Don't count on it," Devon grumbled. "Tyree will have men back down there guarding his stash. Kingston is obviously using the tunnels for something as well, given the supplies we saw. He's involved in all this, I'm not sure how. There might be some other unfriendlies, so tell the men to be careful."

"Where are you going to be?" A hint of concern entered Harold's voice.

"Good Samaritan. There's someone there we need to talk to," Devon said.

I hadn't agreed to try to communicate with Jane Doe, but I

followed him down the steps and headed toward the hospital. It was either that or walk to my uncle's place alone and face my family.

I wasn't sure which would be more painful.

CHAPTER TWENTY-THREE

RYDER DROVE AROUND the block, parked across the street from St. Timothy's school, and studied the maps of the tunnels he'd added to his cell phone, courtesy of Gator Guy and the Fire Department. The jpegs were a bit blurred around the edges where the flash washed out, but he'd added enough overlap that he had a pretty clear idea of the layout.

Ozzie sat in the passenger seat, nose pressed against the window, giving out the occasional sigh. Impatient with his new human, no doubt. Ryder scratched him between the shoulder blades. "I know you miss her. We're going to find her."

The dog turned his head, meeting Ryder's gaze and nodding his head solemnly, as if accepting Ryder's promise and etching it into his memory.

Ryder put the car back in gear and pulled away from the curb. Christ, now he was talking to a dog. Not to mention sneaking back onto the crime scene he'd just been ejected from. The entrance below Good Sam's ER still looked like his best bet. He parked near the Good Sam ambulance bay and got the dog out.

This wasn't a good idea, wasn't even good enough to be a bad idea, but it was the only one he had.

"You ready?"

The dog wagged his tail and started for the door. Ryder followed.

"WHY DID YOU think Daniel Kingston might be involved in all this?" I asked as Devon and I walked toward Good Sam. "You said he was hiding something in the tunnels."

Devon's jaw began working like a dog gnawing the meat off a bone. "Everything bad that's happened around here, he's responsible. Daniel Kingston destroyed my mother."

That brought me up short. "What happened?"

"She and some of the other women were protesting the conditions in the Tower. My mother organized the women. They even marched over to Kingston's office, delivered a petition. Kingston decided to make an example of her."

His fists bunched, elbows drawn back, ready to hit something. But he forced his hands open, making a flinging motion as if he was throwing something away. "He left her half-dead the first time. The other women nursed her back to health. But Kingston wouldn't leave her alone. He was obsessed with her, I think because she never gave up fighting. Day or night, you never knew, he'd just show up, take her away. And when she came back…"

"Why didn't she go to the police?" I asked. The Advocacy Center had been created to help victims like Devon's mother, but it was only seven years old. The abuse he was reporting would have happened over twenty-five years ago. "If she'd spoken up—"

"She would have been branded a snitch and killed," he said. "Not like anyone would have taken her word over Daniel Kingston's anyway. He may not have been as rich back then, but the Kingston family name was just as powerful as it is now."

He paused, drawing in a breath that had more sharp edges than the broken glass lining the gutter beside us. "It went on for years. He'd leave her be for months at a time, but then, he always came back. My earliest memories are her hushing me, putting me in the hall closet with my crayons and books, telling me to stay there until she came to get me. But I could hear. The screaming and hitting. I'd smell the blood. The things he'd do to her, make her do. But she always fought back, she never surrendered to him.

"The other women took care of her, pretty much raised me. Said she was their hero, would tell stories about her standing up to Kingston, but really, they were protecting themselves. As long as Kingston came after her, he was leaving them and theirs in peace. I didn't figure that out until I was a lot older, and she was already gone."

The lights of Good Sam were visible. But Devon didn't seem to notice, lost in his memories. I had the feeling I was the first person he'd told the story to. And that he needed someone to share it with.

"What happened?"

"I wish I had a picture of her to show you. What she was like before he broke her. It was as if she had this glow about her, more than just being pretty or beautiful—"

He kicked a stray rock into the gutter. "By the time I was eight, she was dead inside. Didn't recognize me anymore. But still when he showed up, the light would come to her eyes—only time she was alive was when she was fighting him. The rest of the time, she was a zombie. Could barely feed herself. And then," he shrugged, heaving the weight of memory aside, "she was gone. Good as dead—in a coma after a hot shot of heroin. All because of Kingston."

"You think Patrice and Jess were doing something Kingston didn't like and he targeted them like he did your mom?" Surely a rich man with connections like Kingston's could find a more effective way to deal with people who got in his way.

"Or he got Tyree to do his dirty work for him. Who knows?" Devon's tone was bitter, making him sound young. Then he straightened, eyes wide. "Maybe Kingston knew Jess called me. Maybe he knew I was coming back for her and Esme."

"Why would that make Kingston want to kill them?"

"Because he hates me. He'd gladly destroy me and everyone I love."

"Why?"

He shook his head as if remembering the punch line to an old joke. A smile played across his lips, but it wasn't a happy smile. It was a smile filled with contempt and dark promises. "Kingston hates me because I'm his son."

CHAPTER TWENTY-FOUR

DEVON DIDN'T WAIT for Angela's response. Instead, he forced a laugh. "Yep. Someday, all this," he swung his hand around to indicate the ravaged blocks between them and the Tower, "could be mine. Well, part mine. Leo was born a few years before me, so he's entitled to half."

Despite his joking tone, inside he steeled himself for battle. Retreating behind locked doors, barricading his secrets. He'd told Angela only part of the story, but what if he was right and Jess had died because she'd asked him to come home?

When would he learn? All he brought to anyone he loved was pain. First, his mother, just by his existence, a constant reminder of what Daniel Kingston had taken from her. Then Jess, lovely Jess, her beauty destroyed by Devon's love. And now Esme at risk.

Because of Devon.

"You can't give up," Angela said. "Ryder will keep searching the tunnels. The little kids aren't talking. But maybe in the morning, after they get some rest. And we might be able to learn something from their families once we track them down."

"Harold's working on the Tower residents, trying to find the families. So, guess that just leaves you and me and Jane Doe."

She hesitated, staring down at her hands. They trembled slightly. She jammed them into her pockets, took a breath, and they crossed the last street separating them from Good Sam. He knew she was scared—hell, just watching her have one of those spells made his skin

179

twitch. Primal fear. Like getting too close to an open flame. Couldn't imagine living through one. But what choice did they have?

They continued in silence, entering the hospital—quiet as it ever was at two thirty in the morning—and up the elevator to the ICU floor.

Devon hated hospitals. Had spent way too much time in them with his mom. The pediatric ICU was worse than he'd imagined. The Asian girl, Jane Doe, looked even skinnier here, dwarfed by machines and people and noises. White sheets clung to her like burial shrouds.

Doubt almost made him pull Angela back. The girl looked half past dead already. What if something happened while Angela was...his mind stuttered, trying to find words for what Angela was about to do...while Angela was with her. What would it feel like to be inside someone's mind as they died?

An image of his mother filled his vision. Eyes empty, staring but not seeing, just like this girl's. Body dwindling away, but the mind already gone. Wouldn't death be a release? A gentle embrace, gathering you to it like a lover's arms.

Sounded like a fairy tale to him. Sounded like bullshit. Kicking and screaming, clawing and scratching at life, that's how death should be for someone so young, vibrant.

The memory of Jess's body, reaching out to him, blindsided him.

Angela didn't seem to notice the beeping and humming and whooshing of the machines surrounding them. Or the other patients cocooned in their beds, surrounded by gadgets and prayers.

Instead, she grabbed Jane Doe's chart, skimmed through it, shaking her head mournfully. "Serotonin syndrome with acute rhabdomyolysis," she murmured, speaking Greek for all the good it did Devon. "Hemodialysis isn't keeping up with the potassium overload." She closed the chart, frowning, as she scrutinized the readings on the monitors. He dared a step closer, taking care not to get near any of the wires or tubes. "It's not good. She's dying."

All that medical mumbo jumbo and he could've told her that just by looking at the girl. He'd seen death too many times not to recognize it. Slanting his gaze at Angela, he realized she had as well. The doctor talk was just a way of denying the inevitable, controlling the chaos.

Hell, maybe all these machines and people scurrying around were doing the same. Living in denial. Needing to be able to tell themselves they tried, they at least did something. Even if it was more harm than good.

No wonder he hated hospitals.

Angela leaned over a big machine with a lot of pens sketching out waves. "EEG. Her brain waves. Minimal activity." She pursed her lips. "Some excitation. Spindle bursts. Alpha and theta waves with synchronized activity."

"Want to translate for us poor slobs?"

"Her brain, the spindle bursts…I wonder if that's the reason why—" She cut the sentence short, glancing around to see if anyone was near enough to overhear. "If this works, you might be right. Maybe somehow, I don't know, we're in sync." She nodded to the comatose girl.

"So you can do it again?"

"Only one way to know." Before he could ask any questions—like what the hell he should do if someone came by while she was doing her trance thing—she grabbed the girl's hand.

"Angela—" Too late. She was gone.

❋

RYDER KNEW THERE'D be a guard on the door leading from Good Sam's basement to the tunnels, had wondered how he'd bluff his way through without getting another officer in trouble, but he needn't have worried. It was Petrosky standing watch at the door.

Not only did she let him inside, she checked that the crime scene techs had left and the coast was clear.

"Looks like it's just you, me, and the gators," she quipped. "Don't let them eat that dog of yours. Do me a favor and don't trip any of those bombs. Wouldn't want to be the one who had to explain how you got into a secure scene."

"Didn't know you cared, Petrosky."

"Care about covering my ass, you better believe it."

The crime scene guys had brought in portable halogen lights and left one behind outside the taped-off and sealed door to the refrigerator, giving Ryder his first detailed look at the tunnels' infrastructure. The walls were dove gray, either by intent or aging, as were the concrete floors. Overhead, a puzzle-knot of pipes of various sizes and colors wove their way below the catwalk. He aimed the work light back down the way they'd come, counting at least three intersections and numerous doors lining the corridor as far as he could see. Some of the blocks were lined with the metal shelving units, like the one Rossi had climbed when she chased after Esme, but others had bare walls.

"CSU check the other rooms down here?" he asked Petrosky.

"Kingston gave us a master key. No signs of any illegal activity, but they only covered the rooms near where the kids were found. They pulled everyone out after that."

"Don't suppose you could lend me that master?"

She thought for a moment, then took a key ring from her pocket. "I'll need it back before shift change."

Almost three now. That gave him four hours. He had no intention of staying in here that long. Not alone, without backup. The dog shifted at his feet, anxious to get going. Okay, without human backup. "Deal."

"You know they found more than just Tyree's bombs. There's also meth labs, other hazmat shit. You sure it's worth it? That girl could be anywhere by now."

He glanced into the blackness ahead of him. Just like Paktika. "I'll be fine."

Petrosky headed back to her post, her flashlight swinging through the darkness until she disappeared around the corner. Ryder checked the maps on his phone again, confirmed what he'd committed to memory. Then he turned his own light on and let out Ozzie's lead. "Find her, boy."

The dog needed little encouragement. He sniffed the air and led Ryder back to where they'd last seen Esme. So far, so good. Now came the tricky part.

Alone except for the dog, he felt a familiar tingle of fear tap-dance between his shoulder blades. Like he had a sniper's rifle sighted on his back. Strange noises echoed through the cavernous space, reverberating so he couldn't pinpoint their locations. With them came an unnerving claustrophobia, as if the blackness was smothering him, walls closing in, even as there was a sense of wide-open space above him—perfect for an ambush.

The dog hesitated, caught a scent, and they were off again.

They passed a few places where it was obvious the bomb squad had dismantled booby traps. The ammonia stench of chemicals wafted out of several closed doors. Ryder made a mental note of them but didn't stop. Tyree would have any product moved before he could get men down here anyway.

Ozzie did a good job, occasionally stopping when the scent trail led them to a dead end when the overhead catwalks continued past the corridor walls. They'd backtrack, find an alternate route and continue on. Ryder decided he liked having the dog with him. Ozzie knew how to maneuver in the dark, was a hard worker, and didn't whine. Better than some of the men he'd partnered with.

They came to a section that was lined with doors the color of rotting Halloween pumpkins. No shelves here, just very strong, very heavy metal doors with no windows. Ozzie kept sniffing at the doors as if confused by other scents, but then tried to pull Ryder down a side corridor.

From the map, Ryder knew the corridor led to one of the unmarked exits Gator Guy had told them about. It came up on Park Avenue, just a block away from Daniel Kingston's brownstone mansion. As far away from the Tower as you could get in the tunnels. The same in the world above ground—the neighborhood where

Kingston lived used to be Cambria's Millionaire's Row, but that was a century before the money abandoned Cambria, the Tower was built, and the city had pretty much gone to hell.

He was just about ready to follow Ozzie in that direction when his light swept over something at the bottom edge of one of the orange doors. A smear of dark red. He crouched and focused the light on it. Blood.

Fingerprints. Smaller than his. Gripping the edge of the door as if fighting for life.

He motioned the dog into a sit. Using the master key, he unlocked the door. Pulled his service weapon, made sure the dog was in the clear, and pushed the door open with his foot as he took cover against the far wall.

Ozzie barked once and lunged at Ryder, barreling into him, pushing him around the corner.

The door swung silently inward.

A bright white light blinded Ryder. Thanks to Ozzie, he was already twisted away from the door, half-sprinting, half-leaping through the air as the explosion hit.

CHAPTER TWENTY-FIVE

FLAMES SURROUNDED ME. Every color imaginable, bursting and dancing and singing and sparking. I couldn't see my body, but I felt the flames firing every nerve. Except they weren't really colors—or rather, the colors were born from music. Painful, discordant notes that drilled into my brain.

I wanted to shut out the blinding chords but couldn't. Instead, I forced myself past the cacophony of light and noise and pain.

And found her.

She'd retreated into a small, peaceful corner. She was lovely. Long, dark hair hanging like strands of silk, face unmarred by bruises or cuts. She wore a shimmering gown that changed colors as she moved. And she was playing the piano, a large, black grand piano, its polished surface reflecting the colors of her gown as if she was painting with music.

Her fingers, no longer swollen or broken, danced over the keys like words in a poem.

The music was haunting. A cry for help but also a sigh of hope.

The fingers of my left hand moved, forming chords, wanting to accompany her. For a few moments, I thought I heard a violin weaving through the piano's voice, as if I really was playing.

Then she looked up. *You came back for me.*

In my head, her voice sounded surprised. Like she was used to being abandoned.

You play beautifully.

She gave me a shy smile and nodded her thanks. *I think I'm dying. Shouldn't I be scared?*

I don't know. I sat beside her on the piano bench. The pain was gone, but the flames still surrounded us, flickering in time to her music.

You should. You're dying, too. She seemed disappointed that I wasn't smarter than I was.

What's your name?

Alamea Syha. My friends called me Allie.

I hesitated, not sure of the rules of this strange conversation. Still half-believed that it wasn't even happening, but I wasn't about to let that stop me from finding out what I could. *Who did this to you, Allie?*

The ground shifted beneath me, an earthquake toppling me from the bench. I was falling, headfirst, spinning out of control like a skydiver who'd forgotten her parachute. The pain returned, accompanied by the same visions that had bombarded me during my first contact with Allie—images of her torture, of all that she'd suffered. The face of the man was never clear, instead morphed with pain and panic into a twisted monster.

I'm sorry, I'm sorry, I'm sorry. Allie cried. *I'll be good, I promise.*

I spun around, flames licking at my flesh, searing me with piercing, high-pitched screams. Found her huddled at my feet, naked again, bruised and battered and broken. She didn't look up when I spread my arms around her, trying to protect her from the memories.

Shhh…it's okay, it's okay, everything will be okay. I lied. I didn't care. She was dying, and we both knew it—but I couldn't let her go this way, in pain, terrified. I wanted her to have the serenity that Mrs. Kowacz had, or at least the sense of release that Patrice had. But I had no idea what to say to help her.

Guilt at having brought her to this point flooded me, fueling the flames. It was hard to focus on her. Every inch of my body shrieked in pain, but it was nothing compared to what Allie had suffered.

Tell my parents I'm sorry. One last plaintive wail, and she vanished, leaving me cradling empty nothingness. The flames turned into popping firecrackers, sparks flaring then dying, black silence in their wake.

I was buffeted, whirling in a blaze of heat and pain and blackness. The emptiness was more frightening than the bright, screeching pain. I tried to look for Allie, but she was gone.

And I was lost with no way out.

☽ ✻ ☾

DEVON HAD SEEN some freaky shit in his life, but the sight of Angela standing there, somehow communing with a girl in a coma, spiked to the top of the list.

Watching her reminded him of being in church. Not the sucker's game of turning water into wine (talk about an easy con—the mark did all the work), but more the feeling of anticipation that something miraculous *could* happen. He may have left the Church behind a long time ago, but he was smart enough to realize there was something out there bigger, badder, and hopefully a helluva lot smarter than humans were.

When he was a kid, the women would come to his mom each time she returned from a visit with Daniel Kingston. They would light incense, clean her wounds, tend to her, forming a circle around her as they prayed, their rosary beads clicking like an abacus calculating a debt.

Delivering her from the devil, Mrs. Anders had told him. Making sure the evil that was Kingston didn't take hold. Of course, the devil who carried Kingston's evil was Devon himself. At Mrs. Anders' hands, he'd paid the price for his mother's healing.

As a kid, Devon would believe in the miracle. No matter how much pain it caused him. If it saved his mother, protected her from Kingston, he'd gladly suffer.

But Mrs. Anders' purification rituals never took hold for long. As soon as Devon's mother was healed enough to stumble down to the street, she would find more drugs and return to her mindless limbo, a land where little things like raising a son or fighting off Kingston simply didn't matter anymore. Despite the fact that by the end she had lost everything, including her looks, Kingston still wouldn't leave her alone. Not until he broke her.

Devon scratched at the scars on his palms. Lord, how Mrs. Anders had worked to whip the devil out of him after that. He could barely remember it, so much of that time he'd blocked out of his memory, but he remembered her tears as she'd whipped him with her rosary beads, striking him harder and harder, as if his blood could heal his mother.

She'd failed, of course. As all her rituals and prayers had. The only lesson Devon had come away with was there was no such thing as miracles. You had to make your own way in this world, couldn't depend on the next for anything. Especially couldn't depend on believers like Mrs. Anders, no matter how strong their faith.

This thing with Angela, though. This was no charade. This was the real deal.

He thought he should have been scared, maybe even in awe, but all he felt was a vague edge of hope. Slippery, sharp, capable of slicing him if he held on too tight.

If Angela helped him find Esme, he couldn't give a good goddamn how she did it.

The monitor beeping above him and the scratching of the pens across the EEG tracing to his right changed rhythms. The monitor became irregular, *beep-beep-beep…beep…beep.* But the pens that measured the girl's brainwaves slowed until they barely made a squiggle on the page.

He was no doctor, but there was no way this could be good. Angela stood rigid, staring without blinking, her face a mask.

Then the alarms began to shriek—three different ones at once. He glanced up. The line that measured the heartbeat had gone flat.

The girl was dying. What did that mean for Angela?

CHAPTER TWENTY-SIX

HANDS GRIPPED MY wrist, spinning me in the dark and toward a deafening light. A wave of white-hot lava seared through me.

"Shit, Angela, you okay?"

It was Devon. I broke free from Allie, collapsing into his arms. He braced me as he pulled me behind the curtain separating the bed spaces, then whipped it shut just as two nurses and a resident ran to Allie's bedside.

I heard the alarms, knew they were too late. Nausea doubled me over, but Devon held me upright. He guided me across to the nurses' station, where we watched the ICU staff try to resuscitate Allie. "I'm taking you down to the ER."

"No." The syllable was a struggle. I was sweating and shaking and needed to pee. But I ignored all that. My eyes were scratchy and dry. I blinked, trying to focus. "How long?"

"Almost half an hour."

Holy shit. A chill raced over me, knocking my teeth together as the implications hit me. This was bad. Very, very bad. This was my-life-was-fucked-forever bad.

"Angela? Jesus, you're white as a—"

I was going to be sick. I pushed myself up, leaning against his chest, and swayed.

"Get me out of here," I whispered, unable to trust my legs to carry me from the unit. He led me into the hallway. I bolted into the public restroom and hurled into the toilet, not even bothering to

189

close the door behind me.

Behind me, I heard water running, then Devon handed me a wad of wet paper towels. I staggered to my feet, flushed and, shaking off his help, rinsed my face, gargled. When I looked in the mirror I saw a wraith—dark eyes burning through pasty white flesh, lips colorless, sweat matting my hair.

"What happened?" he asked. "Inside there—"

My senses reeled, on overload, unable to process everything I'd experienced with Allie when she… God, I couldn't bring myself to even think it, it sounded crazy. Dark spots circled through my vision, and my stomach flip-flopped. "Let's go somewhere we can talk. I need some juice or something."

We went out to the family waiting room, which was thankfully empty. He fed quarters into the vending machine and brought me a can of apple juice as I sat on the couch by the window. The lights of the city held back the night, creating a blurry grayscape. As if Thomas Edison could conquer the dark. As if he knew a damned thing about true darkness, like what I'd seen with Allie.

A laugh escaped me, harsh and throaty and edged with enough insanity it made Devon flinch. "You sure you're okay?"

No. Not at all. Not sure and not okay. Panic skittered along my nerves, tip-tapping over hot coals. What if Devon hadn't pulled me out of my fugue? Would I have been trapped in there? Not dead but not alive…until my body failed?

I pushed the juice away, my stomach revolting. A sour taste filled my mouth.

Devon sat down beside me, wrapped his arm around my shoulders, and I realized I was shaking. Goose bumps lined my arms, even though I felt feverish. We sat in silence for a few minutes until my trembling slowed. Then he held the juice to my lips as if I was a child. "Drink. You'll feel better."

I took a sip and then another. The apple juice stung my parched lips and tongue but felt good. I took hold of the can with both hands and gulped the juice down.

"Thanks," I said when I'd finished.

He took the can and threw it in the recycling bin. I liked him for that, for noticing and thinking twice about a little thing like that. When he turned back, his face was clouded by worry.

"She didn't know anything about Esme," I answered his unasked question.

His head swung up and down in a slow, heavy nod. "Did she say who did this to her?"

"Not his name. I couldn't see his face. It was so hard, what she went through—" I looked away, unable to finish. Placed my hand flat against the windowpane, absorbing the cold like a tonic. "Her name was Allie. Alamea Syha."

Her face replaced mine in the reflection in the window—the face of the girl playing the piano, shy but at peace. Not the face of the girl tortured by pain. I could only hope that there truly wasn't anything after this life, that once she died, all traces of that pain vanished with her.

Who was I to know anything? All these years of playing God, practicing medicine—practicing, that was rich irony—and I knew nothing about anything. Anger spiked through me.

"I need to call Ryder."

Devon's cell phone rang. He listened, asked a few questions, then hung up again. "No need," he said. "Ryder's downstairs in the ER. Seems he went back into the tunnels. Your wonder cop triggered a bomb."

❃ ❂ ❁

Two ER visits in one night—twice as many as Ryder's entire life. And this time brought in an ambulance. Embarrassing. Especially since there was nothing wrong with him. Well, nothing except a pounding headache and the ringing in his ears and his back all scraped to hell from where he hit the corner...but it was a lot better than it could have been, thanks to Ozzie pushing him out of the way and the thick steel door that had blasted shut when the IED blew.

"I'm fine," he growled at the nurse for the third time, sick of her hovering.

Despite the fact that she was half his size, she pinned him in his chair with a single strategically placed hand. "You will be. As soon as the doctor checks your CT scan. Makes sure you don't have any bleeding in your brain."

Another damn waste of time. He let the nurse finish cleaning the abrasions along his shoulder and back. They burned, and he'd lost a lot of skin, but none were deep enough to need stitches. Ozzie sat at his feet, looking up at him with sympathy. Ryder absently scratched the dog behind his ears.

The nurse finally finished and left him alone. He was in another curtained bed space—not the same one Sister Patrice had died in, thank goodness. As soon as the nurse left, he stood, braced himself against the bed rail when his vision went swampy, then tugged his way free of the patient gown.

"How is he?" A familiar voice carried through the curtain.

Rossi. He turned, still holding the gown, just as she entered. Felt the same electricity he'd felt the first time he'd seen her. Funny how that seemed so long ago. Years, instead of hours.

She looked like a lifetime had passed. Her face was drained of color, eyes dark and puffy, hair limp.

"Heard what happened," she said, stopping short just inside the curtain. "Came to check on the dog."

Ozzie lumbered over to her, his head fitting comfortably beneath her palm as he nuzzled her leg.

"Damn dog saved my life," Ryder said, holding back a smile. He didn't care how lousy she looked right now. He was glad to see her.

Instead of crossing over to her, shoving the dog out of the way, and taking her into his arms like he wanted, he forced his energy on wadding the patient gown into a tight ball and hurling it into the laundry bin. It wasn't the right time or place, and he didn't want to overwhelm her when she already looked like she was ready to collapse. He turned away, reaching for his shirt, the pain twisting through his body providing a good distraction from any feelings he had for Rossi.

He caught her gaze on him as he dressed, but it was a clinical appraisal. She was worried about him. Wasn't that sweet?

As he finished buttoning his shirt, she finally stopped giving the dog loving, and moved to sit on the exam bed. He tucked in his shirt and joined her, Ozzie immediately plunking down at their feet. All they needed was a fire and some apple pie.

"Her name was Allie," she said softly. "Alamea Syha."

How the hell did she know that? "Was?"

"She just died."

"But she was talking? Told you her name? Anything else?" Too many questions—this whole damn case was too many questions.

She shook her head, tiny little jerks as if running away from something. Her lips so tight they formed a single, pale line.

"Then how do you know?"

"I can't tell you."

Again, he was expected to trust her and her mysterious information. Still, she'd been right about Esme. He suspected Devon Price was her source, not some patient she had to keep confidential as he'd initially assumed. Just how close were Rossi and Price? The question wasn't strictly professional.

She raised her face and looked at him. Not asking anything, not expecting anything. Resigned.

Her bruised expression overruled his skepticism. Ryder reached for his phone, got the duty officer on the line. "I need anything on an Alamea Syha. No, I don't know how you spell it. Start with missing-persons reports. Juvenile, maybe fifteen or sixteen, Asian, black hair, black eyes, five-three, hundred pounds."

He listened, trying to ignore the weight of Rossi's stare. Now that he'd taken the first step, believing her, he worried she'd start expecting miracles from him.

The officer gave him what info he had and sent Ryder a DMV

photo. She beamed out at the camera as if it held all her hopes and dreams. She'd been lovely—hard to reconcile the girl in the photo with the ravaged victim they'd found in the tunnels. "It's her. She was sixteen. Address in the Tower, but no missing-persons report. Just like the others."

They sat there a few moments, his feet on the ground, hers swinging in the air, dog lying with his chin on his paws, staring up at them both.

He should head back over to the Tower—God, he was sick of that place—notify the parents. Rossi should've been home in bed. She looked wrecked. He probably did as well.

Instead, they sat in silence. It felt good. Comfortable. As if the rest of the world had vanished.

He shook his head. He wasn't prone to such philosophical thoughts. Hell, he still hadn't made good on his promise to buy her dinner.

Swallowing a regretful sigh, he slid to his feet. The dog shook himself and stood beside him.

She sat, looking like a kid, her feet still swinging. "Can I come?"

"I'm going to—"

"Notify Allie's parents. I know. I'd like to come with you." She jumped down from the cot. "I've made notifications before, and I'd like to talk to them. She belongs to us."

By "us" she meant the Advocacy Center and the Sex and Juvie Squad. He considered and nodded. Far better than her venturing into the Tower on her own. Which he wouldn't have put past her.

One thing tonight had shown him: Rossi was good company. Better than most partners he'd worked with. He trusted her, even if she didn't carry a weapon.

First time in a long time that he'd trusted anyone. Including himself.

CHAPTER TWENTY-SEVEN

I COULD HAVE gone home. It was half past three, and chances were the bar would be quiet for a few hours until the family party resumed. Holidays with long weekends translated to marathon jam sessions, the music handing off from one player to the next, virtually never-ending. Jacob and my uncle would have persuaded me to perform with the band, and then after, I'd have been forced to mingle, make small talk as I invented new ways to avoid my mother—while watching her avoid me.

Not tonight. Family was just too hard. And what if I had a spell or something happened in front of them? I couldn't let them know I was sick, not until I had answers.

Ryder had given me the perfect out, a way to avoid my family, avoid my lonely apartment above the bar with the music vibrating through the floors rattling its guilt into my very marrow if I didn't join in, and avoid thinking about, well, too many things to count.

Hell, between Allie and the seven kids we'd rescued from the tunnels, I might be able to avoid my family for days.

I went to expedite Ryder's discharge. He was in favor of ignoring the paperwork and leaving against medical advice, but since we were dealing with workers' comp issues, and I knew he was already skating the edge with his superiors, I figured it was best to take a few minutes to follow the rules for once. And it gave me a chance to double-check that his head CT was really okay.

As usual, my timing sucked. I returned to find Jacob standing in

Ryder's alcove, his coat smelling of sweat, cigarettes, and beer, as he played his role of DA heavy. It doesn't happen very often, but I hate when he gets that way, all, "There's a reason the law works, and it's not up to you to interpret it. Leave that to us lawyers." Treating me and my staff like we're grunts, jackknifing to his commands. Even worse, usually he's right, and when we do things his way, we win our cases. Doesn't always mean the victims win, though.

Another reason why we're still divorced: He puts the law first, I put the victims first.

Then I got close enough to hear what he was saying. He wasn't fired up about the law; this was about me.

"Want to explain to me how a civilian consultant, my wife, ended up down in those tunnels with you, getting shot at? Or why I'm apparently one of the last to hear about it?" Jacob stood facing Ryder, his shirt sweat-stained and wrinkled. He'd come here straight from my uncle's bar, no doubt. Our music, that's what had kept Jacob and I together in the first place. Playing music, riffing off one another, finding hidden gems of chords and unexpected grace in the notes as they soared around us, that was always when we were at our best.

"If your ex-wife wanted you to know, guess she would have called you herself," Ryder said, his voice matching Jacob's level, lethal tone.

It wasn't often Jacob found someone immune to his snake-charmer mojo. If there hadn't been two parents waiting for us to wake them from their sleep and tell them their daughter was dead, it might have been fun to watch.

"Ready to go," I told Ryder.

Jacob didn't spin around when he heard my voice. He wobbled. I realized the smell of beer wasn't only from his clothing—one of the many hazards of attending my family's gatherings—but that he was well on his way to being drunk. For a man who seldom finished a single beer, that wasn't far to go.

"Angie." He made my name sound like a weight, something that had to be pulled out of him. "Are you all right? Do you have any idea how many times I called you?"

Hell. I'd turned my phone off while working with the kids and hadn't turned it back on.

He had no business being worried. It rankled that he was so possessive, as if he still owned part of my heart, belonged in my life.

Of course he did. Just like my family did. Didn't mean I had to like it. "I've been busy."

His chin jerked at my tone. Outside the legal arena, he's a pretty easygoing man, not easily wounded except by those he cares for. Even now, the expression that flashed across his face wasn't anger or hurt, it was concern. Ignoring Ryder, he stepped into my space and gathered me into his arms.

"You look like hell. Sure you're okay? When I got the call—"

God, I hated how good his arms felt around me. I almost succumbed to the temptation of melting into them and letting him carry me away from everything. Would have except I felt Ryder's presence as strongly as Jacob's. I was torn between loyalties, which was idiotic—I didn't owe either man anything.

I pushed Jacob away. It was harder than I wanted it to be. "I'm fine. But our rapist has struck again. This time a sixteen-year-old. She didn't make it."

He frowned, sobering. "Sixteen? Younger than the others."

Ryder settled down onto the physician's chair, straddling it just like he had when we'd first met less than twelve hours earlier. My mind buzzed with everything that had happened since.

"Walk me through this case. Seeing as it's now officially mine," he said, all business now. "I read Harrison's reports, but it's always better to hear things firsthand." Harrison was the detective who had died two weeks ago, the one Ryder was replacing.

Ozzie nuzzled my leg, coaxing me toward the exam table. I slumped onto its thin mattress. Not another fugue. I had no aura of unbidden music, just simple, sheer exhaustion. Ozzie sat on the floor, stretching his head to fit perfectly beneath my hand as I scratched behind his ears, giving him a silent thank-you.

Jacob paced, posture straight, a storyteller weaving his magic, just like he did in a courtroom. "Four women, that we know of," he began. "All taken and held for days—the longest, a week. That was the first, Miranda Elsevier. Twenty-six, single mom, no official employment, but she used to work off the books cleaning restaurants after hours."

"Lived in the Tower?" Ryder asked.

Jacob nodded. "Taken from there as well. Same with the others—"

"Same with this last girl. Well, lived there. We're not sure where she was taken from. No missing-person report."

"That tracks as well. Harrison traced the victims back to the Tower, but when he went to their apartments, they'd all been emptied. No one in the Tower even acknowledged these women existed, much less that they lived alongside them for years."

"Tyree Willard's doing. Easier to disappear someone than deal with the cops."

"That's what Harrison said. Before—" Jacob paused. "Before his accident."

I hadn't really liked Harrison. It was clear he hadn't enjoyed working with our victims, but he'd been more than competent, and I had appreciated that.

"Anyway, the others fit the same profile as Miranda. Single, no documented employment, early to mid-twenties, no one reporting them missing."

"Miranda Elsevier, Bekka Brown, Yvonne Taylor, Susannah DeWitt, and now Alamea Syha." Ryder recited the victims' names like a prayer. "All kept for days. Means the actor has a safe haven, someplace he's certain no one can disturb him or find the victims. All taken from the Tower—"

"We think," Jacob said. "Not sure about Alamea."

"All living in the Tower, possibly all taken from there. He knows the Tower, can blend in—"

"Or he's got pull with the residents there," I interjected.

"Someone in authority."

"Tyree?" Ryder said in a tone of excitement. From the gleam in his eyes, he'd enjoy locking up the gang leader. "No. He doesn't have to go to such extremes to get access to women from the Tower. Not to mention everything pointing back at the Tower. Tyree isn't sloppy or stupid. Way too much risk of it blowing up in his face, with the girls being left alive."

"Wouldn't really call it alive," I put in. "What he did to their brains is almost as bad as the torture their bodies suffered."

"No chance of recovery?"

I shrugged. "Too early to say for sure, but it's been months since the first, Miranda, and there's been no improvement."

His eyes narrowed as he stared at the chains suspending the curtain around the alcove. Then he nodded once, a small movement, and returned his attention to us. "Tell me about that, about this PXA drug."

Jacob looked to me, handing over the baton. I was too exhausted to move, so I stayed where I was. "PXA is a synthetic compound, a variant of ketamine—which is in turn related to LSD—but with devastating properties. It provides the same dissociative state as ketamine, but instead of anesthesia, it activates pain receptors, causing feedback loops so the impact of any painful stimuli is multiplied."

"So this actor," the term the police used for unknown suspects, "isn't just inflicting physical torture on his victims. He's using this drug to amplify the effect of what he's doing to them?" Ryder shook his head. "Is that why the first four ended up in the psych ward? He drove them crazy with pain?"

"There's a bit more neurochemistry involved, but, yes, basically the high doses of PXA combined with the physical stress to overload their neuroreceptors. The problem is, when you jam up the system like that, you jam up everything."

"So he fried their brains. Like a meth head or crack addict, only faster? Sounds like this guy must know his chemistry and maybe something about medicine. I mean, from the tox reports, it seems as if he's trying different doses, shortening the time until he gets the end result he wants." Despite the fact that he wasn't scheduled to officially start working the case until next week, it was clear Ryder had done his homework.

"We'd been working on the theory that he was titrating the drug to make it last longer—maximize the amount of time he had to inflict pain before they became unresponsive."

"Yet the amount of time he's kept them has shortened, not lengthened. Maybe he's more interested in the drug itself? Making the actual assaults on these women some kind of twisted experimental protocol?" Jacob asked.

That propelled me off the stretcher, startling Ozzie and both men. "They're people, not lab rats. This man tortured these women—and it's pretty clear from the physical findings that he enjoyed it."

Ryder leaned forward against the back of the chair he straddled. "We know. But I'm trying to get beyond the presentation of the crime to his motivation. What if this guy is looking to create some perfect form of PXA? Something he can make big bucks with—and the opportunity to torture women is just a nice bonus for him?"

"Maybe he's a meth cook gone amok?" Jacob asked.

Ryder nodded. "Except I don't know of any street value for PXA—in fact, the junkies call it Death Head and avoid it like the plague."

I was still trying to process the idea of someone torturing these women, literally driving them out of their minds with pain, as a means to a commercial end. The pain I'd experienced when I was in Allie's mind—was it all for money? "There are some medical protocols experimenting with variations of PXA. It has potential as a non-addictive opiate alternative."

Jacob jerked his chin at that. "I don't understand. A drug that stimulates the pain centers can be used as a painkiller?"

"Potentially. It's all about the balance of the chemicals available for the brain to process. For instance, capsaicin, the active ingredient in hot peppers—"

"The stuff we use in pepper spray," Ryder put in.

"Right. Painful stuff. But it has also been used to stop pain by overstimulating pain transmitters until they're depleted. As for PXA, I haven't read the research behind it. Louise might know."

"If it is possible, how much would a drug like that be worth to someone?" Ryder asked.

"A safe and effective replacement for opioids is pretty much Big Pharma's Holy Grail. It'd be worth billions."

"And all of it legitimate money." He pushed the stool away as he stood. "I think we need to stop looking for a typical sadistic serial rapist and start looking at someone with ties to drugs and pharmaceuticals."

"It does open up a whole new line of investigation," Jacob agreed. Was that a hint of respect in his voice? "Angie, if we analyzed the PXA found on the other victims, would it be possible to nail down something about this guy's manufacturing process? Perhaps he's varying ingredients or something?"

"Maybe." What he was asking was totally outside my field of expertise. I treated drug overdoses all the time, but the chemistry behind them? I left that all behind in med school. "You should talk to the lab guys. They've got all the evidence. Maybe they can run it through a mass chromatograph or something."

Jacob bounced on his heels, now totally sober and energized. He's as passionate about his work as I am, loves digging in and getting his hands dirty to build a case that's a surefire win once he gets it to court. "I'll head over there as soon as they open."

"Don't forget our other victims," I reminded both of them. "Jacob, could you follow up with tracking the families of our seven kids found in the tunnels? Apparently, Children's Services is getting nowhere." I was loath to put their faces out there with the media, but that might be necessary if we couldn't identify all of the kids and find their families soon.

"No problem. You heading home?"

"No. Ryder and I are going to notify Alamea Syha's family."

Jacob drew himself up to his full height, rigid. His face masked, his voice dropping into the danger zone, he stared at me, not Ryder, as he said, "Could we have the room?"

As if I didn't know that look, that tone? "Hell, no. First, if you're talking about me, you'll do the courtesy of doing it in front of my face. Second, this is my job, and you have no right to interfere. Third—"

I ran out of steam, realizing that not only did I not have a third, but neither man was listening to me. They were too busy playing testosterone tug-of-war. Ryder's hands were open, at his sides, near his gun. His mouth had tightened at the corners, revealing the slightest hint of his canines. Jacob did what I'd seen him do a hundred times right before he ground an adversary into legal dust. He relaxed. Smiled. Like he enjoyed the challenge and would be sorry when the fight was over.

Men. Idiots. Darwin was so wrong if this was the best evolution had to offer.

I threw the curtain open hard enough to make it rattle. "Take it outside. Not in my ER."

Both men blinked and swiveled to look at me. Ryder's face relaxed into an honest, self-deprecating smile, revealing a dimple I hadn't spied before. Jacob looked puzzled, as if he didn't understand why I was angry.

Then Jacob stepped to me, his palms resting on my shoulders as he turned me to block the rest of the room—and Ryder—from my vision.

"I don't like the idea of you going over there, not tonight," he said in a low voice filled with concern. "That place is on the verge of total collapse. I really wish you'd think about this, Angela. Come home with me. Let Ryder make the notification. You can pick this up in the morning."

I've had years of practice, and it was still hard to resist Jacob when he did that. It wasn't just the tone of his voice, it was the way his body curved toward me, offering comfort, protection, everything I needed.

I almost said yes. I wanted to say yes. Exhaustion had melted my bones. Not to mention the fears I'd bricked up behind a wall of denial. It would be so easy to simply leave it all behind, take what Jacob offered.

Ozzie's wet nose tickled my palm, reminding me of what was at stake. No easy way out for me.

Standing on my tiptoes, I kissed Jacob—a brief brush of the lips, more than casual, less than a promise of more. "Thanks, but I have work to do."

He didn't look happy, not at all. He looked over my shoulder to Ryder. "She's your responsibility."

Ryder nodded. It was perfectly clear they weren't speaking as prosecutor to police officer. I wanted to haul off and slug them both, but someone had to be an adult.

Shaking my head, I grabbed Ozzie's leash and walked out.

CHAPTER TWENTY-EIGHT

DEVON WAS GLAD to leave Good Sam behind. The place creeped him out—even more so after watching Angela do her séance thing. As he walked, he absently scratched the scars on his palms.

Angela's spells were nothing like Mrs. Anders and her deliverances. When Mrs. Anders got going, praying and chanting over him and his mom, trying to purge the evil that was Daniel Kingston, she'd leave for another world. But not like Angela. Mrs. Anders' trances seemed like cheap carnival sideshows compared to Angela's.

No wonder Angela was scared shitless. Especially being a doctor. Damn hard to face something like that when you've seen up close what happens to people sick in the brain. Tumor, that's what he figured. Not that she'd asked for his diagnosis. But what else could it be?

He didn't blame her for not wanting to find out for sure. Hell of a death sentence.

His phone rang, and he moved out of the wind, into a storefront to answer. It was Harold. "What did you find out?" Devon asked.

"Remember that Nigerian who tried to hustle in on Andre's territory? Idiot wouldn't shut up, kept blabbering about American freedoms and how they protected his right to try to steal from any fool willing to part with his money?"

"Yeah. Andre stitched the guy's lips shut before he shot him dead."

"Well, these folks got their lips sealed just as tight."

"Nothing on Esme?"

"It's weird. The people in the Tower don't act like they're scared she's in danger, but that somehow she's a danger to them and that scares them. Like if she gets found, the whole place comes toppling down."

"So you got nothing about who took her or where she might be."

"Sorry, boss."

"Cops hassling folks over there?"

"Nope. They've finished and gone. Tyree's folks are on alert, patrolling the halls. The place is on lockdown."

Devon didn't ask how Harold had maneuvered his way past Tyree's men. Harold was good at circumventing obstacles—either with money, talking or, if need be, a well-placed fist. For a white guy, he was pretty handy to have around.

Tyree was protecting someone. If it wasn't Esme, then it had to be the Kingstons.

"Any mention of Leo or Daniel Kingston?"

"Some whispers. About Leo. Folks look over their shoulder when they mention his name, like the devil is chasing them. I think he might be tied to the girl you found in the tunnels, because folks sure shut up fast when I asked about her or those other kids you found."

That room where they'd found the girl and the other little kids, that had felt a lot like Mrs. Anders' old deliverances. The crazy exorcism mood.

Mrs. Anders had always insisted that Devon be purified as well as his mother. Back in her home country, Mrs. Anders had told him, she was a famous witch hunter. Witches and demons liked possessing children best, because their defenses were weak. Whenever a devil visited an adult, it came from a child nearby.

Had she any idea the guilt trip that laid on a little boy? He would have done anything to purify his soul if it meant setting his mother free. He would have died if Mrs. Anders told him that was the only way to save his mom.

He held up his palm, letting the predawn mist settle on his scars.

Burns from holding candles during the purification rituals. A skinny boy kneeling for hours on a hard floor, hands held out in supplication, candles balanced on them, hot wax searing his flesh. Small price to pay for his mother's healing.

"Whatcha want me to do, boss?" Harold's voice broke through the haze of memories.

"Keep working things there. Let me know if Tyree makes a move."

"Will do."

Devon headed back toward St. Timothy's. It was four a.m., but not too late to have a come-to-Jesus meeting with his old friend, Father Vance.

☽ ⚛ ☾

TO MY SURPRISE, Ryder decided to walk back to the Tower. "It'll take just as long as driving," he explained. "Streets are blocked with the emergency crews after the explosion."

"What caused it?"

"Fire guys thought it was phosphorus. Used in making meth. Good thing the door blew shut or else the entire place would have gone up."

He sounded awfully blasé for someone who could have just as easily been blown to pieces. His expression was emotionless—which, I gathered, meant he was feeling a hell of a lot more than he was willing to share.

"One of Tyree's booby traps gone wrong?"

He shrugged. "I'm sick of playing crazy eights." He drew a horizontal figure eight with his finger in the air, Ozzie following the movement with his nose. "Good Sam to Tower to Good Sam to Tower and back and again, with the occasional stop by St. Tim's in between. Makes me feel like a damn cosmic yo-yo."

"Patrice or your friend Father Vance would say it's God's will."

He scoffed. "I say it's the job. It's sometimes like this. You go where the answers are."

"And the answers are in the Tower."

Again, he paused before answering. "Maybe. Or maybe that's just what we're meant to think."

He told me about seeing the bloody handprint right before the explosion. "Forensics won't be able to get DNA because of the heat, but they think they can lift a print."

"Maybe somebody took advantage of Tyree's security to use the tunnels for their own purposes. Allie and the other victims could have been held there without anyone knowing."

"I think there's a lot going on down there that no one ever suspected. Allie could have been dumped with the other kids to divert suspicion and to give the actor time to set up the phosphorus trap. Anyone came knocking, it would destroy any evidence he left behind."

We continued on, crossing the street, Ozzie swinging his head in both directions, checking for traffic. Ryder cleared his throat. "So, I thought you and Voorsanger..."

"Yeah, so did he." I shrugged. Ryder sounded interested, which was nice since I felt the same about him. Except that right now, with my mind taking crazy left turns into la-la land, I couldn't risk it. Shouldn't risk being here at all. What if I had another fugue and he saw?

Now it was my turn to feel panicked. My skin rippled with a sudden need to flee. Before I could surrender to it, he touched my elbow.

That was all. The touch of his hand. And suddenly I was calm.

"Why did you and Voorsanger split?"

"It's not like we didn't love each other. I guess we still do. Only we needed different things. We met when I was in med school and he had just finished law school. He was an intern at a law firm, broke his ankle sliding into third during their company softball game."

"Love at first sight?"

"Kind of, I dunno. Definitely like at first sight. We were

comfortable together. After a long day at work, we'd be together, and it was easy—an oasis, a safe haven. For a lawyer, once he's out of the courtroom, Jacob is the least confrontational or competitive guy I know. Anything I wanted, he was fine with."

He made a noise, remembering the way Jacob challenged him in the ER. I'd never seen Jacob act that way before, except during a trial. Wasn't sure if that should make me angry or not, but I knew I didn't like being the pull toy in their testosterone tug-of-war.

"So you got married," he said.

"Seemed like a good idea at the time. For about a year or so, it was. But then I was in my residency—long hours, demanding patients, life and death decisions—and I just couldn't handle coming home to make more decisions, to take care of one more person. It wasn't that he was demanding, just the opposite. Felt like if I didn't make a decision, if I didn't have a plan, then nothing got done. It was exhausting. Then I'd feel taken advantage of, so I'd try to get a rise out of him, pick a fight, anything to make him stand up and do something. Soon, that's all we were doing, fighting, usually about nothing. We decided enough was enough."

"But you still have sex."

And our music. "Why not? Two people can enjoy and comfort each other without getting tangled up in emotions or causing pain."

"Gee, you make it sound so romantic. Thought it was the guy who was supposed to be allergic to commitment."

"Let's just say I don't want to see anyone else hurt because of me. Besides, why can't people just enjoy the moment?"

We'd arrived back at St. Tim's. Ryder had been right. The street now overflowed with vehicles and people. There were cameramen and reporters interviewing anyone who'd stop and talk, civilian or first responder, asking about imprisoned children.

"Damn," Ryder muttered. "Word's gotten out."

I heard more than one reference to the kids as "feral" and "living like rats in the dark." When one perky female reporter speculated on possible cannibalism, Ryder had to grab my arm to prevent me from rushing her.

"It's our fault they don't have any facts," he reminded me. "Can't have it both ways."

We sidled around the edges, avoiding the lights of the cameras. I shortened Ozzie's lead, not wanting him to get tangled up with the police and firemen hustling hither and yon, all with a sense of purpose in their expressions and gaits. We came to a fire department SUV with its rear gate open, two men huddled over something, one of them wearing a bright orange prison jumpsuit, the other in turnout gear. In the car, a guard was slumped down in the backseat, asleep.

"See you lived to fight another day." The fireman greeted Ryder and reached down to scratch Ozzie behind the ears. "Gotta thank you. The overtime my guys will be getting after your shenanigans will provide them with a very merry Christmas indeed."

"Overtime?"

"Yessir. We've been ordered to follow your guys and clear every inch of those tunnels of any potential fire hazards. Job's gonna take weeks."

The prisoner in the jumpsuit bobbed his head excitedly, grinning. "And I'm the official consultant!"

Ryder looked over their shoulders at the map of the tunnels they had spread out. "Kingston's giving you unlimited access?"

"Of course. Only way to do the job properly."

"Interesting. He threw a hissy fit about me stepping foot inside earlier. Have they been able to get into the room where the explosion was?"

"No. It'll be awhile. You have any idea how hot phosphorous burns?"

"Won't be much evidence left after that."

The fireman grunted. "Won't be much of anything left after that."

"Be safe down there," Ryder told him, and we continued on.

"What was that all about?" I asked.

"Daniel Kingston stopped us—me—from searching the tunnels earlier. Pretty much threatened to have me fired, in fact. Interesting that as soon as that one room is destroyed, he's giving us full access."

"You think Kingston is involved with what happened to Allie and the others?"

"I think there's no evidence left to prove anything, and that's awfully damned convenient. So is the timing."

"You know Kingston owns more than real estate."

"Yeah, he also owns the mayor and the chief of police and probably the DA."

"I mean other business holdings. He bought out Narcis Pharmaceuticals last year, made his son CEO." I remembered because the Advocacy Center had been slated for grant money from Narcis, but the takeover canceled the funding. And yet, they somehow found money to throw a big gala celebration tonight. Guess treating the victims of violence, most of them from Kingston Tower, weren't high on Daniel Kingston's priority list. "He's planning to move their operations here to Cambria. It's supposed to revitalize the economy, save the city from bankruptcy."

Ryder turned to stare at me. "No shit. So we have a tie to our actor's stalking ground, the tunnels where the victims might have been held, and now to a drug company complete with access to the chemicals needed to manufacture PXA?"

"Wouldn't go that far. The company's based in Ireland, hasn't moved here yet, so it's not like Daniel Kingston actually has easy access. Plus, any good high school chemistry lab would have the chemicals needed to make PXA. It's all circumstantial, not enough for trial or even a search warrant," I reminded him. Living with Jacob and working with him on so many cases, I'd become pretty well versed in the rules of evidence. Which is why I hadn't brought up Narcis Pharmaceuticals earlier. Jacob would have read us chapter and verse on proper procedure. I had a feeling Ryder might not be as worried about playing by the rules.

"Warrant, smwarrant," he scoffed, affirming my instincts. "Right now, I don't have enough to go on to even think about a warrant. I need a direction to take the investigation. Sounds like Kingston might fit the bill."

"Or maybe you just don't like the man."

"Maybe I don't like the man because I have damned good instincts."

"Better watch it or those instincts are going to get you fired for real."

We approached the sidewalk leading to the Tower's main entrance. A gaggle of boys and young men lounged around the front steps, blocking the path. Ryder stopped at the edge of the walk and gestured to the nearest, a scrawny kid underdressed for the predawn chill in a windbreaker and Nike T-shirt. He jumped up and ran over to us as if he was a doorman greeting a limo.

Ozzie barked at him once, a friendly warning. He gave the dog a mock salute, and I noticed a zigzag-shaped scar on the back of his right hand—the mark of the Royales. Tyree didn't believe in tattoos for his loyal subjects, too easy to remove or fake. Once you were a member of the Royales, you were branded for life.

It made me think about the brand we'd found on each of the rape victims and Allie. It wasn't the same shape as the Royales' crown, though. The brand my victims had was larger, more rounded. I wondered if Tyree's prostitutes also got branded. The thought made me shudder, the idea of him treating girls like cattle. It would explain why Patrice and Jess had been helping them escape.

Would Tyree kill his own sister? He'd seemed genuinely worried about Esme down in the tunnels, but maybe he was mainly concerned that she'd tell the police he had murdered Jess and Patrice.

Maybe their murders had nothing to do with the sexual assaults? And where did our other victims, the seven kids we'd found with Allie, fit in to things? Any answers were hidden in a thick fog I was too exhausted to fight through.

Ryder said something, the boy took off at a saunter and returned a few minutes later with an older boy in his late teens. Same crown-inspired brand on his hand, more attitude and gold around his neck. "Y'all want to see the Syha family?" he drawled, talking around a toothpick in his mouth. "Not without Tyree's say-so. We're in lockdown."

"You can't do that," I blurted out, much to his amusement. He looked down his nose at me then slid his glance to Ryder, implying that Ryder wasn't much of a man if he couldn't keep his woman in check. Ozzie took a step forward, poised to rush inside with me. "I'm going to see that family, and you can't stop me."

It was Ryder, not the kid, who grabbed my arm, his grip strong enough to hold me in place before I could try to bolt past the Royales.

"You know Doc Rossi from Good Sam," he said, his tone matching the kid's exactly. Not threatening, no edge, just a couple of dudes talking. "You probably want to stay on her good side. Never know when you might be needing her services. Why don't you call up to Tyree and tell him if he doesn't open those doors in two minutes, none of his people will be welcome at Good Sam again."

The kid clamped down on his toothpick, considering, then rolled back on his heels and shrugged. "Aw 'ight. But he ain't gonna like it."

He turned away and pulled out a cell phone.

"You know we'd never refuse to treat anyone," I whispered to Ryder. "Why not threaten him with your men?"

"Tyree deals with threats from cops five times before breakfast. You're a wild card. He doesn't know if you'd follow through on the threat or not. And with you, he can give in and make it seem like a joke, so he won't lose face."

"Oh, so I get patronized by a drug-dealing gang leader pimp, and we're worried about *him* saving face?"

"Yep. Hey, you're the one wanted to come along."

That shut me up.

The kid returned, grinning. "You're in. Tyree's granting you an audience."

CHAPTER TWENTY-NINE

WE WERE ESCORTED inside the Tower. Devon had been right. The inside was clean, in decent repair, except for the fact that only one elevator seemed to work. The Royale accompanying us was joined by another member, this one carrying a gun prominently displayed at his belt. Together, we traveled up to the roof. The men kept looking me up and down then smirking at Ryder.

Ryder smirked right back. I ignored them all.

Not because I can't take a joke—although juvenile misogyny isn't my idea of humor—but now that we were inside and I saw how many Royales were between us and the exit, I was too busy analyzing the possibilities of us not making it back out again. Ozzie felt it as well, crowding his body against my leg, the leash as taut as it would go in the tiny area, ready to lunge into action.

I flicked my gaze to Ryder, who stood to my right and behind me, and saw that despite his smirk, he'd elbowed his coat back, resting his hand on the butt of his gun. Not that a gun would do us much good in the elevator.

The elevator lurched to a stop, and the doors slid open. One of the Royales sprang forward, bracing his back against the door, gesturing for me to exit as if he were a palace guard. "Ladies first."

It would have been more charming without the gold cap etched with a reclining playboy silhouette and the "beg for it, bitch" tattoo on his arm.

I crossed the threshold, not surprised when he turned to block

Ryder's path. "Tyree wants a private audience with the doc."

Trying to look casual, like I did this every day, I turned around. "That works for me."

Ryder's smirk barely wavered as he met my gaze and gave me the slightest nod. "No problem." He slammed his palm against the control panel. "As long as the door stays open."

The younger one frowned and opened his mouth to protest, his elbow drawing back, clearing his way to his gun. The older one shook his head. "Chill."

He inclined his chin to Ryder, cementing the pact, and turned to escort me and Ozzie to meet Tyree. As I crossed the open space lined with red velvet, curiosity trumped my fear. I'd treated so many patients who lived here in the Tower, who kowtowed to Tyree and his gang every day, but I'd never been inside before. Much less had access to Tyree's private rooftop sanctuary.

The man had spent the last twenty years running a criminal enterprise, staying ahead of the police and his competition, so I knew better than to underestimate him, but his tastes definitely skewed more porn-obsessed juvenile delinquent than what I imagined for a underworld kingpin. Of course, this is Cambria—not too many kingpin role models for a young gangster to emulate.

The two scantily clad girls kneeling on either side of Tyree's "throne," facing him, looking eager to anticipate his every wish, didn't raise my opinion. He was talking to someone on the phone as I approached. With the slightest flick of his finger or gaze, people from the sidelines hurried to his side, conferring in whispers or pulling up information on the sleek laptop that graced his otherwise empty desk. Donald Trump would have been proud.

He hung up as Ozzie and I arrived at the large mahogany desk. I ignored the jealous stares of the two women kneeling beside him.

Unsure if he wanted his people to know about his earlier forays into the tunnels, I decided to play it safe. "It's nice to meet you, Mr. Willard."

He pushed his chair back and stood, taking my hand and shaking it like an equal. "Welcome, Dr. Rossi."

Two men arrived and whisked the girls away, along with everyone else who stood near, leaving me and Tyree alone. Except for Ozzie, of course. The dog obviously knew Tyree, but he didn't relax. I glanced over my shoulder. At the far end of the makeshift room, Ryder slumped casually against the wall of the elevator, but his hand was near his gun, and his gaze targeted Tyree.

Once we were alone, Tyree turned his back on Ryder and his guards to look out the windows at the rooftops jumbled beyond. From here we could see all the way to the river, the view framed by Good Sam rising up from the darkness on the right and the angular lines of a Victorian-inspired rooftop greenhouse on the other wing of the Tower to our left.

The greenhouse was totally out of place on top of this concrete slab that had become a prison to so many. Lit by a strange red glow, it reminded me of St. Tim's, the way the candlelight inside the church transformed stained glass into devil's eyes.

"Heaters," Tyree said, noting my stare. "For the plants. They don't like the cold." He turned to face the greenhouse as well. "You know, when Kingston first designed this place in the seventies, he won awards. One of the first green roofs used in urban development. The community garden was meant to feed hundreds, just as the rooftop playground was meant to give the kids who lived here a safe and secure environment, far away from street gangs below. It was his pride and joy back then, put Kingston Enterprises back on the map." His chuckle was a throaty rumble.

"What happened?"

"Usual. Funding dried up, leaving everything half-done. We're standing on the playground." He gestured to the space surrounding us that had become his royal court. "Only part of Kingston's vision that actually became real was his greenhouse. Lovingly designed and built, modeled after the Victorian conservatory on the roof of his family mansion. Transplanted up here to the middle of Cambria City's wasteland." He winked at me. "Guess I don't have to tell you what cash crop I grow in there nowadays."

"How much more time will you need?" I asked. Another gamble, but one that paid off when he turned and arched an eyebrow in my direction. "To finish prepping the Syha family, tell them what not to say to us."

He angled himself so that no one would see his grin except me. "Knew you'd be trouble. Any word on Esme?"

"No. Sorry. While we're waiting, maybe you could get me the list of the families of the other children. I'm sure they're all from here."

"Our jobs are a lot alike. We both have to prioritize, do what we can with what little we have. Whatever it takes to protect our people."

"Finding Alamea Syha's killer and whoever took those children isn't a priority?"

"Finding Esme is my priority. She's the one at most risk. Isn't that what you doctors call triage?"

"You don't think Allie's death has anything to do with whoever took Esme?"

His expression darkened. It took him a full exhalation and inhalation before his jaw unclenched enough to answer. "If it does, I'll handle it. Once Esme's safe."

"You know who killed Allie." I had a feeling. "Did the same person take the other children?"

He gave a little shake of his head, even though he didn't answer my question. "Things aren't what they seem, Doctor. Those children weren't taken."

"What do you call being locked away in the dark?"

"They were being protected."

"What about Allie? Was she being protected?"

He pivoted on one foot, turning into my space so fast I almost took a step back. But I forced myself to hold my ground. Ozzie didn't feel such constraints. He bared his teeth and growled at Tyree's sudden movement. "It's my job to protect my people—all my people—the best I can," Tyree continued, ignoring the dog.

"Sometimes compromises must be made. You may not understand why I do what I do, but don't you dare come into my house and ever question my loyalty to my people."

It took effort, but I met his gaze. Nodded. "My job is to reunite those children with their families and make sure they're safe. Are you going to help me with that?"

A long moment passed. Neither of us blinked, but he settled his weight back, giving me room to breathe.

"Will they be safe with their families?" I persisted.

"I know you don't believe me, but those children would have been better left where you found them. You put them in the foster care system and they're good as dead." He stretched his fingers out, as if resisting pulling them into a fist. "Bring them back here where they belong, and I can guarantee their safety. That good enough for you?"

No. And it wouldn't be good enough for Children's Services, either. But I humored him. "For now. What about the Syhas? Are you going to help me and Ryder find Allie's killer?" I was certain he knew who it was.

Wasn't surprised when he shrugged. "They're free to tell you anything they can. As long as you let me know if you find anything that tells you where Esme is."

A bargain with the devil. I'd made worse. "Deal."

"Your boyfriend won't like it."

"Ryder? He's not—"

He was shaking his head. "Not the cop. Devon. You were down there in the tunnels with him. What did he tell you?"

Suddenly, I realized what all this playacting was about. More than stalling us from talking to Allie's family, he wanted to know about Devon Price. Did he know Devon was Esme's father?

I played dumb. "Showed me where to find your booby traps. How to not get lost in the tunnels."

"He didn't tell you anything about my sister, Jess? How it was his fault she went blind?"

"No."

He twisted his lips together as if deciding whether to unlock a secret. "What did he say about me? About what his plans are?"

"Why don't you ask him?"

Anger reddened his neck and climbed up his face. The veins crawling across his murderous thick biceps bulged. Not used to anyone challenging him, much less a woman, I guessed. The air behind us buzzed as his crew sensed his anger, a nest of hornets protecting their leader. Ozzie growled again, which didn't help matters.

"You treat a lot of people there in your ER," he said.

"Most of them from here." Not the smartest answer, but somehow the more he tried to threaten me, the more relaxed I felt. As if the events of the night had depleted my adrenaline stores to the point where I felt no fear.

Maybe not the best survival instinct.

"You think I don't know that?" he thundered. There was a collective gasp behind us, and someone must have rushed forward, but he waved them back with one finger. "We're at war here, Doctor. You are standing on the front line. I protect my people the best I can, but the enemy is all around us."

"You think Devon is an enemy?"

"That's exactly what I'm trying to find out."

"He's only interested in saving Esme."

Tyree stared down at me again, his chin bobbing in time with the pulse jumping in his neck. "Let's hope you're right."

"If I'm not?" Stupid question, but I couldn't resist.

"Then your ER had better stock up on body bags. And it will be all your fault."

CHAPTER THIRTY

DEVON DIDN'T FIND Marcus Vance at the rectory. Instead, he found the priest inside the church, on his knees, praying at the altar rail, a rosary twisted around his joined hands. Shoulders bent and broken, forehead bowed. Nothing like the tough street fighter Devon remembered from his youth.

"How'd you get this gig, anyway?" Devon sat in the pew behind Marcus. "They let just anyone be a priest?"

Marcus finished his prayer, rosary beads clicking between his fingers. Finally, he looked up to the crucifix, crossed himself, and joined Devon. "Some say sinners make the best priests. Like St. Paul."

Devon rolled his eyes. St. Paul's conversion was a favorite story of the nuns and the older women like Mrs. Anders and Jess's mom. As if Devon would someday find himself on a road to Damascus.

"Did the cops show you the room those kids were kept in?"

Marcus flinched. Nothing obvious, but a flicker of emotion that was like shouting to Devon. Funny, Marcus used to have the best poker face around. Guess being a priest had softened him up a bit.

"So, you knew about the kids." Devon didn't wait for confirmation. "Reminded me of what Mrs. Anders used to do when I was a kid. All that crap about demons and devils possessing children." No child had been immune, but somehow it was always Devon that Mrs. Anders had focused her special attention on. Because of his mom and the way the devil himself, Daniel Kingston, just couldn't stay away from her.

The old lady had used his mom—and Devon—to manipulate Kingston. To curry favor with the church? Buy protection for the other women of Kingston Tower?

He stood, knocking a knee against the pew as he spun away from Marcus. "Do you have any idea what they did to me, to my mom?" He was tempted to pull his shirt up, show Marcus his scars. They weren't all from the burns he'd received trying to save Jess from the fire in the tunnels. There were plenty left over from Mrs. Anders, trying to beat the devil out of him.

Funny, Devon had blocked out most of that. Old memories resurrected. Price of coming home.

Long-buried anger flared. He restrained himself—it took every ounce of energy he had—and shoved a scarred palm into Marcus's sight instead of smashing it into his face. "That's what they did to a little boy, Marcus. You were old enough then, did you know? How about what they did to my mom, all in the name of Jesus? They tortured her as much as Kingston did, and then they'd deliver her right back into his hands."

Marcus's gaze never wavered. "They were trying to protect everyone—all the families over at the Tower, Devon. You were too young to remember how bad things were back then. Not a night went by without another murder in a stairwell or another woman raped. The cops didn't give a shit. The only way to get any help was to keep Kingston happy."

"And do you remember what my mother went through? How beautiful she was before Kingston got to her? Remember what she looked like that last day when they took her away, Marcus? Eyes flat, staring at nothing, drool on her face, worse than dead."

Marcus glanced up as if expecting his God to answer.

"Eight years, Marcus. Eight years she endured that monster. Eight years my family played Judas goat for the rest of the Tower. Don't you think after all that, I deserve some answers?"

Marcus remained silent, his eyes on the crucifix above them.

"You know something." It wasn't a question. From the way Marcus stiffened, he understood how serious Devon was. "Tell me. Now."

"I can't. I'm sorry." All his life, Devon had never heard Marcus apologize to anyone for anything.

"Where's Mrs. Anders? I know she kept those kids down in the tunnels. Did she hide Esme somewhere? Who wants Esme dead and why? Who killed Patrice and," his voice faltered, "Jess?" As the questions poured out, Devon came as close to tears as he had in decades.

Still, Marcus remained silent.

"You want to die?" Devon shouted, his voice echoing back from the stained-glass effigies as if the saints all had the same question. "I don't mind killing a priest. But I'd rather not kill a friend."

"If I told you what I know, I'd just be condemning someone else, wouldn't I?" They must have taught Marcus how to use double-talk in the seminary, because he used to be a straight shooter. Said little, and what he did, you could count on. "Guess that means you might as well kill me. Save me from having more blood to atone for."

"Marcus—"

"It's Father Vance."

Damn. That was cold.

Devon tried another track. "You can't tell anyone anything said in confession, right?" Marcus nodded. "So I'm making my confession, Father Vance. Esme is my daughter."

"I know."

"Who told you?"

Marcus remained silent. Of course. As a priest, he now got to keep everyone's secrets. Made him a powerful man without raising a fist.

He folded his hands together as if praying. "If I knew where Esme was, I wouldn't be here, Devon. I'd be out there, trying to help her."

"You sound almost like your old self, Marcus. Almost." Like he was going to trust a priest to take care of business. As always, it was down to Devon to get the job done. He turned to leave, not bothering with genuflecting or even glancing toward the altar with its silent God.

"Devon. Don't you want absolution?"

"Haven't done anything needs forgiving, Father. Not yet. But you want something on your conscience, Father Vance? My daughter's gone, her mother dead, and someone's gonna answer for that. I figure my best bet for answers is Mrs. Anders. She can't hide behind no confessional."

"Mrs. Anders might have gone too far, but she's always done what she thought was best for the people of the Tower. She loved your mother, and she loved you, Devon. Just as she cared for Jess and Esme."

"You saying she doesn't know anything?"

Marcus considered, his lips twisting as if trying to untangle a truth that wouldn't violate his precious priestly obligations. "I'm saying maybe start with the man who knows everything that goes on in the Tower."

"Daniel Kingston?" No way would Daniel ever tell Devon anything. And why would he be involved in Jess's death or taking Esme? He'd never shown any interest in them before.

"Kingston? He hasn't given a rat's ass about the Tower, not since he finished with your mother. I'm talking about the man who does Kingston's dirty work for him, cleans up after him, keeps folks in line so Kingston doesn't have to worry. Tyree. He's who you need to be talking to."

☽ ⚜ ☾

RYDER'S FINGERS CRAMPED with the urge to draw his weapon and charge in after Rossi as she and Tyree held their tête-à-tête in this crazy-ass rooftop porn palace. Once he was past his initial juvenile impulse, he watched Rossi. The woman was fearless, giving Tyree's shit right back to him, standing toe-to-toe with the gang leader and never flinching.

He kept his calm, followed her lead. Ignored the drip of sweat that inched down his spine. Finally, Tyree waved her away as if giving her a benediction, and then she and the dog were back in the elevator with him, on their way down to the fourth floor to where Alamea Syha had lived with her family.

Here there was no red velvet, no sense of open space. Just anonymous plywood doors painted an indiscriminate color lining the two wings stretching out from either side of the elevator. An armed sentry stood guard at the elevator, two more patrolled each hallway.

Their escort nodded to the sentry and led them to a door a third of the way down the east wing. He pounded on it with the side of his fist then left before it opened.

Rossi moved to stand in front of the door, but Ryder waved her back, and she joined him to one side. His hand was on the butt of his weapon, ready to clear it from its holster. The door opened, revealing a stooped Asian woman with sparse gray hair and the white film of cataracts covering her eyes.

Ryder scanned the space behind her. People sitting on couches and the floor, a few crying, others conversing in a foreign language. He relaxed his guard and let Rossi take the lead, interested in seeing how she'd handle this crowd, knowing they'd be more comfortable with her than a cop.

She used the dog to help soften the blow, just like she had with the kids. Allie's family was Laotian, here illegally except for the children who'd been born in Cambria: Allie and a younger brother. The brother, a fourteen-year-old dressed in baggy jeans and a Penn State sweatshirt, did the translating. His parents, aunt, uncle, and grandmother collapsed in tears around him when Rossi broke the news—news they'd already heard from Tyree's boys, no doubt. But the boy, the brother, he kept looking at Ryder. His gaze wasn't filled with grief. Rather, anger and mistrust.

While Rossi comforted the family, Ryder beckoned the boy to join him.

"I ain't done nothing." The kid's first words confirmed Ryder's suspicion. As did the still-angry-red brand on the back of his hand.

"When'd you get that?" Ryder nodded to Tyree's brand. The boy shuffled his hands, not sure what to do with them, settled for folding them and his arms against his chest and leaning against the doorjamb like the gangster he wasn't.

"Whassit to you?"

Ryder waited. Kid caved fast.

"Few days ago. After Allie went—" Kid finally let some grief filter through the anger. Blinked fast, eyes wet. Turned his face away from Ryder to look at his family. "Someone had to do something to protect the family. Not like you all do."

"Tell me about Allie. What was going on in her life?"

The kid looked down at his feet, embarrassment sprinting over his face when he lost his balance and had to straighten, assume a new pose. "Girl had her dreams, and she stood by them. Decided she was going to play in a band, run away to New York, anywhere but here."

"Sounds like an expensive dream. Did Allie have any money?"

No pose, this time it was pure rage that ratcheted his spine straight. "Tyree told her he could help her make some. Fast. Know what I mean?"

"She was working for Tyree?"

"No. She said no. Girl was such a dreamer. Didn't realize no one says no to Tyree. Not ever." He picked at the fresh burn scar on his hand. "But one thing about Tyree. He protects his own. That's for real."

Right. Until Tyree had no more use for "his own." Ryder tried another track. "If Allie wasn't going to work for Tyree, where did she plan to get the money to go to New York?"

"I dunno. But she had something planned. Dressed real nice—extra nice—that last morning when she left for school."

"What day was that?"

"Monday. Said something about coming home with enough money so none of us would have to worry about anything anymore.

Talked about taking us all with her." He pursed his mouth as if ready to spit. "Girl was such a fool."

He gave the kid the other rape victims' names. "Any of them know Allie?"

His expression immediately closed down. "Don't know nothing."

He turned to go back inside, ending the conversation. Ryder had one last question. "Why didn't you or your folks report Allie missing?"

He figured the answer would have to do with their immigration status. The kid surprised him. "Because that's when the money started coming. A grand every day she was gone. Note said not to tell."

"Money?" Ryder wondered if the other victims' families had gotten money during their absences. "How did it come? Show me the note."

The boy pushed away from the door, out into the hall where they couldn't be overheard. "Can't. Burned it after I found the money. It was in our mailbox—me and Allie are the only ones who check it. Figured maybe it was from her, her way of saying good-bye, taking care of us." He looked over his shoulder at his family. "They don't know anything about it."

"But now you know it wasn't Allie who sent it. Any ideas who could have?"

This time it was fear that drove the kid's balled-up posture, making him less of a target. "That's why I burned the note. Paper it was on, it had like an invisible ink picture."

"You mean a watermark?"

"Yeah, one of those."

"What was it?"

"Everyone here knows that mark. We see it everywhere we look."

"Tyree's crown? Was it the Royales' mark?"

Kid shook his head, holding his hand with Tyree's brand up as if noticing it for the first time. "People are so stupid. It's not Tyree's crown. Never was." He pointed down the hall to the elevators.

Above them was a sign riveted to the cinderblock wall.

Ryder couldn't make out the words, but even from here he saw the logo. A lowercase "d" tilted to one side with a capital "K" perched on it at an angle, zigzag lines joining the points of the letters, making it look like a person wearing a crown.

Daniel Kingston's logo.

CHAPTER THIRTY-ONE

AFTER LEAVING THE Syhas, we trudged back to the elevator. Tyree's men were nowhere to be found, but the car was waiting for us. We both leaned against the back wall of the elevator, Ozzie between us. Ryder reached for my hand, and I let him hold it. Wasn't sure who was comforting whom, but it felt good, and I was too tired to fake being strong anymore.

It'd been hours since my last fugue state. Other than contact with almost-dead-people, they seemed triggered by heightened emotions: fear, especially. Maybe I hadn't had one recently because Ryder made me feel safe. Or maybe I was so exhausted that the fear had been leeched out of me.

Look at me, playing scientist, trying to explain something I was busy denying existed. My dad always said I got that from him—the Rossi ability to argue both sides at the same time, guaranteed to drive anybody crazy.

I shied away from that thought. Standing here with Ryder, I didn't feel so crazy. Despite the circumstances, I felt pretty damn near normal, and it was refreshing as hell.

Ozzie led us outside and immediately did his business on the straggly bushes that lined the walkway. I craned my neck up. Few lights this early in the morning, not until you reached Tyree's rooftop office. And the greenhouse with its eerie red glow. "That greenhouse. Wouldn't be a bad place to hide a kid like Esme."

Ryder looked up. "Easy to guard, hard to approach without

warning. I'll see if the staties can swing a helicopter past, get some pictures." He turned his gaze on me in approval. "I like how you think, Rossi." Stifling a yawn with one hand, he grabbed his cell phone with the other and called to arrange the flyby. "And get me thermal imaging," he added. "I'd love to know how many people are inside."

He hung up. "They say thermal might be tough because of the heaters for the plants, but we'll see. You in a hurry to get home?"

"No. Why?"

"I still owe you a meal, and I'm starved." He turned in the direction of my apartment above my uncle's bar. "You're just a few blocks from here, right?"

Yeah, right. "You know I am. Don't try to bullshit a bullshitter, Ryder. How much did you bet?"

The world of sex crimes is pretty small—and more than a little incestuous. Who else are you going to unwind and share stories of the day's work with when your shift is spent interviewing victims or their rapists?

My team includes Jacob as our ADA—I pretty much inherited him when I took over the Advocacy Center, but we work well together despite our history, or maybe because of it—two dedicated social workers; four SANE nurses who, like me, divide their time between shifts in the ER and working at the Center; an on-call psychologist who volunteers her time to provide counseling for victims and their families; a corps of volunteer victim assistants; one county sheriff's detective; and one city detective, the position Ryder was taking over after Harrison's death a few weeks ago.

All of them—except the volunteers, they were pretty much civilians, didn't socialize with the rest of us—knew I never invited men to my place. Never invited anyone there, in fact. But that didn't stop them from hazing any newcomers as an initiation to our select group of merry mischief-makers.

"I have no earthly idea what you're talking about," Ryder said, but his grin gave everything away. Despite being up all night, almost shot, almost fired, and almost incinerated, he crackled with energy.

Okay, two could play at this game. I recalled his address from his ER chart and turned south. "You're just a few blocks from here, on Riverside, right?"

Without waiting for his answer, I started walking, Ozzie at my side. I turned back and called over my shoulder. "C'mon, you still owe me breakfast."

He shook his head, chuckled, and jogged to catch up. "Hope I didn't cross a line. Is it because of Voorsanger?"

Why did he assume Jacob was still in my life? I mean, he was, but not the way Ryder seemed to think. "No. And don't take it personally. Jacob never gets an invite either."

He considered that, a sly grin slipping across his face as if he was keeping score. I suppressed the urge to roll my eyes. Men. Did they ever think of anything but sex?

We settled into a steady rhythm, the street empty. No Black Friday predawn shoppers here. They were all beyond the city limits, with the strip malls and big-box stores.

As we walked, the darkness punctuated by the occasional streetlamp, I couldn't stop thinking about those kids: Esme, Allie, the other children…it was like catching water, as soon as you closed your fist, everything that you thought you had a firm grasp on drained away, leaving nothing.

𝔇 ⚛ ℭ

RYDER'S HOUSE WAS a Craftsman-style bungalow with a river-rock foundation supporting a wide porch, peaked gable, and wide-lathed siding painted a gentle dove gray with cobalt blue trim. In the soft glow of the porch light, it looked like a house out of a fairy tale, complete with moon gate and a cobblestone path leading to the porch. Obviously a house that had been lovingly restored and cared for. Unlike many of its neighbors.

I climbed the steps to his front door—also cobalt blue—and

spotted matching rocking chairs sitting on the porch, waiting for winter to loosen its grip.

"Nice place," I said as he ushered me and Ozzie inside and took my coat.

"Thanks. My folks live across the river, my sister and her family two doors down from them. But when I came home from the Army, I needed space." He looked around as if noticing his own house for the first time. "And this place needed tons of fixing up. Which worked out fine, since I was in the mood for a lot of hammering and pounding back then."

"You did all this yourself? It's lovely."

He seemed abashed at the adjective. Probably not manly enough for a cop's bachelor pad. But it was lovely—not fussy, just simple, rich colors, clean lines. Not jumbled and messy like my place. Or my life.

Serene. That's what the ivory-colored walls with their black and white photographs and the classic Shaker-inspired furniture on crisp heart of pine floors felt like. An oasis. Safe haven.

I wandered over to the stone fireplace that took up an entire wall of the living room. The wide mantel was cluttered with photos: Ryder and an older couple, him with his arms wrapped around a woman a few years younger on one side and a man a few years older on the other, him rolling in the grass with a young girl and boy and a mixed-breed puppy, and several of him in various types of uniform with his fellow soldiers. He looked much, much younger then—and, despite the stark, mountainous landscape in the background, much happier.

"When did you serve?" I asked.

"The 1-87 was one of the first in Afghanistan. Finally came home in 2004, joined the force, been a cop ever since." He shrugged away his years of service, even as his hand brushed the photo, aligning it just so as if it were a holy relic.

He pushed away from the mantel. "Better take care of the dog."

Ozzie and I followed him into the kitchen. Maple cabinets blended with a modern mosaic-glass backsplash. Instead of the current trend of bulky islands to break up the space, he'd chosen a farmer's table, solid and scarred, the kind the Waltons would have been at home gathered around.

"Yard's fenced in," he said as he let Ozzie outside. Then he surprised me by dragging two large stainless steel dog bowls out of the pantry along with a bag of kibble. "I dog-sit for my sister's kids."

I riffled through family photos stuck haphazardly between duty schedules, coupons, and takeout menus on his fridge. "They're cute. How old?"

"Eight and nine." He finished pouring the dog food and water and leaned against the table, watching me as I shamelessly examined his personal effects. "You're the first person outside family that I've brought here in a long time."

It was an admission as much as an invitation, but I didn't RSVP. With regrets. Given everything going on in my life, it didn't seem fair to him. Or me.

The dog gave a little whine, and Ryder let him back in, pausing to get down on the floor and rub his belly. "Always wanted a dog."

"He's not yours. He'll go back to Esme when we find her." I was surprised by the harshness in my voice. He was, too, his gaze bouncing up to study me.

He climbed to his feet, ending up so close to me that his chest brushed mine when he drew in a breath. I thought he was going to kiss me. But he didn't. Instead, he studied my face as if reading an obscure language.

"You believe that. That we'll find her. I admire that, with everything you've seen, you can still trust, still believe." His tone dropped until it sounded like it had back when we were inside St. Tim's.

He'd misunderstood. What I felt wasn't anything to do with God or a higher power. It wasn't that kind of belief. It was necessity. I'd never rest, not with Patrice's voice rattling around in my head, and she'd never rest, not until we found Esme.

"You're wrong." I gave a little shake of my head. "But you do.

Believe. I saw you in that church. Even after everything you've seen and done, you still think there's a God?" My tone skirted incredulity, fell back to a plea for understanding.

"How could I not? Think about last night. First, I, master of the microwave," he nodded to the appliance over the stove, "inexplicably crack my head open on the exact same night that you, despite your family and ex-husband waiting for you, decide to work late."

It was because of my family, not in spite of. But I didn't interrupt.

"You chose my chart," he continued, "out of all the other patients, came to my room, put up with my bullshit long enough for us to both be there when Patrice arrived." From his tone, he truly believed what he was saying. "Do you have any idea how many dominoes had to fall at the precise time and place to make all that happen?" He shrugged, not quite smiling, but enough to reveal that elusive dimple. "How can you not believe in a higher power after all that?"

It was my turn to shrug. I almost hated to disappoint him, but I gave him the truth. "Trust no one, that's all I believe in."

He tilted his head at my words. "You trust me."

I conceded the point. "I wouldn't be here if I didn't trust you."

"Okay, maybe trust isn't the word. Maybe it's faith. Faith in something more than what we see and know."

"Faith?" I scoffed. The conversation was veering into emotional dark alleys I had no desire to wander. "Where do I find that? The corner 7-Eleven? Trust is all I have to give you. If that's not enough…"

"It's enough." Another heavy silence, as if we both wanted something we couldn't have.

I was about ready to say to hell with the craziness going on inside my head, to hell with good sense and fair play and all that bullshit, and kiss him, when the dog nudged himself between us. The moment vanished.

Who knows? Maybe I'd imagined it. Believing that was the safest bet.

CHAPTER THIRTY-TWO

DEVON LEFT ST. Timothy's and pushed his way through the crowd watching the cops and firefighters, the rising sun casting a red glow that added to the lights of the emergency vehicles. You'd think it was a goddamn block party the way the music blasters and laughter cut the air.

At the Tower he was stopped before he even stepped foot on the entrance walk. Smartass kid who thought he might grow up to be tough some day. Lucky Ryder had taken Devon's gun.

"Tell Tyree I'm coming up."

"No one goes up," the kid argued. A few older Royales had joined them. They knew Devon, watched to see what would happen.

Devon had no time for this shit. As the kid squared up in front of him—had no one taught the idiot how to fight?—Devon took him out with a single elbow to the throat. Kid gurgled from the sidewalk as Devon stepped over his body.

"Way to go, Runt." Tyree himself appeared at the entrance to the Tower. "Still wasting your time on fun and games."

Devon climbed the steps to meet Tyree. "It's no game. You know what Jess and Esme mean to me."

Tyree flexed his arms, muscles rippling beneath his Under Armour long-sleeved shirt. He wore no jacket, impervious to the cold. At least, that was the impression he was trying to give. No wonder his followers went around severely underdressed for the weather. Trying to live up to Tyree's image.

Games. Twenty years since Tyree had taken control of the Royales, and it was still all just games.

An image of Jess, lying in her own blood, flashed before Devon. "You ready to help me save Esme? Or you gonna keep on standing in my way?"

Tyree narrowed his eyes, then shrugged dramatically. "Come with me." He spun on his heel and entered the Tower, not looking back to see if Devon followed.

Eleven years ago Devon would have had to hustle to catch up with the larger man, but not now. Now, within a few paces, Devon was walking side by side with Tyree, matching him step for step.

Tyree nodded to one of his guards who stood before a metal door. One of the tunnel entrances. The kid opened the door and held it as Tyree and Devon passed through. No one else. The door clanged shut behind them, but the steps leading down to the tunnels were lit by LED lanterns spaced every few feet.

"You know the cops and firefighters are swarming all over this place," Devon reminded Tyree. He figured if Tyree was going to kill him, he'd do it where his people could watch, someplace that emphasized his power, like his little throne room upstairs on the roof.

"They're over near the courthouse right now. Got themselves a grid system they're following. Makes it easy for me to keep track of them. We'll have plenty of privacy, don't worry."

Devon knew better than to press Tyree. Man was like a bull—if you wanted something from him, best way not to get it was to force him into a corner. He'd learned that the hard way with his and Jess's future on the line. Wasn't about to risk Esme's as well.

So he bit back his pride and his worry and followed Tyree into the dark. To his surprise, Tyree led him back to the abandoned refrigerator unit where they'd found the children last night. But the more Devon thought about it, the more that made sense.

"You knew the kids were here. You and Mrs. Anders," Devon said. "She's back at her old witch-hunter tricks? Performing exorcisms, making innocent kids believe they're evil demon spawn?"

Tyree stopped outside the closed door to the refrigeration unit. "She did what she did because she was trying to protect you. And your mother."

"Don't buy it, not anymore. Maybe you could convince me when I was eight that I was the real problem, that I was to blame for what Kingston did to my mom, but I know better now. Mrs. Anders, Jess's mom, all those women, even the damn priest—they did what they did to save themselves, and they didn't care if my mother paid the price."

"They didn't just save themselves," Tyree said in a flat tone. "They saved everyone. Think of what Kingston could have done if he'd taken it in his head. White men like him, filled with power and glory, they're used to getting what they want. Sometimes you just gotta learn that the best way to get what you want—what you need—is to let them have it. Then everyone wins. Your mama, she just never could bring herself to understand that."

"But you do, right, Tyree? You parade around like you're the king of the Royales, when all you really are is a lackey, taking orders from Daniel Kingston, doing his dirty work."

Tyree didn't respond. He merely smiled, teeth gleaming in the lantern light. He swung the door to the walk-in refrigerator open, ignoring the crime-scene tape hanging limp to one side.

The stench of blood hit Devon. Blood and other bodily fluids best left unnamed. Tyree shoved him over the threshold.

The room was dark except for a single flashlight in the far corner, propped up against the wall so its light shone up, creating more shadows than it exorcised. Beside it, leaning up against the corner was a cop. His hands and legs were bound, his mouth covered with duct tape. He glared at Tyree.

Tyree pulled a .45 semiautomatic and used it to prod Devon farther into the room.

Devon stumbled and almost tripped over a body. Blood squished beneath his shoes. Tyree kicked one of the plastic LED lights across the threshold to illuminate the rest of the room.

Mrs. Anders lay at Devon's feet, blood covering her chest and belly. She'd been gutted.

CHAPTER THIRTY-THREE

BEING WITH ROSSI, here in his home, was surreal on so many levels. Ryder felt comfortable around her, even when their conversation slid sideways from his usual pickup banter into a discussion of trust and faith—things he didn't talk to anyone about, much less a woman he'd met less than twelve hours earlier.

Some men find God in the darkness, some find only themselves. Ryder had been in and out of so many black holes that he'd found and lost a thousand gods. Some nights he lay awake, certain he was still buried inside a mountain, wandering in the dark, and that this world he woke to every day was the dream, not the reality.

Hard to care much about what happens in a dream...but, still, he managed. He was a good cop, the kind of cop who wouldn't have been doing the job if he wasn't sure he could make a difference. Same reason why he'd been a good soldier.

Only lately, it was getting harder and harder to believe.

On good days Ryder chiseled away at the mountain of corruption that threatened the innocent citizens of Cambria City, hammering in the dark with a badge instead of a pickax, fighting for a city built on coal and the blood of the men who dug it. On bad days...well, lately there had been far too many bad days. Days when the good guys didn't just lose. They didn't even bother showing up.

Not Rossi. She gave her all. Ryder had the feeling that wasn't just last night, but every day.

He fed her breakfast—a mash-up of eggs, hash browns, salsa,

cheese, and sausage all scrambled together in one skillet, eaten from the same skillet because he didn't have any clean plates—and plied her with questions about the Advocacy Center, a topic he knew she wouldn't mind talking about.

Some of the cases she told him about... He'd been a cop for going on ten years. He wasn't shocked. More discouraged. What people did, to themselves, to the ones they loved, to children.

"What's going to happen to the kids from the tunnel?" he asked as they loaded the dishwasher together. They even both agreed on putting the silverware in handle up, something his sister was always fussing at him about. "Even if we find their families, we can't just give them back. Not after they were abandoned the way they were."

She stifled a yawn with the back of her hand. "Pediatrics is full, so I can't keep them there."

"Tyree was right about one thing. You can't put them into the foster care system. Separating them—it would about kill them." He surprised himself with his vehemence. It wasn't his job to play social worker. But those kids, the way they barely made eye contact, much less talked. They were so young. Throwing them into the system the way they were now...so damaged and vulnerable. It would kill them.

"I'm working on it. One of my nurses is watching them today while our psychologist evaluates them. After that..."

He waited, assuming she'd shrug or utter some kind of throwaway cliché, like "it's out of our hands," words intended to let people off the hook and assuage their guilt.

Not Rossi. Instead, she glanced up at him, meeting his gaze, and said, "After that, well, we might just have to get creative. How many bedrooms do you have here, Ryder?"

She smiled, but she was also halfway serious. He couldn't help but smile back.

"You know, in his own warped way, I think that's exactly what Tyree was doing when he hid them in the tunnels," she said.

"Might help if we knew what he thought he was protecting them from." Ryder glanced at the clock. Six twenty. Too early to try to talk to Kingston. And he definitely couldn't go smelling like this—sweat and blood and grime and the chemical stink left from the explosion in the tunnel. Not to mention a shirt soiled and jacket ripped.

Ozzie had curled up on a corner of the couch, watching them with one eye, the other drifting shut as he made a snuffling sound that was almost a snore. Rossi plunked down beside the dog, scratching him behind his ears. "Will he be okay here?" she asked. "I should head over to Good Sam soon."

"Yeah, he'll be fine in the yard. No rain today, they say. If you don't mind waiting a few minutes, I'll walk over with you. Just want to grab a quick shower. Unless you'd like to…" He purposely left the invitation open-ended, interested to see where she'd take it.

She dismissed him with the wave of a drowsy hand and curled her body around the dog, using Ozzie as a pillow. Ryder shook his head and climbed the steps to his bedroom. Couldn't help but imagine a dozen more-attractive what-if scenarios than stripping off his filthy clothing, straining sore muscles, and stepping into the shower alone.

Those fantasies fled fifteen minutes later when he returned downstairs and saw Rossi, fully relaxed for the first time since he'd met her. More than relaxed, vulnerable. First time he'd seen her without her guard up.

He risked a touch, only a touch, of the woman sleeping on the couch. Just a finger, a gentle caress of the area where her neck lay bare, right below the corner of her jaw. Warm, she was so very warm, almost feverish, as if she were more alive than any other woman he'd ever met. Her pulse hummed beneath his touch, steady, strong. Reassuring.

Turning his back on the clock, giving in to temptation and exhaustion, he sank down onto the sofa beside her. The dog whined, shifting his weight, and Rossi responded by sliding closer to Ryder. Curling his arm around Rossi's body, his heart and breathing matching hers, he closed his eyes and dared to sleep.

"WHAT THE HELL!" Devon whirled on Tyree. "You killed her. She might have known where Esme is, and you killed her."

Tyree frowned. "What makes you think she knew where Esme is?"

"Every path I go down searching for Esme leads to the Kingstons. Daniel is too old now, but I figured if Leo is following in his father's footsteps, then he might be using the same place where his father used to take my mother. Daniel Kingston would come for her, take her from me—or sometimes Mrs. Anders or the other women would fetch her for Kingston, take her away. My mom said it was her very own special hell, used to mumble about being surrounded by devils while angels sang." He trailed off. It was a long shot but his last lead to find Esme. Now even that long shot was gone.

"Listen to yourself, Runt. Your mama was strung-out, crack crazy. She didn't know what she was saying half the time. Besides, I didn't kill the old lady." Tyree nodded to the cop. "He did. Trying to get her to tell him what she knew."

Devon frowned, not understanding anything about this scenario. Which was exactly what Tyree wanted—Devon off-balance.

"Think you're so smart," Tyree jeered. "You have no clue. Those kids you so-called rescued last night? Mrs. A and me, we were the ones who saved them. Hid them from the real monster. And we paid a price for it. That's why he," Tyree nodded to the cop, "came after Mrs. A. To see what all she knew. Next on his hit list is taking care of all those kids."

"Did she hide Esme as well?" Devon asked, staring at the old lady's corpse, wondering what secrets she'd taken to the grave. He should have been glad she was dead, after all the pain she'd caused, but he wasn't. The long night had sapped his strength. All he had left was enough to care about Esme.

"Nope. She would've told me if she had."

Damn. "Why did you and Mrs. Anders take the kids to start with?

Who were you protecting them from? Leo? His father?"

"Those kids ain't got no one else. Their mothers are all gone, leaving them behind as witnesses. Me and Kingston's pet cops, we were meant to clean up after, get rid of the kids, but they're my people, my responsibility, so I saved them. I took the risk and told Mrs. A to keep them safe, until you came along and ruined everything. Now's there's blood being shed, and it's on your head."

Devon tried to parse his words. "Cleaning up? Kids as witnesses?" He remembered Angela telling him about the victims who'd ended up with their minds destroyed—and how no one had reported any of the kids as missing. "Kingston. He took their mothers—"

"Life in the big city hasn't smartened you up any, Runt. Kingston's too old. And he's sick. Before tonight, it's been months since he's left his mansion."

"Leo." Rage surged through Devon at the name. "And you're protecting him. Cleaning up his mess like some kind of trash man."

It made sense. Daniel Kingston owned the Tower, would have eyes, ears in the place, some way to protect his investment. Especially his investment in his lily-white son and heir, who just happened to be a psychopathic serial rapist and homicidal maniac. Who better than Tyree?

"Did Leo kill Jess? Is he the one after Esme?" Devon was guessing, but from the scowl on Tyree's face, he was right. "What happened, Tyree? Did Esme see him kill Jess?"

"This is none of your business anymore. It's between me and Leo. I'll deal with it in my own good time."

So it was Leo. Like father, like son. Both destroying the lives of the people who lived in the Tower. But Tyree's betrayal was worse— as bad as Mrs. Anders' and the other women who'd offered his mother up to Daniel Kingston. Devon's gaze measured Tyree in the dim light. "What size you wear, Tyree?"

"Why?"

"I'm gonna get you a new suit. Real nice one. Nice enough for a funeral. You'll be wearing it if I don't get Esme back. Alive."

"You talk big, Runt. But you don't know shit." He whistled, and two men dragging a third emerged from the tunnels behind them.

They entered the room. The third man was Harold. Unconscious, maybe dead.

Before Devon could move, Tyree whirled and fired his weapon at the cop. Three shots, all in the kill zone. The sound boomed through the small room, echoing into Devon's bones.

"You really thought you could come on back to my town and send your men poking and prodding into my business and get away with it?" Tyree shot Harold in the face.

"Don't bother looking for your other two men. Nice thing about having the tunnels connecting the Tower to Good Sam. Hospital has an incinerator that comes in real handy at times." He stepped back to admire his handiwork. Harold, by some miracle, was still breathing, gasps bubbling through the bloody mess that was his face. Tyree shot him twice more in the chest.

He turned to Devon. Raised the gun at him. Devon's heart stumbled, then stopped for a moment that hung between them. Everything he'd done, everything he still had to do—like saving Esme—it was all for nothing.

Then Tyree grinned. He flipped his grip on the pistol, holding it for Devon's inspection. "Recognize this? You should. It's yours."

The one the cops had taken from Devon earlier at the hospital. Ryder. Was he in on this? Devon would have bet good money that the detective was one of the good guys. But, hell, he'd been wrong about so much since he'd come home, maybe he'd been wrong about Ryder as well.

Trust no one. When was he going to learn?

"Here's the deal," Tyree said. "I can't afford pissing off the Russians, so I won't kill you unless I have to. You leave town. Forever. Today. You do, I'll work a deal with Kingston, see to it that Esme lives. You don't, the cops get this gun complete with your prints all over it, and she dies."

CHAPTER THIRTY-FOUR

WAKING UP BESIDE Ryder was an unexpected surprise. Not because of the man. Believe me, I'd love to do more than just sleep beside Ryder. Smart, handsome in an irresistible, weathered, world-weary way, and even more attractive—at least to me—was the way he took nothing and no one for granted. Seven scrawny anonymous kids from the Tower were just as important to him as Sister Patrice or meeting with Daniel Kingston himself.

As much as I'd love for Ryder to share some of that passion with me, it was the worst idea ever in the history of worst ideas. In the past twelve hours, my life had spiraled into a headlong rush to insanity.

I couldn't risk pulling Ryder down with me. Even more, I didn't want to risk losing his friendship. And one thing was becoming clear: If my symptoms continued to escalate, I'd be in no position to pursue any kind of more meaningful relationship.

So, attraction or no attraction, this wasn't going any further than it already had.

I sat up slowly, trying not to wake him—or Ozzie, who was snoring so loudly I wondered if they made CPAP machines for dogs. I couldn't believe how good I felt. A little sore and achy—no surprise, given what my body had gone through during my fugue states last night. But what was surprising was the energy. It surged through me like a shot of adrenaline.

Sunlight streamed in through the bay window. I glanced at the clock. Seven-forty. Amazing what an hour of sleep could do. One hour of sleep in five months? It wasn't a world record. There've been people who have gone years without a full night's sleep, but I already missed it and yearned for more.

I stood and stretched. Ryder's eyes were open, watching me with a definitely non-clinical appraisal. I imagined what it would be like seeing him look at me every morning. Inhaled so fast my gut ached. Not in the cards, I reminded myself with regret.

I used his bathroom and when I returned, he had Ozzie set up on the back porch. "You know," he said as he handed me my coat and helped me on with it, "as a detective, I have keen powers of observation and insight into the human condition."

He grabbed his own coat and held the door for me. I was creating a checklist in my mind, prioritizing everything I needed to do today: find a safe place for the kids, follow up on Allie and the other victims' lab results, come clean with Louise and submit to her poking and prodding, maybe find out what was wrong with me…

"What?" I asked, stumbling over a nonexistent crack in the walk leading from Ryder's front porch.

"I was saying, over the twelve hours I've known you, my keen powers of observation have told me that you find me irresistible. And yet, you were going to sneak out without saying a word this morning, weren't you?" His tone was light, but there was an undercurrent that felt all too heavy.

It took me a few seconds to process what he was saying. Ryder was right. I had been giving him mixed signals. Not because I wasn't sure how I felt. Because I wasn't sure what was wrong with me. Could I really expect anyone to dive down that rabbit hole before I had any answers?

No. Of course not.

"You're right, I'm an idiot." He filled in the silence as if I'd spoken. "We have to focus on what's important. Finding Esme and taking care of the kids and stopping Allie's killer. We work together. It's a conflict of interest. Against the rules, right?" A regretful tone entered his voice. "Right." His tone turned firm, a soldier receiving orders. "Of course. Sorry I even brought it up."

We turned onto the sidewalk. I wanted to tell him the truth about what was going on with me. But how could I? I didn't even know what to say without sounding crazy. Why had it been so easy telling Devon last night? I guess because he was a stranger. I had no real feelings about him, would never see him again once we found Esme.

"Although," Ryder continued, "way the brass feel about me right now, I'm sure it wouldn't be too hard for me to arrange to be transferred somewhere else so we wouldn't have to work together. I'm sure they have openings in the motor pool or maybe as a crossing guard."

"Stop it." I spun to face him, stumbling off-balance. He caught me by the elbow and steadied me. "Just stop it. You can't abandon those kids or the Advocacy Center. Besides, you won't have to—I'm leaving."

His mouth sagged open. "Why would you—"

"I'm sick." There, it was out.

His eyes widened, and his grip on my arm tightened. Not painfully, more like he didn't want to risk losing me. Wind from the river whipped between us, carrying the scent of snow. He edged closer to me, our breath mingling to create a cloud. "You're sick? What's wrong? Is it serious?"

His words tumbled over themselves, as clumsy as my feet. He pulled me to him, his breath in my ear, warming at least one small part of my body. We stood there, oblivious to the cold for a long moment before I pushed away. I wiped my eyes and began walking once more. Two steps later, he was by my side, his hand wrapped around mine.

"I haven't slept in five months," I started. "Not until this morning."

"This morning? That was barely a catnap. Wait. Did you say five months?"

"No sleep. Plus, losing my balance. Tremors in my muscles.

Fevers, night sweats." I gave him the litany of symptoms. Well, the ones that didn't make me sound insane. "And now, last night, I started having spells where my whole body just freezes up."

"Like seizures? When I was a kid, a girl in our class had petit mal epilepsy. She'd stare off into space, frozen. They have medicine for that, right?"

He sounded so damn hopeful, I couldn't steal that from him. After all, the man had known me for only twelve hours. It wasn't his burden to shoulder. "Epilepsy would be the best-case scenario. But I don't know. I'm going to see my friend, Louise Mehta, this morning. She's a neurologist. She'll figure this out."

"You think it's something bad. So bad that you didn't see a doctor sooner. Like what? A brain tumor? Something like that?"

I dropped his hand. God, I was so damn tired of not knowing. "Maybe. I'm not sure. Point is, I've got a lot on my plate right now."

"Oh. I see. This is you letting me off the hook."

"No. Ryder, no." I stopped, turned to face him. I couldn't read his expression, which seemed to happen when he had feelings too deep to share with the world. Maybe that was for the best. "This is me asking you, as someone I trust—as one of the few people I trust—not to give up on Esme or those kids. If I can't be there for them, I need to know someone is still fighting for them."

He stared at me, his eyes matching the sky behind him, a blue so bright it made you want to paint with it. A blue that should have made me feel happy, hopeful, but that instead made me regret everything I was about to lose.

I wanted to be that person, the Hallmark type: brave and strong, facing a life-changing illness with courage and dignity. But, looking into his eyes, it took everything I had not to turn tail and run home, grab my fiddle, lock myself in my apartment, and play, play, play until the music flew me away to another world, another life.

"Okay." His shoulders rose and fell with his exhalation as his posture relaxed. "If that's what you need."

"Thanks, Ryder."

We walked in silence, our hands occasionally brushing. It felt so comfortable, being able to think without worrying about holding up a conversation. Finally we arrived at the staff entrance behind the ER, dodging the horde of media camped out at the hospital's front door.

Ryder rested his hand on the door but didn't open it, blocking my path. I didn't like the look in his eyes—no, that was wrong. I liked it, very much. But it was dangerous. And confusing. Didn't he understand? We couldn't do this.

He leaned forward, and I turned my face away before he could kiss me. But he wasn't aiming for my lips. Instead, he kissed the top of my head, gently, with care. The second surprise of the morning. First, actual sleep, and now this…I didn't even know what to call this.

His eyes crinkled in delight at my puzzlement. "I'll call you later."

"To see what the children say." I tried to put things back on a business platform.

"No. I mean, yes, I want to hear what you learn. But that's not the only reason why I'll be calling." He touched my cheek, brushed my hair away from my eyes. "Good luck."

He was gone before I could figure out a response. I stood there, staring, even after he'd vanished from sight, my eyes foggy with tears. I was numb, not from the cold or exhaustion, but from all the possibilities, each uncertain, each fraught with pain and danger. Not just for me, but despite my best efforts, for Ryder as well.

I wasn't sure if I had the strength to carry that burden. Wasn't sure if I could resist the temptation.

I grabbed the cold metal handle and opened the door to the ER. My true home, my comfort zone. The place where I felt in control. Until now.

CHAPTER THIRTY-FIVE

BRUSHING MY TEETH, showering, and changing into clean clothes—
the slacks and blouse I kept in my locker for court—felt almost as
good as the hour of sleep had. As soon as I finished cleaning up, I
went over to the Advocacy Center. Couldn't resist checking on the
kids, and who knew, depending on what Louise found, if I'd be able
to come back again?

They were asleep, bundled together in a pile of arms and legs and
blankets. The nurse watching them said they'd all eaten—piling their
food together and sharing, but without talking—and then had fallen
back asleep. The psychologist was due in an hour, so no answers as
far as any prognosis or course of treatment.

None of them had asked for their families. And social services had
gotten nowhere.

I watched them from the observation window, tempted to call
Tyree and press him for answers. I hated that I had to trust that he
truly was trying to protect the children. But they were safe here
behind the locked doors of the Advocacy Center, away from the
prying eyes of the press and, with police officers guarding the
entrance, also from whoever had taken them.

Nothing more I could do here. My phone buzzed. Louise calling.
Time to face my future.

"YOUR MESSAGE LAST night," she said as we sat in her office, Louise behind the desk and me in one of the patient chairs. "It sounded, you sounded," she glanced up at the ceiling as if seeking guidance, "agitated."

"Good word for it."

"So it wasn't some kind of joke?" I stared at her. She shook her head, as if chiding herself for even considering the idea. "Okay. Tell me everything. From the beginning. When did your symptoms start?"

She took it better than I expected. After her first reaction of shock, then chiding me for not coming to her earlier, she listened, fascinated by my description of my fugue states and communicating with Patrice, Allie, and Mrs. Kowacz.

"Everything they said—Patrice's voice, her image of Esme, how she got shot, Mrs. Kowacz's ring, Allie playing the piano—it's all true. There's no way I could have imagined it," I finished in a rush, feeling emptied. I sat back and waited for her judgment. Hated the way she looked at me like a patient. Hated even more that she didn't immediately clap her hands together in that funny way she has and tell me the answer complete with a magical cure.

Instead, she frowned. Not an encouraging frown, either. "It could have been your imagination," she said. "Filling in the gaps of what you expected."

"Why would I expect a nun I'd never met to talk to me while I held her heart in my hands and tell me about a missing girl who I also never met?"

"The mind is a mysterious thing. Memories even more so. You know that from your work at the Advocacy Center—how easy it is to accidentally plant a so-called memory by simple suggestion. Maybe it wasn't until after you learned the girl was missing that you thought you remembered the nun telling it to you?"

I shook my head. Not sure why I felt the need to defend the veracity of my visions, spells, whatever the hell they were. After all, if I agreed with her, then I was just a wee bit delusional, something easily explained by sleep deprivation and stress.

But, no. I had to insist on being full-blown psychotic. "I know what I know. You can ask Ryder. I told him about Esme being missing, not the other way around."

She made a note—probably to remind her to verify that Ryder actually existed and wasn't another delusion. Then she made me change into a patient gown and did a complete examination. It was obvious that she didn't like what she found. Next thing I knew, she had me whisked away for an EEG and MRI, tests that, if the results were abnormal, there'd be no hiding it from the rest of my colleagues. No such thing as patient confidentiality when the patient is a physician.

Two hours later, her nurse ushered me into Louise's exam room. I changed back into my street clothes—being a patient was so damn humiliating—and took a seat, waiting impatiently. No, more than impatient. Angry.

Because, damn it, I wanted my life back. In my control. And to do that I needed to know the face of my enemy. Needed something to fight.

She walked in without knocking, head facedown in my chart.

"What did the MRI show?" I asked.

Louise leaned against the closed door, looking down at where I sat in the swivel chair traditionally reserved for the physician. I'd taken the chair by habit and, once in it, couldn't bring myself to move to the patient chair.

Her face, a mask denying all emotion, told me everything, but I needed to hear the words. I felt a twinge of guilt, forcing a friend to give me my death sentence. But better a friend…

She took her time sitting down in the patient chair, adjusting the seat, arranging the papers that had quickly filled my chart. From my vantage point, I saw pages of lab results, EEG tracings, an MRI report. I was too far away to read them. I would eventually, of course—part of being a doctor is being a snoop. But, for now, I waited.

Not so patiently.

She reached past me to bring up my MRI on the computer screen. "No tumor or aneurysm."

Suddenly, I could breathe again. Oxygen rushed into my brain, making red spots dance in my vision.

Louise cleared her throat, and I knew my relief had been premature. "But there is evidence of microvacuolization in the thalamic region."

She zoomed in on the image of my brain. Vacuolization? Part of my brain was filling with tiny holes, turning into Swiss cheese. Even I could see them on the magnified MRI.

"What's causing them? MS? Some other demyelinating disease?" I'd heard of vacuolization before, but always as a result of severe brain trauma or metabolic diseases. Never with symptoms like mine. I braced myself, thinking I might have a rocky road ahead of me but certain I could navigate it. Even diseases like MS are no longer the death sentences they once were.

I was wrong. So wrong.

Louise shifted uncomfortably. "I need a blood test to confirm."

"Blood test to confirm what?"

She didn't answer me.

A frown broke through her rigid mask. She stifled it, sorting the lab results neatly into my chart. Louise was methodical, but I couldn't wait for confirmation. I needed to start fighting this thing. Now. "Test for what?"

"Prion diseases. Specifically Creutzfeldt-Jakob and variants, including fatal familial insomnia."

"Mad cow disease? But I've never been exposed—" Her words caught up to me. "Fatal insomnia? What the hell is that?"

"Hereditary disease discovered by an Italian doctor in the 1700s. He was the first documented fatality from it as well."

Louise was good—but knowing the specifics about a disease that I'd never even heard of? She must have looked it up before coming in to talk with me. "You think that's the one, don't you? Fatal insomnia?"

"I don't know. The blood tests will take a few weeks to come back. The only lab that does them is in Italy."

Fatal insomnia. The words collided in my brain, didn't make any sense. Except... "All those years of medical school and residency, training myself to not need sleep—not to mention the crazy mixed-up shifts I work in the ER. And now you're telling me I might actually die from insomnia?"

"You're young for it." She was hedging. "But the stress of your altered sleep-wake cycle could have precipitated it."

"How many patients we talking about? Is there a cure?"

"A few hundred known cases."

That was pretty damn rare. No wonder I'd never heard of it. "Yearly?"

She shook her head. "Total. Since 1765. From the brief research I was able to do, there are about sixty today. Alive. Across the entire planet. The only research center is in Italy. I'm waiting to hear back from them on treatment options."

"Sixty out of seven billion people on the planet. That's like one in a million."

"More like one in one hundred million."

My brain was struggling to comprehend the odds. Although, who cared about the odds when you were the one? "Luck like that, I should buy a lottery ticket."

She ducked her head, focusing on the papers before her. And it hit me. What she already knew but couldn't say.

Why bother buying a lottery ticket when you weren't going to be around long enough to see if you won?

She reached a hand toward my shoulder.

Toddler that I am at times, I pushed hard with my feet, propelling the wheeled stool out of range of her comfort.

Louise crossed her arms, hugging my chart to her chest. "There's been speculation that quinacrine may slow the progression—"

"Do I have time for speculation?"

"Maybe." She hesitated, her mind scouring a hundred checklists of variables. "The average time from start of symptoms until death is eighteen months." She scribbled a prescription for the quinacrine. "If I'm wrong, it won't hurt anything. It's worth a try while we're waiting for the genetic test results. In the meantime, you need to quit working."

I took the tiny piece of paper, held it between my fingers, waving in the air. "Quit?"

"Take leave." She tried to soften the blow. "And no more driving. At least until we know for sure."

I stood, the blood rushing to my toes in an ice-cold wave of fear.

"Angela, I'm sorry. Maybe I'm wrong. I hope I am."

Louise was never wrong. Not about something this important.

"You can cross it off your list," I said as I opened the door to leave.

She frowned, blinked as if there might be tears in her eyes, and nodded. Neither of us had to say what she would be crossing off her to-do list.

No doubt, some polite variant of: Tell Angela Rossi she's dying.

CHAPTER THIRTY-SIX

I RETREATED TO my office in the Advocacy Center and hit Medline—the medical community's online search engine—hard.

No mention of talking dead nuns or other abnormal communication in any of the fatal insomnia literature. But other almost equally weird symptoms abounded. Catatonic states that sounded like my fugues. People suddenly performing wildly creative feats.

Like a guy who had only a high school education solving a complex math theorem that had stumped geniuses like Einstein for centuries, or a woman who previously had no writing ambition creating a remarkable, award-winning literary gem. As if they were tapping previously unexplored regions of their brains.

Sparks of genius tempering their descent into madness. Four months later, that savant mathematician went on a crazy spree and took his own life by walking naked into the ocean. And the novelist? She ended up in a strait jacket to prevent herself from gouging her eyes out and tearing her skin off after she ate her own lips.

This was the fate waiting for me if Louise's tests came back positive. Who said God didn't have a sense of humor? I mean, just the concept: fatal insomnia. It made as much sense as a platypus.

Except it was no joke.

Finally, I turned the computer off and wandered over to the observation room to check on the kids. The psychologist had finished her initial interviews, and they'd fallen back asleep. Sleeping like the dead. The irony wasn't lost on me. I felt strangely numb, removed from the whole situation. After all, what could I do? I still didn't have an answer.

Damn, I hated being a patient.

A soft knock came at the door. Devon Price. Different designer suit but the same wary, weary expression.

"Figured you'd be here. I need to ask a favor." He shifted his weight as if his Italian loafers pinched.

"Sure. What do you need?"

"Could you take a ride with me?"

I wasn't exactly in the mood for company. "Can't. I have to see what the psychologist learned from these guys. We still don't know where their families are."

He frowned, obviously not accustomed to anyone saying no to him. "You do this for me, and I'll tell you what you need to know about the kids."

"Devon, if you know something—" Anger that he'd use the children as leverage sparked through me.

He ignored me, staring through the observation window, one hand pressed to the glass, watching the little girl he'd made laugh last night flail in her sleep, until another child reached out to soothe her and pull her back into the fold.

"Believe me, there's no rush learning what I know."

"Tell me."

He sighed and turned to face me. "You're not going to find their families. They haven't got any. At least none that can take care of them."

That's what Tyree had said, but I hadn't believed him. "How do you know that?"

"The reason why Tyree hid them was to protect them from the man who drugged and raped their mothers."

I stared at him then past him to the sleeping children. "The PXA victims, the ones up in Psych—"

"The ones still alive. I'm guessing there were others and you'll never find their bodies."

It made sense in a warped way. All our victims were single, I couldn't remember if they were all mothers, but they might have been—we'd had a hard enough time identifying them, plus it wouldn't have been part of their ER chart whether or not they had children. Maybe in the police files—but Harrison had been in charge of the investigation, and he was dead.

Suddenly, I wondered if that car accident of his had been an accident after all.

"Did Tyree tell you who was behind the rapes?" I asked.

He shoved his hands in his pockets, ruining the lines of his silk suit. "Nothing anyone can use as proof. But maybe, if you come with me—" He let the offer dangle like bait.

Not like I was going to be much help to the kids, not if what he said was true. With Ryder searching for Esme, there was nothing more I could do for her. "Is this going to help find Esme?"

"I hope so." His voice dropped. Low and deadly…with a touch of desperation.

"Where?"

"Out to see my mom."

I stared at him. "I thought your mom was dead."

He shook his head, looking at the ground. For the first time, I realized how young he was. Not even thirty. Funny, last night I would have pegged him as much older. "Not dead. Just gone."

"You said she had a heroin overdose—" I remembered him telling me about her last night. But he hadn't actually said she was dead, had he?

"Heroin mixed with fentanyl. Persistent vegetative state, the doctors call it. Since I was eight. Once I had some money, I found her a nice place, just outside of town. Real pretty."

My stomach lurched as I realized what he was asking. "You want me to—"

Finally, he met my gaze. All he did was nod.

I held my breath, fighting my initial impulse to tell him no. Fear knotted my throat. But if it would help find Esme, how could I say no?

❂

FLYNN'S ADRENALINE REFLEX was on hyperdrive as she and Esme huddled in the rear corner of the ER's waiting room. Too many people. Too many eyes.

At least she had their backs to the wall and, since they'd come in through the main entrance, they didn't have to go through the ER's metal detectors, so Flynn still had her gun.

But she hated feeling this exposed. Anyone could report back to Leo or Tyree or the cops or someone somewhere, and next thing you knew, there'd be bullets flying again.

Flynn could count the number of people she trusted in this world on one hand. Angela Rossi probably didn't even remember who Flynn was. Why should she? She saved lives every day. But she was someone Flynn trusted. And she'd been in those tunnels last night, risking her life to help Esme. Who else could Flynn turn to now?

Esme had fallen asleep, her head cradled in Flynn's lap, Flynn's coat wrapped around her, shielding her from prying eyes. Flynn envied the girl. Couldn't remember the last time she'd slept that good—years. Not since the first night Creepy Wayne, her mom's boyfriend, crept into her bedroom. She'd been about Esme's age.

Wished she'd had the gun way back when. Instead, it had taken four years and her almost dying before she'd found the courage to kill that son of a bitch.

That was three years ago. But she still saw Creepy Wayne's bloody face screaming at her every time she closed her eyes.

Finally, a nurse called the fake name Flynn had given. Flynn carefully cradled Esme, the little girl whimpering in her sleep before curling her body against Flynn's chest as she threaded her way through the crowded room and through the door.

The nurse led Flynn and Esme through the maze of tiled corridors that made up Good Sam's ER. Sounds of a man crying mixed with a toddler's laughter and a raspy vibration like a drill, the people creating the sounds sequestered behind closed doors and curtains, leaving Flynn's imagination to fill in the nasty blanks. "Dr. Rossi left already."

"I really need to speak with her," Flynn said in an official tone. The overworked registration clerk hadn't asked to see any ID or questioned Flynn when she'd identified herself as a social worker caring for a patient from the Advocacy Center. Flynn wasn't surprised. Despite her youth, few people ever questioned her authority. One of the perks of being reborn in your own image. She didn't take shit from anyone, and the rest of the world instinctively understood that.

"Reception said this is another one of Dr. Rossi's children from the tunnels?" the nurse asked, unlocking a set of doors that led to the Advocacy Center. Flynn didn't correct her misassumption—not as long as it got her what she wanted. "We're keeping them safe from the media in here. We can let her sleep with the rest. Dr. Rossi said she'd be back to check on them later today."

They stopped outside a large interview room. There was a picture window, its drapes open, revealing a group of kids piled together, sleeping on mattresses covering the floor, a bored-appearing nurse reading in an armchair above them. Flynn shifted Esme's weight, buying time to process the sight and the nurse's words. There'd been other kids down there in the tunnels? And somehow Dr. Rossi had found them and was taking care of them?

Whatever was going on, the Advocacy Center was the last place anyone would be looking for Esme. She'd stay safe for now. Giving Flynn time to figure out how to keep her alive.

Not to mention how to stop Leo. Daniel expected her to do the impossible, and so far she'd never let him down, but maybe saving Leo was asking too much. All Daniel wanted was to make sure his son was safe before the cancer took him, that the family name and business would be protected. At all costs.

Except Leo had turned it into this crazy cat-and-mouse game—and she wasn't sure anymore that she was still the cat. If Leo was the one trying to kill Esme, how could she stop him without betraying Daniel?

The nurse opened the door, the click of the lock startling Esme awake. The girl struggled in Flynn's arms until Flynn set her on her feet. She was half-afraid Esme would take off running, but instead, she threw herself at Flynn, wrapping her arms around Flynn's neck, tight.

"Can I have a minute?" Flynn asked. She didn't sound official, not with Esme clutching at her, but the nurse gave a weary smile, as if she was used to seeing her patients break hearts, and entered the room without them.

They were alone in the hall.

"Don't go, don't go," Esme cried. "I'm scared."

"It's okay, Esme. You'll be safe here. I'll be back first thing in the morning." She turned Esme around so the girl could look through the window. "Do you recognize any of those kids?"

"Sure. That's Andre and Zachariah and Venice. We're all in Mrs. Anders' Sunday School class. Why are they here? Did something bad happen to them, too?"

"I think maybe. But the nurses and doctors here are taking good care of them. And they'll take care of you until I can get back. Can you remember the name I told you to use?"

Esme nodded.

Flynn swallowed hard. It was the name of her real little sister—the one she'd protected by killing Creepy Wayne before he could start messing with her. The one she hadn't seen in three years. Not since she'd died and been reborn.

Dr. Rossi had worked a miracle then, bringing a frozen, drowned girl back to life. Flynn would have to trust that she could work another and keep Esme safe.

"That's right. Listen, anyone asks, that's your name and you were in the tunnel and you're too scared to talk to anyone but me and Dr.

Rossi."

"Who's Dr. Rossi?"

"Did you see the lady in the tunnel who had your dog with her?" Esme nodded. "That's Dr. Rossi. She's one of the good guys. If I'm not back—" Meaning if Leo killed her before she could get back. "If I'm not back, you tell Dr. Rossi everything. Your real name and what happened."

Esme shook her head. "But the bad police, they'll come back."

Flynn froze. "Bad police?"

Esme nodded. Slow and steady, like she knew she'd said too much. "They shot my mommy."

"Esme. You need to tell me everything." Flynn crouched down so that she was at Esme's eye level. "It's really important, okay?"

Esme considered, then gathered herself and nodded. "Yesterday morning, a man called. He said to tell Uncle Tyree that he wanted his ring back or he'd be paying him a visit."

"He called your home, not your uncle's?"

"I told Uncle Tyree what the man said, just like he asked, but Uncle Tyree got all upset. It scared me. And Mommy. They were yelling and fighting, and he told her we couldn't leave the apartment, then slammed out."

"Then what happened?"

"Mommy said she'd had enough of Uncle Tyree, and she called a friend. Guess they weren't home, because then she called Sister Patrice, but she was at the soup kitchen, and by the time she got there—" Her voice trembled, and she looked down at her feet. "That's when the bad people came. They—they hurt my mommy and we ran. Sister Patrice told me to hide, to climb up to the metal sidewalk—"

"The catwalk."

"Yes'm, that. But it was too high, I couldn't reach it, so I stayed on the bookshelves and went as far as I could, away from the door where the bad police would be coming from. But, but they still found me."

She was sobbing now but bit her lip, trying to deny her tears. "Are you gonna let the bad police shoot me? Like they did my mommy?" She threw her arms around Flynn, almost knocking Flynn over. "Please don't let them kill me dead."

CHAPTER THIRTY-SEVEN

DEVON DROVE. A black Town Car, which didn't seem to suit his personality. Maybe the persona he tried to project, but not the man who had coaxed smiles out of seven traumatized children last night. We headed west, up into the mountains.

"You never told me. What do you do? For a living?"

His smile was a slippery one. Fit the car more than the man I'd come to know. "You never asked. I'm in acquisitions."

He was lying to me. I felt disappointed. After all, he knew my biggest secret. "So, you followed in your father's footsteps."

It was cruel. A reminder that I knew his secrets as well. But I didn't apologize.

He jerked his head to face me, ignoring the road. I'd seen that look before, on the faces of angry men, ready to do violence.

"No." He fired the word like a bullet. "Not like my father. Nothing at all like my father."

Another lie. I leaned back in my seat, watching him, waiting.

"Daniel Kingston raped and tortured innocent women to keep control of his property, turn a profit. That's not me, not who I am."

"Who are you, Devon?"

He blew his breath out, his frustration circling between us. "I've killed men. Self-defense, mainly—guess it depends on how you define it. But that was a long time ago. And they weren't exactly what you'd call innocent."

His voice dropped as if he were in a confessional. "Sometimes, when I do the things I do, people get hurt. And sometimes I do feel good about it." He slid a glance in my direction, pleading. "That's not why I hurt them, but sometimes it's just the only way to get the job done."

I knew damn well he was talking about a hell of a lot more than the pain we doctors rationalize inflicting. But I kept remembering how he was last night with those kids, the way he risked his life trying to find Esme. "Sorry. I was wrong."

He shook his head as if I'd misunderstood, his attention focused on the road, anywhere but on me. "All my life I've spent hating him, dreaming about how I'd kill him when I finally came home. Sometimes, that anger is all that keeps me going. I can't give it up. It's an addiction, takes everything I have not to give in to it."

"Which is exactly why you're nothing like your father."

He still didn't believe me. I understood. Some things you have to figure out for yourself, can't trust someone else to tell you the truth.

"You said Tyree told you who was behind the PXA attacks," I said.

He gave a grunt of disgust. "Kingston's son. Leo."

I thought about it. If Daniel Kingston made Leo the CEO of the pharmaceutical company he was bringing to Cambria, it made sense that Leo had a background in chemistry. Which would go with Ryder's theory that the rapes were secondary to the PXA drug being modified. What had he called it? A twisted clinical trial. "Why would Leo kill Sister Patrice and Jess?"

"I'm guessing they saw something they shouldn't have."

"And Esme? You think Leo might have something to do with Esme?"

He didn't answer right away. "Do you think you can do that thing you do? With my mother."

Funny. Louise thought my newfound ability to communicate with the not-quite-dead was a simple delusion—my Swiss-cheese brain filling in details, making them seem real. She was my best friend and doubted me. Yet, this man, a virtual stranger, he believed. Had faith.

In me. "How does your mother fit in?"

"I need something she has."

"You mean something she has to tell me, don't you?"

He hesitated, staring at the road before us. Then nodded. "If you can reach her, I'm hoping she can tell you where Daniel Kingston used to take her."

One coherent memory from a woman who'd suffered years of abuse and drug use before she fell into a persistent vegetative state two decades ago? "You know it's a long shot. Your mom's brain waves probably won't have the right pattern. Why is it important to know where Daniel took her twenty years ago? If Leo has Esme, why would he take her to the same place when he has the tunnels and property all over the city?"

He swallowed so hard his Adam's apple jerked up and down. "If Leo has Esme, the only reason he'd keep her alive is to torture me. Best way to do that would be to make her suffer like my mother did."

I blanched. Esme was just a child—to think of her in the hands of the sadist who'd hurt Allie and those other women was unimaginable. Except I didn't have to imagine it. Thanks to Allie, I'd lived through it.

We pulled up to a large Queen Anne house—almost but not quite a mansion, probably built by some turn-of-the-century banker or railroad magnate as a country home a hundred-plus years ago. The discreet sign in front read: Holbrook Care Facility.

The receptionist knew Devon by sight—as John Smith. So unoriginal. Who'd believe it was an alias? "Mr. Smith, it's nice to see you again." Her gaze settled on me with curiosity. "And you brought a friend."

She signed us in—no tacky sticky name tags here. Instead, Devon got a custom ID badge to clip to his suit coat, and I got a generic visitor's one. I followed Devon through the halls, the only sound our footsteps on the polished dark wood floors and the occasional distant muted tone of a woman's voice.

"John Smith?" I asked once we were out of sight of the

receptionist.

"No one knows about this place. No one. It was the only way I could keep her safe."

I had a feeling he brought me here for more reasons than just one. "You're worried this is your last time here."

He shrugged. "You've met Tyree. I watched him kill a cop this morning. Didn't blink twice."

"He killed a cop? We need to tell Ryder."

"Tell Ryder?" He made a sound that was half-scoff and half-growl. "Seeing as how Tyree shot the cop—who'd just killed an innocent woman himself—with the gun that Ryder took from me... Well, let's just say, I'm pretty sure Ryder already knows all about it."

I reached for my phone. He laid a hand on my arm. Not tight or even painful. Just a warning. We were playing by his rules now.

"Ryder had nothing to do with sending a cop to kill anyone—or with helping Tyree to frame you. He handed that pistol off to patrol officers. Besides, we were together pretty much all night long. And he almost got killed trying to find Esme, don't forget that."

A crease formed along his forehead. Exhaustion rimmed his eyes. "Maybe he didn't know," he conceded. "But one thing I do know is Tyree is taking orders from Daniel Kingston. So that's all the more reason not to get Ryder involved, put a target on his back as well."

He released my arm. "You do what you think is right. But I'm not talking to any cops or wasting any time giving evidence. As of now, I'm not trusting anyone with anything until I have Esme back safe and sound."

I pulled my cell phone out, glanced at it, then returned it to my pocket. "Let's see what happens here first. But, if this is a dead end, we need to let Ryder know. That way, we'll have leverage to use on Tyree."

"Tyree doesn't know where Esme is. If he did, he'd be using her against me instead of running me out of town with threats. Way I see it, the person we need to get leverage on is Leo Kingston. Or, even better, his father."

We reached a bedroom door. He knocked and entered without waiting. He knew no one would answer.

It could have been a room at any upscale bed-and-breakfast: bright chintz curtains, antique dresser and rocking chair, tasteful art prints. Only the bed—a special air bed designed to minimize the risk of pressure sores—and the woman lying motionless in it revealed the truth.

Devon approached the bed and sat on the edge, taking the woman's hand. She lay with her face turned to the left, as if looking out the window. She didn't look old enough to be his mother. Her face was too peaceful, no wrinkles or worry lines. Her hair was neatly braided, one long rope of hair draped elegantly over her left shoulder. She wore a burgundy dressing gown that enhanced her dark complexion.

"Hi, Mom. It's me. This is Angela. Angela Rossi. She's a doctor. Been helping me." He glanced at me. "Angela, meet my mother, Tanesha Price."

There was a single framed photo on the table beside me. A woman in her twenties bouncing a baby boy on her lap. Her smile had a radiance to it that reminded me of the stained-glass saints at St. Tim's. But she wasn't looking up at God or anyone else. Her gaze centered on the boy with such focus and power, it was as if the rest of the world didn't exist. "She was beautiful."

"She still is," he said, stroking Tanesha's arm.

There was a gentle knock on the door, and a nurse entered carrying a basin, a bottle of no-rinse shampoo, and a stack of towels. "Mr. Smith, I heard you were visiting today. I know how you like to help with her hair."

Devon smiled and took the basin and towels from her. "Thanks, Michele. I'll take it from here."

The nurse nodded and left. Devon hung up his suit coat and rolled up his sleeves. Hidden beneath his clothing were scars—old ones.

"Burns?" I asked.

He glanced down at his arms as if he'd forgotten they were there. "Most are from the fire. When Jess…was hurt. We were kids, looking for a place to make out and stumbled across a new lab Tyree had set up."

"Booby-trapped?" I remembered the blackened door we had passed last night down in the tunnels.

"Yes. The room went up so fast. I pulled Jess out, but something splashed in her face…" He turned away, pretended to be concentrating on washing his hands. "It was in the ER we learned she was pregnant. Best and worst night of my life."

I said nothing. What was there to say, except empty platitudes? He dried his hands, positioned the basin on the chest of drawers beside Tanesha's bed and sat on the edge of the bed.

"Nothing compared to her scars," he said. Gently, he slid a palm between her left cheek and the pillow and turned her so that I could see her entire face.

Under her left eye was a brand. Exactly like the one Allie and the other victims had had seared into their flesh.

Tanesha's had healed, and I could finally make out details. Two letters, a D and a K, arranged to look like a crown resting on a man's head.

Daniel Kingston's insignia.

CHAPTER THIRTY-EIGHT

"What caused that mark?" Angela pointed to the brand on Devon's mother's cheek.

"One guess," he said bitterly. He undid Tanesha's braid and combed the no-rinse shampoo through her thick hair. "Daniel Kingston's signet ring. His special calling card."

"Devon." He glanced up at the excitement in her voice. "Allie and the other victims. They all have a brand just like this. It was swollen and inflamed, too fresh to get a decent idea of the details, but I'm sure it's the same."

He finished combing Tanesha's hair and rebraided it. "I already told you it was Leo. How does knowing he's using his dad's ring to mark his victims help?"

"We don't have any proof. But a big heavy ring like that, full of nooks and crannies—almost impossible to clean completely. We might be able to match DNA from it to our victims."

"That will take weeks or months. Esme is out there now, and Leo's looking for her, wants her dead. If he doesn't already have her." Devon tied a burgundy ribbon around the end of the braid, carefully tucking the stray strands inside the bow. Every time he did this, he imagined braiding Esme's hair, Jess sitting beside him, like a normal family.

Imagining? More like wishing. The kind of wish that never came true.

"You ready to try this?" he asked Angela.

She didn't look ready for anything. Her face was pale, eyes sunken. Most of all, she looked afraid. First time he'd seen fear in her. He didn't blame her. This thing she did, who knew where it could lead a person? He'd almost lost her earlier when Allie died.

"I wish there was another way," he told her. It was only half a lie. He'd take any wisp of a clue if it led him to Esme.

She nodded and sat down on the opposite side of the bed, taking care not to touch his mother. She pulled in a deep breath, closed her eyes, and reached a hand to Tanesha's arm.

And then she was gone.

Devon wasn't sure if he'd ever get used to the way she was fully there, so vibrant, alive, one moment and then just…empty. Totally frozen, only the pulse at her neck and gentle rise and fall of her chest revealing any signs of life.

He watched her, realized something was different this time. Her eyes darted back and forth beneath closed lids. Her breathing was irregular, short little gasps followed by long—too long—pauses. The kind of breathing he'd seen in guys with sucking chest wounds, right before they died.

Devon was torn. He wanted to make sure she had all the time she needed, but he also couldn't risk her dying without telling him what she'd learned. He moved to her side of the bed, standing close but not touching her. Finally, when she stopped breathing so long that her lips went dusky and her body slid forward, all tone in the muscles gone, he caught her and grabbed her hand, removing it from Tanesha's body.

"Angela," he called, feeling for a pulse. It took a long time, but it was there. Barely. "Angela, come back now." In the ICU with Allie, just his touch had brought her back, even though Allie had been dying.

No response. At least she was still breathing. He carried her to a chair. She slumped, lifeless. "C'mon, wake up." He crouched beside her and shook her. Again, harder. Damn, what now?

Finally, he slapped her. Once, twice. Hard enough to rock her entire body. Christ, she was burning up. He grabbed the water basin and splashed water on her face, surprised it didn't sizzle.

Her lips moved the slightest bit. He grabbed her, rubbing her hands and arms, then lifting her chin to stroke her forehead and cheeks. "Angela, come back. Please, come back."

She choked and gagged like a drowning woman. Her entire body spasmed. Then, like turning a switch on, suddenly she was back, pushing and flailing and struggling as if fighting for her life.

Her eyes popped open, wide with terror, and she would have screamed if he hadn't covered her mouth.

"It's okay," he told her, trying to get her to focus on him. Her breath came in gasps so powerful he felt them cascade down the length of her body. "Angela, it's okay. Everything's okay."

She shook her head, pushed his hands away, and flung herself from the chair to the floor as she vomited into the basin he'd left there. Her body heaved over and over again, until finally she collapsed back against the wall, hair hanging in her face.

He took the basin, emptied it and rinsed it, then returned to kneel beside her on the floor, handing her a damp washcloth. Slowly, she relaxed against him. Less feverish but still warmer than normal. He gently lifted her back into the chair, then grabbed a glass of water, helped her drink it, her hands too unsteady to hold it on her own.

"Did you see anything?" he asked after she'd downed two full glasses and spilled half of another.

She held a hand up, pleading for time, and finished the third glass. Her gaze was haunted, spiraling around the room, never holding steady for longer than a few heartbeats. But her breathing was back to normal, and her trembling had eased.

Finally, she shook her head. "I'm sorry. There was nothing."

"Nothing?"

"Nothing." Her voice was a pale shadow of her normal clear alto. "Blackness…no, not even blackness. No color. No…anything." She blinked hard, gripped his arms, and stared at him. "I was lost, so lost, falling, it felt like forever. Nothing to measure time or distance, no memories, no…me."

"It was only a few minutes, shorter than when you were with Allie."

"Time doesn't matter. Not in there." She shuddered. "Devon, I'm sorry, so sorry."

He nodded, looking away to his mother lying on the bed. "It's okay." He knew this day would come. Just had always hoped…fool to ever hope. Of all people, he should have known better.

He left Angela and moved to stand beside his mother. She looked so peaceful. As if she were asleep. But now he knew better. "Give us a moment?"

Angela seemed to understand. She squeezed his shoulder. "I'm going to call Jacob, see if we have enough for a warrant to search for that signet ring. If any of our victims' DNA is on it—"

"Can't risk Esme's life on wishes and ifs," he told her. "She won't be safe until Leo is behind bars." Maybe not then. In fact, he wasn't counting on the cops to deal with Leo at all. That pleasure was going to be Devon's and Devon's alone.

Once Esme was safe. That was all that counted.

She nodded. "I'll wait at the car while you say good-bye." Then she surprised him by giving him a quick kiss on the cheek. "Devon. I'm so sorry I couldn't help. I wish—"

He looked away, his vision suddenly blurry. Blinking back unbidden tears, he told her, "You did the best you could. More than most would have been willing to do. Thanks."

She left the room, and it was just him and his mother. All alone. Just like it always had been.

"I miss you, Momma," he whispered as he tenderly pressed the heel of his hand over her lips, sealing her mouth, and then pinched her nostrils.

It had to be done. For her sake as well as his. Some small part of him, the eight-year-old boy who'd let Mrs. Anders whip his skinny body with rosary beads and dunk his head in holy water until he about drowned, that boy who'd held candles until they burned his flesh, willing to do anything if it meant the light in his mother's eyes returning even for one more day…that boy would always be hostage to his mother's memory as long as her body lived.

He stroked her hair, kissed her closed eyelids, crooning nonsense nursery songs to her as he sat with her until his hand cramped. "I love you. Always have and always will."

She never struggled, just one quick jerk toward the end, before the pulse fluttering at her neck faded away.

He released his hand, straightened her covers, and sat with her. Then, one final kiss. "This one's from Esme."

He stood and left his mother behind.

CHAPTER THIRTY-NINE

IT WASN'T DIFFICULT to find Rossi's address. She lived above a bar called Jimmy's Place. A workingman's bar in a working-class neighborhood half a dozen blocks from St. Tim's.

When Voorsanger had called Ryder, asking to meet someplace outside work, he'd been all too happy for an excuse to leave the brick walls he'd been banging his head against all day. He'd gone home, then walked here with the dog, Ozzie being better company for Ryder than Ryder would be to anyone else, mood he was in. Why wasn't Rossi answering her phone? Was she avoiding him? Or was it because she'd gotten bad news from the doctor?

No one objected to Ozzie's presence, but all heads swiveled to give Ryder the once-over when they entered, immediately marking him as an outsider. Ryder didn't mind, he was quickly caught in the spell of the music wafting from every corner of the dark-paneled, high-ceilinged room.

He stood for a moment, letting the cold breeze from the open door sway the tune around him. It sounded haunting, otherworldly, a woman sobbing for a lost love. He shook his head—lost love, yeah, right—and strode up to the bar in search of a little industrial-strength fortitude.

On the large-screen TV behind the bar played a video of another one of Rossi's past performances. The sound was nowhere near the quality of a live performance or even the computer video he'd seen yesterday, yet Ryder was transfixed.

Jimmy himself, according to the name embroidered on his shirt, took Ryder's order and delivered a beer to Ryder's waiting hand. The bartender had an average build, light-colored hair and dark eyes, with the ruddy complexion of someone who maybe sampled his wares a little too often.

"What's the name of that song?" Ryder asked.

"Ain't got no name. When the kid plays, she makes it up as it comes."

"The kid?"

The bartender straightened, aimed his chin at Rossi's image on the nearest screen. "My niece. She's something, isn't she?" The man had no evidence of Rossi's dark, Mediterranean looks. He was Irish, through and through.

"And the rest of the band?"

"Mickey's mine, playing the bodhrán," he indicated the drummer, "and Gino is a cousin from the kid's dad's side—Italian, that's her dad's own concertina he's playing."

"The flute player?" Voorsanger, gyrating his hips against Rossi's in time with the music.

"Penny whistle. That's Jacob. Somehow she let him get away." Jimmy shook his head, acknowledging his niece's mistake. "He plays fiddle as well, but not like her. Sings, too. Once they get back to songs that have words. Folks love when the kid comes to play live, even if they don't know the music—and they'll never hear it again, not the same way. Different every time. That's why we started taping them."

"How often does she perform?" With Voorsanger.

"Not often. Was supposed to play last night, but she had to work." Jimmy looked down as if ashamed. "She needs to get herself a man, settle down."

Ryder felt his pulse throb in his temples. "She" was an immensely talented and hard-working physician in an inner-city trauma center on the front lines. Her "work" as a victim's advocate made her elite even among the cadre of emergency physicians. And last night—well, last night had been a helluva lot more important than playing fiddle in some damn bar.

"But if it's live music you came for, don't worry none. There'll be plenty of it once the band gets a bite to eat." He nodded to a boisterous group at a table filled with empty pitchers and platters of food. A striking blond woman in her fifties sat at the head of the table, holding court.

He wondered if Rossi would be playing with them later tonight. She'd texted him about the brand on their victims possibly being linked to Kingston. Easy enough to get photographic documentation to verify it matched Kingston's ring. Now it was up to Voorsanger to get the DA to sign off on a warrant to search the Kingston mansion. And from the tone of his voice when he'd asked Ryder to meet him here, it hadn't sounded like good news.

As if on cue, Voorsanger came through the door. The atmosphere in the bar changed immediately—very different from Ryder's entrance. Members of the band and others scattered around the room waved or nodded a greeting, while Jimmy had a pint of Smithwick's poured and set on the bar before Voorsanger could get his coat off.

"Where's our lass?" Jimmy asked. He never used Rossi's name, Ryder noticed, wondering what family drama had sparked that. "Her mom wants her here tonight."

Despite his warm welcome, Voorsanger scowled past the bartender to the blonde sitting with the musicians. "Tell Patsy there are things that take precedence over her collecting yet another pound of flesh."

Ryder watched Jimmy, wondering what the uncle who so easily dismissed Rossi's professional accomplishments would say to that. He just grinned. "I'll not be telling her a damn thing, thank you very much. You want to enter the lion's den, be my guest." And he moved down the bar to pull another pitcher for the musicians.

"I take it Rossi and her family don't get along," Ryder said.

"What family does?" Voorsanger took a deep drink. "Let's just say that the Kiely clan—Angie's mother's side—get along best when they're playing music and drinking."

Ryder nodded to the TV screen. "She's really good."

Voorsanger smiled, watching his ex-wife—emphasis on the ex, Ryder thought—and himself play a duet, now both on the fiddle. "Yes. She is. That's a good one, from our Lovers' Laments. We used lyrics from *Sonnets from the Portuguese*, wove them into duets. My favorites are the ones when one part would be sung and the other played by an instrument." He reached behind the bar and emerged with a handful of CDs. "Here, have a listen yourself."

"Rossi sings?" Ryder knew they should be talking about work, but if their case was stalled, what was the rush?

"She hates her voice, but yes. Wait…" He nodded to the TV. A few moments later, Rossi lowered her fiddle and began to sing.

Ryder was not one to notice music. He liked a hard beat to run to or work out on the heavy bag with, but other than that, silence was as good as anything else. But this…this made him want to hold his breath and leap inside the notes, let the music carry him under and fill every pore of his being. It was a new experience, stirred him to want to understand the woman behind the music more than ever.

"You're not so bad yourself," Ryder told Voorsanger when the ballad segued into his role.

"I've had training. My father is a rabbi. I was meant to be a cantor before I was seduced to the dark side." Voorsanger finished his pint, and Jimmy had another in front of him before Ryder could blink. Jimmy raised an eyebrow at Ryder's beer, but Ryder waved him off.

"Speaking of the dark side," Ryder prompted.

"Yeah. Got an earful from my boss—and his boss, the DA himself—when I tried to apply for that search warrant. Same old song and dance about how Daniel Kingston is the backbone of the city and—"

"And without him we'd be facing fiscal disaster, blah, blah, blah." Ryder knew it all too well. "Same routine my chief has down pat."

"Sorry. It was a good idea. Should have worked. But that's not why I wanted to talk to you." Voorsanger got off the stool and led Ryder and Ozzie to a booth at the far corner. Ryder slid in, taking the seat where he'd have his back to the wall and a view of the door. Ozzie, used to staying where he wouldn't trip up his human companion, plopped down beside Voorsanger's feet and nestled in for a nap.

"Why all the cloak-and-dagger?" Ryder asked.

"I tried to look at the evidence from the prior victims, see if there was anything special about the PXA used that would lead back to a source. There was nothing in the database."

Ryder shrugged. Another dead end. He was getting used to them on this case. "It was a long shot anyway."

"No. You don't understand. There was nothing on any of the victims in the database."

"You mean, no results entered? That's not unusual with the lab's backlog—"

"Not no results. No evidence."

Ryder set his beer down. Ozzie stirred below them, sensing something was wrong. "Clerical error?"

"That's what I thought. Some clerk scans the wrong bar code on the wrong evidence bag, and everything gets mixed up. So, while I was waiting on the warrant, I went down to the evidence lockup to see for myself."

"And?"

"All I found were empty boxes. It's gone. All gone."

Silence hung between them. Police and prosecutors were the only ones allowed to handle evidence—and then only under strict supervision, following chain-of-custody rules.

Ryder wished he'd gotten something stronger to drink than beer. "To do that, disappear evidence from lockup—"

"Exactly. It means we have dirty cops covering up for Kingston. Harrison was the last person on the evidence log, but I don't believe it was him. And when I suggested to my boss that we investigate, he suspended me. Said since Harrison and I were the only two connected to all the cases, it must have been one of us."

"Shit. He suspended you?"

Voorsanger waved off Ryder's concern. "What worries me is, who knows how high up this goes?"

Ryder nodded, taking in all the implications. "Or who we can trust."

CHAPTER FORTY

DEVON AND I drove away from the rest home in silence. I was mired in my thoughts. Less than thoughts: memories of that awful emptiness I'd just experienced. It left me feeling queasy and feverish, parched. As if every cell of my body had been torn apart, left to rot in some cosmic desert long enough to shrivel and dry, then reassembled into something not quite approaching human.

So that was death. Or as close as you could come and still have a heartbeat.

Devon's face was devoid of emotion, his driving jerky, and I knew he also was barely holding it together. I wondered what had happened after I left him and his mother. He obviously loved her very much, had devoted his life to protecting her.

But I'd been where Tanesha had lived—could you even call that living?—where she'd been *trapped*. Twenty years of that hell. Knowing that pain, that darkness, I couldn't have not told him the truth.

Watching him now, I couldn't help but wonder what he'd done with that truth.

He pulled into a Sheetz, but neither of us had the energy to go inside the convenience store.

Finally, he turned to me, his face crushed with a grief that reached out to me with the haunting notes of a melody that would never be sung. He wasn't crying. I don't think he could have managed tears without collapsing, and that only made his pain all the more unbearable.

I did the only thing I could. I wrapped my arms around him and pulled him to me. We were both trembling as he lay his head between my breasts and I held him as tight as I could. An almost-song poured from me. A melody so ancient and primal that there were no words.

I rocked him against my body and realized I was also grieving. Not just the fact that if Louise was right, then I was dying, that soon—too soon—I'd be plunged into the same endless void he'd just pulled me out of. No, it was more than that. Even though Devon was only a few years younger than I was, as I held him and rocked and crooned a nonsense song, I couldn't help but wonder if this is what it would have felt like if I'd had a child.

Jacob had always wanted children. I hadn't been sure—no, be honest, I'd been terrified by the prospect. And now...too late.

Loss crashed down on me. Just not what I had and was about to lose, but what could have been, what would now never be. I'd be leaving this life without anything left behind to mark my passing. No legacy, no blood, no one to remember and pass the story of my life down to the next generation.

"My very first memory," Devon said, still pressed against my chest so I couldn't see his face, only hear his voice. "The first thing I remember ever, is her leaving me. She put me in my safe place in the closet. I was maybe three. I heard him come for her, yelling and screaming, and then she was gone. He took her from me. And I was alone."

His breath rattled against my chest like something caged struggling to get free. "I don't think she ever came back. Not really, not ever again, not after that first time."

If Kingston was his father, then the abuse had been going on long before Devon would be able to remember it, but that fact wasn't going to help him, so I kept silent. We sat like that for several long minutes, the November sun slipping past the tops of the mountains, leaving us in shadow except for the bilious glow of the convenience store's neon sign.

"She must have loved you very much." I told him.

"If Daniel got hold of her again, even if she can't feel anything, how could I bear that? And Esme…" He opened his eyes, stared directly into mine. "I can't give Kingston any leverage. I'd sacrifice my own life for Esme, but how can I ask my mother to give more than she already has?"

He shook his head and pulled away, more than physically, emotionally. Wiped his face, left and went inside the convenience store. I sat there, too tired to follow, my entire body feeling heavy, a weight more than gravity. He'd spoken of Tanesha in present tense. Yet, I couldn't help but wonder if I had another death on my conscience.

No. I bore responsibility for my own actions. That was difficult enough. I couldn't take on Devon's as well.

Besides, who was I to judge anyone? Maybe there is a good reason for a higher power to exist—not to worship, but to remind us all that we were merely human.

Devon returned with a sack full of high-energy snacks and a selection of sports drinks. He was more composed. No more talk of his mother, his expression made it clear. Instead, he was businesslike as he handed me the bag. "You need to eat. Rehydrate."

I hadn't realized how starving I was until I had devoured the first candy bar and half a bottle of Gatorade.

"Thank you," he said, his voice a close approximation of normal. And he pulled back out onto the highway. "I appreciate all you've done to help."

I reached for his hand and squeezed it. "We're going to find Esme."

"Don't make promises you can't keep," he chided.

"I don't."

His hand fell away from mine, and I knew he didn't believe. I wish I could explain why I did—me, usually the biggest cynic in the room. Maybe it was magical thinking, maybe it was something even more dangerous. Like hope. Wanting a chance to get one thing right before

I checked myself into the psych ward and Angela Rossi would be heard from no more, banished to my own special dark hell. A shudder ran cold fingers across my belly at the thought of living full time in my fugues.

I couldn't live with it alone. I desperately needed someone who would listen, and Devon was a good listener. Not only that, unlike Ryder, he was safe. No emotional complications to sort through. So I told him about Louise's diagnosis.

"Fatal insomnia?" His tone was one of acceptance. Just as he'd accepted my fugue states and the information we'd gained from them. "At least now you know."

"Now I know."

"Did the doctors say how long? I mean—"

"Average time from start of symptoms to death is eighteen months."

"When did your symptoms start?"

I counted back to the last time I could remember a good night's sleep. Before the muscle tremors and fevers and off-balance gait and the restless, electrical tingling in my muscles that kept me moving all night long. Before the talking to almost-dead people. "Five months."

He did the math. Frowned. I wasn't very happy either. "There's no medicine?"

I remembered the prescription still folded up in my coat pocket. "Some experimental treatments. They don't know if anything will help slow it down. But there's no cure." No stopping it.

We sat in silence, barren oaks lining the twisting road, their limbs scratching at the twilight sky.

"I envy you, doc," he finally said, his eyes on the road. "This fatal insomnia shit, it gives you the ultimate get-out-of-jail-free card, you know?"

Didn't feel that way to me. I felt imprisoned, even though I now knew the face of my jailor. "How so?"

"You can do anything you want. No one to answer to. Don't have to take shit from anyone. You can fight back. And what are they gonna do about it? Lock you away? You've already got a death sentence."

"Wow, I didn't take you for such an optimist."

"I'm not. Just pragmatic. I say, you got a free pass, you use it." His gaze edged over to me. "I say, you stop living your life playing by their rules and you do what needs to be done."

He wasn't talking carpe diem, not like Ryder had bantered earlier. He was talking serious shit here. Killing people.

"Who decides what needs to be done?" Could I kill someone? Not just anyone. But someone truly evil? Like the man behind Allie's death and the PXA attacks?

"You know better than most what needs to be done." He jerked his chin in a nod. "There's folks I wouldn't trust to elect a dog catcher. Then there's folks I'd trust with my life—with my daughter's life. Folks like you."

I thought about Allie and the pain she'd suffered. If I had the chance, could I do it?

Whirling music surrounded me as I relived what I'd seen inside her—not just remembered. Truly, moment by moment, relived. The spell didn't last long, thank God, but when it broke I was flooded by heat. A burning fury.

Because, from the cauldron of all that pain and suffering, I still hadn't been able to retrieve a clear image of the man who'd tortured Allie. Devon thought it was Leo Kingston. Everything pointed to it being him, but we had no evidence to prove it. Except maybe the signet ring.

Which would take weeks, maybe even months, to process. How many more women would suffer or die during that time? How many more children abandoned like the ones we found last night?

Leaning back in my seat, I twisted away from Devon and looked at the landscape passing by, needing privacy while I pondered what he'd said. Options. My options.

Ryder and Jacob would both tell me we needed concrete evidence, beyond a reasonable doubt, to convict a man of murder.

Devon? I knew what he'd say. Trust no one, especially not the son of the richest and most powerful man in the city, a man who could buy a jury or even buy the DA's office so it never even went that far to begin with. He'd say end it now, before any other girls like Allie wound up in my ER, broken and dying.

Could I kill Leo Kingston if I needed to? If there was no other way to stop him?

I wanted to. Vengeance was so damn tempting.

But. No. I couldn't. I was a doctor. I saved lives.

How could I take one—especially after already being responsible for my father and Sister Patrice's deaths? Those two lives, those two deaths, would haunt me forever. Not that my "forever" would be very long.

Just because I might not have had long to live, should I forget about the rules, about all human decency, about the consequences to my soul?

The question shook me to my core, rattled me so hard I couldn't lift the drink bottle to my lips without spilling some. But the answer stripped away all the lies and facades I'd hidden behind since my father died.

Because maybe it was Devon who was wrong and Ryder who had been right all along. Maybe I still believed. In a God, in a soul, in the possibility of redemption.

Maybe I still hoped that in the little time I had left, I could prove myself worthy of forgiveness.

My eyes watered. Could my mother, my sister...my father...could they ever forgive me for what happened twenty-two years ago? I'd thought I'd grown past wispy schoolgirl wishes for what never could be, had long ago decided the best way to honor my father was to live a life worthy of his memory.

Had I? Could I? Time was running out. Fast.

I hid my face from Devon, turning to the window and pressing my forehead against the chilly glass, the world outside a blur as it sped by. It's humbling to learn we aren't who we think we are—not even close, none of us.

CHAPTER FORTY-ONE

WHEN SHE WAS alive, Flynn never had any patience. But now that she was dead, she had all the patience in the world. With Esme safe and Dr. Rossi to protect her, she was free to take her time and stalk Leo, catch him when he finally let his guard down.

After the gala last night, Daniel had given the brownstone's staff the long weekend off. Used the holiday as an excuse, but really he wanted privacy. He was due for chemo today and tomorrow, and it was easier to keep his secret without staff or visitors meddling about.

Flynn crept through the cavernous halls of the old house and up to Daniel's quarters. He slept most of the day now, rousing only when absolutely necessary to deal with Kingston corporate affairs or to put on a brave face for Leo. Not that Leo cared or even noticed.

She didn't understand why Daniel insisted on continuing the chemo. His doctors had told him it was fruitless, could only prolong his suffering without adding many days before the end. But he was a stubborn man, stubborn and full of pride. He'd decide when it was time to give up on life—he wasn't about to allow life to give up on him first.

She admired that about him. Thought maybe he'd seen that same stubborn streak in her when they'd first met in Good Sam's ICU three years ago. Two souls condemned to death and fighting back with everything they had.

With a soft knock, she entered his room. He was in bed, just as she'd expected, but not asleep. Instead, his eyes were wide open, so wide that it looked as if they'd been stretched to twice their size, the whites showing all around, pupils blazing with pain. His neck muscles strained as if he were screaming, but no sound came.

"I quite like the screaming, usually, but not from him. He'd ruin it all, begging or lecturing or wasting my time with useless words," Leo said from where he lounged in a chair moved to the foot of the bed, facing his father's agony like a moviegoer at the cinema. "Besides," he smiled at Flynn, aiming a pistol at her, "Daniel always got the final word. About time someone else had a chance, don't you think?"

Flynn rushed to Daniel's side, assessing his vitals as the doctors had taught her. Heart rate much too high, neck veins swollen like they were ready to pop, a sign that his blood pressure was soaring, sending his heart into failure. "What have you done to him?"

"Relax. I added a tiny bit of succinylcholine, titrated it along with the PXA. It won't last long—just long enough to fry some brain cells so the doctors will assume it's a stroke. Man in his condition, end-stage testicular carcinoma, they probably won't even bother with an autopsy. And if they do, they'll never find any trace of my special formula—guaranteed to be metabolized and gone long before anyone can even think of testing for it."

"PXA—you gave him Death Head? The man gave you everything. Why would you betray him like this?" She whirled on him, fingers sliding the knife concealed in her sleeve into her waiting hand. She could kill him—oh, how easy it would be. She glanced at Daniel, saw the pleading in his eyes, burning through the pain. After everything Leo had done, Daniel still had faith in him.

"Do something," she pleaded. "He loves you, Leo. You mean everything to him."

"Everything except the time of day. He'll give me the money, the business, even hire you to protect me from the police so I'm free to do as I please. But he'll never give me the one thing—the only thing—I ever wanted from him." He stood, approached Daniel on the opposite side of the bed, near the IV pump. Flynn noticed a fresh bag of fluid and tubing running to the catheter in Daniel's chest.

"You've never wanted for anything. What more could Daniel have possibly given you?" She leaned forward, one hand sliding below the duvet covering Daniel's body, searching for the IV line. If she pulled it out—yes, there, a simple twist of her fingers and warm fluid began trickling harmlessly down the silk sheets instead of into Daniel's veins.

Leo sat on the edge of the bed, his back to her. Such a tempting target, but Flynn restrained herself. "Tell her, Father. Better yet, tell me. What was the only thing I ever wanted from you? You gave it to others—even to this street whore bitch you dragged from the gutter."

Daniel's face twisted, whether with pain or an effort to speak, it was hard to say.

"Still can't say it, can you, old man?" Leo chuckled. "Of course not. Because now I'm the one with the power. And you won't be saying anything, not ever again." He adjusted the IV, then glanced over his shoulder at Flynn. "Respect. That's all I ever wanted from him. Simple respect."

He blew out his breath and stood, pocketing the pistol and brushing his hands together as if he'd just finished a particularly tedious job. "We're through here. He's finished. You can call 911 if you like. No matter to me if he lives out his days a vegetable or dies here tonight. He'd choose the latter, I'm sure, so you'd be doing him no favors by saving him."

He strode toward the door. Flynn took a step, ready to end him, but beneath the covers, Daniel's hand grasped hers.

Leo paused at the door. "You work for me now, Flynn. I know it was you in the tunnels last night. I know you have the girl squirreled away in one of your bolt-holes. Bring her to me."

"I don't work for you," she spat, shaking free of Daniel's grasp. "I'll never work for you."

He looked back over his shoulder, a superior smirk creasing his face. "You do. You will. For the rest of your life—which is however long you keep me amused. Because if you don't, that precious little sister of yours, the one you killed a man to protect, she becomes my next guest." He nodded as if they'd sealed a deal. "I expect the girl delivered tonight."

With that, he left. An icy chill filled Flynn's veins, freezing her in place. Daniel grabbed her arm once more. He needed her.

"Hang on," she urged him, pulling out her phone and calling 911. "Help is coming," she told him once she'd hung up. "I'll tell the police everything. You won't have to worry about Leo hurting you ever again."

He frowned, shaking his head weakly. "No." The syllable was barely a scratch. But the fact that he was able to move, to speak, meant the drugs were already leaving his system. Was it enough to save him?

He opened his mouth again. She leaned down closer to him. "You do as he says." He swallowed hard, a grimace of pain twisting his face. "Never forget. *Omnes nominis defendere.*" His voice grew stronger, his color less pale.

To hell with the family motto: Above all, defend the family name. There was only one Kingston she cared about defending. "But, Daniel, we can't let him get away with—"

"Not *we*," he said, contempt filling his eyes. "*Me*. You're nothing compared to the Kingston name."

Flynn jerked away, confusion and betrayal colliding.

"Protect my son," he ordered, gripping her so hard his hand trembled. Sirens could be heard from outside his window.

"Daniel?" Her voice emerged sounding like the girl she used to be, the one who'd died in the river. The weak one, the victim.

He didn't answer.

Flynn stared down at this man, this stranger who she'd thought cared for her, wanted to help her create her new life. Slowly, one finger at a time, she pried his hand away from her arm. He slumped back onto the pillows, face slack, barely breathing, but she did nothing to help him.

By the time the paramedics burst in, she was already gone.

CHAPTER FORTY-TWO

ALTHOUGH RYDER WAS the one sitting facing the door, it was the dog who knew she was there first. While he and Voorsanger mulled over their conspiracy theory, Ozzie suddenly shook himself awake, crawled out from under the table, and turned to sit facing the bar's entrance, tail thumping against the floor.

Ryder glanced up, then Voorsanger turned as well. The door opened, and Rossi entered. She looked even more wrecked than she had last night. Drained. Long day or bad news from her doctor friend?

Either way, she needed to take better care of herself. Ryder wished she'd let him be the one to do it. Her eyes met his. Despite the bad news he had for her, he forced a smile—it wasn't very difficult, not when it was for Rossi—and her face became animated once more, the fatigue falling away. For a split second, he imagined being able to do that, making her feel better with just a simple smile every day. Why was it that Rossi brought out the dreamer in him?

The rest of the bar's clientele grew quiet. More frosty than even Ryder's reception, most of the arctic chill coming from the direction of the blonde at the musicians' table. Rossi's mother. Without leaving her chair, Patsy Rossi created a gravitational pull her daughter couldn't resist. Rossi gave Ryder a self-effacing shrug and, shoulders bowed, obeyed her mother's silent summons.

Ryder was so intent on the family drama that he almost didn't notice the door opening once more and Devon Price bounding through it.

"Had to park in the alley," Price said to no one in particular as he spun to the bar as if he was a regular and ordered a Jack Daniel's. "No ice, no water, none of that soda crap, just the way God intended it."

The rest of the bar returned to its buzz of conversations, the musicians leaning away from Rossi and her mother. The two women sat together: a bright golden sun, all-seeing, all-knowing, commanding a moon into a dark eclipse.

Ryder turned to Voorsanger. "What's with Rossi and her mother?"

Voorsanger made a sound like a sigh cut short. "Ancient family history. It's no secret. Jimmy will fill you in, if you like." He held up his phone. "I'm still on hold with Daniel Kingston's executive assistant, trying to schedule that meet-and-greet."

"Good luck with that," Price said, scraping up a chair and sinking into it. He sipped his whiskey with one hand and patted Ozzie on the head with the other, appearing totally at home. "Price, Devon Price."

Ryder made introductions. "Jacob Voorsanger, assistant district attorney. Mr. Price here has—" What exactly was Price's role in all this? He'd never managed to get a straight answer. "He's been helping us with our inquiries."

Voorsanger looked interested at that, shook Price's hand. Ryder strolled to the bar, trying to eavesdrop on the Rossi family drama. Jimmy poured him another beer without Ryder asking. Seemed he'd been accepted into the fold.

"Can I ask?" Ryder nodded to Rossi and her mother. Another blonde had joined them, a woman Rossi's age adorned in expensive jewelry and wearing designer clothing. At breakfast this morning, Rossi had mentioned a sister, Eve, a year younger than she was, recently divorced. Eve sat on the mother's other side, their shoulders touching, leaning toward each other, leaving Rossi in exile at the crowded table.

Watching them, Ryder remembered something his training officer had said after they'd responded to a particularly nasty domestic: *No one knows how to hurt us better than the ones we love.*

"Jacob didn't tell you?" Jimmy swiped the bar with a rag even though it didn't need it, regarding his niece once more. "Girl can't seem to help bringing heartache and pain wherever she goes."

Heartache and pain? A bizarre contrast to the laughing and dancing on the TV screen behind Jimmy as Rossi and the band threw themselves into a merry dance tune.

At the table, the musicians had finished their drinks and were collecting their instruments, several of the men trying to coax Rossi into playing. She shook her head without raising her eyes.

"She should play," Jimmy said. "Least she could do for her mom. Not to mention helping us a bit. Folks always stay longer, drink and spend more, when she's on stage." He shook his head. "She's wasted in that hospital."

Ryder kept his disdain from his face—if these people couldn't see Rossi for what she was, they were idiots. "You said her father was a musician as well. He around?"

"No." The barkeep pulled himself a beer—something dark and frothy that required him to pour slowly, tilting the glass just so. "We lost Angelo awhile back. Poor Eve was only eleven when it happened."

Which would have made Rossi twelve. Tough age to lose a parent—not that any age was a good one. "What happened?"

Jimmy took a drink, wiped foam from his lip with the back of his sleeve. The music from the TV had died down to a low, lilting lullaby-like ballad. Perfect for telling sad tales. "No one blames the girl. She doted on her father. Two peas in a pod, the dark ones in the family, sharing their looks and their music. And their tempers."

He gave a little shake of his head. "All Patsy needed was for Angela Joy to help out, look after her little sister until she got home from work. All Angela Joy wanted was to rebel, always had to have things her own way, that one."

Ryder drank slowly, waiting for Jimmy to tell the story. Jimmy, who called Rossi only by her given name when speaking of her as a child. There must have been a powerful catalyst for that. You didn't go around stealing a kid's name for no good reason.

"No one blames her," Jimmy repeated. "She'd had detention plenty of times before. So when Angela Joy was kept after school—again—her mom went home to take care of the baby instead of waiting for Angela Joy to be set loose by the nuns."

Eve, "the baby," would have been eleven, Ryder reminded himself.

"So," Jimmy continued, "Angela Joy got to stew at school until her father got off work. The nuns locked up after detention, made her wait outside on the stoop in the rain. Teach her a lesson, they all thought. Let her see the consequences of her actions."

"But it didn't quite work out that way?"

"No. Guess not." Jimmy's sigh caved in his barrel chest as he spun a coaster with his fingers, not looking at Ryder. "Angela Joy figured if she was going to be in the rain, she might as well walk home herself. She almost made it, was less than a mile away when she spotted a car coming toward her in the rain. The road curves there. There's no sidewalk, just trees on both sides, you know, so she was walking on the berm. She tried to jump out of the way, but..."

His voice trailed off, leaving Ryder to fill in the blanks. "It was her father. Did he die in the crash?"

"Not until two days later. Patsy was a mess but stayed at his side the whole time. The girls were at our place. Patsy never got over it. The kid looks just like Angelo. Every time Patsy lays eyes on her... Well, no one blames her." An obvious lie, but Ryder kept his silence. "Anyway, the girl never went home again, stayed on with us from then on."

The music from the TV slowed and died, fading away. Jimmy shook himself, turned away, but Ryder saw him swipe at his eyes. Taking his beer with him, Ryder slid from his stool.

"I wish you'd just once put your family before work," Patsy Rossi was saying to her daughter as Ryder approached. She swiveled her diamond-glint of a glare in his direction.

Ryder gave her his best I-can't-wait-to-bust-you smile and took Rossi's hand. "Excuse us," he said, tugging Rossi from her seat and steering her away from her mother without further explanation.

"Thanks," she murmured.

"Rescuing fair maidens is part of the job description." He nudged her toward the fire exit at the rear of the bar. The alley outside was crowded with two dumpsters and a collection of garbage cans, but it was private. "I called. Just like I promised."

She nodded, her gaze focused on the broken glass at her feet. "I saw Louise."

He swallowed hard, squeezed her hand. She didn't squeeze back. After a long moment, she continued, "It will take awhile for the tests to come back. Before she—we—know for sure."

"What is it?"

She looked up but past him, her gaze scanning the sky visible between the buildings as if searching for a star to wish on. Her expression twisted into a grimace. This was hard for her, he knew. More than trusting him with her secret, relinquishing control over her future.

"Nothing you've ever heard of—nothing I've ever heard of. Louise is pretty sure, though. It's called fatal insomnia. Guess the name says it all."

Ryder took a step back. Not away from her, just enough space to find air to breathe.

She dropped his hand and turned toward the door. "Thanks for watching the Advocacy Center for me."

He grabbed her arm, spun her to face him. "Right now I don't really give a shit about the Advocacy Center. I'm worried about you."

"I don't need rescuing, Ryder. I don't need you. Forget about me. Just do your job so I don't have to worry about what I'm leaving behind. Is that too much to ask?"

She stepped away, but he stopped her, placing both palms on her shoulders to hold her still for one precious moment while he tried to find the right words. Who was he fooling? There were no right words. Not for this.

"Yes," he said.

She jerked her chin up, finally meeting his eyes, even if it was with a glare that would have sent most men running for cover.

Ryder stood, waited a beat, weighing his options. In battle he had been known for never hesitating. But that had been easy. He simply carried his fear with him, strapped it on along with his weapons. But this minefield was far more treacherous than anything he'd faced in Afghanistan. With far more at risk.

Rossi's heart. And his own.

"Yes," he repeated. "It is too much to ask. I'm not walking away."

"Damn it, Ryder." She sucked in her breath, her expression hardening. "I don't need anyone to take care of me. I'm not a charity case. You did the honorable thing, offering, now get the hell out of my life."

She was bluffing, he was certain. To protect him. Okay. Let her save face, deny there was anything between them. No problem. He knew better, could see it in her expression. And now that he had an objective, nothing was going to stop him from completing his mission.

"I can take care of myself, Rossi. How about if we take it one day at a time?" he suggested.

She relaxed at that. "No strings? No commitments?"

Right. The Rossi philosophy of intimacy, like her relationship with her ex. He'd watched the two of them with their little dance of "it's only sex," both protecting their hearts, and he wanted no part of it.

But, if she needed to play it safe, if that's where they had to start, he could go along with her. For now. "No strings. But I'm here if you need me—"

She rolled her eyes and broke away from him, going back into the bar. He followed, glad that she couldn't see his grin. She was sick, maybe dying, but somehow he felt—no, he knew—that everything would be all right. Rossi was the smartest person he knew. No way in hell would this fatal insomnia shit be the end of her. What kind of name was that for a disease, anyway?

Rossi was going to be fine. He'd make certain of it.

At their booth across the bar, Price and Voorsanger were deep in conversation, Price now leaning forward on his elbows, head beside Voorsanger's as they stared at Voorsanger's phone.

"What's the deal with Price?" Ryder asked, itching for an excuse to arrest the man. No way was he happy about Rossi hanging out with a guy connected to the Russians.

"We all want to find Esme. Why not work together?"

She made it sound so damn easy. He gestured for her to slide into the booth before him, putting her as far from Price as possible and keeping his gun hand free. Across the room, the band began setting up while a steady stream of customers entered, swirling between the dance floor and the bar. Thankfully, their booth was as far from the stage as you could get, so they could talk in relative privacy without shouting.

"You two come up with a plan?" he asked Voorsanger.

"Daniel Kingston is in the ICU at Good Samaritan. Apparently, he has end-stage cancer and has been keeping it a secret to protect his company's stock value. His assistant said he's in critical condition."

Ryder slumped back, hitting his head against the wall of the booth. "Well, hell, there goes the one guy who might have the answers we need."

"It was already a dead end. Daniel would never rat on his son," Price argued. "Leo's the one trying to kill Esme."

"You have proof? What makes you so certain it's not your pal, Tyree Willard?" Ryder shot back.

Price rolled his eyes. "Sure, blame the black guy. Because there's just been so very many black psycho-crazy stalker rapist serial killers...oh, wait, no, that's the white man's turf, isn't it?"

"Hush," Rossi said, her tone reminding Ryder of his sister, the kindergarten teacher. "We all know it's Leo. Even if we can't prove it," she added when Voorsanger opened his mouth to protest. "What's important is stopping him before he can find Esme or hurt anyone else. He's probably at the hospital with his father." She slid Voorsanger's phone from him. "Let me call the ICU and check."

"We did find out more about Leo's background," Voorsanger said as Rossi turned away from them and plugged one ear with her finger. The band began playing a rousing jig or reel or some kind of foot-stomping, hand-clapping dance that had the crowd gyrating. Voorsanger paused for a moment, his gaze landing on the musicians, looking wistful. Then he shook himself. "He has a degree in biochemistry and almost finished a research fellowship in pharmaceuticals before he left the NIH."

Ryder wondered if there was a way he could check Leo's alibi for the times the women were taken without alerting the soon-to-be-most-powerful man in the city that he was under suspicion. He grabbed his own phone and began searching. The only time they knew for certain was when Allie was grabbed four days ago.

Rossi gave Voorsanger back his phone. "Leo's not there. Daniel Kingston is in a coma. Stroke. They're not sure if he'll survive the night."

For some reason, Price straightened at that, rocking the table and staring at Rossi like they shared a secret. Ryder frowned. No way in hell was she going off with Price, not again.

"One small wrinkle in your theory." He turned his phone to show them the photo of Leo with the Narcis Pharmaceutical board of directors. "According to this, Leo was in Ireland on Monday."

"That's when Allie was taken," Rossi said.

"He could have hired someone to grab her," Voorsanger said. "Have her waiting for him when he got back into town."

"Or maybe it's not him. Maybe someone else raped and overdosed Allie. And the others. Could even be trying to frame Kingston by using his ring to brand the victims."

Price bristled at that. "No. It's Leo. Has to be."

"We need to focus. What's our priority here?" Ryder asked,

wanting a plan of action. He was tired of dead ends.

"Saving Esme," Rossi said. Price nodded. Ryder glanced at Voorsanger, who was tapping his fingers in time with the beat of the music.

"Agreed," Voorsanger said. "Saving the girl has to come first."

"Okay," Ryder said. "What's our next step?"

Silence thudded through the space between them.

"We're pretty sure Leo doesn't have her already, right?" Voorsanger asked. "At least we hope not, because then she'd probably already be dead."

The others nodded, Price staring deep into his empty whiskey glass. This was personal to him, Ryder realized. Maybe too personal. "So who took her in the tunnels?"

"Someone who knows the tunnels and who would risk their life to save Esme. That's gotta be Tyree," Rossi said.

Price shook his head. "No. Tyree would have told me if he knew where she was."

"Would he?" Rossi leaned forward to better meet Price's gaze. "You said there was bad blood between you and Tyree, that he wanted you gone, didn't want you to have anything to do with his family. He kept Jess from you all those years. Maybe he's keeping Esme as well?"

That struck a chord. The muscles in Price's neck knotted, although his face flattened into stone. The kind of blankness, no emotion, no remorse, that Ryder had seen in men right before they killed.

Ryder straightened, putting himself in the way of Price's gaze. "Don't even think it," he muttered.

Price said nothing, his lips pressed into a tight line.

"You can't go after Tyree," Rossi said, the voice of reason. "If you kill him, we might never find Esme. He was willing to talk with me this morning. Let me try."

All three men turned to stare at her.

"Do you think that's wise?" Voorsanger asked, sounding more like a lawyer than ever.

Price gave a reluctant nod. "She's right. Tyree's all about protecting his turf, saving face. He can do that with the doc better than the cops or anyone else."

Ryder didn't like it, but he didn't see another choice.

Rossi stirred beside Ryder, half-pushing up out of her seat. "Like I said, I should talk to him. Come on, we're wasting time."

Price set his whiskey down. "I can't go near the Tower—unless you want Tyree in a killing mood."

Fine with Ryder. "Wait here with the dog. That way, if we need backup, you won't be far."

"Why would Devon be our backup?" Rossi asked. "Won't we just call the police once we have Esme safe?"

The men exchanged glances. Voorsanger took the lead and explained to Rossi about the missing evidence and the trail that led back to the police, and perhaps even the DA, being in Daniel's pocket.

Ryder was glad he sat between Rossi and the exit. She didn't take the news well.

"All those women, Allie—they'll never get a chance at justice? We can't ever lock up Leo Kingston, stop him from killing again?" Her voice was low but, all the more powerful, a shockwave of indignant fury. "Who did this? How?"

"I'm going to find out," Voorsanger promised her, taking her hand in both of his. "Even if it means my career."

"We can still stop Leo," Ryder added, feeling more than a little jealous of the way Rossi looked at her ex. "We just have to catch him doing something illegal."

"After we have Esme safe," Price put in.

"Before anyone else gets hurt," Rossi said. She nudged Ryder with her hip. "Sooner we get Esme back, sooner we can find a way to nail Leo."

He couldn't argue with that. He slid free of the booth and gave her a hand to help her out. Realized that somehow, despite all the arguments against it, they were doing exactly what Rossi wanted.

Voorsanger joined them and, to Ryder's surprise, he laid both hands on Rossi's shoulders, pulling her so close their foreheads almost touched. Blocking her from Ryder's view as he whispered something to her. Something that made her nod her head and straighten her shoulders. An intimate exchange of encouragement.

They stepped apart, Rossi returning to Ryder's side. And that pretty much said it all.

CHAPTER FORTY-THREE

As I LEFT the pub with Ryder and Jacob, I felt a little bad about abandoning Devon. At least he had Ozzie for company. Although he seemed to fit in with the rest of the crowd just fine, I knew it was a show. He'd much prefer to be stalking the streets alone, searching for Esme.

A lot like Ryder that way. Men of action forced to slow down and behave in a civilized manner in order to fit in with society. Jacob was the opposite—he actually enjoyed people. Whether it was entertaining a crowd at the bar or finessing the power game that was a trial, he loved navigating nuances and unspoken undercurrents.

The door to the bar swung shut behind us, the air instantly lighter, more easy to fill my lungs with. Guess I fit into the same category as Ryder and Devon, only I long ago gave up trying to fit in with society—not even my family. Outsider, outcast, outlier, that's me.

When Ryder had escorted me from my mother's table and her ever-silent demand for contrition—although, after years of playing the game, I knew no matter how much I atoned for the sin of being the one who'd lived, she'd never grant me absolution—I remembered the ache of loss I'd felt earlier when I'd held Devon in the car. And it finally hit me. I wasn't mourning the loss of a possible future family.

The grief that had felt like such a weight, anchoring itself deep in my soul, that grief was for the family I'd already lost. Twenty-two years ago when my father died.

And now I was dying. Probably. No. After the events of the last two days, I couldn't deny that something was very, very wrong. I could fantasize about Louise being mistaken and a last-minute miraculous reprieve when the lab tests came back in a few weeks, but it was time to face reality. I was dying.

These next few weeks might be my last before degenerating into a helpless, bedridden, psychotic zombie.

Because that's the fate fatal insomnia delivers. And why I couldn't let Ryder play white knight—he had no earthly idea what was coming. First, insomnia. Then, delirium. Worse than dementia because you're aware of what's happening to you, even as you lose control of your body and your ability to separate reality from hallucination.

And finally your body fails, abandoning you in an eternal dreamless, sleepless wasteland, where you lie, catatonic, unable to care for yourself, totally dependent on those around you. Only then, after months of this awake-but-paralyzed state, only then does death finally hear your confession and grant you the grace of ending your miserable, pathetic life.

That's what I faced. As much as I loved her, I imagined my mother would still think it not punishment enough.

Saving Esme might be the last thing I did that was truly my own, a choice made of free will, solely in my control, not driven by the demands of my disease.

One last chance to make a difference, save a life. No way in hell was I going to squander it.

"I'll get the car," Ryder said, leaving me with Jacob after giving Jacob an inscrutable glance. More of that silent man-talk, as if testosterone communicated better than words.

Too tired and depressed to care about Ryder's frail male ego, I slumped against Jacob and let him hold me.

I turned to him, our bodies pressed together, raised my face. "I wasn't a very good wife, was I?"

He ran his fingers through my hair. "No."

"Such a *mensch*." My fake Yiddish accent had him smiling again. "I can always trust you to be honest."

"No." He squeezed my shoulders, pulling me close. "You were a great wife. You took care of me. Now, let me take care of you. I know there's something going on, Angie. For once, let someone take care of you."

I took his hand in mine and squeezed. "I can't. You can't. It wouldn't work."

"That's what you said about our marriage."

"Honesty. That was the one thing we always had going for us." I kissed him on the forehead, untwined my fingers from his, and pulled away, standing on my own once again.

Ryder pulled the car up to the curb and jumped out, holding his phone. "I'm texting you a few names of cops you can trust—men and women I trust with my life," he told Jacob. "In case you need them."

While we talked with Tyree, hopefully returning with Esme safe and sound, Jacob was going to the federal prosecutor in charge of investigating public corruption to tell him about the missing evidence and the search warrant the DA had quashed.

"Do you have to do this tonight?" I asked Jacob, suddenly realizing he might be risking more than his job. If Daniel Kingston was the money who bought the dirty cops and politicians, with him in a coma, they'd have no one to protect them. Desperate men used to wielding power and now cornered—it was a dangerous combination.

Jacob nodded and turned to walk down the block where his own car was parked. "I'll call you when it's done. Take care."

Before I could reply, a sharp cracking noise split the night. At first, I thought it came from inside the bar, some strange new sound effect the band had added. Crazy what you think when people are shooting at you.

Last night, in the tunnels, I'd been on guard, anticipating danger, but here on the sidewalk in front of my family's bar, in front of my home? It just didn't compute. Not until Ryder tackled me, throwing me to the ground as more gunshots crackled above us.

He drew his pistol and scoured the street, keeping the car's engine block between us and the shooter, as he searched for where the shots came from. I tried to raise my head to see Jacob and to help Ryder, but he pinned me down, my body pressed flat against the curb, my face hanging over the gutter.

The sounds weren't at all like what you see in the movies. More of a pop than a boom. Thuds and pings as bullets hit wooden walls and metal cars. Broken glass of a shop window smashed. The sledgehammer crack of concrete splintering.

And then the sound I'd been dreading. A man yelling in pain.

🌒 🌿 🌘

DESPITE THE NOISE of the crowd and the band, the sound of gunfire blazed through Devon's awareness like a jolt of lightning. He rushed to the door, the dog at his side, easing it open to assess the situation before committing.

No one else inside the bar seemed to notice anything wrong. Figures, bunch of white folk too busy gyrating, thinking they were dancing. Although, he did like the music.

He gazed into the darkness beyond the bar's door. Ryder had taken shelter behind a car, Angela at his feet, his body protecting her. Two parking spaces down, Jacob Voorsanger staggered against the brick wall of the building beside the bar, blood streaking down one side of his camel-colored wool coat. The lawyer clutched at his left arm, trying to reach Angela. The plate glass window behind him shattered, glass flying everywhere, and he dove to the sidewalk.

Devon spotted the muzzle flash at the alley entrance across from the bar. The shooter was firing shots in pairs or threesomes, definitely not a full auto, probably a pistol. Lousy aim. So far all he'd hit was a few parked cars, a storefront window, and maybe Jacob.

Why would anyone be trying to kill Jacob? If it was because of the evidence tampering he'd discovered, surely whoever was behind it

304

had law enforcement connections and would have been a better shot?

Ryder raised his own weapon, training it on the alley, also tuned in to the muzzle flash. He fired three rounds before their unknown assailant returned fire, this time zeroing in on Ryder's position, forcing him back behind cover.

Devon ran back inside the bar to the emergency exit near where they'd been sitting earlier. The door was propped open by a stray brick, a pile of cigarette butts on the ground nearby. Trash cans and dumpsters littered the narrow alley. Devon navigated them, the dog on his heels, emerging a few doors down, diagonally across from the alley where the shooter was. He was out of the shooter's sight line, safe to cross the street and sprint between two storefronts to circle back behind the shooter.

Ryder spotted Devon and jumped up to provide cover fire, keeping the shooter occupied while Devon made his move. Just as he crossed the street, he saw Angela crawling over the sidewalk to Jacob.

Thankfully, the shooter was aiming at Ryder, ignoring Angela and Jacob. Devon pushed his speed, hoping he'd have time to circle behind the gunman before he shot anyone else. To his surprise, as he hit the opposite curb, a blur of fur sped past him, heading directly into the alley where the shooter was.

"Ozzie, no!" Angela cried out.

Damn dog, now there was no chance at surprise. Ryder knew it as well, circling out from behind the car and advancing as Devon changed his trajectory to race toward the alley, following Ozzie. No more shots came from the alley, but a man's shouted curses carried through the night.

Devon reached the mouth of the alley in time to see Tyree Willard, gun fallen to the ground, as he struggled to get Ozzie off him. The dog had driven Tyree into the side of a dumpster and had his jaws clamped around Tyree's wrist.

"Get this damned mutt off me!" Tyree shouted, pummeling Ozzie's body with his free hand.

Ryder arrived, gun aimed at Tyree. "Good dog," he told Ozzie as he kicked Tyree's pistol farther away. Then he quickly searched Tyree, removing a knife and another gun, while Devon circled behind the two men and grabbed Ozzie's collar. The dog shook his head as if angry, but finally released his hold on Tyree.

"Look, it's not what you think," Tyree said as Ryder pulled his arms behind him and put him in handcuffs. His wrist had teeth marks but not much blood. Devon had the feeling the dog had taken it easy on him—or maybe, given the gang leader's steroid-induced bulk, Ozzie couldn't get a good grip. Either way, Tyree would live.

But sooner or later, he and Devon were going to have to have some kind of reckoning.

Ryder spun Tyree around, and Devon saw his opening. He scooped up the discarded weapon and lunged at Tyree, shoving the gun into Tyree's neck so hard it forced the taller man's chin up.

"Where's Esme?" Devon demanded. "I'm going to count to three, and you'd best tell me before then or—"

"Price, drop it," Ryder ordered, his own weapon now trained on Devon. The distant wail of sirens underscored his words.

"I wasn't trying to kill you," Tyree said. "You know me, Runt. I wanted them dead, they'd be dead. It's Leo Kingston wants you and the lawyer dead," he told Ryder, his words tumbling over themselves in his rush to get it out. "He was going to send one of his pet cops to do the job, but I don't want any part of killing cops. That's serious shit, and it never goes well. But Leo, he's crazy. Thinks cuz his dad's half-dead he's gonna inherit the family name and with it all the power, like he's freakin' Teflon coated, bulletproof and all."

Devon backed off, untangling the truths from Tyree's assorted lies. Tyree would have no problem killing cops—as he'd shown Devon earlier. He glanced at the gun Tyree had used: Devon's own .45. He'd been going to pin this on Devon, hadn't planned on Devon actually being in the company of a cop and prosecutor. Neither had Devon, but he liked how it worked out.

"Slow down and tell us everything." Devon kept his gun trained at Tyree's head. "Starting with, where is Esme? Does Leo have her?"

Tyree shook his head. "No way I'd let that psycho anywhere near her. But he knows where she is. Said she was going to be in his hands by tonight. That's why I had to play along, didn't want him to suspect that as soon as she's safe, I'm done. He's done." He straightened, baring his teeth, the old Tyree, leader of the Royales, back in full force. "I'll kill the bastard with my bare hands. No one touches my family. No one."

"Leo killed Jess and Sister Patrice?" Ryder asked.

"Not him, but two of his pet cops. Under his orders. Esme saw him grab his latest girl. Told Jess, but she was too scared to come to me, so she called him." He jerked his chin at Devon. "Fat lot of good it did her. When he didn't call her back, she asked Patrice for help, thought she could hide them from Leo."

"Guess that didn't work out so well," Devon said with bitterness. Now he knew why Tyree had tortured the cop before shooting him with Devon's gun. Which meant the asshole had had this info all day and still hadn't been able to find Esme. "And fat lot of good you and your gang did, letting her killers waltz right in and out of the Tower."

"If she'd told me—"

"Shut up, both of you." Ryder turned to glance out the alley. Two patrol cars had arrived. Near the bar a group of people had gathered, including Jacob and Angela. The lawyer didn't seem too bad off. Angela had his coat and jacket off and was wrapping a bar towel around his arm. "We don't have much time. Can you find out where Esme is before Leo gets to her?"

Tyree shook his head. "I know where Leo is, but you'll never get to him." He nodded at Devon. "He's using one of his dad's favorite spots from when you were a kid."

"Me?" Devon frowned. "I never went with Kingston—"

"Sure you did."

Stray wisps of memory pinched at Devon. A woman crying out his name, a tall white man, the sound of flesh slapping flesh...no, no, no, don't look, don't listen, it's the devil, the devil...Mrs. Anders' voice intoning prayers, trying to exorcise the demons from Devon and his mother.

"The Tower greenhouse." The words scraped free of Devon's lips before he could swallow them back. Eyes of a devil watching, his mom would say. Not eyes, the light from the heaters filtered through the thick foliage. The acrid smell of fertilizer mixed with the sweet smell of earth and dying. "He's in the greenhouse."

"You'll never get to him there. Not without my help." Tyree shook his arms, the handcuffs rattling. "Lose the cuffs, and I'll take you to Leo." He stared directly at Devon as if Ryder wasn't even there. "I'm the only one who can get you your daughter back."

"You're not going anywhere," Ryder said.

Devon realized there was only one way to play this. He shifted his aim, pointing his gun at Ryder. "Drop your weapon. And uncuff Tyree. We're going to get Esme back."

Ryder raised his gun at Devon. Standoff. But Ryder didn't pull the trigger like he should have—like any other cop would have. Instead, his face tightened as if he'd arrived at the same unsavory conclusion as Devon. "You think that's the only way?"

Devon nodded, wishing he didn't have to involve the cop. But he couldn't see any way around it. "Only way that won't end up with innocents dead." He aimed his chin across the street where Angela and Jacob were talking to the patrolmen. "I can go it alone if you promise to buy me some time."

Ryder lowered his weapon. "No. Too risky. You'll need help if you're going to get Esme out alive." He scowled at Tyree. "Someone you can trust." He holstered his gun. "Let me handle my guys. I'll meet you in the alley at your car."

Devon yanked on Tyree's cuffs, tugging him away from the street. It would take only a few minutes to circle past the cops to the alley behind the bar.

"Hey, aren't you going to take these off?" Tyree protested.

Ryder was halfway out of the alley, the dog trailing after him. He looked back over his shoulder. "Not until you deliver us to Leo."

CHAPTER FORTY-FOUR

RYDER JOGGED ACROSS the street to the rapidly growing crowd on the sidewalk in front of the bar. Many carried drinks, flaunting the city's open-beverage law as they satisfied their curiosity. Even more were on their phones shooting video and tweeting. By morning, Jimmy's Place would top the list of the city's most notorious hot spots.

He grabbed the first uniform he saw and sent him and the others in the opposite direction from the way Price and Tyree had gone. Then he stopped to check on Rossi and Voorsanger. The lawyer had taken some shrapnel from flying concrete and had glass in his arm, side, and scalp, but Rossi already had the worst of it bandaged.

"I've never been shot before," Voorsanger said in a stunned tone, his body swaying. Rossi gestured to Ryder, and between them, they got the lawyer down on the steps, his head between his knees before he could pass out.

Ryder had to try hard not to smile.

"Still haven't," Rossi told her ex. "Most of it was just glass. You'll need to be cleaned up and some stitches, though."

"Oh," Voorsanger said in a weak tone without looking up. "Did you catch them?"

"Got away," Ryder lied. Thankfully, the ambulance arrived, and Rossi went to fill in the medics.

He didn't like not telling her everything, but there was a damn good chance he might not make it back, and he couldn't risk her doing something stupid, like coming after him and Devon.

"Where's Devon?" Voorsanger asked. "The dog made it back, but where'd he go?"

Even wounded and woozy, the lawyer had a sharp eye. Ozzie sat patiently beside him, waiting for Ryder.

"Listen." Ryder pitched his voice low. "We have a lead on Esme. I've got to go. Can you keep an eye on Rossi? Make sure she stays safe at the hospital?"

Voorsanger glanced up, his face pale but his gaze clear. "You and Devon, you're going after Leo? Alone?"

"No other way. Leo's in the Tower, up on the roof in the old greenhouse. That means seven stories of Royales and Leo's crooked cops to get through, all without risking the civilians who live there or Esme."

"Not very good odds."

"No. That's why we're going to use me as bait. Leo sent Tyree here to kill you and me, but Tyree wanted no part of it, which is why we're both still alive. He can get us into the Tower, and together we'll deal with Leo and get Esme out again."

Voorsanger frowned, taking in the implications. "That list of names you gave me. Good cops, you said. Maybe we should—"

"Too risky. Not with all those civilians." Ryder stood. Voorsanger climbed to his feet as well, less wobbly. Ryder handed him Ozzie's leash. "Take care of the dog."

"What do I tell Angie?"

Ryder grimaced. Met the other man's gaze. Voorsanger nodded. "I won't tell her anything."

"Best that way."

"Good luck."

Ryder didn't answer as he took off down the alley to meet Price and Tyree. He didn't believe in luck. He believed in his men, his training, and God.

As he approached Price's black Town Car he realized he was going into a situation where none of the three might be able to save him.

○ ❈ ☾

I KNEW FROM experience that Jacob made a lousy patient. When he got sick, he'd retreat to his bed and ignore my medical advice, relying instead on his mother's long-distance diagnosis and home remedies given over the phone from his parents' retirement villa in Boca. Then I'd end up slaving over a stove, following her recipes for his favorite comfort food.

Tonight was different. Getting shot at seemed to have brought out his inner John Wayne, because he insisted on walking to the ambulance and climbing onto the stretcher without help. Ozzie jumped in with us before the medics could protest or I could find Devon to take the dog.

Ten minutes later we were at Good Sam's ER, bypassing triage and straight to an empty bed. Shari, the same nurse who'd helped me last night with Ryder and Sister Patrice, entered the room warily. "Another gunshot victim?"

"Not really. Cuts and abrasions from flying glass and concrete."

"The bullet ricocheted," Jacob told her merrily, drunk on adrenaline. He held up his hand, thumb and forefinger measuring a small distance. "Came this close to hitting me."

Behind him, I shook my head, but Shari took it in stride and smiled at Jacob. She undid the pressure dressings I'd applied at the scene and began her assessment.

"His tetanus is up-to-date, but those lacerations are going to need to be debrided and sutured," I told her. Then I lowered my voice. "He hates needles, will try to convince you just to superglue them, but—"

"Don't worry, Dr. Rossi."

"I'm going to check on my kids from last night," I told Jacob. "Ozzie might cheer them up."

He looked up, a sharp expression edging past his smile. Poor guy hated hospitals. "You're leaving?"

"Just over to the Advocacy Center. Don't worry, you're in good hands." I patted his arm. "Anyone wants to amputate anything, give me a call. I have my phone."

"Ha ha. You think you're funny, but I know what really goes on in places like this."

I left him telling Shari the story of the great gunfight at Jimmy's Place and headed over to the Advocacy Center with Ozzie in tow. No sign of any press. The officer on duty examined my credentials before allowing me inside.

The kids were wide awake, chasing each other around, over and behind the furniture so that I couldn't keep track of them. I didn't go in. Merely opened the door and let Ozzie loose, eliciting squeals of delight as they pounced on him. Ozzie sat patiently, tail thumping as they stroked and patted and hugged him, while I went to the observation room to talk with the nursing assistant on duty.

"They've been fine," she told me. "Slept most of the afternoon and have already eaten five times today. Your orders said to feed them whenever they asked, so I hope that's okay."

"It's normal for kids like this to have altered hunger and sleep cycles. Any food hoarding?" Another symptom of social deprivation.

"Yes, but I cleaned it all out when they were asleep and then fed them as soon as they woke. Amazing how they do everything together. But, my, they're hard to keep track of, keep huddling up." She looked past me through the window. "Guess it's good they have each other."

I was engrossed in the psychologist's notes, more interested in the prognosis and paying no attention to the children. The psychologist thought they'd recover in time, but she cautioned against separating them too soon. Justification for me to keep them here, where they'd be safe.

Satisfied, I closed the chart. Now for the hard part. "You okay if I leave Ozzie here?"

"Sure," the nursing assistant said. "They love him, makes my job all the easier."

"Thanks." I left before she could ask me where I was going or for how long. A good thing, since I didn't know the answers. It all depended on how close to dead Daniel Kingston was.

My stomach knotted with dread. Every step I took as I climbed the two flights of stairs to the ICU felt like eternity thudding down on my shoulders. But stuck here, it was the only thing I had left to try. Devon had thought Leo would take Esme to the same place Daniel used to take his mother—how could I not try to find the answer?

At least then, he and Ryder could save Esme. Even if it meant exposing my secret to the world.

Maybe not a bad thing. I was tired of all the secrets I was carrying. Not just mine; Devon's as well. But I couldn't judge him or betray him, couldn't even argue that I'd do anything differently if our places were reversed.

The glass doors to the ICU swooshed aside with a breath of chilly air that raised goose bumps on my arms. The last two times I'd done this, Devon had had to pull me out. Without him near, could I free myself from Daniel's mind before it was too late?

Or would I be sucked into that maelstrom of eternal black forever?

☽ ✹ ☾

FLYNN SAT BY Daniel's bedside, hidden in the shadows, unable to bring herself to believe that he'd betrayed her, chosen Leo over her. The man had been like a father to her these past three years, had shared secrets with her that he'd never risk with his own son.

It had been the drugs Leo gave him. The PXA. He wasn't thinking straight. He couldn't have been. He didn't mean she was nothing to him. That her only value lay in serving Leo.

Was she just being foolish and stupid? Or maybe she just wasn't strong enough to handle one more betrayal. Nonsense. She was strong enough to defeat death; she could handle anything. It was Daniel who had taught her that. Gave her the strength and confidence to build a new life.

She drew on that strength now to face the truth: Daniel had never given her all those impossible tasks to accomplish because he had faith in her. No. He'd done it because she wasn't family.

She was expendable.

Flynn stood. Time to prove him wrong.

She didn't want to leave him, but what choice did she have? When he woke, Daniel would hate her for stopping Leo once and for all. But it was the only way to protect the Kingston name. Wouldn't Daniel want that? And if he never woke, then Leo won... She couldn't let that happen. This had to stop. Tonight.

It felt as if time was throttling her, its death grip marking the seconds prolonging her agony. Torn between holding vigil over Daniel and killing his son.

She'd finally gathered the strength to leave when she spotted a familiar figure walking through the doors of the ICU. Doctor Rossi coming to save Flynn, just like she had three years ago.

Rossi had changed. She still had that head-up, shoulders-back stride, as if she owned the world, but tonight her eyes appeared haunted. Flynn felt the same. Had ever since Leo had moved back in with his father and begun his campaign of terror.

"Dr. Rossi. Do you remember me?" Flynn asked, certain the answer would be no. After all, she was no longer the ice-cold, drowned teenager fished out from the river. The girl who'd stolen a gun, forced Creepy Wayne to the wharf, struggled with him, the gun going off, both falling, falling into water darker than night. Blood everywhere, tumbling, clawing, sucking in water instead of air. Both of them dead, dead, dead.

Creepy Wayne had stayed dead. Somewhere at the bottom of the river, washed away, just like Flynn's former life.

Rossi glanced at Flynn. At first she frowned, puzzled, then a welcoming smile lit her face. "Of course. Jane Doe Flynn."

There'd already been one Jane Doe in the ER on the morning Flynn arrived, so instead of making her a number, Rossi had given her the name of the tugboat captain who'd rescued her from the frigid waters of the Cambria River. He'd been one of the best men Flynn had ever known. Died of a heart attack while piloting a barge to Pittsburgh last December. "How are you?"

Good question. How to tell the woman who saved your life that the new one you'd built—based on the lies you told her—was as a killer?

"Still have trouble with the cold." She raised a gloved hand and waved it. Daniel was the only person outside the hospital who knew the gloves weren't just an affectation. They protected her fingers, their nerves permanently damaged by frostbite, leaving her in constant pain.

Rossi frowned in concern. "Reflex sympathetic dystrophy? Tricky to treat. They couldn't find any meds that helped?"

Flynn shrugged. "I need to ask you a favor."

"Of course. What?"

"I saw you there. In the tunnels. Last night."

Rossi blinked. "You were there?"

"I'm the one who pulled the girl to safety. Someone was shooting at her."

"You have Esme?" Rossi lurched forward, eyes wide. "Is she okay? Where is she?"

"She's safe. I need you to take care of her." Flynn turned away when a nurse came to check on Daniel and led Rossi back outside to the empty corridor. "Look. You need to know. It was the police who shot her mother and that nun. She wouldn't tell me any more, just that there were two of them."

"Why would police kill Jess and Patrice?"

"Leo Kingston sent them. He was threatening Tyree Willard, something about a stolen ring. Leo's been kidnapping women from the Tower, raping, torturing them. Killed two so far. At least. Probably more I don't know about."

Flynn paused, waiting for Rossi to protest. In her world, she was the only one who thought Leo capable of anything bad. But to her surprise and relief, Rossi nodded, accepting Flynn's outlandish story. "You've been hiding Esme from Leo and the police?"

"Yes. But now Leo's after me—he knows I have Esme. I need to stop him before he can get to her."

"Where is she?"

"Here." Flynn allowed herself a quick smile at Rossi's look of surprise. "With the other children you brought here last night. Down in the Advocacy Center."

"Esme's here?" Rossi didn't wait for an answer, but headed toward the stairwell. Flynn followed. She needed to be on the move anyway. "How are you going to stop Leo?"

"I'm going to kill him."

CHAPTER FORTY-FIVE

As we hurried down the steps from the ICU back to the Advocacy Center, I cursed myself for not watching the children more closely earlier.

"Thank you," I told Jane Doe Flynn. "For saving Esme. But why were you there? How did you get involved in all this?"

She was dressed all in black, and I realized she moved like Ryder did, as if on constant alert, expecting to enter battle. Had she survived her drowning only to become some kind of vigilante?

When she didn't answer, I asked, "At least tell me your name. I don't know what to call you."

After her drowning, she'd claimed amnesia, but there had to be a damn good reason why a teenager had ended up in the river covered in bruises and blood.

Her shoulders bobbed up and down as if shrugging off a heavy load. "Flynn. Call me Flynn. It's who I am now."

We arrived at the first floor. The police officer was nowhere to be seen—he was probably inside, checking on the children—so I unlocked the doors to the Advocacy Center. We passed the empty exam rooms and turned the corner to the observation room when I spotted a woman slumped on the floor.

I ran to her, skidding to a crouch beside her. It was the nursing assistant who'd been watching the children.

I reached for her pulse. She was dead, a length of surgical tubing wrapped around her neck. I glanced back down the hall behind me, but Flynn had vanished. The door to the observation room was open, but the room was dark.

The children! Panic lanced through me. I stood, but before I could move to check on the children, a voice called to me from inside the observation room.

"Make a sound and the girl dies," a woman's voice came from the darkness. The lights snapped on, and I saw Esme, eyes wide with terror, being held at gunpoint by a police officer.

Officer Petrosky. The woman who'd tried to keep me from going into the tunnels last night. The one who'd shot at us? No, at Esme. Hoping to kill her before we could save her.

"Dr. Rossi, isn't it?" Her tone was one of command. "Pull the body inside and close the door."

What choice did I have? I dragged the nursing assistant's body inside and shut the door. Hopefully, Flynn had gone for help, but I still needed to get this woman and her gun away from Esme and the other children.

Through the observation window I could see the kids and Ozzie chasing each other in the next room. They all appeared unharmed, no idea of the danger a few feet away. A few of them even smiled.

"Imagine my surprise when I come on duty only to find the girl everyone's been looking for. Of course, she," Petrosky nodded at the dead woman at my feet, "wouldn't cooperate. But you will, won't you?" She tilted her head, regarding me once more. "I'll make you a deal. You two come with me, and I'll let those other kids live."

☽ ☀ ☾

"WE'RE GOING TO have to go in through the tunnels," Tyree told them once Ryder, Price, and the gang leader had driven away from the crime scene Ryder should have been working, not fleeing like a common criminal.

Price drove while Ryder sat with Tyree in the back, weapon aimed at him. "Why's that?" Price asked. "Don't trust your own people?"

Ryder wished Price would stop provoking Tyree. They needed his cooperation if they were going to make this work. If the gang leader was desperate enough to partner with him and Price, he obviously couldn't trust his own men.

"There's an entrance to the tunnels on Park, near the old carousel," Tyree told Price.

Price said nothing, merely steered them south toward Millionaire's Row. "How will we know if Esme's really there? If we get there too soon—"

Almost as bad as arriving too late. Ryder nudged Tyree. "What exactly did Leo say about Esme?"

The gang leader shrugged his massive shoulders. "Not much. Just that he had a chick who was bringing her, and she'd be there tonight. Got the feeling Leo doesn't like this chick. Told me he might let my guys have her as a reward."

Ryder met Price's murderous gaze in the rearview mirror. Ryder wondered if he needed to worry more about Price than Tyree.

Price pulled the car behind the caretaker's shed beside the old carousel. He leaned across the front seat, opening the glove box, then handed a small, high-intensity flashlight to Ryder. They got out of the car. Ryder moved Tyree's cuffs to the front and gave him the light to hold.

"Hey, man, that's not the deal." Tyree jangled his cuffs. "Unlock these."

"Not until you get us into the Tower. Then we'll swap places." Ryder hated that his only backup would be Price, but there was no time to follow protocol: surveillance, threat assessment, evacuate the civilians, send in an armed response team. Plus, this was the Tower. A thousand civilians and seven stories filled with well-armed gang members between them and Esme. Not to mention a sociopathic killer.

Tyree narrowed his eyes, staring at Price. "Not you. Him." He jerked his handcuffs, rattling them. "You, Leo only wants dead. Him, he wants alive." Tyree's sudden grin split the night as the light above the door to the shed reflected from his teeth. "You ready to meet your big brother, Runt?"

❂

PETROSKY WAS NO dummy. She knew she'd have her hands full, so she made me dose Esme with a sedative. I chose midazolam; it also causes amnesia. If there was anything I wanted Esme to forget, it was this night.

The back hallway of the Advocacy Center led to the elevator to the basement. All empty this time of night. Soon we were in the tunnels, my wrists handcuffed in front of me, Esme cradled in my arms, Petrosky behind me, holding the gun on us as we headed to the Tower. Still no sign of Flynn or any help. I wondered if maybe she'd set me up, but realized that made no sense. Petrosky had found Esme by accident, without Flynn's help. Surely after risking her life to save Esme once, Flynn wouldn't give up on us now.

My answer came in the form of a whisper high above. Amid the unnatural creaks and groans of the overhead pipes was the rhythmic beat of soft footfalls, someone tracking us. We reached the wide intersection halfway between Good Sam and the Tower. I tensed, expecting Flynn to make her move.

Petrosky had her gun aimed at my spine, only a few inches away, no possibility of missing. But if Flynn timed it right, she could still save Esme.

Two more uniformed police officers stepped out of the shadows. I could almost feel Flynn's frustration boiling up with my own. One of them took Esme from me, and the other held his gun on her, despite the fact that she was oblivious to the world.

"All this for one little kid?" He poked Esme with his gun, and it took everything I had not to rush him.

Petrosky prodded me from behind. "Who cares if it keeps him happy and us paid? As soon as his father dies, Leo will rule this town and we can write our own tickets."

"He'll like the bonus you brought. But we'd better hurry. He's getting impatient."

We doubled our speed down the tunnel. I ransacked my memory of last night, trying in vain to remember any place I could create a diversion, give Flynn the advantage. But all of Tyree's traps had been dismantled, and from here it was a straight shot to the Tower. A few minutes later, we were in the elevator heading to the roof.

They led us through Tyree's throne room—several of his men were there, shuffling about, aimless without their leader—and then across the roof to the old Victorian greenhouse.

With its beautifully arched roof, wrought iron columns, and gracious wide windows, the greenhouse belonged in a different era— and anywhere but on top of this ugly, squalid building. Petrosky shoved me inside. The other cops placed Esme on a stainless steel table, nodding to the man who stood in a cleared area about ten feet beyond the entrance.

The light filtered through the thick, green foliage surrounding him, giving his blond hair and pale skin a sickly hue. His face was narrow, with an angled chin and sharp cheekbones. He stared at me, circling me, hands behind his back. I stared back, forcing my fear aside, even as memories of Allie's torture bombarded me.

Leo Kingston. Had this man tortured Allie and the other women?

Hatred blazed through me. He saw it and nodded in approval. "Well done," he finally told Petrosky. "You watch the girl. The others can guard the door." The two police officers backed out.

The sound of the doors slamming shut sealed my fate. I could handle that. If I could find a way to save Esme.

There was no way in hell Flynn could get up to the roof without alerting Tyree's men or Leo's people. And with the police on Leo's payroll, she couldn't call them. Even if she did, how could they reach us without risking the lives of a thousand civilians?

"I'll do anything you want," I told Leo. What did I have to lose? I'd already lived through what he'd done to Allie. And I had to buy Flynn time. "Let the girl go."

He bounced on his feet like a little boy so excited he was about to pee himself. A gleeful movement that distracted me.

Then I saw the knife in his hand.

CHAPTER FORTY-SIX

DEVON HATED HOW long it took them to travel through the tunnels, but there were cops patrolling and no way of knowing if they worked for Leo or not. Finally, they arrived at the Tower.

Ryder removed the handcuffs from Tyree and placed them on Devon. "Sure about this?"

"Save Esme."

Ryder left the cuffs as loose as possible and slipped the key to Devon. He gave Devon a sympathetic look, then disappeared into the stairwell leading to the roof, armed with Tyree's keys.

Devon entered the elevator with Tyree, forcing himself to think of Esme as the doors sealed them inside. They arrived at Tyree's rooftop office where Tyree's men waited. Then they were a group of seven, parading through a door behind one of the red velvet curtains and across the rooftop to the greenhouse. The night wind from the river whipped across the open space, bringing with it the scent of diesel oil and dead fish.

Tyree shoved Devon through the large, old-fashioned metal doors leading into the greenhouse. The light inside was a strange mix of dusky shadows and the red glow of heaters coming from below. He'd expected the sprawling foliage of marijuana plants, but not the perfumed scent that drifted down from tiny white flowers dangling from vines encircling the rafters overhead. Or the singing.

He stopped in his tracks, unable to pull his attention from the singing. Lovely warbles, like a boy's choir. Only these weren't human voices. Tiny songbirds, bright blue and yellow sparks of color flitting hither and yon through the intricate wrought iron that formed the rafters supporting the curved glass roof.

Blinking back memories—angels, the birds sounded like angels, no, too many memories, rushing over him all at once—he stumbled forward, past the wall of greenery into a cleared area in the center beneath the glass arch.

Lying on a potting bench was Esme, who appeared unharmed, but asleep or drugged. Across from her was Leo Kingston and beside him Angela Rossi, who stared at Devon, not in despair, despite the fact that her hands were handcuffed in front of her and Leo held a filleting knife to her throat, but rather in challenge. Her gaze moved to Esme, and Devon understood.

No matter what happened to her, Esme would survive.

It was a challenge he was happy to accept. He gave her a small nod.

"I brought you yours," Tyree said. "Now, you give me mine."

Leo glared at Tyree and jerked his chin in dismissal. "You get the girl when I'm good and ready."

Tyree backed off to stand beside the police officer, Petrosky, who'd taken position guarding Esme, leaving Devon standing alone about eight feet from Leo. It would be so easy to kill Leo—but not with the knife at Angela's throat. Only as a last resort.

"Welcome, my favorite bastard stepbrother," Leo called in a merry voice. "So glad you could join in on my little reindeer game. In honor of our late, great father, I thought we'd play one of his favorites: sacrifice. Do you remember the rules? We played it last time we met."

"I've never met you before," he told Leo, trying to give Ryder time.

Leo gave a mock frown. "Sure, you have, little brother. Think, think hard. It was the last time our father brought your mother here so we could hear her scream. She was pretty much burnt out by then, but he wanted to try to break her one last time. You were maybe eight..."

Devon shook his head, denying memories he'd locked away for twenty years. That smell. Jasmine. How he hated that smell. And the damn birds singing like the world was beautiful, like everything would be perfect, their voices echoing his mother's screams. "No. I don't know what you're talking about."

He'd hid—just as he always hid when Kingston came for his mother. But it wasn't the closet he remembered downstairs in their apartment, the one his mother stocked with pillows and coloring books and snacks. Against his will, he glanced past Leo to one of the wrought iron pillars that supported the roof. At its base was a large cabinet, the height of a man's waist, perfect size for an eight-year-old boy to seek shelter in. It stank of fertilizer and chemicals, he remembered, the air filled with microscopic flakes of soil and peat, made him sneeze.

"How could you forget?" Leo asked. "Especially that final time. When my father let us play along. He gave your mother a choice: Give in, stop fighting, surrender to him. Or he'd take you from her, raise you as his own. He promised her you'd grow up to be just like him. Just like me."

Suddenly, it wasn't Leo's voice Devon heard. It was Daniel Kingston. Shouting at his mother, telling her how tired he was of her, why couldn't she just shut up and do as he told her? The sound of a slap, a woman's cry, then Kingston. Calm, quiet, giving her a choice. A final choice.

His vision wobbled as the memory of that day became more vivid. The view from ground level, from the height of a little boy peering out through the slats in the cabinet doors, overlapped the reality he saw now. He remembered wanting to rush to his mother's aid, knowing he should help her, wishing he was that brave. And cowering, frozen in terror.

"It was a bluff, of course," Leo continued. "Father would have never brought you home with us. But she didn't know that. She wouldn't take that risk. You were her whole world." His voice rose to a mocking falsetto.

"She chose me," Devon whispered, torn between the memory of his mother's tears and his hatred for the man before him now.

Leo smiled and nodded, a teacher praising an especially bright student. "She chose you. Submitted to my father. Which, of course, meant he was finished with her. He was like that—intoxicated by the pursuit, bored by the actual kill."

He paused, waiting for Devon to catch up to the present. "Good thing he had me around. Do you remember, little brother? You watched. We heard you crying. And I? I held her arm, the needle so bright and shiny. Do your remember her blood rushing back just before I pushed the plunger down?"

Nausea sucker-punched Devon, and he thought he'd be sick right there. If it weren't for Esme, he would have. "You gave her the hot shot that as good as killed her."

"And you wet your pants. Then father took me for ice cream. My reward for a job well done."

"I remember," Devon said, his gaze clear once more and riveted on Leo. It was the truth. He remembered everything—sitting on the floor beside his mother's still body, rocking, crying, and vowing to someday kill Daniel Kingston and his son. "I remember."

Esme made a small noise, one hand rubbing her nose. Devon glanced from her to Leo. "Sacrifice, that's the game? So you want me to choose? Between my daughter and my mother?"

Leo's grin tightened like barbwire. "Not you. You're far too easy, predictable." He tapped the knife against Angela's neck. "Her." He nodded to Petrosky. "Bring in contestant number three."

Petrosky chuckled. Devon felt the draft of the door opening behind him. Two of Tyree's men hauled Ryder inside to the cleared area and threw him onto the floor at Leo's feet.

CHAPTER FORTY-SEVEN

ALL MY HOPE died when Petrosky shoved Ryder inside the greenhouse.

Leo, on the other hand, grew more excited, his knife dancing across my neck, a deadly caress. "Funny how when I have one person with me, they beg for their own lives. Two and you beg for the girl's—guess that's to be expected, you being a doctor, a healer and all. Wonder what will happen now that we have three?"

He stroked the blade across his lips, kissing it, anointing it, preparing for his own holy sacrament. "I saw you two together last night. You seemed very close. Which shall it be, Doctor? The girl or the cop?"

Time froze. Not one of my spells, just pure, unadulterated terror. I met Ryder's gaze. He smiled at me. Nothing fake about it. He truly believed we were going to survive tonight. It would have been easy to dismiss it as fool's courage, but I knew he was no fool.

Trust. No. More than trust. Faith. From the very beginning, Ryder had placed his faith in me. Never questioning what I knew, without the luxury of proof.

Faith. How could I return to him anything less? The most difficult act of courage I've ever performed.

That's when I realized Devon was wrong. I wasn't free because I was dying. I was trapped. Bound and gagged by mortality. Whatever I decided—no, whatever I did, whether I decided it or not—this moment, here and now, was my legacy. An entire lifetime forced kicking and screaming into one frail, too-tiny moment.

Kicking and screaming. I liked that. I might not have much else to leave behind, but at least I could make my passing unforgettable. All I needed was to get the knife into my hand.

Ryder climbed to his knees. Petrosky hauled him up the rest of the way and shoved him against one of the iron columns. He ignored her and the gun pointed at his face. "I know you get your kicks from torturing helpless women," he taunted Leo. "How'd you like to try it on someone your own size?"

"You think I tortured my specimens?" Leo shook his head and clucked his tongue. "You don't understand anything. I might have primed the pump, so to speak. You see, my formulation works best when the fight-or-flight response is already at its peak. All those catecholamines and stress hormones filling the synapses, leaving them ripe for the PXA to block their reuptake."

Leo nodded to Petrosky to stand guard over Esme, while he took a small leather box from the table. He held up a syringe, its needle sparking in the light as he drew clear fluid into it. Then he turned to me.

The memory of Allie's pain flooded me with fear. I stepped back, bumping into a large pot, rocking it. Leo shook his head as if admonishing a child. "Stay still and take your medicine like a good girl," he said. "Unless you'd rather I gave it to the child."

A symphony of soul-rousing music hit me, drawing me into a fugue. Violins this time. Kicking and soaring up and down the scale before leaping into a jig. Music filled with hope and promise. Even if it had hit at the worst possible time.

"Leo, stop," Devon shouted. He'd seen what had happened to me, was trying to distract Leo. I was thankful but hated being powerless, needing protection. "I'll give you a show you won't forget. That's what you really want, right? To get back at me for all the time and attention your father spent on me and my mother. Time away from you."

Leo grabbed my arm. I couldn't resist him, frozen by the fugue.

My only hope was that it would pass quickly, before he saw how vulnerable I was.

"This magic potion is my crowning glory. The one that will leave my mark on history." He plunged the needle into my deltoid.

Somewhere, in the dark recesses of my memory, aided by the fugue state, I dredged up the molecular structure of the chemicals he'd mentioned. Realized that by having them flood the brain and then blocking their absorption, he could keep a person in a perpetual state of pain and terror. Creating a positive feedback loop that basically fed on itself.

But those same chemicals were also tied to endorphin production as well as dopamine, serotonin, and oxytocin. Start playing with those, and you could produce a virtual zombie, someone so dazed and overwhelmed by pain that their own mind would betray them, leaving them vulnerable to suggestion.

The perfect instrument of torture and interrogation, combined into one deadly drug. Worth billions to the government, not to mention other parties.

"I didn't torture those women," Leo continued in a casual tone, his fingers on my pulse, monitoring my response. "They did it to themselves. The right dosage of my new formulation, and a person will do anything I ask them to—anything to stop the pain. One of them chewed her own fingers off when I suggested they'd make a tasty snack. I told another that burning the nerve endings was the only way to end the pain. Then I handed her a blowtorch."

He laughed, a sound that echoed over and over in my mind, replaying itself like feedback from a bad amp. "Wasn't much left of her by the end. Surprised me how long it took her to die. I recorded it all for posterity, of course. In the name of science."

My flesh burned with fever, and my pulse raced, galloping out of control. Pain seared through me. If I could have moved, I would have screamed, been writhing on the ground. As it was, all I could do was fight past it, concentrate all my senses on anything that would help us escape.

A stray draft tickled the plants near Esme, and I realized Flynn had found her way in through one of the windows. Only the slightest rustle gave away her position. Ryder was also working his hands down his back, reaching for the handcuff key concealed in his belt. I stretched my hearing and could sense Tyree closing in behind Devon. Was he suspicious of Devon? Getting ready to hurt him? No, there was the click of Devon's handcuffs being unlocked. Tyree was on our side. Good to know.

Which left me to distract Leo. He caressed my arm, releasing wave after wave of pain in his wake, and leaned to whisper in my ear, "You will obey my every command. If you do, the pain will recede. If you resist, it will grow a thousand times worse."

Then he stood back, glancing at his watch. "Won't be long now. Once the pain reaches her threshold, she'll be mine."

"Stop this," Ryder said. "There's no need—"

"There's every need. This is science. My legacy, my chance to prove to my father that I can accomplish greatness on my own. I don't need anything from him."

"Your father's dying. Wouldn't your time be better spent at his bedside instead of this ridiculous demonstration?"

Leo's face flushed with anger, and he raised his hand with the knife, ready to stab Ryder. Tyree handed Devon a pistol and edged back, out the door. I wondered at that. Wasn't he here to rescue Esme? Then I remembered what Flynn had said, something about Tyree stealing a ring from Leo. Daniel's ring? Did we have this all wrong?

I blinked, finally free of my fugue, but now feeling the full effects of the PXA. Agony doubled me over, knocking me to the floor. Petrosky stepped forward, away from Esme. Through the tsunami of pain, I sensed Flynn sliding behind the table where Esme lay as Leo turned his attention from Ryder onto me.

What I'd felt with Allie, it had been a pale reflection of the real agony she'd suffered. Pain so intense I couldn't describe it, give it any flavor. It was searing and freezing, electrical shocks and choking, wrenching, twisting, breaking... The terror I'd felt lost in Devon's mother's mind would have been infinitely more bearable.

Leo hauled me to my feet. "Stand," he commanded.

Despite the pain filleting me from the inside out, I obeyed.

"Good girl. Now you have a choice." He placed his knife in my hand and folded my fingers around it. "Stab the girl or stab the cop. Now."

His final word blazed through my body, jerking it forward like a puppet on a string. I tried to resist, used every ounce of my strength to fight his command, but the pain grew so intense it felt as if my every cell was exploding, sending fragments of twisted, broken, searing agony across my body. The only things that felt real were my grip on the knife and Leo's voice.

I looked to Ryder. He nodded, his lips curling in the saddest smile I'd ever seen.

I stumbled toward him, Leo following me, while I hoped I was providing enough distraction for Flynn to save Esme, leaving Devon to tackle Petrosky.

Then I was in front of Ryder, my chest pressed against his, my hand holding the tip of the knife to his left rib cage. Over his heart.

Leo practically danced with excitement. Somehow, I managed to take a step back, away from Ryder. Leo blocked my path. He circled one arm across my shoulders as if we were lovers bound for eternity. "Do it. Do it now!"

And I did.

CHAPTER FORTY-EIGHT

STABBING SOMEONE IN the heart isn't like what you see on TV. First, you have all those layers to get through, jackets and shirts and all. Then, the heart is actually well protected anatomically. There's a reason the chest cavity is called the rib cage. Makes it tough to hit, especially when you're aiming blind.

No, if you want to stab someone to death, the heart probably isn't your best bet. Especially if that someone is directly beside you, on the opposite side of your body from your hand with the knife.

Leo had been so wrapped up in his sadistic games that he'd forgotten not everyone responds to a drug in the same way. Especially not someone like me, whose brain is filled with millions of tiny holes interrupting the synaptic connections loaded with the neurochemicals he was relying on to keep his drug active.

I pulled my elbow back, but instead of plunging my knife forward into Ryder's chest, I arced it to my left, directly into Leo's left femoral region. He jerked up in shock, wrenching the blade. I kept my hand on the knife, slicing downward, pushing it in deeper.

"You bitch!" Leo shouted, pushing me away.

Big mistake. I took the knife with me, leaving a gushing wound behind. The femoral artery is one of the largest in the body. Slice that, and you have blood jetting out with each heartbeat. Get the femoral vein as well, and you're dead within a few minutes.

Leo pressed his hands against his groin, slipped in his own blood already puddling on the floor, and fell, writhing as he fought to stop the bleeding.

I had no time to think about what I'd just done. The PXA still had me in its grip—not totally, but enough so I couldn't move, not without pain sizzling down every nerve ending. I stood, frozen, my jaws locked as I fought against a scream.

Across the room, Flynn grabbed Esme from the table, aiming a pistol at anyone who tried to stop her. No one did.

Petrosky whirled, ignoring Flynn, to point her pistol at me. On the other side of her, Devon snapped free of his handcuffs and raised a gun as well.

Too late. Petrosky fired. At me.

Before I could react, Ryder lunged forward—not at Petrosky, she was too far away—pushing me aside and putting himself in the line of fire.

I'm not sure if it was the drugs or remnants of my fugue state, but I saw the bullet race across space as if propelled by slow-motion special effects from a movie. Watched it hurtle and spin, while I was unable to move fast enough to stop it before it hit Ryder.

The sound of the gunshot was quickly followed by two more stacked on another two as both Flynn and Devon fired on Petrosky. Her body jerked right, then left, before she slumped down, her pistol sliding from her slack grasp.

Ryder stumbled against me, off-balance with his hands cuffed behind his back. Blood seeped through his shirt. I caught him with my own cuffed hands and lowered him to the ground.

"I need some help here," I shouted, choking on the smell of gunpowder and blood. At least, I think I shouted. My mind was exploding with the roar of a thousand gunshots echoing, while my body felt each one tear through me, ripping me apart, over and over again. Every time I blinked, I expected to see my own guts and blood pouring out of me.

I tried to focus. I pressed both my hands against Ryder's wound. Not my blood. His. And no guts. Hit in the right lower quadrant, not the worst place to be shot, as long as the bullet didn't fragment and nick a blood vessel or tumble up into the liver.

Flynn grabbed my wrists, unlocking the handcuffs, then freed Ryder as well. Esme lay on the other side of Ryder, still unconscious, thank God. She had enough bad memories without witnessing this carnage.

"I called 911. They're on their way. What do you need?" Flynn asked. Leo moaned beside us, one hand flailing at her ankle, but she kicked him aside.

Devon had disappeared, the sound of gunfire coming from the roof marking his progress. Had he figured out the truth about Tyree as well?

"Hold pressure here." I positioned Flynn's hands over Ryder's entrance wound while I checked his flank. Found an exit wound not far from the entrance. That was good. Very good. I bunched his jacket over the top of it, using his body weight to apply pressure. He gave a little sound, choking back a moan.

I turned to him, one hand at his neck, the other at his wrist, assessing his pulses. Both strong. Breathing regular. Pain still rampaged through my body with each movement, but focusing on saving him kept it at bay. One more gift Ryder gave me—besides saving my life.

"You're going to be okay," I promised him. "Except for the psych eval I'll be ordering. What the hell were you thinking, jumping in front of me like that?"

His eyes crinkled with a smile as he held back his laughter. Time rushed past us, leaving us in an oasis of calm, a feeling not unlike my fugues. Except I was free to move, free to do what I wanted. So I gave in and kissed him.

I stroked his hair with my fingers, taking care not to snag the staples I'd placed there last night when we'd first met. Was it only twenty-four hours? Felt much shorter, like an instant, yet also ages and ages.

Swiss-cheese brain of mine, I had the feeling I'd best get used to more strange time warps. But I saw the gleam in Ryder's eyes and knew he felt the same way.

Then he frowned, his gaze snagging on Leo. Still breathing, but unconscious, barely any blood left to ooze from his wound.

"Help him," Ryder said.

I jerked back. "He's gone. It's too late."

"No," Ryder insisted. "We need to know where he stashed the PXA."

He was right. There was no way in hell we could risk anyone else gaining control of Leo's formulation.

Reluctantly, I turned my back on Ryder and crawled to Leo's side. His lips were ashen, his breathing agonal. He was as close to dead as you could get. Without immediate access to an OR and a dozen units of blood there was no way I could save him.

But I could find the PXA. I hauled in my breath, squared my shoulders, making sure Ryder and Flynn couldn't see my face. Only hoped I wasn't frozen so long that they'd have to pull me out. I wished Devon was here. He'd know what to do if—when—Leo died and I was still with him.

How quickly I'd accepted this curse. So typical of an ER doc—make that former ER doc—to improvise, twist a death sentence into some kind of blessing.

I lay my hand on Leo's neck. His pulse was thready, barely palpable.

The music hit. Different this time, probably because of the PXA still in my system. Painful. Roaring. Buffeting me as if I'd been sucked into an F5 tornado.

At its center, Leo. Larger than life, radiating with a fierce, white-hot brilliance.

I know what you want. You'll never find it. He raised a hand, swatting me aside, sending me reeling, falling into the darkness that swirled at the edges, devouring the light, closing in on both of us. Pain sliced through me as if he'd hit me for real, and not with a hand but with a machete.

I was on my hands and knees, gasping, my body blazing with

agony.

Scream, he commanded. *I like it when they scream.*

No. I climbed to my feet and faced him. *Tell me. Where's the PXA?*

The darkness had collapsed the circle of light that held Leo and I into a small whirlpool, winds buffeting us, waves of light crashing against us. I staggered, fought to keep to my feet. Leo merely laughed, absorbing more of the light to grow taller, towering over me.

Scream for me, he said, raising his hand to strike me down. A death blow.

This was how he saw himself, I realized. Just as Allie had seen herself as a concert pianist, had created that reality that we shared. Leo wanted to go down fighting, conquering, all-powerful. Deciding not just his own fate, but mine. As he had with all those women he'd tortured. How many more had he killed in his twisted search for the ultimate torture device?

Power and control. That's what he wanted with his drug. And now with his death.

I wouldn't let him. Instead, I opened my mouth and screamed. Not a scream of surrender or anguish. A rebel yell of defiance, letting loose all the pain the PXA had brought me, all the pain and suffering Allie had experienced at his hands, even the pain Devon's mother had lived through for so long.

All of it. A tympani of pain crashing down, burying us both in our shared reality. His cries pierced the roaring that filled my mind—his mind—our mind.

And suddenly I saw. Knew what I needed to know.

As the pain swept him away, into the dark, he reached out a hand. *Save me!*

I pushed away, a rush of fever heat forcing me back. He vanished in the darkness.

And I blinked, back in the here and now of the greenhouse. Leo's body lay before me. No pulse. Not breathing. Gone for good.

I shook myself. Pain, but not as intense, nothing I couldn't handle.

I spun around to Ryder. It was obvious I hadn't been lost in the fugue for more than a minute or so, though it'd felt like all of eternity had collapsed into one soul-sucking black hole.

"He's gone," I said. "I couldn't save him."

The gunfire outside had died down. "I'm going to see if I can find some first aid supplies, Flynn. Stay with him and Esme."

"Take this." She handed me Petrosky's service weapon. I held the gun. It was heavier than I expected. Felt powerful in my hand.

I stepped over Leo's body—funny, he seemed shrunken, inconsequential. I'd basically just tortured him to death, and there'd be hell to pay for that, but I'd deal with it later. I went outside. The roof was empty except for Devon and Tyree.

Devon was on the ground, face bloody, glaring up at Tyree. Tyree had one hand braced against the waist-high balustrade, using it as leverage as he swung his leg to aim a vicious kick at Devon.

"Stop!" I shouted, raising the gun. Tyree froze. Devon rolled to his feet.

"Do it, Angela," Devon said. "It's because of him that Jess is dead. Think how many people he's killed, how many lives he's ruined, all those innocent girls he delivered to Leo. He deserves to die, just as much as Leo did."

I could do it—kill Tyree, end this here and now. Just as I had with Leo. Free the residents of the Tower from their reign of terror. Odds were I was dying anyway.

Which meant there was nothing to stop me.

"Do it, pull the trigger," Devon urged.

Freedom coursed through my veins, energizing me, as if the universe was suddenly much, much larger than I'd ever imagined. Larger than the law or the rules or penance. Justice personified.

A hero's end. Here, in my grasp.

Tyree's face morphed from gloating to terrified little boy. Pinched and twisted and desperate. "You're a doctor. You can't shoot me. You save lives."

He was trying to keep his voice calm, but it emerged with a whine that made me want to pull the trigger even more. He must have read that in my stance, because he held up his hands in the universal posture of surrender, his back to the balustrade. "It'll be cold-blooded murder if you pull the trigger. Can you live with that?"

Wouldn't have to live with it for very long. But I said nothing. It took all my concentration to keep my index finger from squeezing the trigger.

"Give me the gun, I'll do it." Devon sounded irritated. Casual. He'd done this before. I'd guessed as much, but now it was hammered home.

I liked Devon. He was a good guy. Better than most. Maybe Hippocrates had it all wrong. Maybe we shouldn't treat everyone the same. Maybe there really were good guys and bad ones. Ones who deserved to be stopped before they caused more harm.

It wasn't philosophy or morals or ethics that stopped me. It was Ryder. He trusted me. Had faith in me. To save Esme, to save him, to do the right thing.

So I did.

I eased my finger off the trigger. "We're taking Tyree with us. He's the one who killed Allie, not Leo. He needs to answer for what he's done."

Devon didn't look too surprised. Tyree chuckled. "How'd you figure that?"

I couldn't very well tell him that I'd been inside Leo's mind, had seen everything that he'd done—and Allie hadn't been any part of it. "Esme said Leo threatened her and Jess if you didn't give back the ring you stole. Daniel Kingston's signet ring. I'm guessing that once Leo finished with his victims, he had you take care of cleaning up. You knew those women's minds were destroyed, figured it was a way to frame Leo without Daniel knowing you were involved. So you branded them with a ring covered in his DNA."

"If you were a real man, you'd've just shot him like the animal he was," Devon said.

"Right. And have his old man take it out on me? Kingston

would've burned this place to the ground, everyone who lives here with it." Tyree's face twisted into a sneer. "You have no idea, riding around in your fancy car, wearing your fancy suits, but I'll always protect my own."

"But you didn't, did you, Tyree?" I asked. "What happened? Did Allie spot you disposing of a body? She'd dressed real nice that morning. Was she coming to tell you she'd reconsidered your offer of a job? Anything to get enough money to get out of here. But you didn't know how to titrate the PXA. You overdosed her. And in the meantime, Leo got back from Ireland, figured out what you were doing, and he came after you."

"You let Leo kill Jess," Devon said. "And you used the search for Esme to cover up you moving Allie into the room with the other kids. Figured if the cops found her and them, they'd finally start to put two and two together."

"Stupid cops. Should've figured it out months ago. Must've all been bought off by Kingston." Tyree chuckled. "Fat lot of good it did him or his son. And you got nothing to prove anything against me."

"He's right," Devon said. "Give me the gun, Angela."

"No. Jacob will find a way to prosecute him, see to it that he pays for what he's done. The truth needs to be told." After everything she and the other victims had been through, I couldn't let Allie down. They deserved justice.

"Truth has nothing to do with the law. When you gonna get that through your head, Angela? Shoot him and be done with it."

"No."

Devon glared at me, his face filled with disappointment and anger. Then he lunged forward, head down like a bull, launching Tyree over the edge of the roof. Tyree's scream shredded the night.

I ran to the edge, looked over. Tyree's body sprawled on the ground far below.

"They'll find a gun on him," Devon said. "The same one that shot the cop I told you about. The same one he would have used to kill me. It was self-defense, pure and simple. Me or him. No choice about it."

My breath coming in gasps, I stared at Devon. He wasn't gloating, but he didn't appear racked with guilt either. Maybe he wasn't one of the good guys after all.

The gun was slippery in my blood-covered hands. Maybe I wasn't either.

CHAPTER FORTY-NINE

I DIDN'T WANT to be here. Ryder was still in the OR, and I wanted to be there when the surgeons had any news. But I owed Devon—even as I worried about the direction he was taking. Tyree's death had only made things worse, although the cops hadn't seemed too interested in pursuing the truth, not after they realized Tyree had killed one of their own.

So I kept Devon's secrets, and he kept mine. He'd guided me through the tunnels to where I'd seen Leo's stash—the last of his various PXA formulations, along with his computer and written notes—and we used one of Tyree's bombs to destroy it all. Then Devon had insisted we come here, that I do him one last favor.

He wasn't the man I'd met last night. Seemed that losing Jess and his mom, seeing Esme in danger, had broken him. Or maybe, like me, he had already been broken, and the events of the last two days had just brought the cracks to the surface.

"I want to make sure he knows what's going on," Devon insisted as we entered the ICU where Daniel Kingston lay in a coma. "It's only fair that he knows about Leo."

"Basically, you're using me to tell him his son was a homicidal maniac and that I killed him." Exhaustion and the need to get back to Ryder had driven me past subtlety.

"You don't have to tell him that part. Tell him Leo died because of me."

"You don't understand." I waved my hand vaguely toward my

341

head, not sure of any words to describe what happened when I was inside someone. Remnants of Leo's final scream echoed through my mind, making me wince. I had the feeling I would never be free of him...or what I'd done to him. "There's no lying in there."

"It's the truth. Leo did die because of me and his warped jealousy of the woman his father was obsessed with."

We reached Daniel's bedside. His vitals were stable, except the pressure monitor revealed cerebral edema, brain swelling. I studied the EEG tracing, hoping there would be no spindle bursts. No such luck.

"Be sure to let him know that as soon as the paternity test is back, the lawyers will arrange for me to be his legal guardian while he's in a coma. I'll be handling all his business and affairs, so they're in good hands."

It was his smile that told me this was his real message for Daniel. The knowledge that the bastard child of the woman he'd brutalized was now gaining control of Daniel's life. Everything Daniel once held dear, Devon now had power over.

Funny how I never noticed before how cruel Devon's smile could be. "You're no better than Tyree or Leo or Daniel himself."

He startled, then a quick, sharp laugh escaped. "Never said I was. But at least I'm trying. Better for folks in the Tower than if any of them had lived and I'd died."

I hated that I couldn't argue with that. "What about Esme?"

His smile jackknifed into a warning. "Don't you worry about Esme. I'll protect her. Just like I'll protect your secrets, Angela. Ryder never has to know about your little fits. At least not from me."

"I don't respond well to threats, Devon. Tell Daniel what you want him to know yourself. I'm done here." I stalked away, returning to the waiting room in time to hear that Ryder was going to be fine, just fine, no major damage.

As I hugged Ozzie and Jacob, I surprised myself by sending a prayer of gratitude—to who, I had no idea. But it felt good. I was starting to understand why Ryder still believed. Maybe too little, too late, but worth a try.

❃

"EVERYTHING'S PAID FOR, and I've set up an account you can draw on if you need anything else," Devon told Flynn when he met her outside the Tower.

"Just like I heard those other kids had some mystery donor pay for them all to go to a fancy group home out in the country?"

"Tyree should have done that himself. Man was a miser, worse than the Russians." He glanced at his watch. He was meeting with his lawyer in an hour to start the court proceedings. Soon, he'd own the Tower.

No more drugs and whores. He was going to put Tyree's people to work turning this place into someplace decent to live.

Flynn had her hand on the car door. "Don't you want to tell her good-bye?"

"No. No, I can never see her again. She starts school next week. A nice one, all girls, real good. She'll have money for college, everything she needs. Can't get into any trouble up there. It's goddamn Vermont. Who ever heard of any trouble up in Vermont? She'll be safe."

"What if she asks about you? About her father?"

"Say he died. Say he loved her very much. But he died."

"But—"

"No." He didn't recognize his own voice—it sounded like an ancient memory, this harsh, all-too-certain man, callously exiling his only family. "This is the best way to keep her safe. I don't want anybody ever coming after her, not ever again. The only way to do that is for nobody to ever know she's mine."

"I understand." But her face said she didn't, not really. No matter. Flynn had already risked her life time and again for Esme. She'd keep her safe. That was all he cared about.

"Here's a private number you can call if you ever need me. No

343

one else on the planet has that number, so don't lose it. You call, I'll get back to you as soon as I can. If I don't get back to you—" They both knew what that meant.

Flynn nodded. "I'll take care of her. Don't worry."

Devon opened the car door for her. Esme was asleep in the backseat, her hands folded under her face like she was praying.

He helped Flynn into the car, gripping her arm, suddenly not wanting to let go. "Don't let her hang out with any boys like me. No smoking, ever—that shit's worse than crack. And if she wants to do any of that Vermont ski stuff, make sure she wears a helmet and pads and—"

She laid her gloved palm against his cheek, and he stopped. "She'll be fine, Devon. I promise."

He nodded. Let her go. Closed the car door. Turned away before it left the curb. And walked inside the Tower. A pair of Tyree's old bangers lounged inside the lobby.

"You boys don't have nothing better to do?" he asked.

Their eyes vacant, they shrugged. Chickens with their heads cut off. "Stand up straight. You all work for me now."

🌙 🌟 🌙

ACTING ON MY feelings for Ryder would be wrong—probably the most wrong thing I've ever done in my life. Worse even than what I'd done to Leo. But nothing had ever felt so right.

Was it so horrible to allow hope guide me instead of the guilt I'd followed most of my life? After all, I didn't know for certain that things were hopeless, that I truly had fatal insomnia. Louise said it would take three to four weeks to get the genetic results back. My answer would probably come around Christmas.

Until then, I needed to be able to feel, to live, to laugh. I needed to believe that after everything I'd done—after my father, Sister Patrice, Leo—that someone, somehow found me worthy of love.

I needed Ryder.

I crept forward, wrapping my fingers around the drape surrounding his bed in the surgical recovery unit. Other than the steady beat of the monitor, it was silent beyond. I filled my lungs as if preparing to enter an unknown world and stepped inside the drapes.

He lay so still, so very still on the bed. It didn't look like him at all. The Ryder I knew was filled with energy, ready for anything—even when he was relaxed. It was his eyes, I realized now. The way they never stopped moving, scanning for danger.

That spark was gone. His eyes were closed, his face slack, the only sign of life the slight rise of his chest.

I reached out to take his hand, feel his pulse—reflex of a physician. But I wasn't a doctor, not anymore. I was still accepting that new reality. It stung, like a fresh wound left open to heal from the inside out. Raw nerve endings exposed, not scarred over yet.

Anesthesia is as close to dying as we get, medically. I stared down at Ryder's still form. Was he still under the influence of the sedatives? What would come if I touched him? If I was able to go inside with him, what would I find? What would he learn about me?

Would he despise me for trespassing into his most private thoughts?

I hated this uncertainty, this feeling like I was out of control. Pretty much how the rest of my life would be. No more guarantees. Of anything.

No rules, no boundaries, no limits. I could do anything I wanted with little to no consequence. Devon was right—and so very wrong.

There would be a price to pay. The people I left behind. Jacob. My family. And now Ryder.

Still, I couldn't resist. I took his hand in mine. Closed my eyes, waiting for the music and bright lights.

Nothing. Just the warmth of his skin. I opened my eyes, realized I was smiling. He was asleep, just asleep. Nowhere near almost-dead.

I sat there so long, I drifted into a comfortable haze of numb apathy. As long as he was okay, I didn't care about anything else. Then I felt him stir. He stiffened with pain, opened his eyes, instantly at full alert. Until he saw me. I loved the way his smile crept up his body, relaxing his posture, quirking his lips, releasing that devastating dimple, and finally lighting his eyes.

He was smiling at me—eyes clear, gaze steady. Everything we'd been through in the past two days, it hadn't shaken him at all. I didn't have to worry about overburdening him, accidentally hurting him. Not like Jacob.

I can trust Ryder not to break.

Maybe I am dying. Who knows? Feels like I'm only just beginning to live.

I'm Angela Rossi. I'm thirty-four years old, and once, I was a doctor.

Now, I am a killer.

This is the story of how I will die.

Someday. Soon.

But not alone. And not without hope.

Dear Reader,

Some people collect stamps, I collect bizarre and gruesome diseases. Of these, Fatal Familial Insomnia is perhaps the worst. I've long been fascinated by its unique symptoms and inescapable clinical progression. In fact, I began writing this book back in 2008.

(If you're interested in the real facts behind Fatal Insomnia, check out the Extras page on my website, www.CJLyons.net)

It's taken me this long (six years!) and multiple starts and stops to realize I wasn't writing a book about a fascinatingly cruel disease; rather I was writing a book about hope.

It was a reviewer who made this clear to me. He wrote me a personal note commenting that he enjoyed my work because I wasn't afraid to tackle grief and explore the consequences of loss.

I'd thought I'd been writing my Thrillers with Heart about ordinary people finding the courage to stand up and change their world. But, after reading his note, I realized he was right. Almost all of my books have dealt with life-shattering loss and how we heal. Many of my characters must go through the stages of grief before they dare to risk everything and become heroes.

Perhaps you can't be a hero until you walk through the fires of hell and emerge on the other side?

If so, then FAREWELL TO DREAMS and the other Fatal Insomnia stories that follow, are the ultimate test of fire, because Angela knows she's dying. Soon. And so do we—it's in the title! Yet, we can learn so much by following her on her journey…because she's going where someday we all must go.

Hope. Faith. Love. What better guides for Angela—and any of us?

Thank you for joining in on the adventure! Angela will return in Fatal Insomnia, Book Two, A RAGING DAWN.

I'd also like to thank some of the people who helped make this book possible: Toni McGee Causey who lent her extraordinary talents not only to the cover art that enticed you to notice this book, but also with her refusal to let me take the easy way out or give up on this project. Jaime Levine for her astute editorial guidance. Joyce Lamb and Sandra Simpson for their eagle-eyed copy editing and proofreading. David Morrell and Eileen Hutton for sharing their wisdom and insights. My agent, Barbara Poelle, whose motto "onward and upward!" is a battle cry that keeps me going no matter the obstacles.

Also, Shari Bartholomew, a special fan who won the right to be a character in FAREWELL TO DREAMS—and who is a hard working ER nurse in real life!

I'm always grateful to my fans who push me to write more great books (usually through messages urging me to write faster because they "need more CJ!") and who I strive to delight and excite with every story I tell.

Thanks for reading!

CJ

PS: want to stay in touch and be the first to hear when I have a new book out? Sign up for my Thrillers with Heart newsletter at www.CJLyons.net

ABOUT THE AUTHOR

Pediatric ER doctor turned *New York Times* bestselling thriller writer CJ Lyons has been a storyteller all her life—something that landed her in many time-outs as a kid. She writes her Thrillers with Heart for the same reason that she became a doctor: because she believes we all have the power to change our world.

In the ER she witnessed many acts of courage by her patients and their families, learning that heroes truly are born every day. When not writing, she can be found walking the beaches near her Lowcountry home, listening to the voices in her head and plotting new and devious ways to create mayhem for her characters.

To learn more about her Thrillers with Heart go to www.CJLyons.net

CPSIA information can be obtained at www.ICGtesting.com
Printed in the USA
BVOW08s1021090915

416364BV00004B/6/P